Beast Be Gone

By A L Billington

Billington Publishing

Copyright © A L Billington 2021 all rights reserved.

First published in Great Britain in 2021 by Billington Publishing.
www.billingtonpublishing.com

The right of A L Billington to be identified as the Author of the Work has been asserted by him in accordance with the Copyright, Designs and Patents Act 1988.

All rights reserved. No part of this publication may be reproduced, stored in a retrieval system or transmitted, in any form or by any means, without the prior written permission of the publisher, nor be otherwise circulated in any form of binding or cover other than that in which it is published and without a similar condition being imposed on the subsequent purchaser.

All characters in this publication are fictitious and any resemblance to real persons, living or dead, is purely coincidental.

1 2 3 4

ISBN: 978-1-7391516-6-9

Cover Illustrations: A L Billington
Inside Illustrations: A L Billington

Beast Be Gone

A L BILLINGTON

Beast Be Gone

1

Eric and Timmy crept down the steps of the crypt, the rhyme making Eric smile in spite of himself. The domed chamber opened up before them, revealing a layer of mist that rippled across the uneven floor. Lanterns illuminated the stone coffins lining the walls, each coated in a mess of cobwebs. Eric wondered who kept all the lanterns lit. It was almost as if someone wanted to make the dungeon adventure-friendly. He shivered. Somehow the air was thicker down there.

'I'm scared, Eric,' whispered Timmy, his apprentice. He was frail, pale as the moon and twice as spotty. His overalls were filthy and oversized, making him seem much younger than he was. Faded text on them read:

Best Be Gone - Pest Control

Eric gave the boy a pat on the back, which knocked him forward. 'Don't worry, we can handle a lich. Easy. Just try to think of it as a disgruntled skeleton and do everything like I told you.' Eric had seen Timmy recite all five hundred and twenty-six undead anti-curses. Poor kid. If only he could have a little more confidence in himself. It was a shame there was so little fieldwork to take him on.

'But that was days ago! What if I forget?' Timmy glanced around. He jumped as he brushed a cobweb, tripped and went crashing to the ground.

Timmy tried to stand but noticed the bodies hidden under the mist. Huge human barbarians, thin elven mages and tiny pixie thieves lay all around. Each adventurer twisted into an inhumane position, all covered in dried blood.

Timmy got to his feet. 'There are so many!' he whimpered, as he clutched Eric's sleeve.

'Well of course. Demi-lich ain't nothing to be sniffed at.' Eric readjusted his leather overalls, which were stained with ghoul blood that refused to wash out. If this went well he might be able to afford a new pair.

'But...where will the lich be?'

Eric chuckled to himself. 'You've got a lot to learn, Timmy. There's some stuff you can't get from books and teaching. Real-world experience like this is invaluable. You see, a lich is always at the end. Usually hiding in the biggest coffin. Even adventurers know that.' Eric pointed up at the altar. 'My guess is right there.'

There was a whooshing sound as the largest coffin at the end of the room burst open and a skeletal form floated out. Blue smoke swirled around its ragged robes, its face a hollow skull beneath a rusted crown. It turned its empty eye sockets upon the pair.

I AM THE LICH KALAKZAR! BOW DOWN BEFORE ME, PUNY MORTALS...

'What did I tell you? Right, hand me my Sack of Clutching, Timmy.'

...AND PREPARE TO MEET YOUR DOOM.

'Now what we need is a Spirit Stone. Probably level three. Hmm… here it is.'

FOR MANY YEARS I HAVE LAIN IN WAIT...

'Oh no, that's a level two. Let me have another look.'

...TO FIND A HERO WORTHY ENOUGH TO DEFEAT ME.

'Here we are Timmy, time to kill your first lich. Ready?'

DARE YOU CHALLENGE THE MIGHTY LICH KALAKZAR?

'Hold the Spirit Stone like this. No, not like that…'

...ARE YOU EVEN LISTENING TO ME?

'Okay, that's it. Keep steady.'

I'M RIGHT HERE.

'Now remember, aim it at his heart, that's the weak spot.'

I USED TO BE KING, YOU KNOW. I WAS KIND OF A BIG DEAL...

There was a flash of light and a high pitched wail as the lich was sucked into the stone.

Then silence.

Timmy looked down at the stone glowing an eerie blue in his hands. It let out a gentle hum as it pulsed.

'Well done!' announced Eric. 'See? Not so hard after all?'

'If it's not so hard,' said Timmy, voice trembling. 'Why did it kill so many adventurers?'

Eric laughed heartily. 'Adventurers are only in it for the glory and "Experience". It would take all the fun out if they just dispelled the monsters or poisoned them like we do. Plus our tricks are a trade secret. Heck, half the time we can persuade the creatures to leave with a few compliments or a bribe.'

'Oh, I see.'

'Now be careful, we don't want to…'

But as he said it, the stone slipped from Timmy's hands and shattered on the ground. Blue flames erupted from the shards as the undead creature rose once again.

Eric sighed.

I AM THE LICH KALAKZAR! BOW DOWN BEFORE ME, PUNY MORTALS...

'Oh no!' shrieked Timmy. 'What do I do? *What do I do?*'

'Relax,' said Eric as he rifled through his Sack of Clutching. 'Let me get a Lesser Dispel Undead Scroll out, we don't have another stone. Here, you take it. You need to learn how to use it.'

...AND PREPARE TO MEET YOUR DOOM.

Timmy took the scroll in his shaking hands. 'I'm not ready,' Timmy stammered. 'I've never done it before.'

'Then now's the perfect time to learn. Go on, just read it out.'

FOR MANY YEARS I HAVE LAIN IN WAIT…

'Lichus disspellus magicum exlodus…'

'No, no, no, not disspe*llus*, it's *diss*pellus'

…TO FIND A HERO WORTHY ENOUGH TO DEFEAT ME.

'I'm not ready! Can you do it, Eric? I'm too scared!' Timmy looked frantically between the lich, the scroll and Eric.

'You need to learn to work under pressure Timmy.'

DARE YOU CHALLENGE THE MIGHTY LICH KALAKZAR?

'Lichus disspell…'

Timmy exploded into a bloody mess. Entrails flew everywhere. The lich laughed as he held out his staff, which emitted a trail of smoke.

Eric winced and wiped a bit of Timmy from his face. Now, why did he have to go and do that? Why couldn't he have just read it out properly? Resurrections weren't cheap. Eric leaned down with a groan and picked the scroll up off the floor.

He read the incantation and the scroll evaporated along with the lich.

* * *

A holy man stood before Eric, his mole costume flapping in the breeze. He raised his head to reveal a frown from a furry hood. 'You took your time,' the priest said. 'I was beginning to think you were dead.'

Eric could hardly hear him. The wind blew through the trees surrounding the temple, and the man's voice was soft as a baby elf's. 'Well, I'm here now,' said Eric with a grunt, cleaning the last of the blood from his face with a rag. He took Daisy the mule by the reins and led her over to the water trough. Draped over his mount a banner read:

"*Creatures in your basement? Undead spooking your castle? Infestation of goblins? Beast Be Gone will clear out those pesky pests and save your health and business. Find us on Tinbottom Alley, Porkhaven - (no dragons.)*"

The priest looked him up and down. '*And* you came three days late!'

Behind him, the temple's tower cast a looming shadow. Eric wasn't intimidated by the structure, however. In the land of Fen-Tessai, temples to the Holy Mole God were more common than inns - and he knew which he'd rather be at.

Eric licked his lips at the thought of his next pint. 'We've been very busy this past week, so this is the earliest we could fit you in.' He waved his calendar at the priest, being sure to do it fast enough the priest wouldn't see it was empty except for his monthly bath schedule. 'We apologise for any inconvenience caused.' He did his best to sound sincere but was sure his apathy was apparent. At least his apathy stopped him from caring about his apathy.

The priest spoke through gritted teeth. 'I shall be sending a formal letter of complaint to your manager.'

'I am the manager.'

The priest crossed his arms and his two thick fur sleeves enveloped one another. 'Then I bid you register my disapproval on your report.'

'Right you are then,' said Eric, pretending to write on his notebook while the priest watched intently. 'Was it just the lich that was the problem?'

The priest looked at Eric with disgust. 'Yes, it was *just* a lich.'

'Oh yeah, lich. Sure. That's all sorted now. A grand-lich, I believe?'

'A demi-lich.'

Eric drew an intake of breath. 'Demi-lich, right. He needed special equipment, mind you.'

The colour drained from the priest's face. 'Oh my. It has killed a lot of adventurers. Although I thought a demi-lich was *less* powerful than a normal lich?'

'That's why they need special kit.'

'Oh.'

'Lucky for you I brought everything I needed. But it'll cost extra I'm afraid.'

The priest narrowed his eyes. 'How much exactly?'

'Well, let's see,' Eric paused and scratched his chin. 'Say ten gold for the Spirit Stone... twenty for a Scroll of Undead Resistance, plus my standard rate...' Eric murmured to himself as he added it up. 'Say ninety gold?'

'But we agreed on fifty!'

'Alright, call it eighty.'

'Sixty. You were late.'

'Deal.' They shook hands, the priest's grip weak in Eric's palm. 'Had much problem with all those adventurers?' asked Eric.

'That is *precisely* why I need your services.' The priest's face turned from white to beetroot red. 'The beastly adventurers have been running amok! The undead creature has lived in the basement for years, but he was never a problem until all these adventurers started to show up. They blunder in, breaking pots and rifling through my things. They have the audacity, the *sheer audacity* to steal temple property right in front of me.'

The priest went quiet. He took a few breaths, flapping his hands in front of his face in a failed attempt to hold back the tears. 'They just *know* I could never stand up to them. Have you seen the size of their swords? It's humiliating is what it is.'

Eric shook his head. 'Once word spreads, there's no stopping 'em. But you won't have to worry about adventurers no more, just make sure you post a notice in town saying the crypt is cleared out. We do also offer a prevention package, along with a…'

The priest cut him off. 'That won't be necessary, thank you. I'm sure everything will be fine now.'

'If you say so.'

The priest hesitated a moment. 'Didn't you have a companion when you arrived?'

'Yes.'

'Oh.' The priest paused a moment, a sly smile crept onto his face. 'Of course, we do also offer a resurrection service. Only four hundred gold coins...'

Eric cut him off with a wave of his hand. 'Not at those prices.'

'If you say so.' The priest cleared his throat, produced a pouch from his sleeve and handed it to Eric. 'Well, anyway, thank you for your help, here is your payment. Sixty gold coins, as agreed.'

Eric did his best not to seem too desperate as he accepted the pouch. It was barely enough to cover the cost of the Lesser Dispel Undead Scroll and the Soul Stone. He took Daisy he mule by the reins and produced a Scroll of Town Portal from his belt. After muttering the words, they both vanished in a cloud of smoke and lightning.

Eric and Daisy materialised outside his familiar shop front, startling rats who scampered away across the muddy cobbles. The peeling walls revealed crumbling bricks, which some may have considered trendy. To Eric it was home.

Barely visible from grime, the window's lettering read:

Beast Be Gone
Clear out those pesky pests
to save your health and business.
(No dragons.)

He didn't know how people ever lived without Scrolls of Town Portal. Wherever you were, they would take you home. Although he wasn't exactly sure how they knew where home was. Occasionally they would teleport him to an inn instead. He was suspicious the Scrolls were being sarcastic.

Eric tied Daisy inside the shelter behind the shop. It was more like a large cupboard than a stable, but Daisy seemed to like it. He fed her a carrot and went indoors. The room was empty, except for a bookshelf full of faded books, a crossbow on the mantelpiece and a lonely desk in the centre. He'd made very little pawning his things, but it was the only way he could afford food for himself, an apprentice and Daisy. At least there was one less mouth to feed.

He slumped onto the chair at his desk, produced a bottle from the drawer and poured himself a large glass of cheap whisky. The fiery liquid disappeared in a single gulp. Wiping his mouth, he dipped his quill and then scratched onto a piece of parchment.

Dear Mr and Mrs Binny,

I am writing to sadly inform you that your son, Timmy, was fatally injured as part of his apprenticeship. Enclosed is a vial of his blood for resurrection, along with sixty gold pieces to help pay for it.

I'm sorry.

Regretfully yours,
Eric Featherwick

Eric put down the quill and leaned back. He sat, drumming his fingers and staring at the wall. That was the last of his money. Poor families like Timmy's rarely bothered with resurrections. It was far cheaper and more enjoyable to make a new son.

After a while, he stood up and produced a sign from the cupboard.

It read: "*Apprentice Vacancy - Enquire Within - (Five Copper Coins Per Day)*"

He placed it carefully in the window, then went over to the plaque on the wall which read "*Days without injury - 42*" and flipped the numbers to "*00*".

Finally, he sat back in his chair, put his head in his hands and let out a deep sigh.

2

Skwee scurried through the dark tunnels of The Master's lair, sweat dripping from his brow. The walls were thick with soot and claw marks, carved out by a domesticated demon. Screams echoed in the distance, followed by dull groans. One of the latest prisoners would be cooperating soon.

Skwee nimbly leapt over a poison barb trap, being sure not to trigger the tripwire or spill the tea tray, then turned a corner. The Master wouldn't like the news he had for him. Then again, he never seemed to like any news he brought.

Skwee had only been The Master's Personal Assistant for a few weeks, and it had already been the most stressful time of his life. At least the position was one minions rarely kept for long. Or so he'd heard.

He'd been promoted late one night, curled up in his comfy nest, deep down in the warrens with the other goblins. A senior officer had booted him in the side, grunting, 'You've been promoted, *Survivor*.' And that was that. Being the sole survivor of The Glogville Caves massacre had somehow attracted some attention. What his superiors didn't realise is that he only managed to avoid the massacre by hiding under a table. Then there'd been a job opening as a result of his predecessor not making the tea right.

Skwee tried to find his predecessor to ask for some advice. Such as, what were The Master's favourite biscuits? That sort of thing. But there had been some kind of violent accident in which his predecessor had tripped and fallen backwards onto a dagger several times.

As stressful as it was, being such a high ranking goblin had its perks. They gave him an extra soft pillow and he was allowed to eat scraps directly from The Master's table. That was premium grub. Skwee licked his lips. Maybe there'd be some roasted pheasant bones he could nibble on.

Skwee's heart pounded as he arrived outside The Master's chamber. Before him stood a tall, dark door, with hundreds of expensive-looking human skulls carved into it. Each painted pink.

The pink skull symbol was introduced a few years ago as part of what The Master called a 'rebranding exercise'. Apparently inventing the logo had cost a small fortune. Skwee thought he could have come up with something much better. Like a nice traditional white or black skull. But pink was supposed to give better brand awareness as The Master said it "popped". Now he had to spend his days in a tight pink tunic, which he thought made him look rather silly.

Skwee's green hands shook, clattering the tea tray as he rapped against the obsidian panelling.

'Enter,' came a booming voice.

Skwee turned the handle shaped like a severed demon's fist and strained to push open the door.

The Master sat behind his desk at the end of the high-ceilinged chamber, a fire crackling beside him. He wore a smart tunic covered by a cloak, all black with the exception of his signature pink skull logo shining out from a pin on his breast. The Master always looked regal, which was unusual for a human. Goblin guards lined the walls, standing like statues. Skwee didn't envy them. He knew how hard it was to keep still during guard duty, you couldn't even scratch your nose. The Master looked up, drumming his fingers against the lacquered wood. 'Well, what *is* it?' he said, wearily.

Skwee put down the tray on a side table and held up his notes, squinting at them in the light. He cleared his throat. 'Someone has managed to kill The Demi Lich Kalakzar, my lord. Our sensor runes have indicated that...'

The Master waved a dismissive hand. 'Impossible. My mages have *assured* me demi-liches are undefeatable. Kalakzar should have regenerated as soon as they left the raided crypt.' The Master cackled and twiddled his goatee. 'Those foolish adventurers keep coming back, resurrection after resurrection. They never learn. We're making a fortune from resurrection stones alone.'

Skwee wiped the sweat from his palms onto his pink tunic. 'It was a man called Eric Featherwick. A pest control agent at Beast Be Gone in Porkhaven. He used a Dispel Undead Scroll...'

'*Pest control*? I thought we'd run them all out of business?'

'Most of them my lord. Apparently he's one of the last ones. Him and Glorp & Co. Both are in pretty desperate financial situations. We purchased their debts a few years ago.'

The Master's lips twisted. 'Our swarms of adventurers will have been making it hard for them to find work. Still, to be on the safe side, we should put an end to their interfering. They must be living off the substantial loan from us. Alert our Doom Bank division and send in the bailiffs. Let's apply some pressure. They need to be made an example of.'

'At once my lord.'

'And let's get more adventurers out adventuring. I want all teenage boys and girls living near any pest control businesses orphaned. They'll be adventuring in under a week, freed from the tyranny of The King. Then train up more mysterious old folk to give them plenty of quests. I don't want this *Eric* having another contract *ever* again. Bankrupt him by the end of the month. Do I make myself clear?'

'Perfectly, my lord.'

'Oh and make sure all the other liches get resistant to these *vulnerabilities*. A simple weakness like that is laughable.' The Master frowned. 'In fact, I want *all* our minions inspected for weaknesses.'

'I'm not sure that's possi…'

'Get it *done*.'

'Yes, my lord.'

'Excellent. Did you bring my tea?'

Skwee held up the tray. 'Yes my lord, as requested.'

His Master's eyes narrowed at him. 'And *where* are the biscuits?'

Skwee's heart stopped. 'Oh… no my lord. My apologies, it… it… must have slipped my mind.'

The Master stood up, face blazing red. A glowing wind whipped around him, lifting up his cloak. He pointed a finger at Skwee and said in a deep, hollow voice, '*You have failed me for the last time, worthless wretch!*'

A jolt of pain hit Skwee in the chest. The air rushed from his lungs. Choking, he fell to the floor, trying to draw breath.

Faintly he heard The Master speak. It was distant, as if he were in another room. '*You*, step forward.'

Skwee closed his eyes as he convulsed on the ground.

'Me… my lord?' said one of the nearby goblin guards, his voice wavering.

'Yes, *you*. Congratulations. You've just been promoted.'

3

Eric's head pounded when he was awoken by the sounds of explosions. This was not uncommon in the city of Porkhaven, as it had the densest population of magic-wielding lunatics in all Fen-Tessai. They were usually throwing poorly aimed fireballs or messing up some experiment or other.

The explosions faded into a light tapping. He ignored the sound and rolled over, pulling the tattered bedsheet over his head, but it wasn't long before the noise became a constant banging.

Eric muttered, stood up and rubbed his temples. A jabbing pain blasted through his skull. How much did he drink last night? He'd got carried away. Now he wouldn't be able to afford another drink for at least a few weeks. What was he supposed to do to pass the time now?

He pulled back the curtains to release the waft of his nightly emissions and winced at the shower of morning light. Porkhaven sprawled out before him, a chaos of wonky rooftops and gravity-defying towers. He breathed in deeply, relishing the familiar stench of magic and gutter water. The acrid tang was especially strong around the neighbouring Alchemy District. It made him feel at home.

The banging continued.

'I'm coming, I'm coming,' he mumbled, fumbling his way into his breeches. He tripped and bashed his knee on the chest of drawers, cursed, *'Giant's balls!'* then threw on his tunic and hobbled downstairs. He entered the barren shop and approached the door, swiping up the letter on the doormat labelled in red print: *'Debt Overdue - Foreclosure Warning.'* He grimaced, crumpled it up and tossed it to where the bin had previously been.

More banging.

Eric sighed, opened the door halfway and poked his head into the fresh air.

A girl stood below him. She couldn't have been more than about fifteen, her pale skin in shining contrast to a bun of dark hair. She wore a curious golden backpack that chugged quietly, emitting a cloud of steam behind her head. A series of levers and dials poked out of the straps.

'Howdy and good morning,' she said cheerfully.

Eric put his hand up to shade his eyes. 'What do you want?'

'Why, I'm here to apply for the position of your apprentice.'

'What?'

'I came as soon as I heard there was a vacancy.' The girl pointed to the dusty wooden panel he'd propped against the glass a few months ago that read: "*Apprentice Vacancy - Enquire Within - (Five Copper Coins Per Day)*"

Eric ran his fingers through his thinning hair. Once it had been thick and dark, but in the past few years, it had become depressingly spattered with grey, making him appear even more boring. He'd always considered himself average looking, even painfully so. His chin was flat, his face was soft and his eyes a mundane brown. People never remembered him. In fact, as a child, his mother had accidentally left him at the market and taken another child instead. That evening, after Eric had finally found his way home, he switched back with the bewildered imposter and his mother had been none the wiser. Eric turned the sign over, hiding the text. 'That vacancy has expired.'

'Then let's not waste any more time. I should like to start immediately.' The girl strolled past Eric and into the shop. She glanced around, then wiped a finger along a dusty shelf. 'Well?'

It was far too early for this kind of nonsense. Her shrill Western voice was doing nothing for his headache. 'Well… it's not for girls, I'm afraid.' He was far too embarrassed to admit he couldn't even afford the measly five copper coins to pay her each day.

'Don't be absurd. Whyever not?'

Eric scratched the back of his head. 'Bit dangerous this line of work, you see.'

'Utter rubbish! So you're one of those old-fashioned types.' She shook her head. 'Times have changed Mr Featherwick.'

'Call me Eric.'

'Right, times have changed Eric. Gender equality is much more important than it was ten years ago. If you read any of the latest books, all the best protagonists are girls.'

'Is that so?' Eric gently edged the strange girl towards the door.

'Come to think of it, there aren't very many *without* a heroine...' She stepped backwards.

'Uh huh.' Eric nodded, another step.

'In fact, without fully representing gender equality in your workplace you could have your fingernails pulled out for discrimination.'

'How interesting.' The girl was backed all the way to the open doorway. He may be able to have that lie-in after all.

In one quick motion, the girl jerked one of her levers.

An arm sprung out of her metallic backpack. It flung itself backwards, almost life-like in a hiss of steam. The claw at the end of the arm grabbed the door and slammed it closed behind her.

'Rose,' said the girl, extending a hand.

Eric ignored it, stunned. 'Beg your pardon?'

'My name's Rose.'

'Oh.' Eric weakly shook her hand, then turned back towards his desk. He poured himself a whisky, draining the bottle, and sat down.

She stood over him, watching intently. All he could hear was the gentle hum of her mysterious bag. He took a deep swig from the glass and let the sweet oak flavour burn its way down his throat.

'I'm from the Western Lands you see,' said Rose, breaking the silence.

'I gathered.'

'From my accent?' She stared at Eric with a frown. 'Gee, have I said something to offend you? Sorry if I don't know your funny customs. This sure is a strange place. My boat arrived in Fen-Tessai only this morning and I'm still trying to figure things out.'

Her accent was undoubtedly annoying. It was as if she was trying her best to make everything a question when it wasn't. 'No, it's not that. But I wouldn't worry, it really isn't complicated.'

'It's certainly a lot more *moist* here than where I'm from.'

'I expect so.'

'Can you explain to me why there are so many horses everywhere?'

Eric rubbed his temples, kneading-out the pain. 'How else do you get around?'

'Zeppelins, chuffers and cart-mobiles of course! Not to mention the railsteams. It all seems so *old-fashioned* here.'

Eric rolled his eyes. They were so obsessed with steam in the Western Lands. Eric would take a good old enchantment over some crazy gadget. So much simpler. The West was an awful place full of brash, tech-touting loud-mouths. There, even the most humble of Westerners had elaborate gadgets. Things that couldn't possibly need moving parts, like tables or mugs, had cogs inexplicably plastered all over them.

'Oh Eric, now I've gone and offended you again.' Rose chuckled to herself. 'You Easterners are just too funny.'

'Why did you come here?'

'To apprentice with you of course!'

'Then why don't you just go and apprentice at Glorp & Co Pest Control? They're much more successful than I am.' Eric winced at the thought of his rival.

Rose scoffed. 'They're far too corporate. And besides, I've heard you're the best.' She smiled warmly. 'I'm happy to pay top coin for that kind of experience.'

'Pay?'

'Of course,' she gestured to the overturned sign. 'I think five copper coins per day is a bargain for an education like this.'

'You want to pay *me*?' He cleared his throat. 'I mean, yes, of course, you'll pay me. Well, you ain't getting much education here anyway, Glorp & Co steal all the good jobs. Then the adventurers take the rest.'

'I'll take my chances. And besides, my father spoke very highly of you.'

Eric stopped lifting the whisky to his lips. 'Your father?'

'The High Governor of Murica.'

He thought for a moment. 'Oh yeah, funny looking fellow with a big nose.'

'That's him alright. He told me you saved his life.'

Eric took a deep swig of his drink. 'Long time ago that was. I ain't the same man I was back then.' He could barely imagine the man he'd been, practically a boy. He'd saved The High Governor of Murica's life after a dire-beetle decided to lodge itself in a chandelier while he was visiting for a diplomatic ball. The King had insisted the ball must go on, even with the overhead threat. Naturally, it was a disaster, but at least Eric's insect net broke rather than The High Governor's neck. The High Governor could probably afford to buy the entire city of Porkhaven ten times over and turn it into a mechanical walking city. Eric licked his lips. Perhaps Rose could be useful after all.

'Even if you are half the man my father described, you'd be better than twice most other people.' Rose grinned at him. Eric decided she was possibly one of the most precocious little teenagers he had ever met. 'Father said you were the best.'

Eric grunted, but sat up a little straighter, shuffling in his chair. 'Maybe once. Before all these adventurers got out of control.'

'That's partly why I'm here.' Rose's face was impassive, yet the corners of her eyes twitched. She turned away from Eric and put her hands to her face. 'My brother died after running off with a band of adventurers.' Her shoulders shuddered. 'The whole party got ambushed by wandering ogres. By the time anyone found them... the blood was too stale for resurrection.' She turned back to Eric, her cheeks glistening wet. 'My father sent me here to learn from you, so we can put an end to adventuring for good. In the Eastern and Western Lands both. Clear out one dungeon at a time and leave nothing left for adventurers to plunder.'

Eric felt a wetness in the corner of his eye. It must have been a bit of sweat. 'Clearing out a few caves won't stop 'em,' he said, wiping his face. 'I'm not sure where they're all coming from, but they're everywhere. It used to only be the odd lone hero; I could compete with that, but now I can't even get a measly job killing rats in tavern basements.'

'I can help you, Eric. We can work together. It doesn't have to be that way.' She banged a fist into her open palm. 'When you see a problem with the world, doesn't that make you want to change it?'

This strange little girl certainly had big dreams. He'd probably been like that once, back when his shop stood for something. Pest control made a difference a long time ago. He protected innocent people from dangerous creatures and dangerous people from innocent creatures. Now everyone only wanted to go out and slaughter one other.

How could he get this girl to leave him alone? His hangover screamed for him to go back to bed. 'I don't think so. It's far too late now. There's nothing we can do.'

'I'm convinced it's part of a larger conspiracy. The infrastructure supporting adventurers is too convenient. I don't have a plan yet, but you're going to help me whether you like it or not. I don't give up that easily Mr Fea…'

A duck flew through the door and landed on the counter behind them. It made a loud quack and stared at Eric.

'Is that a…?' asked Rose.

'Yup.'

'Can't you Easterners afford owls or crows? Much more elegant, don't you think?'

The duck tilted its head and quacked again.

'Carrier-ducks are much better suited to this climate.' Eric went over to the duck and removed the note from its leg. 'A duck will push on, rain or shine. Plus the duck postal service runs exclusively on payments of breadcrumb. Those owls demand fresh mice and are too self-absorbed to deliver during the day, and the arrogant crows will shi...' He stopped himself. 'Not that it's any of your business.'

'Fascinating.' Rose's backpack claw handed her a funny-looking metallic quill that didn't have a feather on top. She scribbled in her notebook.

Eric frowned as he read the duck's note.

Rose leaned across, 'What does it say?'

Eric covered the note. 'Also none of your business.'

Rose snatched the paper from his hands and read it. Eric was too shocked to react.

'Ohh! A call to action!' Rose exclaimed, 'Lord Egglewort wants an infestation of kobolds removed from his old fort so he can renovate it for his new son-in-law. Sounds fun! Can I come? This could be the perfect way for us to get to know each other.'

Secretly he wanted to jump for joy at the chance of work. Finally, something to sink his teeth into. But all the feelings of happiness melted away as soon as he realised Rose was still beaming up at him. He couldn't possibly operate with such a busybody trailing behind him. Even if she was paying. And what if she died? What would her father say? The last thing he needed was a powerful international enemy. 'No. You're not my apprentice, so you can't come.'

'You can't stop me from following you.' Rose folded her arms. 'It's a free country.' She stopped herself. 'Well, maybe not *country*… and not really *free*.' She tapped her chin. 'More, poorly defined landmass with a strictly autocratic feudal social structure.'

Eric sighed, then filled out a reply to Lord Egglewort on a bit of parchment. He attached it to the duck's leg and fed it some bread crumbs. The duck quacked with glee, then fluttered out the window.

Eric grabbed his cloak and left the shop with the irritating girl following behind him.

He stopped in his tracks.

Outside, a small crowd of people tittered around a large lump of metal sat in the street.

Rose walked right up the lump and patted it on the side. The form sprung to life in a whirr of clunks and clanks, lifting off the ground to reveal dozens of tiny legs. The crowd of onlookers cooed as steam seeped from the crevices in its armour. Eric coughed and fanned his face. The thing looked like some kind of giant mechanical woodlouse.

Rose leapt up into its back. 'What's the matter? You look like you've never seen a chuffer before.'

Eric ignored her and went to the stables next door. There he filled up Daisy's saddlebags and smiled as she chewed on a carrot. She was the only one in the world who understood him. Probably because she was happy with the simple things in life. He climbed on her back and led her outside to the road.

Rose's chuffer rattled and spat as it followed alongside him. The contraption drew all sorts of attention from the passers-by, and almost crushed some overly curious and enthusiastic children. Rose had put on a ludicrous pair of brass goggles; Eric wondered if they actually improved her vision or were merely a fashion accessory.

Heads continued to turn as they passed through the main city square. Although most people here were too distracted by their daily shopping to do more than watch the strange invention chugging by. A long shadow fell on the Porkhaven's main square, cast by a great structure at the far end. It gleamed with freshly polished stone and across the front, a colossal sign read:

The Guild
Career Advice and Services
Your Adventure Starts TODAY
"Why farm animals when you could farm Experience?"
Proudly Brought To You By The Doom Bank

A pair of goblins handed out fliers and Elixirs to the cityfolk, 'Get your free Elixir sample, courtesy of The Guild!' they cried. Merchants, craftsmen and beggars alike all gathered around them, clamouring for their free taste. Elixir was awful, addictive stuff, Eric thought. Only adventurers were mad enough to drink it. No doubt those grabbing samples would be joining The Guild and becoming adventurers before long.

They carried on through the city, and soon there weren't many honest work-hands left on the streets. Most of the folk wore chainmail and brandished an assortment of weapons.

A pointy-eared person stepped out from the throng, blocking Daisy and bringing her to a stop. The elf's armour left him almost completely naked, as if his enemies were only intent on cutting off his nipples. He looked Eric dead in the eye, 'Got any quests?' he said.

'No, get out of my way.' Eric tried to go around him, but Daisy wouldn't budge.

'Come on I know you've got a quest or two for me.' The elf put his hands together. 'Missing a family heirloom? Bandits kidnapped a loved one? Troll scaring your cattle? Give me something, *anything*. I'm begging you, please. I need the Experience, *please*.'

'I *said*, get out of my way.' Eric kicked Daisy and she trotted forward, knocking the adventurer aside.

Typical adventurers. They truly were a sad, mad lot.

Eric and Rose exited the city gates. Tall trees cast shadows across the winding road ahead. Eric shivered. It was autumn, and the air was as bitter as a vampire's temperament.

'How far is it?' asked Rose.

'Not far.'

'I thought there'd be more magic here in the Eastern Lands. Why can't we just teleport?'

Eric scoffed. 'You think I'm made of money? Scrolls of Town Portal are costly enough as it is, but they only take you home. And besides, we're only going a few miles out of the city.'

'I knew I should have brought father's zeppelin…'

'Uh huh.'

There was a pause. 'Wanna know how I control my backpack?'

Eric grunted.

'Well, it's very clever actually. It's *thought* activated. There's a strong bond between me and my pack, not unlike the bond between a witch and her pet familiar. It doesn't only move because of these levers, I have to *will* it.'

'Is that so.'

'It's highly sophisticated.'

'Wow.'

'Are you even listening?'

'Amazing.'

Rose huffed and they were left with only the sound of the breeze and the incessant spluttering of the mechanical steed.

After a while they turned off the main road and followed the track into Lord Egglewort's vast estate. Fen-Tessai's countryside was depressing at the best of times, but this was worse than he'd ever seen it. Normally it looked like a painting by a lazy artist who'd thrown green paint down and added the exact same trees, houses and fields over and over. But now barren farmlands blanketed their sorrow across the land. Limp wheat lay on the earth and piles of apples rotted beneath the trees. Eric couldn't hear the bleating of a single sheep.

Rose pulled out a metal tube from her sleeve. She somehow extended its length, then thrust it into her eye. Humming, she scanned the miserable horizon. 'Where are all the green and golden fields I've heard so much about? It's all a bit… you know, *grey*.'

Eric spat onto the road, but the wind flicked it onto Daisy's side. Eric pretended not to notice. 'All the young farmhands want to run off and go adventuring these days. Ain't nobody left to work the land. Damned shame it is.'

'And that doesn't make you want to try and stop them?'

'Not right now, no.'

A crossroad appeared before them. Eric stopped Daisy and pulled a map out of his Sack of Clutching.

'Are you lost?' asked Rose.

'No, just making sure.' Eric rolled up the map. 'Navigation's tricky in Fen-Tessai, you see.'

'Oh? How interesting.' Rose cocked her head. 'Is that because you people have bad spatial awareness?'

Eric gritted his teeth. 'Let's just say mountains and forests tend to migrate a little.'

'Are you serious?'

'I'm always serious. Anyway, it should be up that hill.'

The old fort soon loomed in front of them. Its walls were made from large grey blocks that crumbled away at the corners. They rode up and stopped at the closed gate.

Eric cleared his throat. 'Hello there!' he called up to the battlements. 'Is Grom, The Slayer Of Men there?'

There was a quiet tittering above them, then a pointy-eared creature poked its head out between the crenelations.

'Who askin'?' said the kobold.

'Tell him Eric's here.'

There was more whispering overhead.

Rose turned to Eric and muttered, 'You *know* these creatures?'

'Of course.'

'What are they?'

'Kobolds.'

'What's a kho-bald?'

'You'll soon find out.'

'Okay!' yelled the kobold from above, 'but who with you?'

'It's…' Eric looked across at Rose and said weakly, 'It's my apprentice.'

Rose beamed as the gate slowly lifted before them.

'Come on then.' Eric gave Daisy a kick, and she strolled into the dark entrance.

He had a strong feeling he was going to regret it.

4

Eric and Rose rode through the fort's passageway. Furry, loincloth-clad kobolds stood in rows along the walls, their spears pointed and ready. Rose let out a whimper.

'No need to worry,' said Eric. 'They're more afraid of you than you are of them.'

They dismounted at the fort's stable and were immediately surrounded. The kobolds clinked as they shuffled along, their mismatched ill-fitting armour no doubt harvested from inexperienced adventurers. Every kobold had managed to find an item to wear that made them unique, either a jazzy ribbon or pink pauldron, making them easy to tell apart. Kobolds had curiously dog-like faces that almost made them look cute. However, their scowls ruined what little affection humans might have for them. The poor devils weren't welcome anywhere, which was especially telling in a land where even goblins could find jobs if they tried hard enough. After a bath and some training in politeness, goblins made surprisingly good lawyers.

The little creatures glared at Rose's chuffer in disbelief. One tapped it with his spear, the machine hissed a cloud of steam and the kobold fell back with a squeak. The others decided to keep a safe distance.

The guards escorted Rose and Eric deeper into the ruin, murmuring amongst themselves and flashing wary looks. The ones taking charge were the largest and held wonky candles that sent a flickering light along the corridors. The further they went, the more the place stank like a gryphon's litter box.

They came to a great hall packed full of kobolds perched on hay bales and wooden chests. At the end of the room sat a kobold on a makeshift throne, one who was around twice the size of all the others and had a halberd sitting across his lap. The human doublet he wore was bursting at the seams and squished the creature into a hunch. He glared at Eric and Rose with beady eyes.

Eric approached the throne and stood before him. The other kobolds scuttled off into the shadows. For a moment, Eric and the large kobold stared at each other in silence. He felt his heart thud in his chest. Last time he met this tribe he'd bribed them to vacate a disused warehouse with some magic beans. They were only regular beans of course, haricot if he remembered correctly. So long as they hadn't figured that out he'd be fine. His fingers tightened around the emergency smoke bomb in his pocket. The chief kobold loomed over him, furrowing his brow.

Eric bowed. 'Hello, Grom.'

Grom burst into laughter. 'Eric!' he said, standing up. 'It been long time!' He embraced Eric, which made Eric's back click. His nostrils were bombarded with the musk of sweat and hay.

He held his breath.

'How are the kids?' asked Eric, exhaling.

'Good thanks, very good.' Grom sat back down on his throne. 'Little Grom set up own tribe. Very proud. Magic beans good luck.'

'Glad to hear it, glad to hear it.' Eric looked around the room, then back at Grom. 'I suppose you know why I'm here.'

'Who this time?'

'Lord Egglewort,' said Eric. 'You weren't to know.'

Grom groaned. 'But just decorated bedroom! Can't leave now.'

'I know, I know, but he inherited the land last month. He's going to renovate the place and have a nice spot for his new son-in-law.'

'We not leaving.' Grom crossed his arms. 'It nice here.'

Eric knew it was time to play hardball. 'I didn't want to tell you this, but…'

Grom leaned forward, taking the bait. 'What? Tell what?'

'Lord Egglewort said he's already put this place on a tavern noticeboard.'

Grom nearly fell off his throne. 'He not dare!'

'Adventurers could be here any minute.'

'Adventurers!' Grom yelped. The crowd of kobolds around them began to murmur.

'I'm here to give you a polite warning. Give you a good chance to get out while you can.'

'He evil man. We have families. We bother no one.'

'Now I know you're just trying to make a home for yourselves, but you've got to find somewhere else. It's not safe.'

'Where we go? Nowhere safe. Adventurers everywhere.'

'Well, maybe that's where I can help you.' Eric produced a piece of folded paper from his Sack Of Clutching.

Grom took the paper and looked at it intently. 'What this?'

'It's a pamphlet showing the new rehousing scheme that's been set up way over in the west. There's an extensive list of nice unused cave systems. All perfect for your tribe to live in peace. Plenty of space and the area is a haven for bees, so you can make all the wax candles you desire.' Eric had personally been out to find the rehousing locations a few months ago when he didn't have much else to do. He was a little jealous, as with the exception of the ones near swamps they were all rather lovely spots. Running off to hide in a cave would certainly solve a lot of his problems.

Grom's eyes glowed with joy. 'Many candles!' He shook his head. 'How know caves safe?'

'For one thing, there's no ancient treasure hidden in any of them, so you don't have to worry about adventurers blundering in. But the best part is there ain't no nearby taverns. Adventurers would have to travel for *days* without taking a rest. So even if they did reach you, they'd be too weak to fight.'

Grom scratched his oversized nose that was filled with clumps of hair seeking daylight. 'Seems too good. What catch?'

'You need to be out of here by sunrise.'

'Hmm.' Grom frowned and looked intently at the pamphlet. Eric realised he was nervously tapping his foot, and stopped. Grom had better take the deal, he would hate to have to use stink bombs to flush them out. These poor things never hurt anyone. Maybe the odd inexperienced adventurer or two, but they didn't really count as people.

Grom remained silent. Eric needed to sweeten the deal. He cleared his throat. 'Okay Grom, how about this. You can take anything you can carry too. Then you'll have some furnishings for your new home.'

The kobold grunted. 'Hmm. Okay Eric, deal. But only because you. Not Lord Egg.' He spat on the ground and they shook hands.

Lord Egglewort wouldn't even know what was in the fort yet, so taking a few chairs wouldn't matter. But the kobolds didn't know that.

Eric turned back to see Rose furiously scribbling notes in her book, her backpack rumbling in time with the featherless quill.

Back at the stables, Rose and Eric mounted their steeds while a mob of kobolds gathered to wave them goodbye.

Grom smiled, revealing a thick set of wonky teeth. 'Visit any time friend.'

'I will,' said Eric. 'Just keep off people's properties, or I may see you sooner.' He winked and Grom chuckled.

'Tell Lord Egg we gone by sunrise.'

'Bye then,' said Eric, turning Daisy around.

Eric and Rose trotted back through the passageway and out into the forest, steam trailing behind them, emitted vigorously from Rose's chuffer.

'Are there really adventurers on their way?' asked Rose once they were back on the path. The trees along the road were eerily calm, their amber leaves practically motionless. 'The note didn't say anything about that.'

'Who knows?' said Eric. 'There usually are.'

'So you *lied*?'

'Of course. All part of the job.'

Rose jotted down more notes. 'And where are we going now?'

'Well, *I'm* going to pay Lord Egglewort a visit.'

'And as your newly appointed apprentice,' said Rose with a grin, 'You won't mind me tagging along too.'

It was dark by the time they rode up to Lord Egglewort's castle gates. Guards appeared on the battlements above.

'State your business peasant!' one called down.

Eric ignored the presumption about his status and craned his neck upwards. 'We're from Beast Be Gone, here to see Lord Egglewort and collect on a kobold contract.'

Unseen, the guards mumbled to one another. The portcullis rumbled upwards before them.

The guards footsteps echoed as they led them to the spacious dining hall. A surprising number of stewards stood along the walls, surrounding a sea of empty tables. The party approached the end of the hall, where Lord Egglewort sat alone at his long-table, gorging on a leg of mutton. He was thinner than most lords, and yet still grotesquely overweight. His faded purple finery attempted to hold the shape of his body, leaving little to the imagination and provided a shield for food smatterings. Working with Lords always left a sour taste in Eric's mouth, and Lord Egglewort was no exception. Especially after what happened last time.

'Ah, the chap from Beast Be Gone!' said Lord Egglewort without getting up. Grease dripped down his chin as he spoke. 'Did you fix my little problem? I recall you did sterling work for me before. With some giant spiders in the forest, I believe?'

'That's right,' said Eric. 'Got through about four barrels of repellent.' The repellent in question had been cripplingly expensive. He'd almost made a loss as Lord Egglewort refused to negotiate.

'And the pine trees still smell of lemons to this day.' Lord Egglewort chortled as bits of meat spattered down his front. He looked over to Rose. 'And a new apprentice too! What a fine bit of Western technology you have there. Delightful.'

Rose beamed and made the claw on her backpack spin. 'Why thanks. A pleasure to meet you.' She bowed.

Lord Egglewort turned his gaze back to Eric. 'So what's the news?'

'The kobolds will be gone from the fort by morning,' said Eric.

'Jolly good! Colour me impressed, I knew you were the man for the job. I'm glad I went with you, your competitors at Glorp & Co cost a bleeding fortune. Times are tough don't you know?'

Eric winced at the mention of Glorp & Co. Times were tough indeed. Tough enough to lower his prices to rock bottom.

Lord Egglewort leaned in. 'So how on earth did you manage it?'

'Trade secret.'

'Of course, of course.' Lord Egglewort tapped his nose with his forefinger. 'If you couldn't manage it I would have had to get some adventurers in. Dreadful, the lot of them.'

'That they are.'

'They would have wrecked the place. Especially if they had a blasted mage with them.'

'Fire-burns don't come out easy.'

'Precisely.' Lord Egglewort undid his breeches to release his belly. 'Ahh that's better.' He breathed out deeply. 'So how much damage have those wretched creatures done?'

Eric scratched the back of his head. 'Not too much, my Lord. But they have stolen most of the furnishings. It will need a good renovation.'

Lord Egglewort tutted. 'That's a shame. I would quite like to get my new son-in-law moved in there as soon as possible. He's a layabout you see, need him out of the castle.'

'Right.'

'I was hoping a project might liven him up a bit. Having the run of the place, you know?' Lord Egglewort raised his voice as if reaching him in another room. '*Be a man for once!*'

'Uh-huh.'

The contempt in Lord Egglewort seemed to subside. 'Anyway, I digress. I'm afraid you'll have to wait until tomorrow for your payment, once we've confirmed the fort is clear. Feel free to stay the night. I'll have the servants make up some beds.' He clapped his hands and some of the hovering stewards hurried out of the room.

'That's very kind of you.' Eric performed an awkward bow. 'Oh and um… we also offer a "Prevention Package", three years of guaranteed security from beasts and…'

'No, no,' Lord Egglewort cut in, 'that won't be necessary.'

'Perhaps you may be interested in one of our partners' packages?'

'What partners?'

'I work with a number of partners who can offer an excellent "Tax Protection Package" and a "Renovation Package".' Eric handed him a pamphlet. 'Oh and the "Platinum Package" combines both of these with the "Prevention Package", for a monthly sum of...'

Lord Egglewort waved at him to stop. 'Enough. I don't want any of your damn packages.'

'There's a five percent discount if you sign up today.' There was a five percent bonus in it for Eric too.

'Only five percent? Pitiful.'

Eric tensed his fists as the rage inside him simmered. This pompous oaf has been walking all over him for years, but not for much longer. Eric opened his mouth to shout, to scream...

Rose stepped forward. 'If I may.'

Eric, startled, held his tongue.

Rose cleared her throat. 'The fort has been left in an awful state by those creatures. It really could use a makeover.' She pointed at the prices on the pamphlet. 'You'd make a great saving signing up with us today. If you tried to get a better price in the city, they'd screw you. *And* then take months to get going. We could have them here tomorrow, it says so right on the pamphlet. Your son-in-law could be living there in luxury in a matter of weeks.'

Eric stared at her in disbelief. Damned Westerners and their overconfidence.

'I suppose so,' said Lord Egglewort drumming his fingers. 'Fine. Just the Renovation Package will do.'

'Thank you.' Eric felt a great wash of relief. The five percent commission on a job like this would keep him alive for another few weeks. 'I'll tell them to come by tomorrow.'

Lord Egglewort went back to his food. 'Now get out of my sight before I change my mind.'

As they walked out of the great hall, Rose flashed Eric a smile. Eric did his best to ignore it.

5

Skwee scratched at the scales on his head. His goblin eyes had long since adjusted to the gloom of the cave, so he didn't have any trouble seeing, yet the wonky rock shapes of the dead-end didn't look familiar to him at all. He'd arrived in Darkfill Cave the week before, immediately after his resurrection, and was still having trouble finding his way around. The winding cavern was supposed to be easy to navigate, with conveniently placed boxes and barricades to create a linear journey, all of which eventually circled back to the main entrance. Although you had to pull a lever on the other side so newcomers would still have to take the long way round. It was all very confusing, and yet none of the other goblin minions appeared to mind. They wandered the corridors without much awareness of where they were going, blank expressions plastered onto their pointy faces.

Skwee wondered why they'd been sent here in the first place. There didn't seem to be any strategic reason that they should occupy this particular cavern, but The Master had been very insistent. Something about being bait. For who or what, Skwee didn't have the foggiest idea. There was a very shiny sword that they seemed to be guarding, but it wasn't locked up or anything. In fact it sat on a big pedestal, right out in the open. Of course they weren't allowed to touch it. But what good was having a powerful weapon if they couldn't even use it to defend themselves? Maybe The Master was worried they would break it.

This had been his third position in two months with the Dark Army and he was still desperate to fit in. "Fitting in" meant not asking too many questions and keeping your head down. After having upset The Master as an assistant, he'd been crushed into a tiny ball, promptly healed and relegated back to the lowest of the low. Level one minion. That was fine by Skwee, as he was just happy to be involved. Even if it included the most excruciating and humiliating experience of his life.

It had been Skwee's dream to work for an evil overlord. He'd been over the moon when his minion application had been accepted. Tears had filled his eyes as he read the letter to his brood-mother. Then he'd packed up his bindle, waved goodbye to all thirty-three siblings and left the swamp for good.

Skwee stopped tapping his chin and turned back. This wasn't the way. He was feeling rather peckish now as he'd been looking for the fire pit for over an hour. Maybe he should have taken the other left past the not-so-secret loot room?

A scream echoed through the darkness. Skwee froze, heart pounding. It was unmistakably goblin.

This was it. Time for action. Follow the steps from the training seminar.

He yelled, as if by instinct, 'You'll regret coming here, stranger!' Then headed towards the sound.

His little feet slapped the stone as he veered around the corner, but stopped dead at the sight of the room. Three goblins lay motionless in the cavern, green blood decorating the walls. Skwee felt the bile build in the back of his throat. His eyes darted around the emptiness as he panted, sweat dripped down his sides. There was a phrase he was supposed to use at times like this. What was it?

'Must have just been the wind,' he said with deliberation. That was it. It was a phrase to make it less embarrassing for you that there was actually no-one there. Then you were just talking to yourself. But on the off chance there *was* someone there, they would think you thought there was no one there. Or something like that. It made his head hurt when they'd tried to explain it to him.

A swarm of goblins scuttled in through a side passage and scattered into the room, daggers drawn. They must have heard the commotion too. Skwee let out a sigh of relief. They would know the protocols and he could follow along.

A shadow flickered. Were his eyes playing tricks on him?

A squeal. A goblin dropped to the floor, throat spilling blood. The flicker moved. Another goblin fell, head sliced clean off.

Panic set in. The other goblins ran in all directions, frantically shouting the lines from training.

'Die, adventurer!'

'Not so cocky now, human scum!'

'Must have been the wind.'

All the while Skwee could see the fear and helplessness in their eyes. He felt it too. He didn't want to die, not again. Not like this. The resurrection had been the second most painful experience of his life, dying being the first.

Figures burst into the cavern. Humans clad in shining armour, weapons glowing with magical power, faces strong and confident. Skwee was in awe.

The armoured woman pointed her mace forward. 'Xenixala give me an enchantment of bolster before I cast my shadow rune. It'll give me a bonus to my casting power.'

The robed Xenixala waved a dismissive hand, 'Oh *shut up* Panella.'

'We discussed this before the raid!' Panella shouted. 'And for hell's sake watch out for Jimmy, he's being stealthy.'

But Xenixala had already begun chanting, a glow sparking from her hands. She stumbled and threw her arms forward. Skwee yelped, dropped his rusty dagger and dived to the ground. The stone floor sent a sharp pain through his side as a fireball flew overhead. It exploded behind him, sending a pulsating wave of heat through the cave. Goblins screamed in agony, their faces melting as the flames engulfed them.

Skwee rolled across the floor towards a pile of his decapitated colleagues and thrust himself under their warm, motionless bodies.

'I don't want to die,' he whimpered to himself. 'Oh please don't let me die. I have so much left to take.' Tears streamed down his cheeks, mixing with the blood of his comrades.

He needed to stay quiet and still, but he couldn't stop trembling. He clenched his eyes shut and thought of his brood-mother, of freshly baked rat-pie and summer mornings by the bog.

If he had known minion life was like this he never would have applied.

6

The High Sorceress Xenixala of Xendor, Breaker of Demons, Oracle of Elendar and treasurer of the Bagwell Library Club, lay in a pool of her own vomit, her mouth bitter with the tang of bile and stale Elixir.

'Wake up, witch,' came a deep voice.

A hulk loomed over and nudged her with its boot.

Xenixala rubbed her eyes. 'I'm awake, Gronk. Snuff off.'

Gronk crossed his mighty arms. 'At last.'

Xenixala smiled. Thankfully, Gronk was a man of few words. Typical barbarian.

A cold drip landed on her from the cavern ceiling high above. Darkfill Cave was truly a depressing place. The air was clammy, the light was dim, and the ceiling full of stalactites that looked like a bored sculptor had got sloppy and copied the same design a thousand times. Yet Gronk never once complained about the cold in the two weeks they had been adventuring together. This was especially strange as all he wore was a tiny leather loincloth and a strap to keep his oversized axe on his bulging back.

Xenixala sat up and rubbed her temples. How many Elixirs had she had last night? Things were a blur.

There was a groan at her side. It came from her upturned spellbook. Its ancient papers twitched and fluttered, then snapped shut. A gap appeared between the pages along the book's fore-edge, forming a sort of mouth. 'I have a suspicion we overdid it last night Xeni,' it said.

'Oh stop moaning, Wordsworth,' said Xenixala. 'I don't recall you asking me to stop.'

'I don't remember all that much to be honest…'

'Enough of this!' shouted Panella. Why did the Clerics of The Holy Mole have to be so self-righteous?

Xenixala and Wordsworth turned to face her. Panella had turned bright red, her face shining against her white surcoat and neat blond hair.

Panella lunged at Xenixala.

Gronk's great hands clasped Panella. Lifted from the ground, she wriggled with the violence of a cornered bugbear.

'Let me go, you beast!' she screamed. 'She deserves death!'

Gronk held her effortlessly. 'Remember your oath, Panella.'

'Relax, Panella,' said Xenixala. 'Go cast a calm-spell on yourself.'

Panella glared at Xenixala, shaking with rage. 'Aren't you even going to *apologise*?'

Xenixala continued to rub her head. 'For what?'

'For last night!'

Xenixala looked across at Wordsworth. He curved his spine into a shrug.

'By The Holy Mole,' said Panella, broken. Gronk let her go and she crumpled to the floor. 'You're officially out of the party.'

'Wouldn't be the first time.' Xenixala glanced around, only just noticing the carnage in the cave. There were huge black gashes scarring the walls. Rubble littered the floor, interspersed with splatted goblin corpses and stinking pools of green blood. She held back a retch. 'Where's Jimmy Lightfoot? Hiding in the shadows as usual?'

'He's *dead*. No thanks to you.'

'Oh, what happened?'

'You really don't remember do you?'

'Enlighten me.'

Panella snatched up a discarded empty Elixir bottle and waved it at Xenixala's face. *'This happened.'*

Gronk shook his head but said nothing.

Xenixala stood up carefully, trying to stop the world spinning. 'I get it. I had one too many Elixirs, no big deal.'

'No big deal? *No big deal?!'* Panella raised her voice, throwing the Elixir bottle to the ground, it shattered. 'You drank *every* last Elixir we had! Enough to last at least ten adventures!'

'No sweat, I'll buy us some more when we get to the next town.'

'Jimmy *needed* those Elixirs, Xenixala. He bled to death because of you. Just *one* Elixir would have healed him. *One.*'

'Run out of healing spells did you?'

'You know I did! Healing *you*!'

Xenixala looked down to see the five or six goblin arrows poking out of her side. The wounds glowed with the afterburn of Elixir and healing incantations. She tutted. She'd never get another robe to fit her like this one. Especially not in blue. 'I had enough Elixirs inside me to keep me going. You shouldn't have bothered.'

'Well I know that *now*. Besides, I had to use my spells on Gronk too. After *you* hit him with a stray fireball.'

Gronk scowled and scratched his thick beard, half of which had been singed off.

'Sorry, Gronk,' said Xenixala.

'So *now* we get an apology?' said Panella, exasperated.

'What do you want from me?' Xenixala shrugged. 'I'm sorry ok! By The Mole, just relax. You're giving me a headache.'

'Don't blame me for your Elixir burndown, you did that to yourself. And you know what else? You killed everything yourself again! Grom and I won't get *any* Experience from this dungeon, we'll never be the most Experienced adventurers with you around.'

Wordsworth licked his lips. Or rather, a kind of leather bookmark protruded from his pages and flickered along the edges of his cover. 'Did we get any good loot? Any nice books perchance?'

Panella flashed him a cold stare. 'You're not getting anything, you stupid *book*. In fact,' she paused and crossed her arms, 'We're going to sue you for damages.'

Xenixala and Wordsworth looked at one another. Then they both let out a hearty laugh. Xenixala gasped for air, then wiped a tear from her cheek, 'Good luck with that.'

Panella stood firm. 'Resurrecting Jimmy will cost us a small fortune. And we'll have to go *all* the way back to The High Temple. As it's your fault, we think you should pay.'

'Go stuff yourself. He got himself killed.'

'Oh really?' said Panella. 'He'd crept right up behind the Goblin Lord, then you two buffoons ran in screaming incantations. Those goblins were on him faster than a dragon on heat. He didn't stand a chance.'

Xenixala scoffed. 'Serves him right for being such a dirty sneak.' You never could rely on thieves in your party. They were too damn fragile, and their egos were so big they always insisted on being the first into the room. They thought they were so brooding and complex. 'He had it coming. What sort of a name is Jimmy Lightfoot anyway?'

Wordsworth chuckled. 'It'd be like calling you Sally Spellhands.'

'Exactly, utterly ridiculous. Pretentious is what it is.'

'Totally pretentious.'

Panella sighed and drew the mace from her belt. 'Enough of this.' She pointed the weapon towards the pair. 'Pay us what you owe, then get out of our sight.'

Wordsworth coughed. 'Xeni, perhaps we do a page four hundred and fifty-three?'

'Oh excellent idea, Wordsworth,' Xenixala said with a grin.

'Right you are.' Wordsworth leapt into her arms and riffled open to page four hundred and fifty-three.

Panella frowned. 'What's on page four hundred and fif…?'

Before she could finish her sentence, she froze on the spot. Her skin turned a stone-like grey, her face twisted in confusion.

Wordsworth's pages stopped glowing. 'Nicely done, Xeni.'

'And a nicely done to *you* too, Wordsworth.'

Gronk stood watching them with his mouth hanging open, clearly deciding whether to run or attack. It amused Xenixala that he thought he might stand a chance to do either.

Xenixala ran her finger down four hundred and fifty-three again and read the incantation a second time. The words glowed a bright blue and lifted into the air like smoke, then raced towards Gronk.

Gronk tried to lunge aside, but was too slow. He froze in a half jumping pose of panic, then toppled to the floor. The stone Gronk clattered and splashed into goblin's blood.

Xenixala shut Wordsworth. 'They'll be alright in a few hours won't they, Wordsworth?'

'Yeah, I'm sure they'll be fine. A little stiff perhaps. But alive.'

'I guess we don't stay around for long after we cast that one.'

'Probably for the best,' said Wordsworth. 'So what's next? Go back to the local inn and find another party? Get another quest or two?'

'I dunno, I'm getting sick of these adventures. They're all so *boring*. It's always ruddy bandits or goblins.'

'We just need to keep looking. We'll find something good eventually.' Wordsworth excitedly leapt from her arms. 'Come on, let's see what glorious treats they've found. That's bound to cheer you up.'

Xenixala went over to Gronk and pulled the Sack of Clutching from his belt. She stuck her arm inside and rummaged around.

Adventuring had been such a nightmare before Sacks of Clutching came along. They were a real revolution in portability. You could put anything in there, so long as it fit through the mouth of the bag. Then it weighed a consistent fifteen pounds, regardless of what you put inside. All you had to do was put your hand in, think of an item and it would come to you. Fortunately, this bag had a search function, so she simply thought "recently added".

A cold metal handle materialised in her palm. She pulled it out.

'Oh great, a useless shortsword.'

'Keep looking!'

Xenixala tried a second time. She groaned. 'Another shortsword. They must have really needed cash.' You couldn't expect more than a couple of gold pieces for them at the blacksmith. Perhaps it wasn't going to be such a good haul after all. No wonder Panella was so grumpy.

'Try refining your search, think "recently added, no shortswords".'

Xenixala did so, and felt a soft sheet appear in her hand. She pulled the canvas from the bag and unfurled it. It seemed to be a map.

'Map to The Treasure Of Yal...ahn...akes? Ylalanaks. Who came up with these names?'

Wordsworth bounced with excitement. 'Wondrous! That sounds like an excellent adventure! Seems like that Sack of Clutching read your mind. Literally.'

'The treasure is a valuable long lost family heirloom, why is it always a lost heirloom? It says the reward is two-hundred gold pieces.'

'We could buy Elixir for weeks with that kind of money!' Wordsworth flapped with glee. 'Perhaps this could be the perfect adventure to get you out of this rut?'

'Maybe. But first things first, we need to get out of here. I can't stand this stench of goblins for much longer.'

The smell brought back the memory. A memory she visited all too often.

'If you're not the best, Xenixala. You are the worst.' Professor Mogg loomed over her.

The whole class stared. She had a potion in her hands. It reeked of goblin blood.

'Drink it. Drink the poison,' barked Professor Mogg. 'Maybe next time, you will do the spell properly. I will not tolerate failure in my classroom.'

Xenixala shuddered, picked up her own Sack of Clutching and wiped off the spatters of sick. It was only last week she'd customised it with jewels to match her now-ruined robe. It glinted in the torchlight. Another thing she'd have to replace.

She sighed, stuffed the map into the bag, then walked back towards the cave exit.

Wordsworth bounded along behind her, his pages clapping each time he hit the floor. 'Time to find ourselves a nice refreshing Elixir, don't you think?'

7

'I haven't heard from you in *months,* darling,' said Sylvia, in a tone of feigned concern. The interior designer stood in Eric's doorway, looking over the top of her pink, crescent-moon shaped spectacles. 'I was beginning to get worried.'

Eric got out of bed and stretched. 'Good to see you too.' Lord Egglewort's guest room was modest, but had a damn comfy bed. Eric had enjoyed his sleep immensely.

'I was so relieved when your carrier duck arrived last night. Finally word from Eric. I came as soon as I could.'

'Still five percent, isn't it?'

Sylvia waved her hand dismissively. 'Yes, yes. Just send a message to my assistant Sarah. She'll arrange your commission.'

'Assistant?'

'Business has been *booming,* darling.' Sylvia walked over to the desk, thumped down her large wad of carpet samples and plopped herself into the chair. 'All these new adventurers really tear these places apart. Gives us a lot to *sink* our teeth into.'

'Uh-huh.'

'Just last month they blasted a hole right through a castle wall, so we made a beautiful veranda.'

'Oh, great.'

'I suppose they're not good news for you, are they darling?'

'Not so much, no.'

Sylvia tilted her head to the side, as if analysing some kind of rare and delicate bird. 'You need to evolve with the times, Eric. Have you ever considered becoming an adventurer yourself?'

Eric scowled. 'No bleeding chance.'

'Just a thought darling, just a thought.' Sylvia stood back up. 'Lord Egglewort's going to inspect the fort now. He's *insisting* you come. In case there are any rogue beasts lingering around.' She walked to the door, paused and turned back. 'Do *please* get some nice clothes on.'

Once dressed, Eric made his way through the castle's corridors in the direction he believed to be the fastest way to the courtyard. A gentle hiss followed him as he went. He strode faster, trying to outpace it, yet the sound grew louder and louder until it was upon him. He turned to see a small cloud of steam. It dissipated to reveal Rose, slightly out of breath.

'Good morning! There you are, finally,' said Rose, with a far-too-cheery smile. She pulled a lever and her backpack stopped sputtering. Somehow it had been propelling her along. 'The way you negotiated with those kobolds yesterday was amazing! I've never seen anything like it.'

Eric carried on walking. 'Well, maybe you won't be seeing anything like it again.'

Rose hurried to catch up with him. 'Now look here Eric! You're going to stop this nonsense if I'm to be your apprentice.'

'You're not my...' Eric stopped himself. He thought back to what had happened to all those other apprentices. Could he really put her in the same danger? To a friend's daughter? She did seem surprisingly more competent than the others. Her father, The High Governor of Murica was wealthy and powerful. Upsetting powerful people was a dangerous business, and having someone kill your daughter was supposed to be quite an upsetting experience. It could be quite nice to have someone keep him company, not to mention the extra few coppers she'd be paying. He made up his mind.

'Not my what?' asked Rose.

Eric shook his thoughts away. 'Nothing. When do you reckon you'll be making your first apprentice payment then...?'

'I'll have a cheque for you next week.'

Eric wasn't sure what a cheque was, but he looked forward to finding out.

By the time Eric and Rose arrived to meet Lord Egglewort the fort's courtyard was packed with wagons, all full to the brim with boxes. On the side of each hung a pink banner that read: "*Sylvia Perriweather - Renovator, Designer and Spaceweaver*", in an almost illegible twirling font. Dozens of servants ran to and fro, clutching furniture and fabrics.

'There you are Eric darling,' said Sylvia, looking up from her clipboard as they approached. 'And who's this?'

'Rose,' said Rose, stepping forward and shaking Sylvia's hand. 'Eric's new apprentice.'

Sylvia looked Rose up and down with her cat-like eyes. 'A Westerner? How *quaint*. A pleasure to meet you, Rose.'

'Eric!' cried Lord Egglewort across the courtyard. 'Finally decided to join us?' He waddled over to them, his belly rolling with each step. 'Care to join me and Sylvia for an inspection? She's going to show me its... what did you call it Sylvia?'

'Architectural potential.'

'That's right, architectural potential.'

'I'm sure that won't be necessary,' said Eric.

Lord Egglewort put his hand on Eric's shoulder. 'I *insist* Eric. You can't be too careful. You *do* want to get your payment don't you?'

Eric nodded wearily.

Lord Egglewort led them around the now-abandoned fort. Sylvia babbled her ideas and Lord Egglewort gushed with agreement. Eric and Rose followed along a few paces behind.

'What's the deal with her?' Rose whispered to Eric.

'Chevron rugs are so thirteen-twenty-one. I think a distressed look would be more contemporary.'

'We have a long-standing arrangement,' Eric whispered back.

'Have you thought of an accent colour yet...? You haven't?!'

'What kind of an arrangement?' said Rose as they turned into the now-empty great-hall. The smell of straw still hung in the air.

'Of course, all the fireplaces will need large mirrors propped on them.'

'I send jobs her way and she pays me a finders fee. It's where we… *I*, make the most coin these days. The upsell packages.'

'We should get lots of antiques for a timeless touch.'

Rose scribbled into her notebook and eyed up Sylvia's pink silk dress. 'But she gets paid more than you.'

'... and once that's decided, we can talk tablescapes.'

'I suppose so.'

'We mustn't give this room a focal point. It really ruins the energy.'

There was a scream.

Everyone froze.

A creature leapt out from the shadows. It wailed and jabbered, pointing a spear at Lord Egglewort.

'Good gracious! Do something!' squealed Lord Egglewort. Sylvia hid behind her carpet samples.

Eric got out his Sack of Clutching and rummaged through it.

'Quickly! He's getting closer!'

Eric produced a piece of dried meat and dropped it at the kobold's feet. In an instant, it threw down its spear and leapt on the morsel. Eric walked over and stroked its head. It chewed and whimpered with glee.

'Don't worry,' said Eric. 'It's just lost and hungry.'

Lord Egglewort mopped the sweat from his brow. 'Aren't you going to kill the ghastly thing?'

'No need, that meat's packed full of sedatives.'

'Full of wh...?' said the kobold, as it slumped to the ground.

Lord Egglewort clapped his hands together. 'Well done! Truly marvellous.'

'All part of the job.' Eric stood up as two guardsmen came over and dragged the unconscious kobold away.

Lord Egglewort beamed. 'Colour me impressed Eric! You know, I may have another job for you…. I was going to offer it to Glorp & Co. or some filthy adventurers, seemed like too big of a job for you, but after that capable display, I think you've proven yourself. Interested?'

'Depends on what it is.'

'Well, one of my villages has been having a dreadful time recently. Clopcod it's called. A pesky dragon has been terrorising…'

'*No* dragons,' Eric cut in firmly.

'What? Whyever not?'

'Way too much trouble. I wouldn't even go near the thing if I were an adventurer. That's a sure way to end up as a roast dinner.'

'I'll give you five hundred gold pieces.'

A sum like that could almost buy him a new shop. Eric shook his head. 'No dragons.'

'Alright, six hundred gold pieces.'

Sylvia pouted. 'Oh come now Eric, I've always wanted to convert a dragon's lair, you can do wonders with the fire pits.' She cooed. 'Don't forget your commission.'

'I *said*, no dragons.'

Lord Egglewort sighed. 'Perhaps I'll leave it to the adventurers after all. Although I doubt any will have the experience to take it down. *Do* let me know if you change your mind.'

Eric shuddered as visions of scales and fire darted through his mind. 'Don't worry, I won't.'

Back in the courtyard, Sylvia's decoration carts had been emptied, their contents now neatly piled against the castle walls. Sylvia dashed off to scold a servant for chipping a candelabra, leaving Rose and Eric with Lord Egglewort.

'Can I get my payment now?' asked Eric.

'Of course, you've more than earned it.' Lord Egglewort handed Eric a small coin purse, but paused as three tall men dressed in long black tunics walked towards them. They had an air of pretension Eric could spot a mile away and a way of moving that suggested they were better than everything under the sun.

'Oh not these stinking creeps,' Eric muttered under his breath, snatching the purse and slipping it in his belt.

'Greetings Lord Egglewort,' said the tallest of the men, bowing with his hands behind his back. 'I hear you have recently inherited a delightful property.' The air seemed to grow colder as he spoke.

Lord Egglewort frowned. 'That's none of your business.'

'Actually Lord Egglewort, it is *precisely* our business.' The man produced a little piece of dark card and handed one to Lord Egglewort. Lord Egglewort turned it over in his hands, confused. He bit down on it to check the material, then regarded it closely, noticing the text written on the front.

Eric already had a small collection of their little cards back at the shop, most of which were being used to prop up wobbly furniture. He already knew what was written there in a golden, rigid font, "*Geiston & Geiston - Property Agents*".

Lord Egglewort looked up from the card. 'I don't understand, what do you want?'

The tall man's face twisted into a grotesque, patronising smile. 'We are here to oversee your legal obligations, Lord Egglewort. It is in your interest for you to cooperate.'

Lord Egglewort looked across to Eric, who shrugged. 'I told you, you should have got the tax package with me. Would've avoided all this.' Nobody ever got the ruddy packages, thought Eric. Served him right.

The man in black continued. 'You owe The King a large sum of property tax, based on the value of your fort and treasure therein. Clearly, your properties are due to be *revalued*. We can administer all this… for a small fee of course.'

Lord Egglewort's face went bright red. 'This is a damned outrage!'

'Please remain calm, Lord Egglewort. If you refuse to cooperate we will be forced to summon all The King's men. And we wouldn't want *that* now would we?'

Lord Egglewort stood still, paralysed with anger.

Eric saw his opportunity to leave and stepped away. He walked towards his mule as Rose scurried along behind him.

'What was that all about?' said Rose.

Eric stuck his hand down into his Sack of Clutching and rooted around. 'Just some vultures swooping in.'

'Is that really true? Everything they demanded?'

'Of course. You can't expect to inherit a castle and not pay property taxes on it. Here you have to pay the crown a proportion of your property's value as taxes. Unfortunately for Lord Egglewort here, the value of his fort's just gone way up. Plus Geiston & Geiston are notorious for overvaluing.'

'Doesn't seem very fair.'

'That's because it isn't.'

Rose crossed her arms. 'How'd they find out about the fort so quickly?'

Eric tapped his nose. 'Trade secret.'

'You *told* them?'

Eric ignored her and pulled out a Scroll of Town Portal from his bag. Geiston & Geiston hadn't paid him much for the tip-off, but he needed every copper he could get his hands on.

Rose looked intently at the scroll. 'What's that?'

'Scroll of Town Portal of course.'

'Why didn't we use that on the way here?'

'It's a one-way deal.' Eric chuckled. Westerners were so innocent of even the most basic magic.

He read out the scroll and they vanished in a puff of smoke and lightning.

8

Elite Warlock Xenixala of Xendor, known to the Elves as 'The Graceful One', known to the Treefolk as 'The One Who Walks' and known to the Gnomes as 'Oh No It's Her', flicked her wrist and sent another frostbolt towards a walking skeleton. Bones shattered in a blaze of ice. The ancient stones of the dungeon fell silent.

It was obviously a dungeon because of all the chains on the walls, so at one point it must have held prisoners. That meant this was a proper dungeon, not a crypt, temple or warren that people *called* a dungeon, but an actual, "throw you in a dark hole" kind of dungeon. The real deal. Unfortunately, proper dungeons only ever contained skeletons. Ex-residents, as Xenixala liked to think of them. Once they'd rotted off enough flesh, it was only a matter of time before they slipped through their manacles and started wandering the corridors.

Xenixala sighed and looked down at the spellbook in her arms. 'Sorry Wordsworth, not much for you to do here. It's all just boring undead.'

'That's alright,' said Wordsworth, pages flapping as he spoke. Having a spellbook as a magical companion was her own work of genius. Most witches went for a cat or owl or something else mundane, whereas Wordsworth helped her power her magic to limits most spellcasters could only dream of. Simple cantrips like frostbolt spells, however, were very much beneath him.

Crawling through this dungeon had been utter tedium. The only adversaries were the walking dead, who were pitifully easy to defeat. For some reason that she never fully understood, they were incredibly weak to frost based magic, which meant that using any other tactic besides a frostbolt spell was a complete waste of time.

Something clattered. A skeleton appeared, shambling around the corner, coated in wisps of ancient cloth, dead eyes and rusted sword. Its jaw rattled in a comical fashion. The deluded creature was probably trying to be menacing.

Another flick of the wrist, another frostbolt, another pile of bones. A familiar tingle flowed into her. Experience, the life force of adventuring. Although these skeletons were far too weak to give her much. She was far too Experienced already for it to make any difference, so the increase in her power would be negligible. She would never be the most Experienced adventurer at this rate.

Professor Mogg's words rang in her head. '*If you're not the best, Xenixala. You are the worst.*'

She strolled over and scuffed at the remains with her heel. There were a few copper pieces, but otherwise nothing. She bent down and pocketed them, wondering which bit of bone had contained the loot.

Perhaps they were already on the floor when the bones fell on top of them.

If she found anything good in this dungeon, she could sell it to Adventurer's Supply. All she needed was money for more Elixir. Of course, the jackpot would be finding more Elixir, but they went stale after a few weeks, and Holy Mole only knew how long they'd have been down in a place like this.

Exploring dungeons was much more fun with a party. She could berate them and watch them get stabbed while she could relax. Now she had to do all the menial chores of adventuring. Rummage through drawers for loot, draw the little map to stop you from getting lost, keep an eye out for traps. It was tedious and exhausting. She needed some companions. Basically, meat and muscle who could carry everything and distract all the dangerous creatures.

The problem was, she got through parties like a dragon got through virgins. Once they realised how much she used them, they sent her on her way. Even the evil parties couldn't handle her. Although they usually weren't as evil as they claimed to be. Sure, they dressed in black and were a bit mean to shop keepers, but when it came to actual torture to get a quest done nice and quick, they rarely had the stomach for it. Panella, Gronk and Jimmy had managed four dungeons with her, a new record.

A casket twinkled in the candlelight at the end of the room. Finally, a chance for decent loot. Caskets were always hidden at the end of a dungeon and would invariably contain the most valuable stuff. This also meant that this particularly boring dungeon was finally finished.

She licked her lips, strode over to the casket and pulled at the handle.

'Oh!' the handle cried in alarm, its hinges formed a crude mouth. 'If my contents you want to take, first a riddle you must break.'

Xenixala rolled her eyes. Riddles in dungeons were almost as bad as the button puzzles. Clearly whoever designed dungeon defences these days had had a damaged childhood. 'What is it?'

The handle twisted upwards into a self-satisfied kind of smile. 'No beginning nor end have I, yet the longer you look, the more I die.'

'Light, time, darkness,' Xenixala listed, 'Nothing, a favour, a sponge, man, time, a piece of string, a river, water, time, and uhh… a mirror, or ageing.'

The handle clicked and turned.

'Excellent,' said Xenixala. 'Well, which answer was it?'

'You cheated,' said the handle. 'You ruined my fun, so I'm not going to tell you. Do you know how long I've waited to tell someone my riddle, all alone in the darkness?'

She sighed and opened the casket. 'Does it look like I care?'

The Treasure of Ylalanaks glinted before her in the torchlight. It appeared to be some kind of bracelet.

'Bingo,' she said, taking the artefact.

She could finally get out of that stinking cave.

* * *

Xenixala knocked on the door of Ylalanaks Manor. She waited, tapping her feet in time to the evening's cricket chirps. The manor had probably once been the pride and joy of this lesser lord, but the half-shattered windows and ivy coated walls now said otherwise.

The door creaked open and an old man poked his head out. The light from inside bathed the porch. 'What do you want?' he said, eyeing her up and down. He was thin and wearing his nightgown.

'Are you Lord Ylalanaks?'

'I am. What's it to you?'

'I've got your family heirloom.'

'Not interested, good day.' Lord Ylalanaks tried to shut the door, but Xenixala forced it open with a wave of her hand. Lord Ylalanaks backed away into the house. 'I don't want any trouble,' he stammered.

Xenixala stepped inside the sparsely furnished home. 'You owe me two hundred gold for this piece of junk.' She held up The Treasure of Ylalanaks and waved the map she'd found. 'See? It says right here on the map.'

'Please,' said Lord Ylalanaks, tears in his eyes. 'I can't afford to pay for another reward, I'm begging you.'

Xenixala paused. 'What do you mean, *another* reward?'

Lord Ylalanaks gestured to a pile of golden bracelets beside the door. Each identical to the one in her hand.

'Why does your family have so many heirlooms?' Xenixala asked.

'It doesn't!' said Lord Ylalanaks. 'There was my great-great-grandmother's bracelet, but it got stolen *years* ago. Now someone's been making copies to hide in dungeons and leaving maps to find them.'

Xenixala pondered this. 'That's all very well, but I do still want my reward.'

'You're just like all the other *adventurers*,' he spat, as if adventurers were an insult. 'You don't care what you do as long as you get your reward and more quests. It's not as if I stand a chance at fighting you off. So if you want to rob me, go ahead. I don't have anything left to give.'

Xenixala eyed the food and tableware laid out for dinner behind him.

'The Doom Bank's already been round,' he continued. 'They demand I pay inheritance taxes on all these useless family heirlooms, King's orders. They're going to take my home!' Lord Ylalanaks collapsed to the floor, bowed his head and gently sobbed. 'I'm ruined…'

Xenixala decided to leave, being sure to grab a few candlesticks and a wheel of cheese on the way out. It was better than nothing, and you never know when a candlestick or some cheese could come in handy.

Probably at a dinner party.

9

Eric, Rose and their steeds materialised outside the Beast Be Gone shop in Porkhaven, their feet landing on the cobbles. The gloomy sky overcast the rows of shacks that barely constituted a street. People hurried past, shopkeeps, traders, bankers alike all going about their mundane lives with a vacant stare. With each of their outfits being so similar, Eric wondered if they all visited the same tailors. Interspersed between the city folk were heavily armoured adventurers, relentlessly demanding quests, knocking back Elixirs and challenging each other to duels.

In spite of the adventurers, it was good to be home.

Eric led Daisy to the tiny stable beside the shop, then tied her up and fed her some kind of knobbly vegetable he'd found deep in his Sack of Clutching. Rose appeared beside him, her face beaming. 'This has all been quite informative so far.'

Her chuffer had followed her inside, taking up the rest of the space. Its many legs collapsed down, settling itself into the hay. It let out a long wheeze of steam and went quiet.

Eric patted Daisy on the nose. 'Glad to hear it.'

There was a crash.

Eric and Rose exchanged looks, then hurried outside. Eric felt his stomach lurch. Adrenaline kicked through him.

Six burly dwarves were leaving his shop, carrying out a large chest of drawers through the smashed down door. Broken glass sparkled on the ground. The dwarves all wore black tunics emblazoned with unusual pink skulls. They glanced up at Eric and Rose, then continued to steal the furniture.

'Hey!' Eric exclaimed, running over to them. He pulled at the chest of drawers, but the dwarves didn't even flinch, they simply grinned.

'There you are, Mr Featherwick,' boomed a voice over the sound of the crunching glass. It came from a man in the shop doorway, who had a jaw to compliment his caveman-like brow. The pink skull on his robes was larger and had more detail, implying that he was in charge. 'You owe The Doom Bank a lot of money.'

Anger pulsed through his veins, a fire of hatred burned in his belly. 'Get off my property!' he shouted.

'Now, now Mr Featherwick,' said the man. 'We don't want to have to call the city guards,'

Eric shook with hatred, poised to punch the man in the face. Something gentle caught his arm. He looked round to see Rose. She smiled at him.

'Come on, Eric,' she said. 'It's alright.'

The rage washed away, leaving behind only shame. He hung his head. 'I... just need more time,' Eric pleaded. 'Please.'

'You've had plenty of time,' said the bailiff.

Eric removed the money pouch from his belt and begrudgingly held it towards the man. 'This is all I have.'

The bailiff snatched the bag and stuck his nose in it, inspecting its contents. 'If you don't pay us the rest by the end of the month, this shop is ours.'

Eric grumbled and nodded.

'You should join The Guild. Free access if you have an account with us.' The man thrust a parchment into Eric's hands, smiled with satisfaction, turned and strolled away.

Eric looked down at the paper in his hands.

The Guild
Career Advice and Services
Your Adventure Starts TODAY
"Why farm animals when you could farm Experience?"
Proudly Brought To You By The Doom Bank

He was going to lose everything and there was nothing he could do to stop it. He wanted to scream and throw rocks at their big fat heads, but held himself back. Something about Rose calmed him down, but he couldn't quite put his finger on it. He scrunched up the paper and tossed it onto the floor.

'Who were they?' asked Rose.

'Bailiffs.' Through the window he watched the group leave on their pink cart with their newly claimed furnishings. Eric froze. Had they taken...? He ran over to the fireplace and breathed a sigh. His crossbow was still sitting where it always had been, right above the mantelpiece. 'Thank The Mole,' he mumbled as he caressed the wood.

Rose raised an eyebrow. 'Probably not worth their time, looks pretty rusty.'

Eric frowned. 'It's a... family heirloom.'

'Quite an interesting heirloom.' Rose turned around and looked at the shattered doorway. 'Right then, where do you keep your brooms?'

They spent the rest of the morning clearing up the remains of the shop door. The sun beat down on their backs, while city folk wandered by, being careful to avoid eye contact. Life in Porkhaven bred a basic survival instinct of staying out of other people's business, especially when violence and broken glass was involved.

A few addicts stumbled by, their skin green, soft and withered. The Alchemy District was full of these fools. At least once a week Eric had to clean up some purple or green bile outside the shop.

Although living there did have its perks, namely a cheaper mortgage and an unlimited supply of empty bottles.

'Stop that,' Eric snapped as he inspected the wonky frame.

Rose's mechanical arm poked from her backpack, holding the dustpan while she swept up into it. 'Stop what?'

'You know what. That humming. Stop it.'

'Was I humming?'

'You were definitely humming.'

Rose paused and leant on her broom, her metal appendage whirred and retreated into her back. 'You're a real grump, you know that?'

Eric grunted and ignored her, going back to hammering the door frame. It wasn't ever going to be straight again, but he couldn't exactly afford to buy a new one.

'Why didn't you take that new job from Lord Egglewort?' she continued, 'Seems like you need the money.'

Eric stopped hammering. 'I don't do dragons.'

Rose took a step closer, leaning in conspiratorially. 'Why not?'

Eric shuddered. He could still hear his father's screams some nights. Feel the burning on his skin. 'I don't want to talk about it. They're a damn cliche is what they are. The adventurers can have the stinking dragons for all I care.'

'Well you've got to find work somehow,' said Rose resolutely. 'If I'm going to be your apprentice I'll need to have some experience out in the field.'

Eric glared at Rose. 'Why did you want to work with me so much anyway?'

'After what you did for my father. How you stopped that direbeetle with only a net...' Rose stopped herself. 'Why gee, it was so heroic. I've grown up with that story. It's what made me want to be a pest controller.'

'Things had been so much simpler back then,' said Eric, fondly. 'That was a time when being a pest controller meant something. The King himself hired me for that job, and more too. Once I spent weeks fumigating his palace against a nest of lesser-hydras. Now I bet he can't even remember my name.'

'My father remembers,' said Rose.

'I was just doing my job.' Eric's face decided to blush.

He still couldn't wrap his head around her. She seemed old and yet so young, all at the same time. Maybe it was something to do with her white blouse and tidy hair.

'How old are you anyway?' he said.

Rose stood up straighter, puffing out her chest. 'I'm fifteen and three quarters.'

'And in those fifteen long years, have you had any other experience with wild creatures?'

'My father owns a lot of plantations in the Western Lands. I've seen my fair share of bogglet invasions and goblin pillaging. But our land seems much less forgiving than here, so it's only now that we've been hit by the same adventurer craze.'

Eric spat on the ground. 'Damned adventurers.'

'Where did they all come from?'

Eric shook his head with sorrow. 'There have always been heroes. But I guess people realised how much treasure was sitting around unattended. I even heard they were all inspired by some knight who butchered an Elder Dragon. Then once word traveled, everyone wanted a piece of the glory and they all got addicted to drinking Elixirs and absorbing Experience. They're obsessed with endlessly getting stronger and stronger, until eventually they die and there's no one left to resurrect them. They only use their power to make themselves more powerful, it's totally pointless.'

The thought of Experience made Eric shudder. For some twisted reason, the universe decided that killing something meant you deserved a tiny piece of its life force. You would have to kill thousands of people or creatures to make it worth the while, of course, but that's exactly what adventurers planned on doing. The believers would say it was all part of The Holy Mole's plan to turn the world into a molehill.

A familiar voice, silken and sickly, suddenly trickled from behind. 'My guess is they wanted to have as much fun as we do.'

Eric grimaced. He knew that voice all too well. 'Hello Freddy,' he said, turning around.

Freddy Glorp posed in the street with his legs wide, violet cloak flapping in the breeze. 'Good to see you old boy. I was just passing through and thought I'd come and check how my little buddy Eric was doing.' Freddy glanced at the limp door hanging from the hinges. 'Had a bit of an accident have we?'

'Nothing to worry about. Only a break-in.'

'What hooligans.' Freddy smiled in such a way that made Eric want to punch him right in his chiselled jaw. 'Take anything of... *value*?'

'Nothing much.'

'Glad to hear it. How's business?' Freddy swept back his handsome golden hair as if to mock Eric's receding hairline. 'I heard you recently helped Lord Egglewort with a little kobold problem?'

'That's right.'

Freddy absentmindedly neatened his sleeves. 'We were too busy for that job ourselves. The reward simply wasn't worth our time you see. We had to turn him down.'

'Is that so.' How had Freddy managed to get so many jobs? His wealthy father was probably still propping him up. It had to be.

'If you are struggling Eric, *do* let us know.' The words seemed to slither out of Freddy's mouth. It made the last of Eric's hair stand on end. 'We'd make a good offer for your shop. You know. For a *friend*. I think it would convert wonderfully into a stable.'

'I'm doing just fine.'

Freddy's expression twisted into a mocking grin as he looked back at the door. 'Of course you are. Have any other jobs lined up?'

Eric crossed his arms. 'None of your business.'

Freddy laughed and patted Eric on the back. Eric flinched at his touch. 'I understand Eric, I understand.'

Eric felt his face flush. 'We do have one job. If you must know.'

Freddy raised his eyebrows. 'Oh? And what job is that?'

'A big one.'

'Oh yes? How big? A few large bats in an attic? A couple of gremlins stolen a farmer's family daughter...?'

Eric ground his teeth. 'Much bigger than that.'

'I'm *sure* it is...'

'It's a dragon.' Eric blurted out before he could stop himself.

Freddy froze, mouth slightly agape. 'A dragon you say? My, my, my Eric, I didn't think you had it in you. Especially after, you know. *The incident*.'

Eric remained silent, fists clenched. He caught Rose's eye and breathed out.

Freddy turned his gaze onto Rose. 'And who's this little one? Not *another* apprentice?'

'Howdy, I'm Rose,' said Rose, setting down her broom and extending a hand.

'Ah, a *Westerner,* how darling. Charmed to meet you.' Freddy took her hand with both of his, enveloping them. 'If you fancy some *real* experience, you're more than welcome at Glorp & Co.'

'Oh. Thank you,' said Rose, pulling her hand away from Freddy's grip. 'But I'm doing just fine here.'

Freddy appeared perplexed by the rejection but quickly regained his composure. 'Well, I must dash. Good to see you, Eric. And Rose, I hope to see you again *very* soon.' He winked at her and strolled away, whistling.

'Who was that latrine-for-brains?' said Rose after Freddy had disappeared down the street.

'Freddy Glorp. His father owns Glorp & Co.'

'Your rivals?'

'You could say that.'

Rose picked her broom back up. 'Definitely glad I took my apprenticeship here. He seems like a bit of a prat. Why doesn't he like you? What did you do to him?'

Eric sighed. 'We apprenticed together. Things got ugly.'

'Oh. What happened?'

'It was a long time ago. I don't want to talk about it.'

'You don't want to talk about anything.'

'Talking's overrated.'

Rose turned to him with a look on her face that suggested she'd uncovered some kind of juicy gossip. 'Well, you talked to Freddy. And you *lied* about having a job.'

'We do have a job. From Lord Egglewort.'

'I thought you said you didn't want to do it? Something about not liking dragons?'

'I don't remember saying that. I said I would think about it. And well... I've thought about it.'

'And?'

'And maybe we could give it a go. It'd be good learning for you. And it'll help pay for this door.' *Not to mention the crippling debt,* he thought to himself. He'd even get to shove it in Freddy's smug face.

Rose smiled and carried on sweeping. Soon she began to hum tunelessly again, but Eric didn't stop her.

10

The Demi Enchantress Xenixala of Xendor, Toppler of Tyrants, Great Seer of The Void and winner of "most likely to succeed award" at Trolltop College, stared down at the half-empty pewter cup in her hands. Chattering fools filled The Crow's Wort Inn, and the unmistakable musk of peasantry assaulted her nostrils. It was as if a horse had pissed on a mouldy blanket, and then the blanket had become sentient and decided to get itself a drink, only to discover two dozen other piss-blankets arriving at the same establishment. Xenixala shuddered and knocked back another swig of beer. It was weak and tasteless, much like the inn, but at least it masked the smell of the other patrons.

Wordsworth the spellbook sat quietly on top of the long table in front of her, shuffling ever so slowly away from a creeping puddle of spillage. In public places it was better for him to pretend to be a regular book as neither of them desired the attention. Peasants had grubby fingers, and they loved nothing more than to prod curious magical items, no matter how much it put their lives at risk. That was usually the reason why they needed saving from curses so often.

Xenixala's fingers trembled as she clasped the cup with both hands. She could still feel the Elixir coursing through her veins. That tingling bliss of strength and confidence, that burning knowledge that everything was going to be alright. Even if someone stabbed her now, it would feel like a mouse scratching her back. Wordsworth's pages turned up with a hint of a smile. He could feel it too, their souls inextricably bound. Summoning and binding a magical familiar to yourself was the first task at witching school, and she was the only one cunning enough to make hers an actual spellbook.

'I'm bored,' Wordsworth whispered discreetly through a tight gap in his pages.

Xenixala groaned and took a swig of her drink. 'Me too. But there's nothing else to do, so suck it up and keep quiet.'

'Couldn't we set something on fire?'

A wicked smile appeared on Xenixala's lips. 'As much as I would like to burn this place to the ground, I don't think it would be very… citizenly. Now would it?'

'I bet there's a wolf or two out in the woods. Why don't we go out and take a look? Get some Experience?'

'We'll hardly get any. I really can't be bothered.'

Wordsworth ruffled his pages. 'Why don't we ask some of these villagers if they have any quests? There's always at least one good quest at an inn.'

'Look at them though,' Xenixala gestured to a nearby group of men guffawing over their unconscious friend. 'They're clearly morons. At *best* it would be a missing daughter who's eloped with some farmhand.'

'You never know…'

'I'm just going to enjoy my beer in peace and we'll think of something tomorrow.' It would be great if she could bed someone as well, but the pickings were awfully slim.

Wordsworth muttered then clamped himself shut.

Xenixala looked up, then smiled. It was as if the world had read her mind.

Standing in the doorway was the most striking man she had ever seen. He had long, shimmering blond hair and a chin that looked strong enough to break a log in two. His fierce eyes surveyed the room with the confidence of a man who knew what he wanted. Probably a drink, as he strode over to the bar, golden armour clicking with every stride and blue cloak flapping in his wake.

Xenixala couldn't take her eyes off him. Finally, something exciting in this forsaken place. She stood up with purpose, and walked towards him, leaving Wordsworth lying dormant on the table. He would only chime in and ruin things.

Xenixala reached the bar and stood beside the towering hulk. She flicked back her hair and tried to catch his eye.

The man didn't notice. Instead, he raised his hand and waved at the barkeeper. 'One of your finest ales, good sir.'

Xenixala cleared her throat and the man's eyes locked onto hers. He scratched his nose. 'I'm sorry, my good lady, have we met?'

'We haven't had the pleasure. I'm Xenixala, but you can call me Xeni.' She smiled as sweetly as she knew how to, then caressed his arm. Her charm spell tingled through her fingers, a wave of warmth and irresistible passion trickled out of her. The glow embraced the man's armour, then vanished.

'A pleasure to meet you Xeni, I am Edwardius Ironwell, Defender of The Light of The Mole.' He bowed.

By the gods, not a goody-two-shoes paladin. She should have guessed; all the most attractive men ended up as paladins. It was almost as if charisma alone was a prerequisite for the job. It was no wonder her charm spell hadn't worked, he was coated in every 'resist-evil' spell in the book. Looked like she would have to do things the old-fashioned way.

Xenixala did her best to discreetly push out her bosom. It wasn't her best feature, but it often worked as well as a charm spell. 'Could I buy you a drink, Sir Ironwell?'

'Please, call me Edwardius.'

'Could I buy you a drink, Edwardius?' Maybe he wouldn't be as resistant to her poisons.

Edwardius smiled. 'Perhaps we could speak a little later in the evening my dear? I'm here to watch the performance, and I don't want to miss a word of it.' He pointed to the stage at the back of the room, now garishly lit with cheap enchanted lamps. 'Look, it's about to begin!' His face beamed and he clapped his hands together.

Xenixala sighed as Edwardius turned to face the stage, then she went back to her bench. It seemed like she wouldn't be getting any action tonight after all. She was so much more *powerful* after she'd had a man. It was better than any Elixir.

Wordsworth pouted his pages as she sat down beside him. 'Made a new friend have we?'

'Perhaps. He's a paladin though.'

'It hasn't stopped you before.'

The incessant hubbub of the inn dropped to a faint murmur. All heads turned towards the stage as footsteps rang out across the wooden boards. A pixie appeared in the spotlight, her sickly sweet lips smiling vacantly to the crowd. She couldn't have been more than three foot tall. Carefully, she swept her blond hair over her shoulder, raised her lute and closed her eyes as if she were about to reach some kind of silent erotic climax.

Damned pixies with their stupid little faces and annoying high pitched voices. They were such do-gooders as well, almost as bad as paladins. She'd never met a pixie who wasn't vegan and they never stopped going about it. The worst. And how had this little creature managed to get everyone's attention so easily? What made her so damned special?

Xenixala also felt a burning irritation that she was going to be subjected to some amateur music. This pixie was clearly a bard and was undoubtedly going to burst into a tuneless mess about some mundane quest. Considering it was their profession, you would think that a bard would be able to invent something more compelling. Simple folk enjoyed their ballads because of the charm spells woven into them, but being a sorceress made Xenixala naturally resistant to such basic magic. To her, they sounded like a cat-bear being strangled.

The pixie on stage cleared her throat. The room went silent. She strummed her wooden lute and sang softly.

'Have you heard the tale,
of The Chosen One? The Chosen One?
With highest Experience, and never undone.

'The greatest adventurer,
Gentle and kind,
A stronger man you will not find.'

Xenixala sat up straight. They were calling him The Chosen One now? Everyone knew the most powerful adventurer existed, yet no one actually knew who he was. He was what made people crave Experience at all, and it niggled at her to no end. Something inside her needed to be the best, strongest, most powerful, top of the leaderboard. It was infuriating that she had never been able to catch up to his level, but there was nothing left to kill that gave her enough Experience.

She pictured Professor Mogg smiling at her across the classroom, all those years ago. A cold smile, ready to turn into suffering. It was the smile before she made her drink another poison. The taste of failure. Do better. Be the best witch in the class. The best witch in the school. The best witch in the whole land.

'If you're not the best, Xenixala. You are the worst.'

She *knew* she couldn't be far off, she could feel it in her bones. This Chosen One would have had to kill hundreds of thousands of creatures to gain more Experience than she had.

It was hard to ignore the wretched singing when everyone else was being so quiet.

'Grenden the dragon,
Would rage no more,
When he shot its mighty maw.

'Our great King,
Learned of his might,
So sent him many beasts to fight.

'The Fen Legion of dead,
Falls at his knees,
With all his skill, done with ease.

'Great spiders of Wortwood,
Would he destroy,
Only a stick need he employ.

'He'd conquer the thieves,
Of the Bandit King,
And off his head with a piercing sting.'

The pixie's voice seemed to melt the air. This Chosen One almost had as many claims to fame as Xenixala did. Not that she'd made a list of them all or anything.

'Dark Masters end,
Will he bring,
And for that, we'll sing and sing.

*'Have you heard the tale,
of The Chosen One? The Chosen One?
With highest Experience, and never undone.*

Xenixala and Wordsworth exchanged glances. Wordsworth shuffled in closer. 'Are you thinking what I'm thinking?'

'That we could kill The Chosen One and become the most Experienced adventurer?'

'Oh.' Wordsworth's pages crumpled in a deflated fashion. 'I was going to suggest getting another Elixir. But that's an excellent idea too.'

Xenixala licked her lips. 'If we're not the best, then we are the worst. This Chosen One could finally get us out of this rut. If not to fight him for the huge amount of Experience, then at least to follow him on one of his quests.' She spoke quickly, surprising herself with a new found excitement. 'If he truly is the best adventurer, then he'll only look for the most challenging and exciting adventures. Then we can become the best too. It's perfect.'

'So how are we supposed to find him?' The tone of Wordsworth's voice was incredulous. 'What if he doesn't even exist?'

'There's a good chance of that. But if he does, I bet that bard is a good place to start.' With that, Xenixala stood up and marched herself over to the pixie, who was in the process of stepping down from the stage. Xenixala pushed past the sea of doe-eyed peasants that had closed in on her. They cooed as if mesmerised.

Xenixala reached her and crossed her arms. 'Good evening bard. I am The Sorceress Xenixala of Xendor, I demand you tell me more about this "Chosen One" you were wailing about.'

The creature giggled and fluttered her eyelashes. 'A pleasure to meet you Xenixala, I am Felina Flickfoot. Have you not heard the tale of The Chosen One before?'

Xenixala scoffed, 'I don't have time to learn *every* silly little prophecy.'

Felina sighed. 'Oh, isn't it a wonderful tale? It's all they sing about at the inns right now. They say it's all the rage! I did my best with my little number. Although, I must say I'm not too confident about my rhyming scheme. The fourth and fifth stanzas still need a little work...'

'I don't care about the song, *pixie*,' Xenixala cut in. 'Where can I find him?'

Felina threw back her head and let out an obnoxious titter. 'Funnily enough we are hunting for him ourselves. We're scouring as many inns as we can to pick up more words of his movements.'

'Who's we...?'

'My love! You were marvellous!' came a booming voice, as if to answer her question.

'Thank you, my sweet!' Felina gushed and embraced Edwardius the paladin. 'Your presence breathed life into my song. I couldn't have done it without you.'

Edwardius beamed. 'And I couldn't have done it without you...'

The pair proceeded to conjoin each other's faces in a way that could only be described as stomach-churning. After an uncomfortable amount of time, the lovers broke off their embrace and finally realised Xenixala had been glaring at them the entire time.

'Where are my manners!' announced Edwardius, face now smeared with glitter and lipstick. 'My love, this is Xenixala the sorceress. She introduced herself to me at the bar. Perhaps she could be of use to our quest?'

Felina's eyes lit up. 'Of course! In fact, she was just asking me about The Chosen One. She's searching for him too.'

'Oh err, I prefer to travel alone,' said Xenixala. 'If you could point me in his direction, I'll be on my way.'

'Nonsense! Nobody adventures alone, you need a party.' Edwardius grabbed Xenixala by the shoulder and gave her a friendly shake. She tensed at the unwanted contact, yet felt a surge of joy. 'As luck would have it, we're missing a spellcaster after last week's unfortunate… fatality. So you're a perfect fit!' He gave her another shake.

Xenixala brushed off his hand and straightened her robe. 'Why *are* you searching for him exactly?'

'Firstly to thank him!' Edwardius beamed. 'He's the one who inspired me to ask for more than a dull life, to seek excitement and glory. When I heard how he defeated Grenden, The Great Elder Dragon all those years ago, how he became the most Experienced adventurer, I knew I had to run away from my humble farming family, join The Order of The Holy Mole and become the paladin you see before you today. To seek power and be the best. I've been looking for him my entire career!'

Felina stepped between them, as if to remind Xenixala she still existed. 'But the *main* reason is that we need his strength at our side. A great plague of goblins blights the land with raids and pillaging. Filthy goblin scum. They call themselves The Dark Army.'

'Please don't be racist my love.' Edwardius' face turned grave. 'Goblins are people too.'

'They're scum and deserve the release of death.' Felina spat. 'And besides, it would be "species-ist" if it were anything.' She turned back to Xenixala. 'Regardless, I'm convinced their banner is controlled by an evil presence. A great dark force is growing. The soothsayers have seen it. They call him *The Dark Master*.'

Xenixala rolled her eyes. 'I've defeated, like, nine Dark Lords. No big deal. And he's only got goblins. They're the weakest possible minion.'

Edwardius put his hand to his plated chest and dipped his head in sorrow. 'This Dark Master is different. He threatens the entire world with his power…'

'Yeah, yeah, heard it a thousand times. I'll pass. And besides, what makes you so sure it's a man?'

Edwardius hesitated. 'Yes of course… uh women can be evil overlords too, I simply mean…'

Xenixala knew full well that the overlord would probably be a man. They were much better suited to the insecurities and loneliness of a megalomaniac lifestyle. She also enjoyed watching people squirm over their political-feudal-correctness. 'Whatever, I don't care. I'm only interested in this Chosen One. Which way are you heading?'

'We go north, towards Clopcod.' said Felina. 'A soothsayer has told us of his next location.'

Edwardius cut in with a pleading tone. 'Listen, if money is an issue, you don't have to worry, my father is very wealthy.'

Xenixala wasn't impressed by his desperation. 'I'll find him on my own. Thanks.' With that, she turned and walked back to her table.

'What do you think you're doing?' said Wordsworth from under her arm. 'This could be our ticket to some decent Experience!'

Xenixala sat down and helped herself to a beer someone had left unattended. 'I can't *stand* that sickly-sweet pixie, plus they've told us everything. We don't need them. We'll find this Chosen One on our own. How hard could it be?'

11

Eric shivered and tightened his cloak. The countryside air was bitterly cold, its unique aroma combining pine with damp. He didn't care for it, especially not in Porkwood. He swayed gently with Daisy's strides and considered getting off to give her a break, then looked at the state of the muddy road and thought better of it. His boots were barely holding themselves together, and a new pair was a luxury he couldn't afford.

The branches obeyed the wind's command, moving overhead with a gentleness only the trees understood, and that was because they didn't have much else going on. The thick undergrowth made Eric uncomfortable. The warped limbs and dense foliage provided far too much cover for lurking highwaymen. Such things were a cliche, but bandits were staunch in their traditions and clung to the same old methods - like hiding in the bushes. The Bandit King ruled Porkwood, and he was said to be predictably ruthless and ruthlessly predictable. Eric looked back to check on Rose, but she seemed gleefully oblivious.

After a day's ride north, Eric had almost become used to the chug of Rose's metal contraption, which had rumbled the entire way from Porkhaven. But every now and again it would violently splutter, making him wince. He was surprised that they hadn't drawn more attention to themselves.

'Why can't you just use magic and enchantments like a normal person?' he said. 'It's not *natural*.'

Rose smiled. 'You need to get with the times Eric. Technology is the future.'

Eric mumbled something about a troll's nether regions and turned back. He patted Daisy on the side as if to reassure her that her job wasn't threatened by metal gadgets. Rose's chuffer was pulling the usual wagon that was full to the brim with equipment, which meant an easier job for Daisy, but also made her less essential.

'Wonderful day isn't it?' said Rose.

'No, it ain't.' Eric scowled. 'Can't you turn that thing down a bit?'

Rose patted the metal shell. She sat at the peak of her machine, operating levers either side while its little legs scurried obediently under the great dome. 'I'm afraid this is as quiet as it gets.'

Eric had managed to find a spare banner for it, which made it stand-out a little less. However, the sign's words of: 'no dragons' had been crossed out with a hasty blot of paint.

'I think we should call it a day,' Eric squinted at the last of the daylight trickling through the leaves. 'Keep a lookout for a clearing to camp for the night.'

Rose called out from behind him. 'Excellent! I'm starving.'

Shortly after the sun set, a glade opened up beside the road, a great circle of dark green. High above, stars twinkled through the awning of the trees, and below, the marks of old fires pitted the floor, ones probably made by adventurers rather than honest folk. This was confirmed when Eric saw the array of discarded Elixir vials, their Adventurer's Supply symbol blending into the twigs and mouldy leaves.

Eric led Daisy over to a tree and tied her to it, being careful to ask permission. The tree didn't reply, so he took it as a yes.

Rose leapt down from her chuffer, which hunkered down and went blissfully quiet. She stretched and pulled off her goggles, then casually picked up one of the many wrappers littering the forest floor. 'Adventurer's Supply ration,' she read out loud, 'A days sustenance guaranteed with only two small bites. *Warning*, do not consume more than six bites.' She turned it over in her hands. 'What happens if you eat more than six bites?'

Eric smirked. 'Try to imagine having six full meals magically appear in your belly all at once.'

Rose grimaced and put her hands over her stomach. 'In spite of that thought, I'm famished. Have we got adventurer rations too?'

'No bleeding chance.'

Eric stopped.

There was something in the mud, something living. A shivering patch of green fur amongst the litter. He hurried over and knelt beside the poor creature.

'What is it?' asked Rose, coming up behind him.

'A dire-badger.' He noted the puddles of bile matted into its fur. 'He's been drinking up all these bleeding leftover Elixirs.'

'So isn't that a good thing? Doesn't Elixir heal you?'

'Yes and no.' Eric gave Rose his best stern look. 'Highly addictive. Adventurers can't get enough of this damned poison, it's probably why they're so loopy. They leave their old vials all over the place, so a little guy like this could have gotten addicted fast. Now he's got The Flux.' Eric caressed the creature's grey fur. 'Too much too soon can kill you. Poor fella.'

'What can we do?'

'If he survives 'til morning, he should be fine. But I should induce more vomiting. Go and get some bark from those greywillow trees. That'll ease his pain.'

Rose nodded, then hurried away.

Eric put his fingers into the dire-badger's mouth and caressed the back of his tongue. Green ooze shot out, along with flashes of lightening. Eric jumped back in pain, wiping his hands on his overalls. The animal remained unconscious and his breathing became deeper, but still not regular. It's eyes became less green. Eric knelt back beside him and stroked his head.

A scream pierced through the forest.

Eric whipped the poisoned darts from his belt and ran towards the sound. Hopping over twigs and brambles, he followed the noise of Rose's hissing backpack. He found her cowering, backpack-claw outstretched in an attempt to cover her face.

He glanced around. 'What's the matter?'

Rose jumped at his voice. 'The tree! It spoke to me!'

Eric laughed. 'Of course. You never spoken to a tree before?'

'No!' she stammered. 'I didn't think they *actually* spoke. I thought it was a metaphor.'

'Don't they talk in The West?'

'Of course not!'

'How do they communicate then?'

'Why do they need to? They're just trees!'

'*Just* trees?!' boomed the tree. Its two main branches folded into crude crossed-armed shape.

Eric swatted Rose on the back. 'She didn't mean that. Did you Rose?'

Rose trembled and shook her head.

The tree shook its leaves. 'Damned foreigners. You're as bad as all these adventurers.'

Eric looked up to the tree. It was hard to tell which way they were facing when they didn't have a face, but there was usually more moss on their backside. 'Sorry about that Mr…?'

'Barkwellington Thunderbranch. But all my friends call me Barkwell.'

'Friends?' said Rose, startled.

Eric laughed. 'Trees are very sociable, you know. Barkwell's probably got more friends than you do.'

Barkwell rustled his leaves with pride. 'He's not wrong, I've got loads.'

'I'm not his friend,' chimed in a nearby tree.

'Nor me,' said another.

'Oh shut up, the both of you,' Barkwell blurted. He twisted his trunk slightly towards Eric. 'You see what I have to deal with round here?'

'Time for a move, maybe?' Eric suggested.

'Don't you think I tried that? These two keep following me around. It's taken me two months to move from over by the road. All this rushing around is doing my bark in.'

The trees around them sniggered, resounding into the forest. It sounded as if the wind was joining in too.

Beads of sap started to seep from Barkwell's trunk.

'Don't listen to them Barkwell,' said Rose. 'We'll be your friends.'

'I don't need your pity!' Barkwell sniffed. 'Especially not a Westerner. You're more machine than human.'

'There's nothing wrong with a bit of technology.' Rose shuffled her pack. It gurgled and emitted a whiz of steam.

Eric clapped his hands together. 'It's been lovely chatting guys, but we were really only looking for deadwood. Mind if we take some?'

The trees murmured.

'By all means.'

'Sure.'

'Enjoy my dead bits you pervert.'

'No problem at all.'

Eric bowed in acknowledgement, grabbed a few handfuls of twigs and walked back into the clearing, making sure he had enough extra for firewood.

Rose followed suit, but noticeably neglected to use her mechanical arm and struggled with her small bundle of twigs. 'Why'd you ask them permission like that?' she said, bending down to pick up the branch she'd dropped.

Eric threw his bundle down beside the dire-badger. 'It's just polite. Also, trees can be jolly annoying, they'd be moaning at us all night. Nothing worse than a moaning tree.'

He began to set up a fire but struggled with the damp wood. Rose simply watched, scribbling notes in her book.

Eric frowned at her. 'What are you writing? Don't you know how to light a fire?'

'Of course, I do. I just wanted to see how you did it.'

Eric stood up, flustered by his failed attempts. 'Well, why don't you show me how you do it in The West then?'

Rose smiled, put on her goggles and produced a small metal disc from her bag. She twisted the device and tossed it onto the pile of wood. It erupted in a spurt of white flames, sparks and smoke.

Eric coughed and fanned his face. 'Very clever. Couldn't you have done that in the first place?'

'I thought you didn't like technology? You said it wasn't *natural*.' Rose put her hands on her hips, her face illuminated by the now roaring fire.

'It ain't. But I never said it wasn't *occasionally* useful.'

Eric set to work brewing a concoction of greywillow bark, ash and a little Elixir residue. Once it was done, he spooned it into the dire-badger's mouth. It wasn't long before the creature's breathing was regular again. He wrapped it up in some canvas and carried it over to the fireside. Eric pulled out the camping gear from the wagon and dragged them over to the least muddy looking patch in the clearing. Under normal circumstances, Eric would have been sure to stay at actual lodgings like a normal traveller, not camp in a forest like a filthy vagabond adventurer. But he had to save in any way that he could, which included forfeiting warm beds and tasty dinners. He didn't understand how adventurers could enjoy their lives tramping through the countryside. Sleeping rough was worse than sharing a bed with a were-mole.

Rose sat down beside the fire on one of the strategically placed logs. 'So what's for dinner?'

'Porridge and oatcakes.'

Rose raised an eyebrow. 'Do all Easterners eat such bland food?'

'The poor ones do.'

'It's that bad huh?'

Eric hung his head and sat down in front of her. 'They're going to take the shop and I'll have nothing. I can't exactly afford chimaera tail soup.'

'Is this to do with those bailiffs?'

He took a deep breath. 'I had to borrow a lot of money after there was... an incident.'

Rose made a knowing look. 'Was that with a dragon by any chance?'

Eric felt a pang of fear at the thought. 'None of your business.'

Rose continued to stare at him with her irritatingly kind eyes, eyes that didn't possess even the slightest malice. Eric had never seen anything like it. No one in Porkhaven looked at him like that, not in the forty years he'd lived there. People who looked at people like that got their teeth kicked in if they weren't careful.

Eric sighed. 'When I was a teenager... I wanted to be an adventurer.'

Rose drew an intake of breath. 'Really? Why?'

'I thought being a hero was exciting, and that everything my father did at Beast Be Gone was a boring waste of time. That you should be out slaying demons, not catching them. I'd never been so wrong in all my life. He tried to take me as an apprentice to teach me the right way to do things, along with Freddy Glorp.'

'Your pest control rival?'

'The very same. Anyway, my father got a job to stop a dragon. As soon as me and Freddy heard about it we snuck off with our adventuring gear to slay the dragon the fun way. Father was only going to put it to sleep. This was years before Adventurer's Supply, mind you, so I stole the crossbow from our shop and bought some potions from the Alchemy District with my pocket money. We wanted to show my father we were men, not boys. Then maybe he'd listen. We even left him a note.'

'Did he come after you?'

'Thank The Mole he did. He'd already laid traps and sedative-coated sheep around the dragon's lair a few days before. The dragon was weakened. Even so, by the time father got to us I'd been burned pretty bad. Luckily I'd drank a cocktail of potions to keep me alive. My father hadn't, that was for adventurers. The smell of Elixir makes me feel sick even today, I've never had a potion since.'

'So what happened to him?'

'He died. As he was roasting alive, he screamed at me to fire my crossbow, screamed like I'd never heard before, "Shoot it in the eye!" The only weak spot. But... I was too late.' Eric took a deep breath and wiped a tear from his cheek. 'Did everything I could to get a resurrection to work. But my dad, he... was beyond it. Burned to a crisp. I spent all of our savings on failed resurrections, no refunds. From then on there have been more and more adventurers, fewer and fewer jobs, and less and less money.' Eric paused, staring deep into the fire. 'And that was that.'

'That's awful Eric.' Rose shifted in her seat and there was a moment of silence. It lingered as the fire flickered it's comforting melody. 'Well, I look forward to giving this one a good thrashing.'

Eric held back a sudden wave of emotion. He pushed it back deep down until he felt normal again, clearing his head. 'Dragons ain't anything to look forward to. They're not romantic like they are in the tales. They're nasty things that'll burn you up and slice you to ribbons in seconds.'

Rose gulped. 'I see. Well, at least it'll be exciting. I've never seen a dragon before.'

'And they're real ugly too.' He could still see the dragon's face. The one which tore into his father. The man who taught him everything he knew, gone in a flash of teeth and cinder.

'With me by your side, I'm sure we can sort out this big ugly dragon. Then we'll save your shop and buy you a new door.'

Eric emptied the oats into a pan over the fire. 'I'm not sure this job will be enough to cover the debt. And even if it was, all these adventurers take the good work from me. I can't even get a contract clearing out goblins from caves, that used to be my bread and butter.'

'Sounds like we need to put an end to this adventurer craze.'

'And how do you expect us to do that?'

'I'm sure we can think of something.'

Eric poured water into the pan from his waterskin and gave it a stir. 'It'll figure itself out eventually. We've just gotta weather the storm.'

Rose stood up. 'What kind of attitude is that?! It's all happened with too much coordination, it can't be just a coincidence. We need to take action! Fight back! Do you just want to roll over and take it? Let them kill their way through every creature in the land? They're going to make everything extinct!'

It was infuriating what the adventurers had done to the world. Maybe she was right. What he wouldn't do to go back to the way things were. When people were compassionate to monsters, when you could walk down the street without a threat of violence, when the world was a quieter, more peaceful place. Perhaps there could be a way.

'I'll think about it,' he conceded, 'But first things first, let's stop this ruddy dragon. Alright?'

'Alright.' Rose sat back down, content. 'Thank you for taking me on, Eric. I want to help as much as I can.'

'Don't mention it.'

In the background, the trees mumbled their approval, but it was lost in the sound of the wind.

12

Eric dismounted Daisy and stretched. Rose climbed down from her chuffer and lifted her goggles over her head, curiously glancing around at the village they had arrived at. There were only a handful of houses, all dotted beside the central pathway. Each looked like an eerie copy of another, yet all had their own distinct flavour, such as a stack of barrels or a rickety porch. Barren fields stretched all around, providing no salvation from the tedious breeze.

'Are you sure this is the place?' asked Rose.

Eric unravelled his faded map and peered at it for the hundredth time that day. 'This is where Lord Egglewort marked for us, and there hasn't been anything else for miles. It's gotta be Clopcod.'

It had taken another day's ride, and Eric had managed to avoid most of Rose's incessant questions along the way. None of his other apprentices had ever been this chatty, and Eric preferred to watch the bland farmlands pass by instead of making small talk. She'd even asked where the dire-badger had wandered off to in the morning. How was he supposed to know? Probably to forage for another hit of Elixir. Eric rubbed the sleep from his eyes. He'd stayed up all night tending to that badger, but didn't tell this to Rose in case she'd think he'd gone soft.

Eric shoved the map back into Daisy's saddlebag and patted her side, then led her over to the hitching post and tied her up.

'Only one way to find out,' said Rose, as she skipped over to a passing farmer. The young man was surprisingly well dressed for a peasant and hardly had any muck on him. Rose nodded to him and gave a warm smile. 'Howdy and good morning, sir! Is this Clopcod? We've come to deal with a dragon problem.'

The young farmer didn't seem surprised at all, or even thankful. He simply stared at them with a blank look on his face. 'You'll be wanting to speak with Old Ted then,' he said and spat onto the dry earth.

Rose's smile didn't falter. 'And where can we find Old Ted?'

'Probably in his house.'

'And *where* is his house?' said Eric, trying to be patient.

The young farmer started to pick at his nose. 'That house there,' he pointed, bogey on the end of his finger. 'The one with the wonky roof.'

As far as Eric could tell, all the little houses had wonky roofs. And there couldn't have been more than a dozen of them. However, one was wonky to the point of collapse. That must have been it.

Eric turned and walked away from the infuriating man. 'Come on then Rose, let's go see this old fart Ted.'

After a few knocks, a wrinkled and hunched man poked his head out of his doorway and suspiciously eyed the pair. 'What do you want?' he said through toothless lips.

Eric wiped the spittle from his face. 'Are you Old Ted?'

'Aye, that I am.'

'I'm Eric, from Beast Be Gone. This here is my apprentice, Rose. We've come to sort out your dragon problem.'

The door creaked as it opened and Old Ted beckoned them inside. 'Oh. Yes… of course. Do come in.'

Eric drew an audible breath. The old man's house was much too lavish for a farmer. Golden trinkets glistened in the candlelight, rich fabrics adorned the plush furnishings and an oversized chandelier hung in the middle.

Eric ran his finger along a spotless golden orb on the sideboard. 'Awful lot of loot here. Did you use to be an adventurer?'

'Heavens no,' said Old Ted with a chuckle. 'I… inherited all this from my late uncle.' He slumped down onto a cosy looking armchair and gave them a quizzical look. 'And you're not adventurers?'

'No, we're pest control.'

'Hum. How very odd. Don't see many of your sort around here.'

'Times are tough.' Eric tapped his foot impatiently. 'So where's this dragon then?'

Old Ted's eyes glinted with glee. 'It's a tale as old as time, young man. You see, far across this land, an ancient…'

'Yeah, yeah, ancient curse. Piles of treasure. Lost sheep and maidens.' Eric waved a dismissive hand. 'Textbook. Just tell me where it's nesting and we'll be away.'

Old Ted slumped his shoulders. 'Don't you want to hear my story? It's a tale as old as time...'

'We need to get there before nightfall.'

Old Ted crossed his arms. 'Well, maybe I don't want to tell you then.'

'It's like that is it?'

'Afraid so.'

Why did everyone in this rotten town have to be so difficult? 'We've come under the orders of your Lord,' said Eric sternly. 'If you don't assist us, Egglewort will hear about it.'

'*Fine*.' Old Ted huffed. 'It's nesting up in the ancient mines a few miles north of here. Follow the river, you can't miss it.'

'And what sort of dragon is it?'

'It's a dragon.' Old Ted smiled sarcastically. 'You know, scaly, long, angry. Loves gold?'

Eric clenched his fists. 'No, I mean what *sort* of dragon. Greyskin, Snubnose, Hornfoot, Tuftwaggle, Goldscale…'

'I said I don't know.'

'Well, what does it look like?'

Old Ted tapped his chin musingly. 'Kind of orange, with a spiky neck?'

'And a long tail?'

'I think so. I didn't get a good look at it.'

'Guess it's a Clawridge then. Shouldn't be too much of a problem.' Eric walked back towards the door. 'It's been a pleasure. But we've got to be off to exterminate a dragon.'

* * *

Eric and Rose peered into the darkness of the entrance to the mine. The hole had been cut into the sheer rock face and propped up by thick wooden beams. Shoddy carpentry, though. Eric pushed back the thoughts of the pointy teeth lurking within.

'What's wrong?' asked Rose.

'Nothing,' said Eric. He took a deep breath. 'I can't smell sulphur, so it won't be using this cave as its entrance.'

Rose's voice wavered. 'Are you sure about that?'

'Positive. We can set up camp in the trees over there. Then we'll scout the caves and start setting some traps.'

They led the wagon over to the spot under the trees and unpacked some essential gear. Dragon repellent, fireproof cloaks, torches and comfortable shoes for running away in. He shoved as much as he could into his Sack of Clutching. Then they lit their torches and stepped into the mine.

'Let's just hope it's a male,' said Eric as they descended into the darkened tunnel. The cut stone was smooth beneath their feet, but years of disuse had coated it with dust and grit.

'Why?' Rose's voice echoed in the emptiness, along with her rumbling pack. She winced and turned it off. The chugging stopped and there was blissful silence. She mouthed 'sorry' in the torchlight.

Eric tutted. 'How would you feel about crushing dragon eggs?'

Rose held her torch high, cautiously glancing around at the vast stone walls surrounding them. 'Seems a little cruel.'

'It's not easily done. And it's worse once they've hatched. They don't die so quietly.'

'Surely it can't be so bad? They're only small.'

'They can still breath fire.'

'Ah.'

'And they don't know how to use it. Makes them unpredictable.'

'Fair point.' Rose paused. 'Then I hope it's a male dragon too.'

Eric scribbled a map of the tunnels as they went along, being careful to mark any identifiable points. Not that there were any. He had to make do with comments such as, "sheep shaped rock," and "funny-looking crack."

They managed to find three other entrances and seven chambers, each larger than the last. All empty.

After a while, Rose stopped. 'I don't understand, where could it be? Is it hiding?'

'Unlikely. Where would it fit? There's only one last place it could be, right here in the central cavern.' Eric pointed at the blank space in the middle of his map.

'How do you know there's a central cavern?'

'These are man-made mines, there's always a main cavern. That's where the worst monsters hide, and where the best treasure is hidden. So it has to be down that path.' A foreboding sense of dread crept over him as he looked towards the tunnel. 'Follow me.'

They extinguished their torches and continued along, using their hands to guide them on the rough limestone walls. There were some claw marks etched into the rock. Eric's heart pounded, his stomach twisted into burning knots.

The main chamber appeared before them. A vast open space, lined with shelves and tools along the walls, the floor littered with the bones of adventurers. A single sharp beam of light shone down from a hole in the ceiling high above, illuminating a chest on a central stone plinth.

But no dragon.

Eric breathed a sigh of relief.

'Maybe it's out hunting?' whispered Rose.

'Maybe,' Eric whispered back. 'But this doesn't feel right to me. There's no dragon dung anywhere.'

'Perhaps some adventurers have slain the dragon already?'

'I don't see any dragon bones, do you? Nah, it's still alive. If it ever was alive. But if something's been bothering these villagers, we'll find it.'

Rose stepped a little closer to Eric. 'What should we do?'

'We'll lay a trap, then we'll catch it when it comes back.'

'Shouldn't we go and look at that chest? We could take a little treasure.'

'No,' said Eric, firmly. 'We never steal, just neutralise the threat. We're not horrible adventurers.'

Rose helped Eric unload the equipment from the wagon. She wheezed and strained but never uttered a word of complaint. Eric laid out the metal spikes, pulleys, and rope on the dirt. He inspected each element, ticking each one off his list. Rose watched everything, fascinated.

It took them an hour to drag everything deep into the tunnels, where they managed to find a perfect spot at a crossroad. It had a nice low ceiling and a tight corner.

It had been a long time since Eric last set up a dragon trap. But he tried not to dwell on what had happened then. He just hoped that the equipment was still in working order. Some parts seemed as rusty as rain buckets.

They raised the supports, wedging them into the rocks. Eric scaled a ladder, which Rose dutifully held steady with the aid of her metal claw. He hammered spikes into the ceiling, then coated them with anti-dragon venom.

Using the existing beams left by the miners, they strapped up a series of ropes and pulleys. Finally, Eric wound the whole structure up tightly using the lock-pulley winch.

Eric licked his lips. The floor was now a thick web of taut ropes, ready to snare its unsuspecting victim.

'How will we know when we've caught anything?' asked Rose as she jotted into her notebook.

Eric held out his hand, revealing a red crystal in a silver casing. 'This is a trapgem. It'll let us know when the trap's been sprung.' Trapgems were always exciting. There was a sense of anticipation to them that made him feel alive, although in this case it made him feel the opposite. A trapgem had only only failed him once, when a team of rat-men had tricked him with a wheel of cheddar and he'd ended up inside his own trap. Fortunately he knew enough squeak-speak to negotiate his way out.

Rose's eyes gleamed. 'Fascinating.'

'Careful now, take a step back,' Eric warned Rose. 'Let's go back to camp. We could have a long wait ahead of us.'

The sky outside had fallen dark in their absence. Now only the moon cast its light upon the forest clearing, blotting out the stars. Eric insisted that they didn't make a fire, as it would attract unwanted attention. So instead they depressingly ate wheatbiscuits for dinner and lay down in their tent to get some much-needed sleep.

Eric closed his eyes. All he saw was fire and horns. Sharpened, deadly fangs flashed and snapped. Then a scaly, gaping jaw enveloped him, burning his skin and melting his flesh. He screamed.

Eric sat up, wide awake. Heart thumping.

The crystal glowed in his hand, vibrating gently.

Rose stirred beside him. 'What is it?'

Eric gulped. 'Looks like we've caught ourselves a dragon.'

13

The next morning, the Great Spellmaster Xenixala of Xendor, Queen of Lightning, Slayer of Wyrms and inventor of the patent-pending 'Xeni-Ointment' for intimate hair removal, regarded the naked young man beside her. His ivory skin gently heaved as he slept, shoulders covered by his messy golden hair. He was cute, but not nearly as handsome as that Edwardius. Younger men never had any *presence*.

The boy blinked and stirred. The charm spell had probably worn off by now. Charm spells weren't strictly necessary for Xenixala to get what she wanted, but she did it all the same. Men were so much more *compliant* under a charm. It saved an awful lot of time and energy rebuffing their letching and cat-calling. After missing out on Edwardius the night before, she'd needed some kind of replacement to cheer herself up, and this young man had been most persistent. She'd tried to get Edwardius away from that damned pixie girlfriend of his but hadn't been able to shake her. She clung to his arm like a barnacle. It was almost as if she knew Xenixala's game.

Xenixala had never suffered from a lack of attention from men. In fact, if she were to believe their compliments, she was the most beautiful creature on the planet. However, she was at the tail end of her one-hundred-and-thirties, and there was only so much magic one can do without making things more saggy in the long run.

The boy opened his eyes and stared at her in mild confusion. He wiped the drool from his mouth and sat up slowly. 'Where am I? Did we…?'

Xenixala nodded. 'Of course.'

The young man smiled to himself with gentle satisfaction. Then he looked around the room with a furrowed brow. 'Are we still at the inn?'

'You generously rented us a room last night. In fact, you were quite adamant about it.'

'Oh Gods, I can't afford this. Father's going to kill me!'

Wordsworth sat on the bedside dresser, ruffling his pages in disapproval.

'What?' said Xenixala.

'Aren't you getting too old for this sort of thing?' said Wordsworth.

The boy's eyes became wide. 'Is that a *talking book?*'

Xenixala sighed. 'He's my book of spells. Haven't you ever seen a familiar before?'

The boy shook his head without taking his eyes off Wordsworth.

Xenixala yawned and stretched. 'Our souls are linked, I made him from a part of my essence, yadda yadda. Isn't it time you left?'

The young man looked down at Xenixala's exposed torso and licked his lips. 'Perhaps we could…?'

Xenixala got out of bed and rubbed her temples. 'I'm not really in the mood.' She needed some Elixir.

The young man sidled over to her, putting his arms around her waist. 'Are you sure you don't want...' But he started to choke. He dropped to the floor, clutching at his throat.

'I *said*, I'm not in the mood.' Xenixala picked up the boy's scattered robes while he writhed in pain on the ground. She released her hold-spell from his neck and he made a deep intake of breath.

'You witch!' he spluttered.

Xenixala threw his clothes on top of him. 'Indeed I am. Now get out before I turn you into a toad.'

The boy went paler than a vampire. He snatched up his garments and scurried out of the room.

'Oh, *Xeni*,' said Wordsworth, once they were alone.

'I've got needs too, you know.'

'But they're such poor young chaps.'

Xenixala snorted. 'It's nothing they haven't already done to all the "poor" maidens in town.'

'It just seems so… unsavoury. Couldn't you find someone more stimulating?'

A grin crept onto her face. 'Oh, he was stimulating all right.' She thought again back to the mighty Edwardius. His broad shoulders and strong chin. How much sweeter a prize he would have been. All of a sudden, an emptiness filled her. As if her encounter had left her without something. She ignored the feeling and started to get dressed.

Wordsworth stuck out his leather bookmark tongue in disgust. 'I mean *intellectual*. The conversations you have with these boys are beyond banal.'

'I'm not interested in their conversation.' Xenixala went over to the mirror to rearrange her hair. She pushed back the irritating white streak under the black layers of her fringe.

'Not to mention the *power* we absorb from the better male specimens.'

It was true, and one of the main perks of being a witch. Wizards, however, lost power and Experience with sexual congress. It made them such shy and awkward little creatures, always terrified of being seduced. She smiled. 'Elixirs give us more power than any man could.'

Wordsworth licked his lips. 'Speaking of which...'

'You read my mind. Come on, let's go and find an Adventurer's Supply.'

Xenixala left The Crow's Wort Inn, having hastily dressed. In the fresh morning air, she proceeded to pace the town streets, her face and hands damp with sweat. She needed health potions and she needed them fast.

The town of Gladmore was much like any other provincial town. Xenixala could remember when such places barely had a spot to hitch a horse. Now they were practically bursting with life. Every other person she passed seemed to be an adventurer of sorts. They were easy to spot due to their audaciously impractical armour and stony gaze.

Besides the recent influx of temporary populace, Gladmore was a rather unremarkable town. The roofs were layered with quaint little red tiles, the walls had a charming slant and the townsfolk had the heartwarming innocence that a city would have strangled and left for dead. It was an exact replica of every other town in the land.

It wasn't long before Xenixala arrived at a shop with the all-too-familiar logo hanging on a fresh wooden sign. A potion bottle on a shield. Green on black. Adventurer's Supply.

As she approached the door, Xenixala noticed a faint smell of freshly baked sweetloaf. This probably once used to be the town bakery, recently converted. There were more profits to be had in swords than food these days. Adventurers consumed mostly potions and supply rations, and stabbed more than they ate.

The smell brought back a memory. She was back in Porkwarts School for Witches Not Wizards. Professor Mogg standing over her. The whole class staring.

'Xenixala, was your spell supposed to create a sweetloaf? No, I asked for longbread. What did I warn you about failure? If you're not the best, you are the worst. Pick another poison as your punishment. Let that be a reminder. The rest of the class will watch.'

The doorbell tinkled as Xenixala entered. A tiny gnome poked his head out from behind the counter and smiled vacantly at her. Xenixala scowled back. She hated gnomes as much as pixies. There was something unsettling about the uncontrolled hair sprouting from every crevice of their little bodies. Not to mention the fact that they always drove such hard bargains. She was unsurprised to find one running an Adventurer's Supply.

Xenixala walked over to the counter, concealing her quivering palms behind Wordsworth, who remained dormant in her arms. The shop was dingy, with shelves full of wonderful items. Everything from jars of blood to huge iron maces. Behind the counter the more exotic items were hidden behind an enchanted force field. A metallic tang hung in the air, a side effect of all the anti-spell charms laced into the walls. Adventurer's Supply owners were always so damned paranoid. Thief-classed adventurers really ruined everyone else's fun.

'Good day weary traveller, can I interest you in some wares?' The gnome spoke in a jangly tone, swaying in rhythm to his chime. 'Some armour perhaps? I've the finest swords in the land!'

'Twelve Elixirs please,' said Xenixala, her eyes twitching with anticipation. These would be freshly brewed. And when it came to Elixirs, the newer they were, the better.

'Certainly traveller.' The tiny gnome disappeared behind the counter, then returned with an armful of glass vials. He carefully laid them out on the counter.

Xenixala picked one up, inspecting it in the light. The Elixir glistened its inviting green hue. She grinned. 'How much?'

'For you traveller, a bargain.' The gnome dipped his quill, then scribbled onto a scrap of parchment. Adventurer's Supply shopkeepers had a habit of writing a price down rather than saying it. Xenixala tapped her foot while she waited.

'One hundred and forty-four gold pieces!?' Xenixala exclaimed. 'That's nearly triple the value!'

'That is the price traveller. We do not bargain.'

'How about we say one hundred and twenty gold pieces?'

'That is the price traveller. We do not bargain.'

'One hundred and thirty?'

'That is the price traveller. We do not bargain.'

Xenixala groaned. 'Fine, have it your way.' She pulled out her purse and counted out her last gold pieces. 'Oh hellfire, I've only got fifty pieces.'

The gnome's face remained impassive.

Xenixala slammed down her coins. 'How many can I get for this?'

The gnome carefully slid three vials towards her.

'That's outrageous! It's even more expensive!'

The gnome nodded.

Xenixala tried to remain calm. There wouldn't be anywhere else to buy Elixirs for miles around. 'Deal,' she said, grabbing the three little green bottles.

'Stay safe on your travels adventurer!' called out the shopkeeper in a cheery tone, as she turned and stormed out.

Xenixala muttered as the door swung shut behind her.

She scurried around behind the shop and trembled as she cracked the wax seal on one of her newly acquired Elixirs.

The liquid rushed down her throat, sweet and bitter all at the same time. A power grew through her, starting in her chest, then making its way to her fingers and toes. She breathed in deeply, feeling the sparks tingle on her tongue. Her heart fluttered and she leant back against the shop wall.

But as soon as the feeling arrived, it had gone. All that was left was the mild afterglow that would last for a few more hours. She blinked. Had the world always been so dull and lifeless? She needed another. Just one more.

'That felt good,' said Wordsworth beside her. They shared a knowing look.

The second seal broke as easily as the first. But Xenixala barely tasted it this time, her mouth still numb from the sparks. The warmth grew faster than before. She closed her eyes and let it take her. Silence. No more voices. No more dark memories. The Elixir pushed them away.

Then it was gone again.

'If you are not the best, you are the worst.'

Xenixala looked down at the final vial in her palm. The green liquid sloshed as she let it roll smoothly back and forth. She bit her lip.

Wordsworth craned his spine up to look at her from the floor. 'That's our last one Xeni. You don't have money for any more.'

'You think I don't know that?'

'I'm just saying we should *savour* it, that's all.'

Xenixala smiled.

Her tingling fingers pulled off the last seal with ease. She put the glass to her lips, threw her head back and let the happiness glide down her throat.

Warmth. Bliss. Joy.

Xenixala cast the three empty vials to the ground.

Wordsworth hopped away from the shards of shattered glass. 'I think we need a bit of income Xeni. Maybe we could pawn off some of our old...'

'I'm not selling anything,' Xenixala cut in with a scowl. The world span in an Elixir haze. She pushed back against the wall and slid to the floor. She closed her eyes and breathed deep.

'Are you feeling alright?' came a confident voice.

A shadow loomed over her. Broad and twinkling.

Xenixala winced up at him. 'I'm fine Edwardius, I was just...' she leapt to her feet and brushed down her robes, 'taking a rest.'

The paladin nodded. 'Ah, very wise. One needs to be on top form before setting out on an adventure. It's the best way to get the most Experience from your adversaries. *"If one can't progress from one's battles, one can never progress in life."*' He smiled with satisfaction at his quote, which Xenixala recognised as being from a half-witted motivational scroll. 'Perhaps you have had a chance to reconsider our proposal? Are you sure you don't want to join our quest to find The Chosen One, and defeat the Dark Master?'

'As I said before, no. So if you'll excuse me, I'll be on my way.' Xenixala started walking, but Wordsworth shuffled into her path.

The book tilted his cover to look up at her, his pages folding into a pleading expression. 'Come on Xeni,' he hissed. 'Perhaps we just go with them for a little bit?'

'Why do you care?' Xenixala whispered.

'You said so yourself, we need some real Experience for a change!' Wordsworth lowered his voice even further. 'And besides, we can steal a few of their Elixirs.'

Xenixala regarded the six-feet-of-handsome who smiled pleasantly at her. She had a strong feeling that she may be able to bed Edwardius. The power she could absorb from a paladin would be a fantastic high. All she had to do was get rid of his pathetic girlfriend.

She could even bed The Chosen One and steal his power too, assuming he was a man. Not to mention the exciting quests he could take her on. Better than any she had ever seen. And if neither of these worked out, then a duel with him would be glorious. No one was really a challenge these days. She could be the best. She *needed* to be the best.

'Alright, fine,' Xenixala conceded, picking up her Sack of Clutching.

Wordsworth jumped up and down with joy. His pages clomping together with each bounce.

Edwardius beamed. 'Excellent! We're just about to set off, let's make haste.'

Xenixala sighed. 'There had better be plenty of Elixirs on this damned adventure,' she mumbled at Wordsworth.

14

Eric stared in disbelief at the dragon trap.

Two bodies lay in the closed device, now more soup than solid. Red ooze spattered the walls, lumps of flesh trailed across the floor. A head lay at his feet, eyes glazed over. It stank of bile and entrails. Rose retched and turned away.

Eric bent down to inspect the enchanted-looking helmet affixed to the decapitated victim. 'Damned adventurers,' he muttered.

Rose's eyes were in a wide panic. 'We killed them! What do we do!?'

Eric stood up and scratched his chin. 'We don't do anything. They're adventurers. Everyone expects them to go into a dungeon and not come out again. That's two more we don't have to worry about.'

'But they're *dead*! They're people too you know!'

Eric chuckled to himself. 'Don't you worry, look at those footprints.' He pointed to the trail leading away from the bloody mess. 'One of their party members survived, so it's not a total party kill. They'll have taken blood samples for a resurrection.'

'Really? You're sure?'

'Positive. But I'm curious why they're here in the first place. How did they know about the dragon?'

'Same way we did?'

'No, we heard it directly from Lord Egglewort. Someone's been spreading rumours.'

'Old Ted?'

'Maybe...' Eric sniffed the air. There was a hint of... inanimate magic. It was there before, but it was stronger now. He needed to get away from the smell of guts. 'Something's not quite right Rose, follow me.' His nose led the way, through the passages, slowly, carefully. Sniffing the rocks and ground. His heart pounded in his chest. It wasn't a dragon, he was sure. Further, deeper into the caverns.

Until it led to the main chamber.

The large beam of light still struck a glinting chest at the centre, surrounded by hordes of motionless skeletons and decomposing bodies. The perfect trap.

Rose let out a sigh. 'So no dragon then?'

'Shh,' Eric hushed.

Rose obeyed.

He crept towards the chest, stepping over the scenes of death at his feet. Closer and closer. The box was before him, adorned with gems and gold.

He picked up a discarded sword.

'What are you doing?' said Rose. 'I thought you said we weren't thieves?'

'I said sshh!'

This had to be it.

Eric opened his Sack of Clutching and rummaged around. The vial he was looking for appeared in his hand, cool and smooth. Inanimate-Be-Gone, his own recipe. He dribbled half of it onto his sword, then stowed the rest in his belt.

He lunged, sword swinging down. It hit the wood with a solid clunk.

'Arrrrghhh!' screamed the chest. 'Bleeding hells!' It tumbled away, quivering. Blue steam emitted from where the sword had landed.

Eric raised his sword again.

'I yield I yield!' The chest pleaded, its lid lolling open. A few gold coins rolled from its mouth and tinkled onto the stone floor. 'Ach, that stuff burns! What is it? Am I going to die?'

'It's only a bit of repellent to keep us safe. You'll be fine in a moment.'

The mimic nodded its lid thankfully as it groaned. 'Why'd you go and do a thing like that?'

Rose stood at the ready, claw outstretched from her now-chugging backpack. 'What is it exactly?'

'This here is a mimic. I know his smell anywhere.' Eric stood up and patted the mimic on the lid. 'He's a magical being. He can turn into any inanimate object he likes.' Eric saw what a mimic's original form looked like once. He pushed the thought away. Why did they need that many teeth on their tentacles?

Rose edged towards the creature. 'Are you sure he's safe, Eric?'

'Positive.' Eric smiled at the mimic. 'We're not a threat. I know mimics, they ain't so bad.'

The chest smiled back. 'That's right, we're not.'

Rose tentatively patted the creature on the lid too. It purred with satisfaction. 'Oh, sorry. I've just… never met a mimic before.'

'I wasn't going to eat you,' said the mimic. 'Honest.'

'Oh yeah?' said Eric. 'What about all these bodies?'

'I was only defending myself! I can't live in peace with all these adventurers blundering around. When I'm a chest they can't resist shoving their filthy hands in me, then they get aggressive when I tell them to get lost. Although they are rather tasty.'

Eric nodded and discarded the sword. He crouched down beside the chest and lay a hand on its warm wood. It felt soft in a way that wood wasn't supposed to be. 'Sorry about that, but I had to be sure. You'd bite us otherwise.'

The mimic hesitated. 'I was only going to bite you a little bit. What are you doing here, anyway? You don't look like adventurers.'

'We're looking for a dragon,' said Eric. 'Pest control. But it doesn't seem like there is one.'

'That's what all these adventurers keep coming in for,' said the mimic. 'I overhear them talking about it, before I kill 'em of course. What's that all about?'

Eric shrugged. It was curious indeed.

'What's your name, friend?' asked Eric.

'I'm Larry,' said the mimic. 'And you are…?'

'I'm Eric, and this here is my apprentice, Rose.' He gestured a thumb towards her. 'From Beast Be Gone, Pest Control.'

Larry rocked back upright and bounced towards Rose. The bottom of the wooden chest thumped as it hit the stone floor. 'Well you're not adventurers, so you're alright in my book.'

Rose patted Larry again, who wiggled with joy at her touch.

'So, do you reckon you can get these adventurers to keep out of my house? They make an awful mess, even if they are delicious. You could tell everyone you've slain this dragon and you'll look like a hero. I've still got a few years left on the lease, I can't really afford to live anywhere else.'

Eric became lost in thought. He fiddled with the his stubble. There was something going on here. The job wasn't done. 'I don't think that will do it,' he said, determined. 'Someone's been spreading rumours to get people going on this quest.'

Rose looked at Eric with a knowing smile. 'It's got to be Old Ted. He knew everything about the dragon.'

Eric nodded. 'I thought his house looked too nice. I bet someone's been paying him off handsomely. But who?'

'We'd have to ask him.'

'That won't do, he'll deny it. We need to catch him in the act, get some proof.'

'And how are we supposed to do that?'

Simultaneously they both looked at Larry.

'Me?' said Larry, who shuffled away.

Eric crouched to Larry's level to where he assumed his eyes were, somewhere around the keyhole area. 'You'd be the perfect undercover agent, Larry. You could pretend to be his desk, then listen in and find out what he's been up to.'

'Ha! No chance.'

'What if…'

But Larry had already started hopping away, clomping over the dead bodies, some of which made a satisfying splat.

Rose and Eric shared another look, then ran after him.

Rose yelped and tripped over a loose skull. Her robot arm whizzed into action and propped her back up. The thing seemed to have a mind of its own.

Eric reached the exit to the chamber and looked left and right. But only emptiness echoed down the corridor.

Rose caught him up. 'He can't have gone far, he can only hop.'

'He would have shifted forms. He could be anything now.' Eric breathed in deeply. He would have to rely on his nose again. But the smell wasn't there anymore. He sniffed, the air only held the tang of blood.

Rose rifled through her backpack and took out a small orb. She shook it until it emitted a high pitched whine. Faster and faster she shook, her face tight with concentration, before tossing it in the air. The mechanical claw protruding from her bag snatched it between its two pincers, keeping it spinning. The orb burst into a ball of white light above her and the tunnel became as bright as day. She pointed at the ground. 'Look, Larry squashed those dead bodies and left a trail.'

Sure enough, a square stamp of blood clung to the floor. One stamp after another, leading left down the passageway. 'Let's go!' She hurried off, her lamp-like orb bouncing and flickering light. It made Eric dizzy.

Eric conceded that she had the right idea and followed along.

They delved deeper into the mine, always keeping an eye on the ground at the rapidly thinning trail of blood. The imprints would suddenly change, from squares to circles to a thin line. Eric assumed Larry must have transformed into some kind of wheel. Fortunately, they had already mapped all the tunnels, so Eric wasn't concerned with becoming lost. Although all the unexpected exercise was making him sweat more than during a health and safety inspection.

The trail disappeared, along with the last of Eric's breath. He hunched over, wheezing and panting and wishing he'd never left home. Rose seemed unaffected and instead cast her lamp around the cavern they'd found themselves in. It was barren, aside from loose rocks and stalactites.

'Larry, we know you're here,' Rose lulled cautiously, 'Come on out, we just want to talk.'

Silence.

'That won't help,' Eric leant against a wall, trying to take the weight off his jellied legs. 'He doesn't want to be found.'

'Eek! Okay, I yield again!'

Eric leapt as the rock he'd leant on tumbled away and rolled at his feet.

'Ah, there you are Larry. Just as I suspected.'

The rock melted into a soft brown, warping so that all the pointy-bits were in the right places. Larry shook himself, now back in his treasure chest form. 'Why can't you leave me in peace?'

Rose folded her arms. 'You're quite the coward, Larry.'

'What do you expect?' said Larry, puffing out his chest's chest. 'All the bold mimics end up dead. Hiding keeps you alive.'

Rose stepped towards him with an outstretched finger and prodded him in the panelling. 'But you won't be alive much longer with all these adventurers coming by. We plan on stopping them, and we need your help.'

'You don't need me.'

'Course we do. You can help us find information. All we need you to do is pretend to be a desk in an old man's house and listen in on what he's up to.'

'I couldn't do that! What if he caught me? What if...'

Eric cut him off. 'As far as I can tell from all those dead bodies, you can handle yourself just fine.' He felt quite sorry for Larry. Mimics were close to becoming extinct with this adventuring craze. Their mating habits were too infrequent to keep up with the rate of slaughter, although the former was because they were too good at hiding. Mimics would often mistake real inanimate objects for a mate, leading to a lot of destroyed property and very few pregnancies.

Larry paused in the glow of the compliment. 'That may be. So why should I care?'

Rose spoke fast and passionately. 'They'll never stop coming, the world's full of them now. You either have to fight it or accept it, and we're planning on fighting it.' She winked at Eric. 'How about this, if you help us you can come and stay in our shop until we get rid of all the adventurers. Deal?'

Eric scowled at Rose. He wasn't running a damned hotel.

Larry let out a gentle hum, his lid slightly ajar. 'Now that does sound like fun... alright, deal.' He hopped up and down. 'I hope your place is nice and damp though, or my allergies will be a nightmare.'

'That's the spirit.' Rose smiled and patted Larry on the lid. 'Now let's go and pay Old Ted a visit.'

15

The Master Illusionist Xenixala of Xendor, Conqueror Of The Nether, Destroyer Of Blight and owner of one of the seven enchanted toothpicks of Blobton, pushed her fingers into her ears even further, but could still hear the racket. She could take it no longer. 'Will you *please*, shut up?' she snapped.

Xenixala, Felina and Edwardius rode along the forest path of Porkwood as the afternoon sun cascaded down, dappling the path at their horse's feet. Felina stopped strumming her lute, surprised. Felina and Edwardius had tediously average brown steeds, while Xenixala rode a fine summoned demon-mare, Death-Bringer. He was semi-translucent and emitted a blue shimmering gas as if he were reacting badly with the air. She had defeated and tamed him many years ago in the Plains of Despair, deep in The Underworld. Despite his upbringing, Death-Bringer was very well behaved and had a fondness for lemon sugar bites.

'Are my majestic tales not bolstering your spirits, Xeni?' said Felina with a sincere pixie smile.

Xenixala scowled, swaying on her steed. 'It's Xenixala to you. Stop that noise before I smash your singing wooden bowl.'

Felina looked crestfallen, lowering her head and instrument.

'I was enjoying your beautiful tunes, my love,' said Edwardius, in a tone so sickly sweet it would have made a hummingbird vomit. Xenixala shuddered with both pleasure and annoyance. How could one man be so annoying and attractive at the same time?

Xenixala cracked open another Elixir that Edwardius had shared, then chugged it back. The warmth took her, all her past failures dissipated in a flash of numbness.

'I will not tolerate failure in this classroom, Xenixala. Drink another poison. The class will wait until you finish every drop. When you cast the spell correctly you may have the antidote.'

She cast the empty vial to the side of the road and felt capable of enduring her two companions once again. She'd only been travelling with them for a day and she'd already been stretched to her wit's end.

'What are we doing with these two creeps?' Xenixala whispered to Wordsworth, who sat in her arms, absent-mindedly fluttering his pages.

'Come on, Xeni,' he replied. 'We need to find this Chosen One. We'll ditch them as soon as we meet him.'

Xenixala groaned

'And there's always Edwardius…' Wordsworth whispered conspiratorially.

'What about him?'

'I see the way you look at him.'

'What? He's handsome. That's an objective fact. It would be wrong to deny a glance or two.'

'You were gaping so much your jaw dragged in the gutter.'

Xenixala didn't respond. Perhaps she could expedite her escape from the pair. All she needed was a little more information.

'Felina?' she said, as politely as she could manage. Xenixala pulled the reins on Death-Bringer, slowing him down to bring her alongside the bard. 'How about you tell me a little more about The Chosen One? I'd *love* to know about what we're chasing.'

Felina whipped out her lute faster than a bolt of chain lightning. 'The song of The Chosen One?'

'Without music.'

Felina muttered something and put the lute away. 'If you insist. But the tale won't be nearly so… *dynamic*.'

'I'll live. Now get on with it.'

Felina cleared her throat. 'Written in the ancient scrolls of The Holy Mole is a prophecy that a powerful warrior will one day come to the land. He will be so *Experienced* that neither man nor beast can defeat him. He will rid us of all the evil that plagues the world.' Felina nodded with self-satisfaction. 'From what we've gathered, we believe that a man is The Chosen One from this prophecy.'

Xenixala frowned. 'It would stop anyone adventuring if all the "evil" creatures were gone. That wouldn't be much fun. And besides, evil is subjective.'

Felina cut in, 'Evil is evil, and that's that. This evil Dark Master needs to be stopped. His Minions of the Dark Army are gathering. If we don't act soon it will be too late.'

Xenixala yawned. 'This is just some dumb story made up by the Holy Mole priests to sound impressive.'

Edwardius shot her a stare and pointed a gauntlet-clad finger. 'Say nothing against the Holy Mole, for you insult my Oath.'

'Whatever.' Xenixala rolled her eyes. There he goes again with his damned paladin nonsense. What a turn off.

Felina continued, her eyes glinting with delight. 'It is said that in a single afternoon, he defeated an entire colony of owlbears. He strolled into an Arch Warlock's tower and destroyed an army of the undead without a scratch. He's even running errands for The King, slaying evil on his orders. All without a party.'

'All without a party?'

'All without a party.'

'What does he look like?'

Felina paused. 'Ah, that we do not know.'

Xenixala was more certain than ever that this Chosen One character could get her some real Experience for once. Just the thought of it was enough to still the nagging voice within. 'So… where are we going exactly?'

Felina tapped her disturbingly pointy nose. 'We cannot tell you until we are there. Some former companions have used our information against us in the past, then they ran off to get there first. Can you imagine?'

Xenixala gave a forced chuckle. 'Who would do such a horrible thing? Imagine. Just awful. Terrible.'

Felina continued, 'Suffice it to say, we spoke with a very reliable soothsayer last night about the last known location of The Chosen One. That is where we are heading.'

Edwardius sniffed the air. 'Danger is close. Be safe.' He drew his sword and spun his head, inspecting the trees. In return, the trees drifted lazily with the breeze, ignoring his concerns.

Xenixala tutted. 'It's just the wind.'

Someone yelled. Five shapes swung from the treetops. They surrounded Xenixala, Felina and Edwardius, thrusting their blades. The bandits had a wild look in their eyes and were covered in a layer of filth that implied they'd spent far too much time sleeping in the middle of a forest.

The meanest looking bandit stepped forward. Although he mainly looked mean because of his eyepatch, which Xenixala suspected was simply a fashion accessory. He licked his lips and bared his teeth. 'This is gettin' too easy. We heard you coming for miles.' Xenixala glared at Felina, who seemed oblivious that her irritating bard song had got them in this mess. 'Now hand over your horses and loot, before we make you.'

'Hold on Greg,' said one of the other bandits to the eyepatched one. 'These guys look like adventurers.'

'So?' spat Greg, 'If you don't want their loot, Bill, you can bog off.'

'They're the reason bandits are dying,' said Bill, his voice wavering. 'Adventurers are hunting us down. Plus, they've got big swords and magic armour and things, and we've only got tatty tunics and rusty daggers. We don't stand a chance. Can't we just pick on farmers and peasants and things?'

Greg lowered his voice. 'Can we talk about this *later,* Bill. I'm trying to be menacing.'

'Actually,' piped up one of the other bandits. 'I'm not too keen on fighting adventurers either. They slew my last band. I barely made it out alive.'

'Nor me,' said another.

'Nor I,' came another voice from the back.

'Fine!' Greg burst, his face red. 'By a show of hands, who wants to leave these adventurers alone?'

All the other bandits slowly raised their arms, including Edwardius and Felina.

'You yellow-bellied cowards!' Greg screamed at his companions. 'I'll be sure The Bandit King hears of this. He'll have your heads on spikes, mark my words.' He turned back to face Xenixala. 'I'll take them on myself.'

Xenixala grinned. She clicked her fingers and her demon-mare faded away. She glided slowly down through where the creature had once been, assisted by her lesser-gravity spell. Wordsworth leapt into her arms and flicked open to a useful page in anticipation.

'I don't care who you are,' said the eye-patched Greg, shaking with rage. 'I've got plenty of experience killin' adventurers. Plenty. Now hand over your loot.'

'Are you sure you want to do this, Greg?' said Bill, as he and the other bandits backed off into the trees.

'I'm no coward, Bill.' Greg remained alone and stood defiantly before Edwardius, Felina and Xenixala. Xenixala saw the doubt flickering across his eye.

There was a tense silence.

Greg lunged at Felina, pulling her from the horse. She screamed, somehow managing to keep hold of her lute.

'Felina!' Edwardius bellowed.

Greg thrust a knife to Felina's throat. 'One move and your girlfriend here gets a new air hole.'

Felina put her hand dramatically up to her forehead, wilting her body in submission. 'Save me, Edwardius, you're my only hope.' She closed her eyes, but kept one slightly open to watch Edwardius' reaction.

Could this be the moment to impress Edwardius? She could save Felina and be the hero. Or maybe she should let Felina die and have him all to herself? Her mind made up, she flicked Wordsworth open to page fifty-one and took a deep breath.

Edwardius had sprung from his horse, his sword held high, shouting 'Felina!' over and over again in a wild rage. He pirouetted in the air, as if in slow motion. Xenixala had never seen anything like it - except when she cast slow-motion spells.

There was a flash of steel.

Xenixala's spell nudged Felina's head to the left.

Edwardius landed beside Greg and Felina's dire embrace.

Two heads thumped at his feet, blood sprayed across his shining armour.

Edwardius choked and stumbled to his knees. 'What... have I done?!' Tears filled his eyes as his bottom lip quivered in a childish blubber. 'Mole forsake me.'

The other bandits had already fled with terror the moment Edwardius started flailing. They clearly had keen survival instincts, so they probably stood a chance at being able to make it past the age of thirty-five. Practically ancient in bandit years.

Edwardius cradled Felina's limp body on the ground, rocking back and forth with a whimper.

Xenixala thought Felina's head looked much better on the floor. Something about its relaxed expression complemented her features.

'Time for a nice Elixir don't you think, Wordsworth?' she said with a sigh.

Wordsworth snapped shut in her arms. 'You read my mind.'

16

Eric took a deep swig of his ale and let out a purr. Beer was one of the few things in life he still enjoyed, and he wasn't going to let Rose's glares ruin it for him. They both sat at a table in the only tavern in Clopcod, located conveniently across the road from Old Ted's house. The tavern was as pathetic as you'd expect for a village like Clopcod. The ceiling was low, the floor dusty and the only other patrons were the three local drunks, who were probably the only reason the place maintained any kind of profit, and a mysterious man with a dark cloak in a shadowy corner. He would have been paid by the owner to be there, as every inn had to have one mysterious stranger to make the place seem "with the times". It was either that or saucy tavern wenches. Eric wondered if the tavern was turning better profits than him, which were none and therefore very likely. Why hadn't he followed his dream and opened a pub? He should never have listened to his father.

Rose sniffed at the tankard that dwarfed her hands. 'I can't believe you actually like this swill. It tastes like dishwater.'

Eric finished the amber delight and slammed his tankard onto the table. 'Fond of dishwater in the West are we?'

'Our beer is actually refreshing. This is warm and gross.' She slid the tankard away from her and grimaced. 'Beer is supposed to be cold and fizzy.'

'Fizzy? You mean stale?' Eric scoffed. 'And do you really think they can afford ice charms on *every* tankard?'

'What about compressed air? You Easterners are so behind the times.'

Eric thought compressed air sounded like an accident waiting to happen. And when alcohol was involved, everything was an accident waiting to happen. 'This is plenty refreshing for me. Now stop moaning and drink up.' He nodded to the barkeep. 'You've only had one drink in two hours, the bartender's giving you the evil eye.' The barkeep had also been polishing the same glass for an hour. They'd been waiting in the tavern for almost two days (only leaving to sleep in their nearby tent) and the barman was never without a glass to polish in his hands. It must be a nervous tic.

Rose stuck out her tongue. 'I'm not thirsty. And besides, I shouldn't drink and chuff. Handling a chuffer is more dangerous than it looks.'

Eric thought it was exactly as dangerous as it looked. 'That's why animals are better.' Eric wagged his finger. 'You can be drunk out of your mind, and nine times out of ten a mule or horse will take you right home.'

'What about the other one time?'

Eric smiled. 'That's usually when the horse is drunk too. Then things don't pan out too well.' Eric had a few scars he didn't remember the origins of. He partly blamed Daisy.

'Oh.'

'Anyway, we ain't chuffing anywhere. We're waiting for Larry.'

'What if he never comes back?'

'Oh, he'll come back.'

Rose gave him a level stare. 'What makes you so sure?'

'Because that beer barrel's been edging its way over to us for the last ten minutes.'

Rose turned and leapt out of her chair when she realised the barrel was right at her elbow.

Eric chuckled as Rose tried to regain her composure. 'Hi, Larry.'

'Aww,' said the upright beer barrel, the sound emanating from the open bung. 'How'd you know it was me?'

'Let's just say I know a real beer keg when I see one. Did you find anything out?'

'Sure did!' Larry whispered with glee. 'This spying business is a right lark. I wish I'd tried it sooner.'

Rose ran her fingers along the wooden staves in wonderment, then sat back down and scribbled into her notebook. Larry wriggled with glee.

Eric leaned in with anticipation. 'So what did you hear?'

Larry's uncorked bung stretched into a kind of wooden grin. 'Well, I pretended to be a table in his front room, see.' He spoke fast and with a hint of pride. 'Then I waited to find out who came to speak to him, just like you said. After a while, these two blokes arrived and gave him a bag of gold.'

'What did they look like?'

'Like real rough sorts. You know, eye patches, lots of stubble, facial scars, that sort of thing. Real evil-looking. And they had these funny pink skulls on their cloaks.'

The pink skull symbol seemed awfully familiar. Eric shuffled in his chair. He didn't like the sound of being up against rough sorts, he valued his face and kneecaps too much. 'And then what?'

'They asked Old Ted how many adventurers he'd sent into "the filthy mimic den". The cheek of it! So I er… got a bit carried away. Come and take a look.' Larry stretched open his lid, the wood melting aside.

Eric stood up, peeked inside and was surprised to see Old Ted curled up inside the barrel, covered in bruises and splattered blood. He burst into life, squinting in the light. 'Let me out of here you sons of harpies!' He bellowed, 'Do you know who you're dealing with?! 'The Dark Master will…' The hole snapped back shut and the shouts became a distant muffle.

'You *kidnapped* him?' Rose hissed, warily glancing around the tavern.

Larry jostled himself from side to side, and soon Old Ted went quiet again. 'Yeah, uh, things kind of got out of hand after he insulted me and all. So I ate the two goons and grabbed Old Ted here. He's been banging on about this Dark Master all the way over.'

'I *told* you all these adventurers are from a conspiracy!' said Rose.

Eric didn't know who The Dark Master was. Probably some megalomaniac with too much money but not enough attention. He stood up. 'We best get going then.'

Rose got up too. 'I'll get our steeds.'

* * *

They retreated back to Porkhaven with a Scroll of Town Portal, resupplied and had a brief rest. Then the three (or four counting Old Ted in Larry's belly) of them rode to Lord Egglewort's castle. The mimic had reverted to his favoured form of a treasure chest, claiming it was what he "identified" as. Rose's chuffer didn't seem to mind the extra weight, so Larry had sat himself on the back of the lolling contraption as it rode along. Eric was astonished that as a square he managed to keep perfect balance.

The castle guards ushered the group into the main hall, two of whom reluctantly carried Larry. They clearly hadn't realised he wasn't an actual chest and Larry didn't correct them. The main hall was much sparser than Eric remembered. There were no tapestries or servants standing by. In fact, the cavernous room was empty with the sole exception of a table at the far end. There sat Lord Egglewort, with two dark figures looming over him. The discussion they were having was heated, and ended with Lord Egglewort screaming a collection of obscenities. The two figures bowed, turned and walked away, sneering as they passed Eric. He recognised the pair immediately. Pompous black tunics and a gait that suggested they were in charge of the very ground they walked on. Geiston & Geiston, Property Agents.

Lord Egglewort noticed the new arrivals and wearily gestured them forward with a finger. They complied and strode across the room, boots clopping, to where Lord Egglewort sat at his high table in his stained undergarments, thick bags under his eyes. The guards carrying Larry put him down before Lord Egglewort, bowed and left them alone.

Lord Egglewort licked his lips. 'My my, what's this treat. I do hope you bring good news... uh, Edrick was it?'

'Eric, my Lord. From Beast Be Gone.'

'Ah, that's right. You were supposed to sort out a dragon problem for me?'

Eric chose his words carefully. 'Indeed I was my Lord, dragon won't be a problem no more.'

Lord Egglewort cleared his throat awkwardly. 'Unfortunately, uh, I've got a bit of bad news for you. I'm afraid I'm not entirely sure I can reward you… just now. Seems I've come into a little financial crisis.'

Eric gritted his teeth. It was as if the whole world wanted him ruined. His face flushed and he scowled, ready to scream at the pompous oaf. He caught Rose's eye and she gave him a calming smile. He relaxed his jaw and shuffled his feet. 'What do you mean, my Lord?'

Lord Egglewort glanced down at his miserable outfit, tugging at a hole in the vest. 'I'm sure you saw those fiends from Geiston & Geiston. These property taxes are ruining me. I'm *sure* they hired actors to make offers on my fort of *absurdly* high sums. Of course the offers vanished when I tried to accept. But that's all Geiston & Geiston needed, that is the fort's new value, and a fat slice of it must be paid to The King.'

Lord Egglewort should never have rejected the tax protection package he'd offered him. 'Bunch of sharks.'

Lord Egglewort continued his whimpering. 'And on top of that, this adventuring craze just won't go away. I haven't any useful loyal subjects left, only the elderly and infirm. Everyone else is running off, plundering temples and looting goblin nests. There's no-one left to till the fields, milk the cows or harvest the grain.' He let out a sigh, a single tear rolling down his cheek. 'But The King still wants his dues. So I have to sell everything to pay up. I'm ruined.' He produced a handkerchief and blew his swollen nose.

'I suppose you won't be renovating that fort anymore either?'

Lord Egglewort hung his head. 'Sylvia was very cross about that. The budget she wanted was astronomical too. I can't afford such luxuries.'

Eric clenched his fists. That meant no commission from Sylvia either. He only had one hope left to redeem anything from this disastrous situation. 'Well, funny you should say that, my Lord. You see, we may be able to help you on the adventurer front.'

Lord Egglewort sat up a little straighter, a gleam in his eye. 'Oh, really? How so?'

'In fact there never was any dragon to begin with. One of your "loyal" townsfolk had been making the whole thing up.'

Lord Egglewort waved a dismissive hand. 'What of it? I'll put him in the stocks for a week.'

'I think he's part of something much bigger, my Lord. Men came and *paid him* to lure adventurers on a phoney quest.'

'Interesting…' Lord Egglewort stroked his three chins. 'Do you have any proof?'

'This mimic here overheard the whole thing, then captured the perpetrator.' Eric gave Larry a gentle kick.

Larry snorted awake. 'What?' His lid flapped as he spoke. 'Oh, yeah.' He leaned forward, lid wide and Old Ted flopped to the cobbled floor. An overpowering smell filled the room. Eric put his hand over his nose.

Lord Egglewort got up and looked down at the limp body. He stepped forward and gave Old Ted a tap with his toe. 'He's dead.'

'Nah, he's fine,' said Eric. 'Just needs a bit of air.'

Lord Egglewort gave him an incredulous look. 'I', pretty sure he's dead, my boy.'

Rose knelt down next to the old man's body and put her fingers on his neck. 'He's definitely dead.'

'Oh, hog's balls.' Eric turned to Larry and frowned.

Larry twisted his corners into a shrug. 'What? Why are you looking at me? I don't know how much air humans need!'

'Did you give him *any* air?'

'Well, no.'

Before Eric had a chance to scold Larry further, Lord Egglewort sat back down at his long-table and groaned. 'I don't care for having dead citizens thrown at my feet Eric, so this had better be going somewhere.'

Rose chimed in, right on cue. She'd been itching to make her speech ever since they'd devised their plan that afternoon. 'Well, my Lord, *we* believe that this is part of a large conspiracy. Someone wants adventurers everywhere, and they're willing to send them on any kind of quest they can muster up. Including inventing dragons.'

Lord Egglewort's face illuminated into a radiant smile. 'Of course! How could I be so blind! This is far too widespread to be a passing fad. Otherwise how on earth could it go on for so long? There shouldn't be any dungeons left by now.'

'Exactly.' Rose nodded with satisfaction. 'Someone must be filling them up with loot and monsters, or making up fake quests such as this dragon.'

'But who?'

Larry leapt in with surprising cheer. 'The Old Ted corpse had been going on and on about some Dark Master. Maybe he's behind it all?'

Lord Egglewort wriggled with glee. 'Most excellent! A lead. Right, Eric, I need you to get to the bottom of this Dark Master fellow, then get rid of these adventurers for good.'

Eric winced. Things were getting out of hand. 'Are you sure you don't have some guards or knights who might be able to…?'

Lord Egglewort tutted. 'You think I can afford to spare knights and guards in these times Eric? You're my last hope. I'll pay you handsomely of course.'

'You ain't even paid me for the dragon yet.'

'There never *was* a dragon Eric. Once these adventurers are gone, I can make you all very wealthy and give you plenty of land. A title too if you fancy it.'

'No title. But land I could use.' Eric imagined building a pub of his own, full of the best beer, fresh-baked pies and homemade stew. Maybe even a few tavern wenches for good measure. He could even run the Beast Be Gone business out of the back and have plenty of room for new traps and cages. He shook his head, letting his dreams tumble into nothingness. How could he possibly expect himself to solve all the world's problems? He couldn't even run a successful business. 'Actually, I'll pass.'

Rose turned to him, leaning in and speaking in a hushed tone. 'Just think Eric, we could finally be rid of adventurers! Don't you want to at least try?'

Lord Egglewort coughed to get their attention. 'Let's put it this way, Eric. If you *don't* try to stop all this adventuring, I'll be forced to tell The King how you kidnapped and murdered an innocent old man, then threw him at my feet.'

Eric bowed. 'Consider it done.'

17

Skwee the goblin led the three ogres into the ancient mineshaft, relieved to be back in the dark, cold and damp. He cleared his throat and pointed. 'And if I may bring attention to the wonderful detailing on the stalagmites.'

'Stalac-*tite*,' interrupted the largest ogre, Morg, who was presumably the father of the family. Skwee found it impossible to guess an ogre's age, or gender.

'Yes, that's right,' said Skwee, 'the downy ones. Wonderful detailing.'

Morg grunted agreement, ducking under the stalactites-and-or-mites.

Ogres only knew about one thing, and that was the quality of stone. Skwee had been given careful training on how to sell to ogres. Most of it involved pointing at rocks.

The Dark Army had taken it upon themselves to retrain Skwee again after he'd failed so miserably at being a foot soldier. He quite liked his new Geiston and Geiston uniform. There were no silly pink skulls and the velvet was delightfully soft. He enjoyed his new title too, "Estate Agent". It sounded so grand and proper. It was beginning to dawn on Skwee that there wasn't really an army in the Dark Army at all. It seemed more like a series of business ventures.

Skwee brought them to the cave's main chamber, which he knew had the "wow" factor all good properties needed.

'Wow,' said Morg behind him, staring up at the shaft of light that illuminated the central plinth. His wife and son (or possibly husband and daughter) let out a gasp.

Skwee had personally overseen the clear up of the cave and was so proud of the results that seeing the ogres ogle the place brought a tear to his eye. There had been a surprising number of dead adventurers, and a lot of blood, but with a good team of goblins, anything was possible. Removing the mimic smell had been a bit of a challenge, and in the end they resorted to masking it with scattered sage and turnips. If they'd been leasing the place to humans they wouldn't have needed to bother. Their noses were awful.

It was time to make the sale. He looked up at the three creatures, fixing them with a stare. If you broke eye contact you lost the sale, the training had been very clear about that. 'This cave is only fifteen hundred gold for a ten year lease, paid upfront,' he said. 'Or sixteen hundred in ten easy instalments.'

Morg scratched his head. 'Instal-mints?'

'Yes, instalments,' said Skwee. 'I have the paperwork here. We just need your signature and ten percent deposit.' Skwee's eyes flicked to the gold-filled bags tied to the ogres belts.

Of course the property was valued at almost triple what it should have been. That's what you can do when you had a monopoly like Geiston and Geiston did.

'We hear rumours,' said Morg the ogre, scratching his bare chest. 'Dragon live here. Where dragon?'

Skwee had read the file. There had been a dragon a long time ago, but it had flown off after getting fed up with all the adventurers coming after him (courtesy of The Dark Master's rumour spreading of course). For some reason, dragons absolutely fascinated adventurers. Just the idea of one was enough to get an adventurer salivating. Therefore The Dark Army's dungeon keepers had made the executive decision to keep the dragon stories going, letting a mimic live in the cave to keep the adventurers amused instead. But the mimic had run off, so they needed quick replacement "dungeon fodder".

'I don't see a dragon, do you?' said Skwee, gesturing around the cavern. 'He's long gone, adventurer's probably got him.'

The three ogres flinched at the word adventurers.

'But...' said Skwee quickly, 'there aren't any more adventurers either. As you can see.'

'What if come?' said Morg. 'They everywhere.'

'Ah well, that's the great thing with Geiston and Geiston,' said Skwee with a smile. 'We'll resurrect you free of charge if you die to adventurers on any of our properties.'

Skwee neglected to mention that after the first five free resurrections, the ogres would be charged. Then if they couldn't pay up, they'd stay dead. And Geiston and Geiston could lease the cave out again and again and again.

'Okay, deal,' said Morg.

Skwee breathed a sigh of relief. 'Excellent, please sign here.' He held up the documents and the father-slash-mother signed them with a quill. The ogre dropped a bag at Skwee's feet, it clinked with the sound of coins.

'Daddy, I'm *hungry*,' said the little ogre, who was still twice as tall as Skwee.

Morg licked his lips. 'Me too.'

Their eyes locked onto Skwee.

'I suppose...' Skwee stammered, 'that I'd best be on my way,' He bent down to pick up the bag of gold, but was snatched by the scruff of the neck. The ogres laughed to themselves as Skwee struggled.

Morg brought Skwee to eye level as his jaw opened wide, revealing rows of rotten teeth.

Skwee tensed and tried not to scream.

At least he'd made the sale. All in all, not such a bad day.

18

Prime Witch Xenixala of Xendor, Mistress of The Wind, Dominator of the Halls of Hellfire and finalist at the West Trenton Fishing Competition grimaced at Felina's headless corpse. It was slung over Edwardius' mighty shoulders, while blood oozed down his armour, trickling all the way to his horse's hooves. Edwardius sobbed gently, occasionally patting the body and muttering his apologies.

Xenixala pulled the reins of Death-Bringer, halting him as they came to the clearing. Finally, they'd made it. Time to put an end to his endless weeping. 'Here we are Edwardius,' she announced, floating down from her steed, Wordsworth tucked under her arm. 'One Holy Mole temple, exactly where I said it would be.' Actually a "locate holy" spell had done most of the work. She'd also done her best to take some detours. If they couldn't resurrect the pixie she could have Edwardius all to herself. He'd get over it eventually and she could be his rebound.

The Holy Mole temple's marble tower loomed before them, casting a mighty shadow across the forest clearing. The rest of the structure cascaded out from the base of the tower into uneven mounds, representing giant molehills. It was the second silliest religion she knew of, the first being "The Missing Sock Scriptures".

Edwardius leapt down from his mount and hurried to the temple without even securing his horse, the lifeless pixie in his arms. Xenixala strode after him with limited enthusiasm.

A hooded priest greeted them inside the grand entrance hall. He stood with his hands tucked inside his drooping black sleeves, head bowed. 'Welcome trav…' He looked up, then shook his head, rustling his moleskin robe. 'Oh, not more wretched adventurers. You're here for that lich in the basement aren't you?'

Edwardius and Xenixala exchanged looks.

'No, good sir,' Edwardius held up Felina's limp frame. 'I have a resurrection request, my dearest love has befallen a grave accident and I cannot go on witho…'

The priest raised a hand. 'Easily done. Although I'm surprised you brought her whole corpse... a mere sample of blood would have sufficed.'

Xenixala felt vindicated. 'I tried telling him, but he couldn't *bear* to leave her.' She gave Felina's little body a prod. 'Although I thought pixies couldn't be resurrected?' She'd never actually seen a resurrection, preferring to leave the carnage for other people to sort out. Most of her research involved finding the best way to kill someone, rather than the opposite, so she was still a little hazy on details.

'Of course they can be, any sentient being can...'

Xenixala cut in. 'It's been two days, probably a bit stale now?'

'Not at all,' said the priest. 'We can manage up to three weeks. But the longer you wait, the more damage to that person's soul and, in turn, *Experience*.'

Xenixala cursed under her breath. She shouldn't have bothered getting her killed after all. 'Alright then... any Elixirs for sale?'

'We're all out I'm afraid, we've had far too many adventurers coming through.' He gestured to a large doorway. 'Please, bring the body over to the resurrection altar. Follow me.'

He led them into a room with a low ceiling. There were no windows, instead, thousands of candles coated the floor, shimmering with an unnatural pulse.

'Here we are,' said the priest as they arrived at a large slab of marble. 'Place the body on the altar, then insert the coins into the slot.' He pointed to a tiny hole to the side. It had a sign next to it saying: *"Please insert six-hundred gold coins - Property of The Doom Bank"*.

'*Six-hundred gold coins*?!' Xenixala exclaimed.

'Simple economics my dear.' The priest grew a patronising grin. 'If people are willing to pay it, that is the price.'

Edwardius had tears streaming down his face. 'I will pay anything to have my love returned to me.' He placed Felina on the altar, gave her a tender kiss on the hand, then removed his Sack of Clutching from his belt. He pulled gold coins from it and then slid them, one at a time into the slot, counting under his breath. 'One, two, three, four...'

The priest raised his eyebrows to Xenixala. 'See?'

Due to a mishap with a button and a few mixed up copper pieces, it took Edwardius ten minutes to count out all the coins.

The priest smiled as the altar began to hum. 'She will be ready in exactly twenty-two hours. We offer dormitories for the night... for a price of course.'

Xenixala let out a long moan. 'Urgh, we'll be here forever. Is there a tavern nearby?'

'Not for miles. Have you ever considered the path of patience and the Holy Mo...'

'Quiet, mole man,' Xenixala snapped. 'Didn't you mention a lich?'

The priest shuffled awkwardly. 'I don't know what you're talking about.'

'Spill the beans holy boy before I turn you into a weasel.'

'If I could request to be a mole, actually that would...'

'Not a mole. A *weasel*.'

'Very well.' The priest gulped. 'We've had an issue with The Demi-Lich Kalakzar in our crypt. I *thought* I had dealt with the situation when I paid a handsome price to a pest control agent to remove him. Only to have some burly men in black leather and pink skulls force their way in with a new haunted coffin for Kalakzar. They threatened me, saying they'd, they'd…' he bit his lip, trying to hold back tears, 'Cut off my ears if I tried to get the lich removed again.' The priest put his head in his hands. 'What is a man to do? Why must I suffer such an endless stream of adventurers?'

Wordsworth flapped in Xenixala's arms and looked up at her. 'We might as well have a look. Could be fun? Better than moping around with this blubber guts for twenty-two hours.'

Xenixala watched the sobbing paladin wipe his tears onto Felina's sleeve. This was her chance to get some alone time with him. Plus, as a lich was no walk in the park, there would actually be a chance to break a sweat. 'Come on, Edwardius, how about a bit of adventuring to take your mind off things, loosen you up?'

'I shan't rest until Felina is back by my side,' Edwardius whimpered. 'I cannot go on without her.'

Xenixala put a reassuring hand onto his back, feeling the smooth metal on her fingertips. Didn't he ever get tired of lugging that stuff around all the time? It must have weighed a ton. 'She'll be right here. We're only going downstairs. And besides, do you really want her coming back to life in a *haunted* Holy Temple ruined by evil…?'

Edwardius sniffled. 'I suppose not.'

'And don't you *love* stopping evil?'

Edwardius smiled sheepishly. 'I do rather enjoy banishing evil.'

'Excellent, then let's go downstairs and have some fun. You've done all you can for her now and you need a distraction.'

'Oh… alright. But just for a little bit.'

'We'll be back here before you can say, *Demi-Lich Kalakzar.*'

Xenixala and Edwardius strode down the old stone steps and entered the domed chamber of the crypt. A thick layer of dust coated every surface. Lanterns shone on the stone coffins along the walls and the dead adventurers on the floor. What a bunch of amateurs.

Xenixala waved her hand to melt the mess of cobwebs from their path, her breath misting in the air. She cracked open an Elixir and finished it in two gulps. The warmth held the shakes at bay. It was almost her last one; hopefully there would be some more lying around. Elixirs somehow found their way into even the most ancient of tombs.

'Are you sure about this Xeni?' said Edwardius, his oversized sword at the ready. 'Looks pretty empty to me. Perhaps that priest was lying?'

'Nah, his tears were too pathetic. The biggest undead always hides in the fanciest coffin at the end.' She pointed. 'Probably that one.'

There was a sound of gushing air. The large coffin at the end of the room burst open and a skeletal form floated out. Blue smoke swirled around its ragged robes, it's face a hollow skull beneath a rusted crown. It fixed its gaze upon the pair with eye sockets that betrayed no emotion and pointed a dagger at them with a boned hand.

Xenixala chuckled at the predictability. 'See?'

A deep voice boomed through the chamber.

I AM THE LICH KALAKZAR! BOW DOWN BEFORE ME, PUNY MORTALS...

Wordsworth flipped open in Xenixala's arms, skipping to page seventy-three: Undead preventions and anti-curses.

...AND PREPARE TO MEET YOUR DOOM.

'Begone evil spirit!' Edwardius charged at the enemy, sword high, effortlessly leaping over the sea of victims on the ground.

FOR MANY YEARS I HAVE LAIN IN WAIT...

Xenixala read the incantation and blue flames ruptured from her hands. The ball of energy sailed across the room. The undead figure batted it away like a fly.

YOU DIDN'T LET ME FINISH MY SPEECH.

This might be harder than she thought. Xenixala smiled. Finally. She ran forward, casting a protection barrier. A wall of energy enveloped her just in time to deflect a bolt of lightning from the lich.

LET ME START OVER. I AM THE LICH KALAKZAR! BOW DOWN BEFORE, ME PUNY MORTALS...

Edwardius was upon him, swinging a graceful dance. The lich parried with his dagger and ducked the sword blows, joining the dance, his bared teeth twisted into a macabre grin.

AND PREPARE TO MEET YOUR DOOM!

Xenixala's heart raced. Nothing beat the thrill of the fight. Inches from death. The fear in your enemies eyes, the power, the blood. All condensed into one glorious moment.

'Give me a bolster charm Xeni!' Edwardius cried, dodging the lich's dagger.

'On it.' Xenixala ran forward. She touched Edwardius' armour and chanted '*Protectus Armourus Veritus.*' It glowed red, shining bright in the gloom of the crypt.

Edwardius exploded in a frenzy of new found energy, forcing the lich to back away. He winked at Xenixala. 'Thanks.'

'Don't mention it.'

The lich seemed distressed. He'd stopped his nattering and instead chanted a charging spell. They took longer to cast, but boy did they pack a punch.

Edwardius hadn't noticed.

'Get down!' Xenixala jumped at Edwardius, pushing him out the way. They landed hard onto the floor, in time to see a wave of black energy scream overhead. She lay beside him, panting. Their eyes locked in the breathless moment.

It was time to take things up a notch.

Wordsworth chimed in, upturned on the flagstones. 'Perhaps a page three-two-nine followed up with a connecting enchantment?'

'You read my mind.' Xenixala flicked her wrist, sending the world upside down. Everything flew to the ceiling, dust and bodies shattered against the stone. The lich tumbled upwards too, lost in the confusion. But Xenixala and Edwardius were prepared. Xenixala landed on her feet, running across the roof at the lich, she spun her arms, binding Edwardius to the enemy.

Gravity returned to normal, sending the room's contents hurtling back down. Xenixala drew the lich towards Edwardius, their weights connected by her spell. The lich wailed with despair as they crashed together.

The dazed Edwardius steadied himself, then swung his mighty sword down onto the undead beast. It exploded into a white flame, its soul dissipating into the air with a gush of screams.

Then silence.

All that was left of the lich was a pile of dust and a rusty crown. The Experience tingled through her. More than she was expecting, but still only a measly increase in her power.

Edwardius embraced Xenixala. 'Bravo! What a magnificent display. And a delicious bit of Experience too.'

Xenixala breathed in his sweaty after-battle musk. 'See? Wasn't that fun?'

'I must admit it Xeni, vanquishing some evil did rather get my mind off... Felina. I feel much better now, thank you.' He stared into her eyes for a moment too long.

That's when she knew she had him. He didn't stand a chance.

Xenixala stepped back and dusted herself down. 'Now let's smash open all these pots and coffins to see what we can loot.'

The pair arrived back at the temple's entrance hall, bags packed with old swords, helms and an array of junk.

Xenixala smiled at the priest, who stopped in his tracks. 'How much will you give for all this loot?'

The colour left the priest's face. 'That's my stuff! Where did you get all that?'

'In the crypt and a few of the boxes in the hallway. And down in the stores. Oh, and behind that secret wall that had a different shade of brick.'

The priest gawped over Xenixala's shoulder, noticing the hole in the wall. Scorch marks surrounded the shattered bricks and debris. 'That's what that noise was?! It cost a fortune to brick that up!'

'Well, you should have paid to get matching bricks, it was clearly hiding some goodies. Anyway, we want to sell it all to you.' She dumped the junk at the priest's feet and it clattered unceremoniously, scattering weapons and armour across the marble floor. 'We can't exactly carry it all around, my Sack of Clutching would be a total mess.'

The priest was lost for words. 'But... they're *my* things! You *stole* them from me! And now you're selling them back?!'

'They were left unattended.' Xenixala grinned. 'Simple economics. If people are willing to pay it, that is the price.'

The priest stood, trembling and red faced.

Edwardius stepped in. 'Have no fear priest. We will put the proceeds to good use, our fight against evil. We will make the land a better place with your generous donation.'

The priest glared at Edwardius. 'You think this is part of your holy oath *paladin*? Looting the temples you swore to protect?' He spat at his feet. 'You make me sick. All you adventurers are the same. You think hacking up monsters has *anything* to do with the Holy Mole?! It's about love, peace and understanding for Mole's sake!'

Edwardius furrowed his brow. 'I don't understand, is that a yes or a no?'

The priest grumbled. 'What choice do I have?' He sighed. 'One copper piece per item. Final offer.'

Xenixala grinned. 'Deal.'

The priest handed over the coins from his pouch, head bowed.

Edwardius beamed. 'Thank you, priest. And cheer up, aren't you happy we purged the evil from your holy sanctum?'

The priest looked like he was going to burst. 'The lich *isn't* dead, you oathless oaf!' He yelled, throwing his arms out. 'He regenerates as soon as anyone leaves the room. I'll never be rid of him.'

'You mean he's not un-undead?' Xenixala looked at Edwardius. 'Are you thinking what I'm thinking?'

'Unlimited Experience?'

'Unlimited Experience.' Xeni chugged down one of her newly acquired crypt Elixirs, it tasted weak and watery. 'We've still got another twenty hours to burn in this dump. May as well spend it fighting.' She cast the vial onto the pile of items on the floor, showering it with sticky glass.

'Better, Xenixala. But still not good enough. Do it again. You will not rest until you have mastered this spell. Drink another poison.'

Edwardius smiled, his hand hovering over the hilt of his sword. 'I do love a good bit of questing.'

Xenixala wiped her mouth as the warmth took her. 'Me too. Now let's show that boss who's boss... again.'

19

Back at the Beast Be Gone shop, Eric fell into the only chair and poured himself a whisky. Dust sparkled in the light filtering through the shutters. Rose stood over Eric with her arms folded, while Larry tramped into a corner and tried to blend in as another chair. Eric considered it a pathetic attempt to hide. With such little furniture in the room, a detailed mahogany seat stood out like a sore thumb. On their way back, Eric had tried to dissuade Larry from coming to live with them, but Larry was completely set on the idea, and was excited as a baby with a candy-apple. All things considered, a mimic wouldn't be such a bad lodger. If anything it would give him a bit more furniture.

Rose hesitated, obviously weighing up whether it was appropriate to sit on Larry. Instead, she pulled a lever on her backpack. With a whir, her mechanical arm folded down to the ground forming a kink, upon which she leant. She shifted against the bronze device. 'So what now, then?' she asked.

'How should I know?' Eric took a swig of the cheap whisky, its delights slid down his throat. 'My job is to clean out caves, not chase evil villains. I'm not a damned adventurer.'

Rose's face twinkled with realisation. 'That's it! We're *not* adventurers… right now.'

Eric didn't like the sound of that one bit. He shook his head. 'No, no way. I know what you're thinking. I swore I'd never try adventuring *ever* again. Not after what happened.'

'But it makes perfect sense! We need to find out who's been making all the quests and filling all these dungeons, right?' Rose stopped leaning on her metal arm and paced up and down the shop, a trail of steam following behind her. 'We need to get in their boots, learn their ways, find out who's running the show. We have to *become* adventurers.'

'I know their ways alright.' Eric took another swig. Just talking about them was enough to leave a bitter taste in his mouth. 'Run around, swing your swords, destroy property and kill innocent creatures. Then finally loot what ain't yours.' He put down his glass and leaned forward. 'My father showed me the right way. Care for the living and protect the world from itself. Not murder things for their life-force. It's grotesque.'

Rose tapped her chin. 'There must be more to it than that. Like, how do they find all these quests in the first place? What do they do with all their loot? What drives them?'

'I don't care what drives them, probably a hero complex. This Dark Master chap certainly has one, judging by the name alone.'

'Got any better ideas? We don't have to do much *actual* adventuring, we just need to see what they're up to.'

As much as Eric hated to admit it, he felt Rose was right. They had to learn the inner workings of the adventuring world. He'd never really understood them, even when he tried to be one as a foolish, angry teenager. Adventurers used to be so rare that you could forget they ever existed, but now there were more adventurers than normal folk.

On the other hand, could he ever live with himself after sinking that low again? He didn't seem to have any other choice, as Lord Egglewort's offer was all he had left.

He let out a deep sigh. 'I'd lose all credibility...'

'Credibility?' said Rose. 'You think that matters in a time like this?'

Eric rubbed his temples. He could hardly believe this was happening. It was like he was in some kind of dream. Or more rather, a nightmare. 'Alright. I'll be a ruddy adventurer. But I ain't fighting no dragons.'

Rose let out a little yelp of excitement. Eric frowned at her. She seemed awfully keen to become an adventurer. How did she manage to be so positive about everything? It was exhausting.

'I barely know how to swing a sword,' Eric muttered.

Rose pointed to the dusty crossbow that hung above the mantelpiece. 'What about that? Anyone can fire a crossbow.'

His father's crossbow. The one he didn't fire in time to save him from the dragon. He shuddered. His last taste of adventuring had been the worst day of his life. 'I suppose so.'

'See? It'll be easy. So how about we start at the Adventuring Careers Counsellors shop by the market? We went past it the other day.'

'How do you know so much about all this?'

Rose bristled. 'I don't. But my brother became an adventurer. Remember? For a while at least, before he, you know...'

Eric felt a pang of guilt. 'Right, yeah, sorry about that.'

Rose patted Larry on the armrest. 'What do you reckon Larry? Fancy coming along too?'

Larry snorted. 'No chance. Sounds dangerous! Maybe I'll.... stay and keep things safe for you here?'

Eric nodded. 'Actually, that's a good idea, if any bailiffs come, please eat them.'

The chair did a kind of bow. 'It would be my pleasure.'

Eric and Rose left the shop, and after a short walk through the muddy Porkhaven streets, arrived at the market square. Its usual thrum had long since evaporated, leaving behind a miserable affair. Eric remembered when you could hardly move for people thrusting pots and questionably fresh fish in your face. Now only a handful of stalls remained open, mostly selling knock-off potions and rusty swords. That was all anyone wanted to buy these days. A shadow blanketed the space, cast by the building at the far end. It gleamed white, and across the front, a sign in pink read:

The Guild
Careers Advice and Services
Your Adventure Starts TODAY
"Why farm animals when you could farm Experience?"
Proudly Brought To You By The Doom Bank

Eric recognised the pink skull logo blotted above. The whole place was funded by the same wretched bank who'd sent over the bailiffs to kick his door in.

The pair entered the building through a doorway marked "entry", finding themselves faced with a metallic box behind a desk. The box rumbled and two lights shone out of it like eyes, while steam billowed all around.

'Greetings travellers,' the box spoke with a sharp, broken voice. 'My name is Loading. A pleasure to meet you. How may I serve you today?'

More Western steam technology. Eric frowned at Rose.

'Don't look at me,' she said, defensively. 'I didn't craft him.'

'Well, it came from your weird land,' said Eric. 'It's as bad as your backpack.'

Rose ran a protective hand down her straps. 'There's nothing wrong with my backpack. It's far safer than crazy enchantments.'

'I can't believe that it doesn't have *some* enchantments.'

'Well, fine, maybe a few. But only the *steam* is enchanted, it's so much safer. If it's off, it's off. It won't just blow up randomly in the night.'

Eric thought he would actually get a good night's sleep if there weren't so many nocturnal explosions in Porkhaven, but then again, that was part of the city's charm. 'Whatever you say.' Eric turned to the thing behind the desk. 'Either way, that box of junk reeks of magic.'

Eric could have sworn the metal box looked offended, which was impossible considering its lack of features.

'I am an *automaton*, Sir,' it said with a hiss. 'How may I help you today?'

Eric cleared his throat. 'Is this err… Guild thing, free?'

The automaton whirred. 'Indeed sir. The Guild has been subsidised by the Doom Bank - with your account, you have free lifetime access.'

Eric kicked himself for having a Doom Bank account. The loan repayments were crippling him, and *this* was what they were putting the money into? 'Right. Well, we, uh, want to become adventurers.

We'd like to join The Guild, so we can adventure and kill innocent goblins and things.'

'Excellent,' said Loading. 'Commencing new adventurer protocol.' There was a gentle hum. 'Select your name adventurers.'

'Eric.'

'ERROR. Eric is taken. We have Eric242, Eric682 or Eric762? Do you wish to proceed with one of these?'

'I want to be Eric. My name's Eric.'

'ERROR. Eric is taken. We have Eric932, Eric145 or Eric425? Do you wish to proceed with one of these?'

Eric groaned. 'Fine, Eric-four-two-five. It's not like anyone's going to call me that anyway.'

'Thank you Eric425. Other party members, please select your name.'

Rose stepped forward. 'I'll be Rosepuff'

'Thank you Rosepuff.'

Eric raised his eyebrow.

'What?' she said with a shrug. 'It's what my dad calls me.'

'Really? I never knew he was such a softie. He always seemed so... cold.'

'He's probably changed a lot since you knew him.'

Eric thought back to the calculating man that Rose's father had been, The High Governor of Murica. Calling his daughter Rosepuff seemed very out of character. The loss of his son must have hit him hard.

'CAUTION,' Loading announced. '*Conveyer belt activated.*'

Eric felt a surge of panic. 'Conveyer what...?'

There was a jerk, and the world moved beneath their feet. He grabbed hold of Rose's shoulder. She smiled and brushed him off. 'Relax, it's just a moving floor.'

The "moving floor" dragged them through a hatch and darkness enveloped them.

'This is fun!' cried Rose.

Eric wanted to be sick.

'What is your race?' came the disembodied voice of Loading.

'A bit of a racist question isn't it?' came Rose's voice.

Eric couldn't see a thing. How could he make it stop?

'ERROR,' barked Loading. 'Please repeat.'

'We're humans,' said Rose.

'Human selected,' said Loading. 'Please choose an item from the following sections and you will be assigned a class.'

The floor stopped moving and the lamps in the corridor burst out in radiant yellow. In front of them was a table covered with a selection of objects. There was everything from lock-picks to potions, rope to musical instruments, books to jewellery. It seemed like someone had just gone to the pawnshop and grabbed everything that came to hand.

Rose and Eric exchanged looks.

It all seemed so pointless. How was this supposed to help him choose a class? And yet... one item did call to him. Out of the corner of his eye, it demanded his attention, like a nagging itch. He reached out and picked up the crossbow bolt. 'This'll do,' he said with confidence.

Rose picked up a small metal hammer. 'I could use this to fix my chugger's wonky foot.'

The conveyor belt leapt into action again, pulling them down the corridor and to another table full of seemingly pointless objects. However, these ones were much stranger. There were skulls, orbs, metal rods, plants, rocks, a flagon, some feathers. Eric took the rabbit's paw without too much thought, while Rose picked up a brass key.

The floor moved again as Loading spoke. 'Thank you, Eric425. You are best suited to be a RANGER. A stalker of prey and friend to the animals, you enjoy crafting traps and putting distance between you and your enemies.'

Eric felt a swell of annoyance that he could be judged solely on arbitrary objects.

'Rosepuff, you are best suited to be a TINKERER. A manipulator of the world, using gadgets to destroy your enemies and trinkets to guide your path.'

Rose nodded. 'Seems like the obvious choice.'

'The final step of the character creation process is facial reconstruction options. Are you happy with your appearance, or would you like a modification?

Rose poked her nose with her forefinger. 'I've always wondered what I'd look like with a smaller nose...'

Eric cut in. '*No* reconstructions, Loading. Thank you.'

'As you wish.'

The conveyor belt stopped again at the end of the room and mechanical arms placed scrolls in each of their hands.

'Here's a list of recommended starting equipment and an assigned trainer for your tutorial,' said Loading. 'Good luck *adventurers*.'

Eric winced at the final word. A door opened in front of them, bathing them with the light. They stepped through it and back into the fragrant streets of Porkhaven.

Rose opened her scroll like it was a long-overdue love letter. She smiled as she read.

Eric looked down at his scroll but decided not to open it. 'What does yours say?'

Rose cleared her throat. 'Congratulations Rosepuff The Human Tinkerer,' she read. 'And welcome to the new world of adventuring. A world of possibility, excitement, Experience and treasure awaits.'

'Excitement my foot,' Eric mumbled.

Rose ignored him and continued. 'There are a few more steps before you can begin your journey. First, go to your nearest Adventurer's Supply store to collect your complimentary *TINKERER Starter Kit.* You may wish to collect further equipment at your own cost.'

Eric snorted. 'Fat chance of that.'

'After this, please attend your local mentor to guide you through your *Tutorial*. Your nearest mentor is: *"Wise Wally, 37 Alchemy Alley - Porkhaven".* Good luck.'

Rose looked up from the scroll. 'How exciting! Guess we should head over to an Adventurer's Supply then. Know where to find one?'

The familiar logo hung on a wooden sign at the end of the street. Potion bottle on a shield, green on black. Eric pointed. 'There's literally one right there.'

'Oh.'

'You can't walk for more than two minutes without seeing one these days. Come on, let's get this over with.'

20

Supreme Conjuror Xenixala of Xendor, Bringer of Destruction, Champion of Fenakkur and owner of a 'Broomstick Proficiency Badge', shuddered. The kind of hot, pleasant shudder she enjoyed more than anything. Her fingers popped the cork off another Elixir and she savoured its chemical aroma. Heaven.

Edwardius spoke with a concerned tone. 'How many of those have you had today Xeni?'

'Not enough.' As Xenixala pushed the door open to the crypt a waft of stale air hit her. Had Edwardius been a little more observant, he would have noticed that she hadn't even made contact with the wood. Telekinesis was rather excellent at preventing broken nails.

Professor Mogg echoed in her head, her voice biting. *'Your telekinesis pushed too far, Xenixala. You nearly destroyed the desk. You need to CONTROL your power. You will never be the best. And if you're not the best, you are the worst.'*

'I've got plenty more to go around if you want one?' she asked, pushing the memory back down. Deep down. 'They're a bit old but they'll do the job.'

'I shouldn't,' Edwardius bit his lip. 'I've had one, and that's plenty. It's better to keep a clear head.'

'This will *give* you a clear head.'

'You think so?'

'Guaranteed. The more the better.' She held out one of the larger vials, waving it so the green liquid made a satisfying slosh. 'Go on, one more won't hurt.'

'I suppose... *one* wouldn't hurt.'

'That's the spirit.' Xenixala handed him the vial and produced another for herself. 'Bottoms up.'

The vials clinked and the Elixir drained.

'Oh my.' Edwardius put his hand on his forehead, his pupils wide with delight.

'Good stuff eh?' She decided not to tell him about the little modifications she'd made to give them a bit more *zing*. Notably gin and rat tails. 'Right, let's do this.'

Xenixala and Edwardius strode down the steps, batting aside the cobwebs as their eyes adjusted to the darkness of the crypt. Somehow the room had returned to the exact layout from an hour before. Dust still coated every surface, lanterns illuminated the repaired coffins along the walls and the dead adventurers remained motionless on the floor. The lich must have had a tidying enchantment.

Xenixala lowered her voice. 'Okay, he'll appear as soon as we step towards the back. What's the game plan?'

Edwardius rubbed his mighty, clean-shaven chin. 'How about you cast a reflecting enchantment on me as I approach. Then I'll be immune and can make the first strike? Are you experienced in that kind of spell?'

Xenixala scoffed. 'I know every spell in the book, and more besides.' Although she rarely used supporting enchantments, Xenixala considered herself more of a "one woman army", one that other people should get out the way of. However, this could win her some points with Edwardius. She rested her fingertips on his golden-clad arms and waves of energy pulsed forth. 'There you go.'

'How about we do a Holy Balm too? They work marvellously against evil.'

Xenixala rolled her eyes. 'Is that some kind of lame paladin trick?'

'I suppose you could say that. I'll show you if you like.' He came beside her, so close she could almost taste him. 'I don't have any holy water, so we'll use this Elixir instead. Any liquid will do, really.' He put his arms around her from behind, it sent a tingle down her spine. He cupped her hands onto the Elixir bottle. 'Hold it just like this. Then pour in all your own hatred, all your inner demons, all your malice into the vial.'

Xenixala felt awfully silly. But she obliged, savouring their proximity. She focussed, thinking of all the wasted quests and tedious people in the world. Weakness, ugliness, futility, fragility, mediocrity. Her teacher, Professor Mogg. The poisons she made her drink. The punishments for failure. The pain. Her peers laugher and mocking.

'If you're not the best, you are the worst.'

Edwardius muttered a prayer and the Elixir sparkled. He stepped away. 'There we are, an anti-evil balm.' He drizzled the liquid onto his sword and gave her a wink.

They nodded at one another, then stormed towards the end of the chamber. The central coffin lid launched off in a fury of smoke, clattering to the floor. The lich appeared once more.

I AM THE LICH KALAKZAR! BOW DOWN BEFORE ME, PUNY MORTALS...

A ray of fire hit Edwardius in the chest, but the enchantment glowed bright. The spell flipped in mid-air, returning back at the lich. The undead ducked and narrowly evaded the ray. It fizzled into the wall.

...AND PREPARE TO MEET YOUR ...BLIMEY.

Edwardius was already there, his sword swishing. The lich backed away, the hollows of his eyes warped with panic.

NOT YOU TWO AGAIN.

Xenixala held Wordsworth open and read the words, '*Tunnelus Libris Enchantica,*' which lifted from his pages, turning in the air, swirling larger and larger. In a moment, the words had spread through the entire room, spiralling in a wind of confusion. The lich spun his head, frantically searching the floating words. Xenixala let out a hearty chuckle. She ran in, letters parted before her, a tunnel of spells ready for her taking. She plucked one from the air, tossing it at the skeletal figure.

The lich batted the word aside as if it were a fly. It was his turn to laugh, teeth bared.

A sword plunged through his skull.

The blue smoke flushed away, leaving silence and a pile of ash at Edwardius' feet.

Xenixala smiled. 'Good job.'

Edwardius wiped the ash from his sword and smiled back. 'That was too easy. Maybe next time we try without the enchantment? Make it more of a challenge?'

'Agreed. Here,' Xenixala tossed him another Elixir. 'You'll want another one of these.' This time he didn't even pretend to resist.

They ran back up the stairs, left the crypt and immediately came back down. The room was fresh, just like how they found it. Curious. Perhaps other dungeon rooms did that too? She'd never bothered going back on herself after a plunder.

I AM THE LICH KALAKZAR! BOW DOWN BEFORE ME, PUNY MORTALS...

She needed a new tactic, spice things up. Time slowed with her enchanted words. The lich's speech became a deep drawl, his movements crawled to a standstill.

...A...N...D... ...P...R...E...P...A...R...E...

Edwardius and Xenixala ran to him, a flurry of destruction.

The lich dissipated into a pile of ash with their first strike.

Xenixala scuffed his remains with her boot. 'Hmm, that was even easier than before.'

'But rather good fun. I've never moved at double speed before.'

'There are a lot of new things you could try with me around.' Xenixala winked, hoping he would catch the message.

'Again?'

'Again.'

Another potion shared. The door opened and closed.

I AM THE LICH KALAKZAR! BOW DOWN BEFORE ME, PUNY MORTALS...

Xenixala let Edwardius take the lead. He ducked and dived at the creature, sword raised high. Her lightning flew past him.

SERIOUSLY?! AGAIN?

It wasn't long before the lich became dust a fourth time.

Up the stairs, down the stairs, potion.

Xenixala hurled a fireball just as the lich burst from the coffin.

I AM THE LICH KAL… OH, WHY DO I EVEN BOTHER.
Edwardius was there, swiping a graceful attack.

It was odd. Working together as a team felt… right. A demi-lich was a mighty foe, and they cut through him with barely a sweat. It was as if she had doubled her power. She'd never felt it before. Normally a party just got in her way. She only kept them around to soak up some damage and talk to all the boring villagers who needed help. But with Edwardius it was different. They were simply a great fit, or maybe it was his handsome face spurring her on. Either way, she knew she had to keep him.

They went again and again. Guzzling Elixirs, thrusting blades, hurling spells, over and over. Things became a blur. She lost count of their successes. The swell of battle consumed her into a mist of magic, Elixir, Experience and joy. More, she wanted more. She could barely think, a perfect state of numb bliss that took her from the wretched world. Darkness was her friend, a shadow that blotted out her mind.

She was everything.
'You will never be the best.'
She was nothing.
And that was just how she liked it.

* * *

Xenixala awoke from her haze with a headache that could kill a troll. Where was she? Opening her eyes made her head spin. The room was bare, with only a bed and a large carving of a mole on the wall. How had she made it to bed? And where were her clothes?

Someone moved in the sheets beside her.

Xenixala rubbed her temples. 'Keep still Wordsworth.' She burped, bringing up a little Elixir, then winced and swallowed it back down.

'Xeni?'

She turned over to find Edwardius staring back at her. 'Oh, it's you,' she mumbled. Her chest filled with pride. At least she'd finally managed it.

'By the Mole!' Edwardius threw the sheets back, revealing his hairless torso. 'Did we…? Tell me we didn't.'

'Not too sure. Probably.'

Wordsworth leapt between them and rifled his pages. 'I'm pretty sure you did.'

Edwardius jumped out of bed and paced back and forth. Xenixala took the opportunity to examine his sculpted rear.

'Oh no, no, noo, no no no,' he moaned. 'This can't be so! What have you done to me?!'

'Relax,' said Xenixala. 'No use crying over spilt piss. I'm sure it was fun. How about we go for another round? Then we'd actually remember it.'

Edwardius glared at her. 'Get away from me you *wicked* creature. You've soiled my good name!'

'Whatever, loverboy.'

He folded his arms. 'You're out of our party. I never want to see your face again. Do you hear me?'

'It's like that is it?' Xenixala grinned. 'If you say so. But it would be an *awful* shame if someone were to tell Felina about your... transgression.'

Edwardius' mouth hung open. 'You wouldn't dare.'

'Wouldn't I?' Xenixala got up, stepping slowly towards Edwardius until she could feel his breath on her lips. 'She's probably been resurrected by now. Maybe I should pay her a little visit?'

'You're a monster.'

She lay back on the bed and stretched out. 'I've been called much worse.'

* * *

Felina sat on the resurrection plinth, where she looked more petite than ever compared to the colossal slab. Seeing her made Xenixala glad she had yet to experience resurrection. Felina's face was pale and puffy, her tiny eyes sullen, her once silky-golden hair frayed and limp. She looked like a low-level vampire. True death would be preferable to that.

Felina would have lost a lot of her Experience too. It only just occurred to Xenixala that Edwardius would have taken a chunk, having been the one to kill her. She could probably bring that up later to annoy them.

The little pixie pulled a weak smile when she saw Edwardius enter the temple chamber. 'There you are, my love.'

Edwardius ran over, lifting her into a warm embrace. 'I've missed you so much, my sweetheart. Please forgive me for... killing you like that.' He hadn't even had time to wash and probably still smelled of Xenixala's perfume, Chant Hell No. 9 - a must-have for any witch.

Felina coughed into her hand. 'You were trying to protect me. It was so romantic. I would die a thousand times for you.' Xenixala rolled her eyes. The pixie looked around the room. 'Where are we?'

Xenixala waved a dismissive hand. 'Some back-end temple out in the middle of nowhere. We should get going, it's as boring as death here.' She paused. 'And I suppose you would know.'

Felina got to her feet. 'I think I can manage.' She stumbled and Edwardius caught her.

'She's fine,' said Xenixala. 'We should go.'

'Never,' Edwardius said with gravity. 'We should wait for Felina to gather her strength.'

Xenixala made an overt cough into her fist.

'Ah yes, I mean… maybe…' Edwardius hung his head. 'Maybe we should listen to Xeni.'

'Good to hear it.' Xenixala clapped her hands together and strolled towards the door. 'Now let's make like a centaur and split.' She enjoyed watching Edwardius squirm almost more than having an Elixir.

This was going to be a lot of fun indeed.

21

The doorbell jangled as Rose and Eric entered Adventurer's Supply. The shop's shelves were full of odd items: vibrating books, glowing hammers, snazzy rucksacks and lumps of ore. Behind the counter, the shiniest loot sat safely behind a protective barrier. Eric sniffed. It stank of anti-spell charms.

A gnome poked his head out from behind the counter, only his hairy face visible. What was visible was dark and unkempt. Gnomes were famously unclean, so the little creature probably hadn't bathed in years. In his experience this made them much easier to track down.

The little thing smiled vacantly at them. 'Good day, weary travellers, can I interest you in some wares?' The gnome spoke in an irritating tone. 'Some armour perhaps? I've the finest swords in the land.'

All of them claimed to have the finest swords in the land. Damned salesmen, they knew full well they all came from the same factory.

'We've come from The Guild,' said Eric, holding up his scroll. 'To collect our free ranger and tinkerer starting kit.'

'Certainly travellers.' The tiny gnome disappeared, then returned with two boxes. He lifted them up on the counter.

Eric opened the box labelled *Ranger Starter Kit.* Inside was an Elixir, a dagger and a rusty crossbow that looked like it wouldn't even load. He let the lid fall back down. 'Is that it?'

The gnome nodded.

Rose opened her box. 'I've got a wrench, a dagger and an Elixir.' She took the Elixir out and popped off the cork.

Eric knocked it out of her hand and it smashed onto the floor. 'Don't,' said Eric forcefully. 'That stuff's poison and highly addictive. You don't want to end up like that dire-badger. The free one's there to get you hooked.'

The gnome was already beside them, sweeping up the broken shards.

'This starter set was a waste of time.' Eric frowned, then noticed the deep, glowing crossbow on the shelf. He caressed it, feeling the cool wood. The engraving on the side of the handle read, "*Fine Crossbow of Plus-Two and Fire Resistance*." He had no idea what a "plus-two" was, but he felt like he needed it. Fire resistance sounded useful. 'How much for this one instead?'

'For you traveller, a bargain.' The gnome dipped his quill, then scribbled onto a scrap of parchment.

'Forty-four gold pieces!?' Eric exclaimed. 'I'm not made of money!'

'That is the price traveller. We do not bargain.'
'How about we say ten gold pieces?'
'That is the price traveller. We do not bargain.'
'Fifteen?'

Rose cut in. 'What about that perfectly good crossbow on the wall in your shop? You could just use that.'

That cursed crossbow. Could he really bear to use it? The one in the starter set didn't look like it could harm a fly, let alone a giant-fly, which were much more common and terrifying. Giant-flies were best dealt with by applying a sticky paint to the latrines. Once stuck stationary, you could send them to sleep with venom tipped darts. Then you could sell the wings to the cape-makers, the body to the pie-makers and the legs to the dog pound. 'Fine, have it your way. Are you going to get anything?'

'I've already got plenty of equipment,' said Rose. 'Plus I think this place is a rip-off.'

'I'm inclined to agree.'

'Stay safe on your travels, adventurers!' called out the shopkeeper in a cheery tone, as the pair walked out the door.

They stopped off to pick up Eric's crossbow at the Beast Be Gone shop, then strolled over to Alchemy Alley, the place Loading had told them to get their tutorial. Whatever that was. Naturally, the place stank of every chemical Eric could think of, along with a few unknown ones thrown in for good measure, all of which made him a little light headed. Eric felt awkward carrying his father's crossbow, and not only because every non-adventurer they walked past gave him a wide berth. It was as if he were back on his first, and last, dragon hunt. It was surreal. Something about the weight on his shoulders took him right back. He stiffened his lip and shrugged off the uncomfortable thoughts.

'Here we are,' said Eric, stopping outside house number thirty-seven. Its rotten shutters hung loose and its walls were coated in an odd blue moss. Eric sighed. 'Although I've lost track of what *here* is. I thought we were trying to stop adventurers. Now it seems like we're just doing a bunch of awful quests.'

'One step at a time, Eric,' said Rose cheerily. 'If this is where the adventurers start, then maybe that's where we can make them stop.'

Eric banged on the door, being careful not to let it fall off its hinges. It creaked open. A wrinkled man emerged from the darkness, stooping as he strained with the door. He smiled through his grey beard, revealing a set of crooked teeth.

'Welcome travellers,' he spoke slowly and in a hushed tone as if he could barely breathe. 'I've been expecting you...'

'Weird Wally?' said Eric.

'Wise Wally.'

'That's what I meant. I'm Eric, and this here is Rose. We want to get a mentor.'

'Eric and Rose? You must be mistaken, there are already great adventurers by those names...'

Eric sighed. 'I mean, Eric-four-two-five and Rosepuff.'

'That makes more sense.' Wise Wally cleared his throat. 'Anyway, where was I? Ah yes.' His voice returned to a whisper. 'I've been expecting you... for I have seen it in my dreams.'

'You must have pretty dull dreams.'

Wise Wally ignored him. 'Come inside, travellers, and rest yourselves, for you have a long journey ahead of you, and much to learn.'

They followed Wise Wally into his house. Eric had to bend down to get through the doorway. The front room was larger than he'd been expecting, full of ancient furniture on top of a mish mash of rugs. Candles dotted the space, with little to no regard for fire safety, bathing it in light.

Wise Wally was already in a rocking chair by the fire. 'Come, sit with me, friends,' he wheezed.

Eric and Rose exchanged a look, then went and sat by the fire too. There weren't any more chairs, so Eric chose the largest cushion he could find.

'Ahh,' Wise Wally breathed out, stretching his legs and wiggling his toes towards the warmth of the fire. 'Many moons ago, a dark power…'

Eric cut him off. 'Listen, we're just here to get our training. If you could hurry things along, that would be great.'

Wise Wally's cheeks flushed. 'You.... don't want your Main Quest?'

'I'm not even sure what a Main Quest *is*. But it sounds long and boring.'

'It usually is,' Wise Wally nodded. 'That's why adventurers tend to do the side quests first.'

'Fine, give us one of those instead.'

Wise Wally let out a hearty, breathy laugh. 'The Main Quest *leads* you to the side quests. Don't you see?'

'Not really.'

'Well, look at it this way. You need a purpose in life, a path, a destination.' He smiled. Eric tried not to look at his teeth. 'That gets you moving towards a goal. Then when you head that way, you get distracted, you meet exciting people and discover new places. That's when you realise that the *journey* was the real adventure all along.' Wise Wally flourished his hands as if he lived up to his name.

Eric scoffed. 'Journeys are the boring part. Everyone knows that. Why do you think that teleporting is so popular?'

Rose chimed in. 'And in The West, the railsteam takes no time at all.'

'But adventures are much *richer* without too much fast travelling,' pleaded Wally.

'And definitely more boring,' said Eric.

Wise Wally sighed. 'You really aren't getting it.'

'Do we actually *need* a Main Quest?'

'Strictly speaking, no.' Wise Wally leaned in and lowered his voice even more. 'Just between us, most adventurers get bored or die before they finish it. But you do need a reason to adventure, or you won't get your adventuring certificate and I don't get paid. If you like, I'll give you the same one to do together. How does that sound?'

Eric rolled his eyes. 'Alright then, give us a nice simple one.'

'Okay let's see…' Wise Wally produced a list from his pocket. He squinted at it in the light. 'Looking for your long lost father and/or mother?'

'No, I knew them. And now they're dead.'

'Right. How about... you're the secret heir to the throne?'

'Am I?'

'I don't know. Maybe.'

'Seems a bit of a stretch.'

'Alright then,' Wise Wally continued to read. 'There is a rift in the astral plane and demons are scourging the land, only you have the power to…'

'I don't see any demons, do you?'

'There are always demons around somewhere.'

'Next.'

'Looking for a cure to a deadly disease that afflicted your village?'

'What disease is that?'

'I'm sure we could infect your village with something.'

'Doesn't seem very ethical.'

'Uhhh…' Wise Wally ran his finger down to the bottom of the list. 'Lost pet...?'

'That'll do.'

'Excellent!' Wise Wally paused. 'Wait, do you actually have a pet?'

'I suppose I do, Daisy, my mule.'

'Perfect. Then it's settled.' Wise Wally stood up. 'Now it's time for me to teach you the basics of combat, follow me.'

Wise Wally led them down the rotting staircase into the basement. He lit the brazier, revealing a long room filled with half a dozen scarecrows. Each had crude targets painted on their chests.

He produced a notebook from his robes and read. 'Worthy adventurers, it is time for you to learn… what were your classes again?'

'Ranger and tinkerer.'

'Exactly. Time for you to learn how to be a true ranger and tinkerer. As a ranger, you will harness the power of your bow to defeat your foes. I see you already have one of those - and a fine one it is too.' Wise Wally turned to Rose. 'And as a tinkerer, you'll craft powerful trinkets to deceive and decimate the enemy.'

Rose beamed. 'Sounds good to me.'

Wise Wally clapped his hands together. 'Though first thing's first, I'm going to show you how to jump.'

Rose and Eric exchanged looks.

'I know how to jump,' said Eric.

Wise Wally tutted. 'Look, it's all part of the protocol. I've seen that you can walk forward, but I have to make sure you can jump before I can progress you to the next stage of your training. You'd be surprised at how badly adventurers jump, even the smallest ledge can be a challenge. Please demonstrate.'

Eric and Rose jumped into the air, Eric winced at his poor landing.

'Excellent!' Wise Wally grinned at their efforts then ticked something off of his notebook. 'Next. Rosepuff, behind you, is a workbench. A tinkerer's closest friend. Have a play with the tools there and see if you can craft some iron daggers and such for the Experience.' Rose skipped over to the bench, her backpack whirring into life. Wise Wally turned to Eric. 'And mighty Eric-four-two-five, the ranger. Let's see how well you fire that delightful weapon of yours.'

Eric loaded his father's crossbow, raised it and breathed out. He fired. The bolt missed the scarecrow target by so much it almost hit another one.

Wise Wally rested a gentle hand on his back. 'Try to relax, take a deep breath.'

How could he relax? As soon as his eye went down and he felt the smooth stock on his cheek, all he could see was that dragon's teeth staring back at him. Hear his father's screams. Sweat dripped from his brow as he pulled the trigger again. The bolt went wide and lodged itself in the wall.

'Try putting your front foot a little further forward.'

'That won't work,' Eric snapped.

'At least *try*,' Wise Wally raised a finger. '"For trying is the start of betterment".'

Eric wondered if Wise Wally had memorised a book of annoying sayings. He moved his front foot forward and fired. This time the bolt grazed the scarecrow's arm.

'Excellent!' Wise Wally had smug plastered all over his face. 'You two keep practising for the Experience, I'm going upstairs to nap.'

Eric had been too irritated by Wally to think about his father. But at least it was something. He reloaded the crossbow and raised it.

This time he focussed on all the adventurers ruining the world. Their pretentious armour and ridiculous matching haircuts, of which there were about seven. Their greed, their arrogance, their carelessness. He fired. The bolt hit the scarecrow dead between the eyes. Eric tried not to seem too pleased, but he couldn't help himself.

After a few more hours of practice, Eric got eleven more bull's-eyes. Rose, on the other hand, had somehow managed to craft a small pile of bombs and a moving box coated in about fifty iron daggers.

'I think I'm getting the hang of this!' Rose exclaimed, sparks flying out of the tool protruding from her backpack.

Eric muttered some obscenities and tried to focus on his aim. He fired and hit the target.

'Wonderful!' came the voice of Wise Wally behind him. 'You both seem to have come along a treat. That means it's time for your final lesson, the special secret to adventuring. But you must promise not to tell any non-adventurers, alright?'

'Promise,' said Rose and Eric in unison. Eric kept his fingers crossed in his pocket.

'Lovely,' said Wise Wally. 'The secret to adventuring is *Experience*. If you kill anything, you get a small piece of its essence. Then whatever you're good at, the Experience will make you *even better*. Sword-fighting, sorcery, woodwork, juggling, sneaking, anything!'

'Everyone knows that,' said Eric, folding his arms.

Rose chimed in. 'Did you know it was first discovered one-hundred-and-twenty-three years ago by the scientist Robert Irwell Experience?'

'I did!' said Wise Wally, impressed. 'But let me tell you the real secret…' Wise Wally tapped his nose, 'Elixir gives a *massive* boon in Experience gain. Over one hundred times more than normal! As long as you have some Elixir in your stomach, killing things will give you a colossal increase in your power.'

Eric thought on this. It was no wonder adventurers were so obsessed with Elixir. 'Is that why they drink so many?'

'Drinking more Elixir doesn't mean more experience,' said Wise Wally. 'One is plenty, but if you want to indulge, then knock yourself out, it is delicious. In fact, I can sell you some for a *very* reasonable price. Fresh today from the Doom Bank's factory.'

Eric shook his head. 'No chance.'

'Your loss,' said Wise Wally. 'Anyway, I suppose that's your training complete,' he trailed off and stepped over to the wall. 'Oh nooo… look at that, a wild swarm of ooze creatures. How did that happen?'

Sure enough, a handful of green balls now glistened on the floor, slowly inching their way towards Wise Wally.

Eric raised an eyebrow. 'You pulled that lever and let them out from those secret doors.'

'No, I didn't,' said Wally as he moved his hand away from the lever. 'Oh help, please! If only there were some adventurers here to save me!'

'Well don't look at me,' said Eric. 'A crossbow won't hurt an ooze, the bolt will go right through. You need a repellent or alkaline solution.'

'You're an *adventurer* now,' said Wise Wally through gritted teeth. 'Use the damned crossbow.'

Eric sighed and lifted his weapon. He hesitated, finger on the trigger. The creature before him was a living thing. It deserved a humane death or some proper care, not to be tormented by a bolt through the head. The oozed trickled closer.

'Quickly!' Wise Wally moaned. 'You're my only hope!'

Eric fired. The bolt shot straight through the ooze and into the floor. Just as he expected. Oozes were liquid, which made them somewhat immune to physical harm.

'What did I tell you?' said Eric, lowering the crossbow. 'Useless.'

'You killed it!' Rose said, pointing.

Eric looked back. The ooze did indeed seem to be dead. It was now more of a puddle than "ooze shape", a shape that had always reminded him of a muffin.

'Rosepuff, use one of your bombs!' shrieked Wise Wally.

Rose hesitated. 'Won't that take down the whole house?'

'Don't worry it's all reinforced. I had it made for adventuring.'

Rose tossed her device. It ticked and hissed, rolling in between the oozes. There was a flash of light and a colossal thunder. Everyone dived to the ground.

Eric coughed, the air thick with dust. He stood up and wiped himself down. 'Everyone alright?'

Rose's backpack chugged, the arm pushing her up. She grinned. 'That was exciting.' She stopped, her expression dark.

Wise Wally lay motionless on the floor, oozes covering his body.

Rose ran over to him. 'He's alive!' She pushed the oozes away, who compliantly rolled off and trickled away into their secret hatches.

Wise Wally's breath was shallow and rattled. 'Avenge me… young ones… And find Daisy…' Wise Wally's tongue lolled out and he closed his eyes.

'He's… he's dead.' Rose hung her head.

The room went silent for a moment.

'No he ain't.' Eric gave Wise Wally a sharp kick.

'Ow!' Wise Wally burst back into life. 'What'd you do that for?'

'Get up, you're not fooling no-one.'

Wise Wally stood up, much taller than before without his stoop. He rubbed his side. 'That really hurt you know.'

'Why'd you pretend to be dead?'

'An adventurer's mentor always has to die.' Wally's voice was no longer husky, it sounded fresh and articulated. 'That's the first part of starting any adventure, gives the hero motivation to move onto Act Two of their story arc. It's how they trained us to do it.'

'And they couldn't train you to be a better actor?' Eric stopped. 'Hold on a minute, who trained you?'

'Why The Guild of course. I have a certificate and everything.' He pointed to the framed paper on the wall. It was titled *"Official Adventuring Mentor"* and the grade said *"C"*. A logo of a pink skull sat at the top of the faded certificate. 'I used to be an ooze breeder.'

Rose took a closer look. 'That pink skull, we've seen it before, haven't we?'

Eric nodded as thoughts formulated in his head. 'It's the symbol of The Doom Bank. Their bailiffs took the last of my stuff.'

'And they were the ones who paid off Old Ted and they fund The Guild too.'

'And didn't Wally just say that Elixirs get made at The Doom Bank?'

Wally scratched the back of his head. 'Oh, ah, I wasn't supposed to say that bit.'

'The Doom Bank must be behind all this,' said Rose. 'They're setting up quests, making new adventurers and flogging them Elixirs. But why?'

'Beats me,' said Eric. 'Wally, d'you know what's going on?'

'No idea,' said Wally, stroking his beard. 'I'm just doing my job, I'll get paid either way.'

An ooze wobbled in and went right up to Wise Wally. A note slivered out of its body, which elongated up to Wise Wally's hand.

Wally read the note. 'Excellent, it seems your Main Quest is ready.'

'I don't think we want that any more,' said Eric.

'Ah,' Wally stopped and drew an intake of breath. 'It's a bit too late for that now, I'm afraid. I sent the messenger duck while you were busy practicing.'

Eric scowled at him. 'Already?! Cancel it.'

'They'll already have your pet by now. You wanted adventuring, you got adventuring. Your Main Quest has already begun.'

Eric felt his stomach turn over. The world span. He leant against the wall.

Daisy. They'd actually taken Daisy.

22

Key Alchemist Xenixala of Xendor, The Mighty Conqueror of Eenokeea, Diviner of The Chaos Orb, and eater of 'The Apple of Anguish', smiled knowingly at Edwardius riding beside her, who did his best to avoid eye contact. Instead, he kept his gaze focussed on the hillsides, pointlessly scanning the dirt and dust that lolled across the horizon.

'How much further Felina?' Xenixala winced into the sunlight. 'I'm starting to chafe.' She wriggled on her demon-steed's saddle, but it didn't help.

'Not much further, Xeni my darling!' Felina's words were like nails on a chalkboard. Pixies had such ridiculous high pitched voices. It was like someone was pinching their nipples.

'This so-called "Chosen One" had better be here, Felina, or I'll turn you into a worm.'

Felina chuckled. 'Oh, Xeni, have no fear! The soothsayer was very particular.'

'You said that days ago.' Xenixala made a mental note to ready a worm enchantment.

Felina looked back at Xenixala, lips pursed. 'As my mentor used to say before he died, "*the journey is more important than the destination*". We'll reach him eventually, so try to enjoy the ride.'

Xenixala rolled her eyes. Felina had returned rather too quickly to her sickeningly perky self after the resurrection. It had been impossible to get any more alone time with Edwardius. Instead, she had been subjected to days of tedious riding while Felina sang her songs and blew kisses. Bards really were the worst. The only thing that kept her going was Edwardius' obvious discomfort. He could barely look either of them in the eye, preferring to ride in sullen silence. It was astonishing that Felina was yet to pick up on it.

Edwardius held up a fist, bringing his horse to a stop. 'Did you hear that?'

'Hear what?' All Xenixala heard was the clopping of hooves.

'That. Listen closer. It's like... someone weeping?'

'I thought that was you, Edwardius.'

'Shh.'

As much as she hated to admit it, a faint sobbing was indeed coming from far below the narrow hillside path.

'Quickly,' Edwardius' eyes glinted. 'Follow me.'

They took their mounts down the slope and towards the sound, their steed's sliding on the loose rocks. At the bottom, they followed the maze of the ravine, turning this way and that. Closer and closer. Louder and louder the blubbering became.

Until they saw the source.

Before a cavern entrance sat a pathetic looking creature with a dog-like face. Tears glistening on its snout as it cradled a corpse, coating its mismatched armour in blood. Smoke billowed from the cavern, filling the air with the aroma of burned hay and candles.

Edwardius released his grip from the hilt of his sword and ran his fingers through his blond hair. 'This is a fresh assault. The Chosen One can't have gone far.'

'Let's speak to this poor thing,' said Felina. 'Perhaps it knows which way he went?'

The three dismounted and cautiously approached the wretched monster. The creature didn't even look up at them, it remained transfixed on the corpse on its lap.

'What is it?' Felina whispered.

'Looks like a kobold to me,' said Edwardius.

Xenixala wiped her mouth and threw the empty Elixir bottle to the floor. 'Isn't he a bit big for a kobold?'

'He'll be a leader.' Edwardius strode forward, addressing the oversized kobold. 'Hail, friend. What brings you so much sorrow?'

The kobold recoiled at the sight of them. 'Adventurers!' It hissed. 'Go away! You take all. No more for you here.' It hung its head, defeated.

Edwardius bowed. 'It's a pleasure to meet you, my name is Edwardius and these are my companions, Felina and Key Alchemist Xenixala of Xendor, The Mighty Conqueror of De...'

Xenixala coughed. 'We don't need to go through all that now. Xenixala will do.'

'But last time you insisted that...'

'Just don't alright?' She turned to the kobold. 'Okay creature, why are you so whiny?'

It wiped tears from its furry cheeks. 'Grom.'

'What?'

'Grom. My name Grom.'

Xenixala laughed. 'You have a name? Cute. Creatures don't have names.'

'We do.'

'Well, how come I never heard of one then?'

'You no ask.'

Xenixala couldn't fault that logic. 'Whatever, *Grom*. What's the deal? Let me guess, some hero clad in armour ran through here and killed your whole nest and took all your gold and heirlooms?'

Grom nodded.

'How long ago?'

Grom caressed the bloody mess on his lap. 'Still here.'

'What do you mean?'

'He no go. We doomed.'

'Care to elaborate?'

Grom looked up. 'He kill everyone. Son, friends, *wife*.' He raised the bloody body towards them. 'This wife. He stab her. He burn too. Burn all things. Now nothing I have.'

Felina put her hands on her heart. 'You poor dear.'

Grom spat on the dirt, scowling. 'Me no need pity from *adventurers*. You do this all time. Every place adventurer go. You kill. You take. How so heartless? No care for life?'

Edwardius shuffled uncomfortably, making his armour clatter. 'I am a Holy Paladin, of The Order of The Mole. I treasure all life, I live to protect the weak and…'

'Protect weak?' Grom scoffed. 'You kill weak.'

'I do not.'

'You kill kobolds other times?'

'Well of course. I fight evil in all its forms.'

'Kobold not evil.'

'Of course you are.'

Grom glared at him with his beady eyes. 'No, we not. Why?'

'Well… look at you.' Edwardius waved his hand. 'You're, you know... evil.'

'Me not know. Me good person. Me loved family. Me want peace.'

Edwardius stood proud, confident. 'Kobolds aren't peaceful. Creatures like you attack us whenever we enter their lair. We're simply acting in self-defence.'

'We self defence. Come to *our* home.'

'But… but you're born of evil. You serve the Dark Master. You worship the evil gods...'

'Me worship no-one *Pally Din.* Me just want home. Be safe. But nowhere safe. Not here. Not nowhere.' He waved a crumpled, blood stained pamphlet. 'Eric promised we be safe here. No adventurers here he say. He lie. Nowhere safe.' The tears streamed down his face. 'Kill me. Get done. Me no want life. Not in adventurer world.'

Edwardius turned back to Xenixala and Felina. 'The beast is clearly deranged with grief. Should we put him out of his misery?'

Xenixala shrugged.

Felina stepped between Edwardius and Grom. 'My dear, can't you see this poor thing is in pain? Surely we can help him?'

'Indeed we can,' said Edwardius. 'We can purge the world of his evil.'

'He says he's not evil,' said Felina.

'That's exactly what an evil creature would say.'

'Me not evil.' Grom piped in. 'I hear you.'

Felina raised her eyebrows. 'See?'

'My darling,' Edwardius pleaded. 'The monster *wants* to be killed. Surely, on a utilitarian level, the kindest thing to do would be to treat him as…'

Grom exploded in a splatter of blood.

Edwardius and Felina both looked at Xenixala, who smiled, her fingers still outstretched from the spell.

'What?' she said, closing Wordsworth. 'Evil or not, I don't care. The Chosen One's here so let's look inside.'

Edwardius wiped the blood from his face. 'You could have given us a bit of warning.'

Felina remained motionless. 'Xeni… that was most *unkind*. How could you?'

Xenixala opened Wordsworth again. 'You want to end up like Grom?'

Felina stood, mouth agape.

'I thought not.' Xenixala froze. Dozens of kobolds ran out of the entrance of the cave. They streamed in all directions, screaming and shouting.

Behind them, a silhouette appeared from the shadows. The man stood, stance wide, cape flapping in the breeze, chest bare.

Then he moved. Steel flashed, cutting, slicing the kobolds with precision. They wailed and yelped. Some desperately thrust their spears at the figure, but he stepped aside with no hesitation and decapitated them. Xenixala was sure the man yawned. Others fled, but the man tossed their discarded spears, catching them perfectly between the shoulders and pinning them to the ground.

The last kobold fell and there was quiet.

The man stopped, wiped his sword on a rag, then levelled his gaze on Xenixala, Edwardius and Felina. His piercing eyes betrayed nothing.

Edwardius drew his sword, Felina pulled her lute from her back, Xenixala flicked Wordsworth to page three-two-six.

Silence ensued.

'There you are, right on cue.' The figure finally spoke. His voice was high pitched, like a child's, yet it carried far. 'Nice to meet you. I'm The Nuub, but some people prefer "*Chosen One*".'

23

Eric's heart stopped when he saw the stable door of the shop. Or rather, saw the empty space where the door used to be. He clenched his fist and stepped through. Darkness and the musk of hay were all that remained.

Daisy was gone.

He felt a deep hollow in his soul, the kind that never fills back up. He'd felt it once before, and he'd vowed never to again. Shaking, he wiped a single tear from his cheek.

The gentle hum of Rose's backpack came up behind him and a small hand laid itself on his shoulder.

'I'm sorry, Eric,' said Rose. 'This was all my fault. We should never have tried to be adventurers.'

Eric spat on the ground. 'I'm just as sorry, don't you worry.'

A moment of silence passed between them.

Rose straightened her back and spoke resolutely. 'Well, you didn't need to punch Wise Wally like that. It wasn't his fault.'

'I'd say it was. I never wanted a stupid Main Quest. And he's been making adventurers, so he deserved it.'

Something caught Eric's eye. He reached out and pulled off the note pinned to the wall. Holding back his rage, he read the scrap of paper.

Dear *ERIC425*,

We have your dear *DAISY* in our possession. Please pay us *937* gold pieces within the week or we will chop off his/her head. Bring the money to North Porkwood and we will rob you of it.

All the best,
The Bandit King

The letter had been made using an official-looking font, but the words, *Eric*, *Daisy* and *937* had been written in by hand. Eric crumpled the note and stormed through to the Beast Be Gone shop.

The door slammed behind him. Larry, in chair form, burst awake and sprung forward, his wooden legs clomping on the bare floor. 'Oh, you're back already. That was quick. Found the bad guys?'

Eric scowled at the plush chair. 'Larry, I thought you were supposed to be watching the shop?'

'I have been! And a good job too, if I don't say so myself.' He pushed himself upwards as if proud. 'Not a soul's been by.'

'Even in the stable?'

'There's a stable?'

Eric sighed and went over to his desk, one of the last pieces of furniture he owned. He took out the single glass and whisky bottle from the bottom drawer, then poured himself a drink.

Rose entered the shop and smiled weakly at Larry.

'What's got his goat?' said Larry through the gap between the cushioning and the wood.

Rose pulled a lever to turn off her metal backpack, the chugging stopped. 'They took his mule so we could have an adventuring quest.'

'Oh,' said Larry. 'But did you find out who's behind the adventuring?'

'We think so. Seems like the Doom Bank has a lot to do with it.'

'Excellent, then off you go!'

Eric took a deep slug of his whisky. 'You two can go after them, I'm done with that nonsense. I've gotta get Daisy.'

Rose crossed her arms. 'Stopping the adventurers is a little more important than a donkey, Eric. Once we stop them, I'm sure they'll let Daisy go.'

Eric saw Daisy's eyes, full of simple joy. She was the only creature he knew that was truly content in this wretched world. 'This is more important.'

'What is she, like fifty?'

Eric sniffed. 'Probably around that.' He finished his drink and stood up. 'You don't understand, Daisy's the only family I have left.' She was also the only one who really understood him, stayed by him. If that wasn't family, he didn't know what was.

'We don't have much time!' Rose pleaded. 'We *need* to get to the bottom of these adventurers.'

Eric stopped midway through pouring himself another drink. 'All you've been going on about is stopping adventurers, right from the start. I'm beginning to think you don't want to be in pest control after all.'

Rose's face was impassive. 'Of course, I do. It's just, you know, after you saved my father from… the things. I had to apprentice with you.'

'Things?' Eric narrowed his gaze on her. 'How close are you with your father?'

Rose pulled a weak smile. 'Well, he raised me. Why'd you ask?'

'How old is he?'

'He's about sixty… three?'

'No, he isn't. He'd be eighty-five now, at least.'

'Why yes, now you say it. That was awfully silly of me. Of course, he's eighty-five.'

'Wrong again, he's fifty-two.'

Rose gulped. 'Ah good one.' She pretended to laugh. 'You got me.'

Eric towered over Rose, she backed away towards the wall. Eric prodded her in the stomach. 'You don't know the Governor of Murica at all do you?'

'He's my dad... don't be ridiculous.'

Eric raised his voice. 'Don't play *dumb*. Why are you really here?'

'I...I...' Rose sighed and dropped her head. 'Freddy sent me.'

'Freddy Glorp?!' Eric couldn't believe what he was hearing. His business rival, Freddy Glorp was interfering with his life. What's worse is he'd fallen for it, hook line and sinker. 'But... why?'

'It's not important. We should get back to finding Daisy.'

'Why?'

Rose hesitated. 'He hired me to apprentice with you, then find out how you're managing to stay in business when he's been struggling so much. And if I could, also get you to stop the adventurers. You'd been one before, after all.'

'I thought he was doing fine? All he does is boast about the work he gets clearing out dungeons and trapping minions.'

'He thought you were the same. It's all an act. He's as bad off as you are.'

Eric's mind raced. 'So what are you then, an actress? Are you even a Westerner?'

'Of course I'm a Westerner!' Rose tutted. 'I'm just a girl who's down on her luck, like everyone else in this town. I came to Fen-Tessai looking for work, only to find adventuring is worse here than it is back home.'

'So it was all for nothing.' Eric rubbed his temples.

This is why you don't get your hopes up. This is why you don't trust people. This is why you keep to your bleeding self and stay out of trouble. Trouble is trouble. And the less trouble you have, the better.

Rose smiled weakly. 'We could still try to stop them you know?'

'Who?'

'The Doom Bank. The bad guys. I'm sure it's them. It has to be.'

'I'll pass.' Eric went back and slumped into his chair. 'Why don't you and *Freddy* go and do it. You've already wasted enough of my time.' He could imagine Freddy's face when Rose ran back to him and told him the news. They'd probably all have a good old laugh about poor old Eric.

Now he had nothing. Not even Daisy.

'For what it's worth, I'm sorry.' Rose tried to put her hand on Eric's arm, but he flinched away.

'Get out of my shop.'

Rose turned her backpack on. Its chugging sounded melancholic. She walked out, then stopped in the doorway and turned back. 'There was one part that was true though. My brother did die trying to adventure. I still want adventurers gone.'

Eric grunted and sipped his whisky.

'If you ever change your mind, I'll be at Freddy's. I don't have anywhere else to go.' Rose continued. 'I'm sure we could use your help.'

The door closed behind her, Eric didn't look up. He finished his drink slowly, and in silence.

'I'm a little confused.' Larry spoke from his hiding spot in the corner, now shaped like a lamp. The lampshade tassels wobbled with his voice. 'Why did you two fall out? I thought you were inseparable.'

'It doesn't matter.' Eric got up, picked up his crossbow and slung it over his shoulder. 'I'm off to hunt bandits. Wanna come?'

'Ah, no,' said Larry, quivering. 'I think I'm better off... home. Staying hidden. That's kind of my thing. The outdoors is a little daunting for our kind. If you know what I mean.'

'Fair enough.' A part of him was relieved, he deserved to be alone. 'Same deal again? You stay here and watch out for the bailiffs.'

'Right you are,' said the lampshade. 'Good luck.'

Eric nodded. He had a hunch that he'd need all the luck he could get. It was a shame he couldn't afford to buy any at Adventurer's Supply.

24

Adept Transmuter Xenixala of Xendor, Defender of Grondrol, Fellow of The Knights of Kran-thun and the first person to ever attempt a custard and beetroot soup, grinned with relief. Finally, they'd found the so-called "Chosen One", the most Experienced adventurer. He wasn't quite as good looking as she'd hoped, but he did have strong cheekbones. His slim frame was strangely exposed, revealing his sinewy rib cage. All he wore was a maroon cape and a pair of leather pantaloons.

He strolled towards Felina, Edwardius and Xenixala, his shoulders swaying. He stopped short of them and performed an odd little jig.

'How's it going?' he said. His voice sounded as if his balls had yet to drop. 'You wondering why I'm here?'

Xenixala folded her arms. 'Well... yes, actually.'

The tiny Felina blushed and bowed. 'I apologise for my *brutish* companion. She can be a little direct.' She shot Xenixala a cold stare. 'I am Felina, a bard by trade, and this is my dearest Edwardius, a great and powerful paladin.' She paused. 'And that's Xenixala.'

'Yeah, I know,' said The Nuub. 'Nice to meet you, anyway.' He performed his jig, identical to before. Xenixala began to think she'd made a terrible mistake. 'You finished off that last kobold.' He gestured to the bloody mess that had once been Grom.

Felina bowed even lower, speaking fast. 'Sorry about that, we didn't know you had laid claim to...'

'I know, it's fine.' The Nuub gestured for her to stand. 'I was expecting you. Now I have one-hundred percent completion in this region.' He held up a glowing rock, a lattice of blue lines shimmered across its surface. 'This spellstone tells me my progress. It's all that keeps me going these days.' He sighed and dropped it back into his side pouch. 'That's why I'm here, but also to meet you guys.'

Felina continued. 'We've been searching far and wide for you, oh great Nuub, for we are in dire need of your help. The Dark Master's Army is growing in power. A power so great that it threatens the whole land of Fen-Tessai with total destruction.' She took a deep breath. 'You are in fact part of a great prophecy, you are The Chose...'

'Chosen One, yeah yeah.' He finished her sentence with a wave of his hand. 'Not quite yet. But sure. What's your point?'

Felina looked crestfallen. 'Oh? You already knew that?'

'Of course. How else am I supposed to fulfil my destiny?'

Felina straightened herself and nodded with deliberation. 'That's excellent, you won't need us to persuade you then. We can set off at once to destroy the dark forces of...'

'Nah, pass. I'm not the guy you're looking for.' And with that, The Nuub turned and walked away.

Felina stayed frozen, her mouth agape.

'But... The Prophecy! Your destiny!' she hurried up to him and reached out to his shoulder. His hand batted hers away before she even made contact.

The Nuub stopped and groaned. 'Sure, I'm *A* Chosen One, I'm just not *The* Chosen One. You've got the wrong guy.'

'How can you know?' Felina stammered. 'There's a whole prophecy!'

'There's plenty of prophecies going around. Which one is it?'

Felina's pointy nose quivered with delight as she whipped her lute into position. She cleared her throat and started singing in her sickly sweet tone.

'Have you heard the tale,
of The Chosen One? The Chosen One?
With highest Experience, and never undone.

'The greatest adventurer,
Gentle and kind,
A stronger man you...'

The Nuub winced and held up his hand, beckoning her to stop. 'Yup, okay enough of that.'

'You don't like it?'

'Sure it was a... lovely rendition. That's just one of the other guys.'

'Other... guys?'

'Sure. Other Chosen One's. I've met most of them at the annual Prophesied Anonymous meet-up.'

'Prophesied Anonymous...?'

'We've got a lot to live up to, you know. It ain't easy being prophesied. We kind of support each other, it helps.'

'Well we could still use your help,' said Felina. 'Even if you're not the right Chosen One.'

'Sorry, but it's not foretold. I can't deviate from the prophecy.'

'That's absurd, surely if...'

The Nuub shook his head. 'I don't think you understand. *Everything* about me has been foretold. Even this conversation. Do you think I wanted to hear you sing for the fun of it? It can't be stopped.'

'What? That's not...'

'Possible? I know, it's exhausting.'

Xenixala stepped in. 'If that's true then what am I about to say now...?'

'Sandwiches.' 'Sandwiches,' they both said in unison.

'Sentences.' 'Sentences.'

'Bunching.' 'Bunching.'

'Fundoop.' 'Fundoop.'

Xenixala smiled. 'Impressive. How?'

The Nuub sat down on the dirt and leaned back, resting on his hands. 'Well, it took a few years, there was loads to get through. Some monk had a real freaky dream about everything I would ever do and he spent *his* entire life writing it all down. He called it "reading the code". A real nutter he was. Then oddly enough, reading about me reading about my prophecy made some weird feedback loop.' He started playing with the dry earth, running his fingers in circles. 'I woke up two years later having read the whole thing. And it was scarred into my brain, every painstaking detail. I'm special mind you, most Chosen Ones don't end up with my curse.'

Xenixala raised an eyebrow. 'Curse? This doesn't seem so bad. You can see what's coming, you'll never be caught unawares.'

The Nuub stood up. 'Not so bad? *Not so bad?!'* he exclaimed. 'Nothing is exciting! Nothing is new! I'm literally just going through the motions. It's totally depressing.' He threw his arms into the air. 'I know *exactly* how this conversation is going to turn out, she's going to temporarily turn us into stone.' He pointed at Xenixala. 'I even know when I'll die. It's the most tedious form of invincibility.'

'Is that so…' Xenixala leapt to one side, tossing a fireball.

Felina screamed. *'Xeni don't!'*

But it was too late. The fireball exploded in a rage of heat, enclosing The Nuub in flames.

The smoke cleared. The Nuub was still standing perfectly as he had been, except with his shield drawn. She hadn't noticed he'd been carrying a shield.

The Nuub pulled a weak smile. 'I appreciate you trying, but I won't be dead for another thirty years, so I wouldn't waste your energy.'

Xenixala didn't give up that easily. This could all be an elaborate bluff. She lunged again, flinging an icy shard through the air.

The Nuub didn't even move. The shard slid past his face, missing him by an inch.

The Nuub smiled again. 'I know you'll try one more time to be sure, so let's get it over with.'

Xenixala didn't like being told what to do, that made her angry. She flicked her wrist, sending forth a wall of acid.

The Nuub casually stepped aside as a fault in the spell left a narrow gap. The acid passed him by, splashing to the ground behind him, hissing with disappointment.

The Nuub yawned. 'Ok, I think you're already bored.'

Xenixala wiped a little sweat from her brow. *'Fine*. Maybe you are invincible.' Fighting him was no fun. It was like trying to catch a fish with your hands. It felt futile, and at the end of the day, you'd only ever end up with a stinky fish. 'Why haven't you tried to do something interesting with your power? Like bet on the races? Or win at cards?'

The Nuub shrugged. 'I wish. If it's not in The Prophecy, I can't do it. The only thing keeping me sane is emptying out dungeons. One after another. I've had to come this far out to avoid people. Or at least that's what the prophecy says.'

Felina looked bewildered. 'But... you're still a Chosen One! You're still destined to save the world!'

'Sure,' said The Nuub, matter-of-factly, 'I'll save the world one day, but it won't be for another seven years. I've just gotta hang around till then.'

Xenixala was actually a little relieved. His child-voice was most unsettling, she didn't think she could put up with him for very long.

Edwardius stepped in after an uncharacteristic silence. 'Perhaps you could help us locate The Chosen One we're looking for? You said you knew them all.'

'Well, I don't know them *all.'* The Nuub scoffed. 'Not all Chosen Ones know they're Chosen. We're usually orphans, so we don't get much in the way of an upbringing. We often find out from some fans such as yourselves.' He rubbed his chin. 'But I do know your prophecy. The Most Experienced Adventurer, that one's a classic. Sorry, but none of us knows who that is. He wasn't ever found.'

Felina looked like she was about to collapse with exasperation. 'But a soothsayer said he'd be here. You must know *something*?'

'Let me see. He was the first person to ever slay an Elder Dragon, right? He would have gotten a ginormous amount of Experience from that, so it's no wonder he's the most Experienced adventurer. Well, he probably *has* been here, but left a while ago. Your soothsayer didn't specify *when* to find him did they?'

Edwardius didn't seem convinced. 'Haven't you ever thought of looking for him?'

'Yeah sure, we sometimes look for new Chosen Ones. It's surprisingly easy to find them, as you know where they'll be eventually. It's been prophesied ain't it?'

The three stared back at him in silence.

The Nuub rolled his eyes. 'Right, so when you've got a long list of his prophesied achievements, all you've gotta do is find out which ones they haven't done yet, then go there and they'll show up eventually.'

Xenixala groaned. 'That could take *years*.'

'I suppose,' said The Nuub. 'I always forget people can't see what's going to happen. Either way, that's your best bet.'

Edwardius slumped to his knees. 'This is hopeless, all is lost. This whole journey has been a disaster.' He buried his head in his hands.

Felina put a reassuring hand on his back. 'Come, my love, we can still look for The Chosen One. We can't give up now, or we'll never go down in the history books as The Chosen One's Champions.'

Xenixala leapt to attention. 'Ah, there it is. You're only doing this so you can write a boring song about it.'

Felina crossed her arms. 'There's nothing wrong with wanting a little publicity. I'll be saving the world, after all, I'd deserve a little recognition.'

Xenixala scoffed. 'Pfft. Sounds like it's all foretold anyway. Doesn't seem like you have much power over how it turns out. In fact, if the prophecy says he'll save the world, why bother at all?'

'Now you're getting it,' chimed in The Nuub.

'That's not how it works!' Felina's face turned bright pink. 'My love and I will find The Chosen One and go down in history and there's nothing you can do about it!'

'I'm not stopping you. Knock yourselves out.'

'All you do is hold us back, you, you… *witch*!'

Xenixala let the silence linger. 'I see.' She made a thin smile as Wordsworth leapt up into her arms and rifled open. 'It's like that is it? Well, perhaps you'd like to know what your precious *love* did with me while you were dead...?'

The colour drained from Edwardius' face. 'Don't.'

Felina looked at Edwardius, eyes fearful. 'What did she do to you my sweet?'

'We…' Tears welled in Edwardius' eyes. 'We were intimate together. I'm so sorry, my love, she got me high on Elixir, then she… used me.'

'You demon!' Felina spat, drew her dagger and bared her teeth at Xenixala. 'How could you! I knew we should never have brought you on our quest. You're nothing but a soulless *beast*.'

The Nuub stretched and put himself into a comfortable position. 'Go on then, turn us into stone.'

Felina lunged at Xenixala, blade held high.

But she never reached her target. Instead, she clattered to the ground, stiff and grey. Edwardius and The Nuub were motionless too, their skin solid stone.

Xenixala closed Wordsworth.

'Guess it's just the two of us again Wordsworth.'

Wordsworth's pages folded into a grin. 'About time. I was getting rather weary of those two. That Nuub was an odd chap as well.'

'Agreed. Do you remember the prophecy, Wordsworth?'

'Of course. I transcribed it straight away onto Chapter Ten.'

'Excellent.' Xenixala smiled. 'Then we may be able to find this Chosen One after all.'

Wordsworth's bookmark tongue licked his pages. 'I could really use an Elixir though.'

'Do better, Xenixala.'

'You read my mind. Let's steal theirs and get the Holy Mole out of here.'

25

The afternoon light fell through the Porkwood trees, sending ripples of pink onto the winding path. Eric ignored it. Just put one foot in front of the other, he told himself. His feet burned in his shoes, his back ached under his haversack and his knees screamed for him to stop. But he refused. It was what he deserved. He'd been walking from Porkhaven since dawn, which made it possibly the longest walk he cared to remember. He didn't have much choice without Daisy to lug him along. That's what he had to focus on. Getting Daisy back. Don't think about Rose and what she'd done. How he'd actually trusted her, how she betrayed him. Poor innocent Daisy. Think about Daisy.

He kicked a brittle leaf, taking satisfaction as it tumbled to the side of the road. That leaf didn't have a care in the world. Unless someone had put a spirit charm on it. Then it was in real trouble.

Although it was he who was in real trouble now. He'd half hoped to form a proper plan as he walked, but instead he'd drunk the last of his whisky. All he had so far was written on a scrap of paper in his hand. It read: "Step one, look for the bandits who have Daisy", with a lot of empty paper underneath it. Whenever his mind tried to formulate anything more, it went blank and decided to focus on his miserable pain instead. He scrunched the paper and put it in his pocket.

Eric stopped.

A rustle in the undergrowth. He was sure of it. Eric raised his crossbow at a nearby bush nestled between the trees. 'I know you're in there,' he called. 'Come on out and let's get this over with.'

'I don't know what you mean,' The bush muttered. 'I'm just a bush.'

'Cut it out.'

'Are you an.... adventurer by any chance?' said the bush, leaves fluttering.

'No chance.'

'I'd like to believe that, but... that crossbow looks awfully *adventurey*.'

'It was my father's,' said Eric, trying not to let thoughts of his father distract him. 'Merely self-defence, you know.'

The bush muttered to itself in a number of voices, then eventually said with certainty, 'Alright then.'

Three men erupted out of the leaves, each with a wary look in their eyes and a layer of filth that implied they'd spent far too much time sleeping on plants. If Eric had to imagine what a bandit looked like, it was exactly that. Everything was textbook from the scruffy bandanas over their mouths, to the tattoos up their arms. The men surrounded Eric, holding crude sticks and blades.

'Looks like you three have hit a bit of a rough patch,' said Eric, keeping a firm hold on his crossbow.

The three exchanged glances.

The tallest stepped forward, with all the swagger of a man who knows he's in charge. 'Well banditin' ain't easy with all these adventurers around. You're the first non-adventurer on this road in weeks.'

'And you want all my things presumably?'

'That would be lovely.'

'Just doing your job?'

'Just doin' our job.'

Eric sighed. 'What's your name?'

The bandit pointed to himself to clarify. 'Oh ah, I'm Bill. That's Derek and that's Graham.'

Graham and Derek waved. Eric nodded back.

'Pleasure to meet you,' said Bill, who flinched as if he were about to raise his hand for a handshake but thought better of it. 'Sorry we had to meet under such, uh, *bad* circumstances. You know, times are tough and all. Nothin' personal. But we will need all your stuff, thanks.' He gestured with his rusty dagger.

Eric smiled. 'No problem, I'll give you my things without a fight. But under one condition. How's that?'

Bill narrowed his eyes. 'Depends on what it is.'

'Take me to The Bandit King, you can have my sack and I won't shoot any of you. Nobody gets hurt, everybody wins.'

'Ah,' Bill scratched the back of his head. 'Might be a bit of a problem that. See, we kind of... deserted The Bandit King. Can't really go back.'

'How about you just tell me where he is?'

'Nah, that won't work neither. Not easy giving directions through these woods, we'd have to show ya. Why'd you want to talk to him anyways? Thinking of being a bandit yerself?'

Eric thought the bandit life wasn't a bad idea. Abandoning the shop would certainly solve his debt issues. His failing business without Daisy wasn't much to stay for. 'It's tempting, but seeing as you had to run away from him, I'm not sure he's such a nice bloke. Why'd you leave?'

The three sheepishly looked down at their feet and scuffed the floor with them. Bill cleared his throat. 'Didn't want to fight adventurers no more. It's too dangerous.'

'Of course it is,' said Eric. 'They're armed to the teeth with spells and enchanted swords and all you have is cutlery. What in Mole's name makes you think you can take 'em on?'

'Well, we usually only try to take on the newbies. You know, fresh off their tutorial training like. But The Bandit King... he wants more.' Bill lowered his voice. 'Rumour has it, he's got a deal with some kind of evil overlord to keep the adventurers entertained. So us little guys don't stand a chance, we're just meat. Plus the benefits are awful.'

'Awful,' chimed in Derek.

Graham simply nodded.

Bill continued, 'You have to work your way up to Commander Bandit if you want to get resurrected, and even then it comes out of your pay. Then he makes you have this kind of... *vengeance pact* with the adventurer who killed you. So you have to go hunt them down and fight them again and again until one of you runs out of coin for a resurrection.' Bill took an intake of breath. 'Which is usually us.'

Eric was taken aback. He had no idea even the bandits were having such a hard time because of the adventuring craze too. No-one was safe. He began to feel sorry for them. He lowered his crossbow and smiled. 'So how about it? Will you take me to The Bandit King or am I going to have to shoot you?'

Bill held up his finger, then the three bandits huddled together, muttering. Eric waited, tapping his foot impatiently.

'Alright then,' Bill lowered his weapon and grinned.

'Lovely.'

'You're a strange fella Eric.' Bill pulled the bandana down from over his mouth, revealing his misshapen nose. 'You do know that if he doesn't like you, he'll chop you up in an instant and feed you to the hounds?'

Eric swallowed. He was glad they'd accepted his bluff. His crossbow could only really stop one of them before a reload. And that was only if he had the mettle to pull the trigger. He still felt a little hesitant after the ooze incident. Now he seemed to be swapping his current crisis for another.

'Excellent,' he said. 'Lead the way.'

Bill took them through the trees until the safety of the path became a distant memory. The light dimmed as the sun set, exchanging its warmth for the cold embrace of moonlight. They pushed on through the tapestry of trees and shrubs, stepping over logs and avoiding bear traps. Eric felt like the stupidest man alive. But with so little to lose, and so little care left, he continued, one foot in front of the other.

They made it to a river, and the bandits stopped to take a breath. Eric wanted to take off his pack and shoes, but felt like his new companions may have a change of heart, snatch his things and run off into the night. So he leant with his back against a tree with his crossbow loaded and close to hand.

Bill sat down in front of him and stretched out his legs. 'So what's your story, Eric? Why are you so keen to get yourself stabbed? Wife left you?' He clapped his hands together. 'That's it, the bandits took her.'

'I ain't ever had a wife.' Eric grimaced. 'The Bandit King took my mule.'

'Not your wife?'

'No, Daisy. '

'Oh yeah, kidnappin's another business he's been getting us into. Apparently quite lucrative.' Bill rubbed the back of his head. 'The adventurers don't half make a fuss when they arrive to rescue 'em. Usually, they slice up all the new recruits to get their loved ones back. Then they loot all the stuff we've left for them in the boxes and it's job done.'

'You… leave things for the adventurers?'

'Yeah, gotta leave 'em something to loot or they'll come after the good stuff. Or at least that's how The Bandit King puts it.'

'What kind of stuff do you leave them?'

'Oh, you know, handfuls of coin, apples, leather jerkins. Nothin' of any value, but the adventurers can't get enough. They spend about five minutes killin' and half an hour huntin' every nook and cranny for worthless scraps. Strange folk, they are.'

'Strange indeed.'

'We had a particularly nasty run-in with some adventurers a few weeks back, didn't we lads?'

Derek and Graham murmured agreement.

Bill carried on with his tale, spurred on by his companion's assurances. 'They were practically insane. Their paladin only went and chopped off the head of their bard. Nearly made me sick to see, so we ran away as fast as we could. Haven't been back to The Bandit King since. Although he probably hasn't even noticed we're gone.'

Eric wished he hadn't paid Bill the morsel of attention he so clearly craved, as now he didn't seem to want to shut up. And not wishing for them to split him open with a pointy blade, Eric held his tongue. 'What a shame.'

Bill shook his head. 'It used to be such a noble profession when I was a wee lad. Back then it meant something. People feared ya name and ladies secretly enjoyed your roguish charm as you winked and took their purse. Now it's all adventurer this, adventurer that. And somehow we've ended up the scum of the land hiding in dirty bushes and living off berries and nettles.'

An idea popped into Eric's head. He let it sit there for a moment in the darkness, then smiled, licked his lips and leaned in. 'It's funny that you say that... I'm actually trying to get rid of the adventurers myself.'

Bill scoffed. 'Good luck with that.'

'That was exactly my response when I first heard the idea. Then I realised... I might as well try. They've destroyed *everything* good in this world and left me with nothing. Like a plague of bleeding locusts. Even if I can't stop 'em, at least it'll hold 'em back. And that's only the beginning.' Eric felt strange. As if Rose was in his body, controlling his words. Suddenly everything she'd pestered him with over the past few weeks made so much more sense.

Now all three bandits were paying close attention. In the low lighting, he could see the gleam of their silver teeth turning into sharp grins.

'Yeah,' said Bill. 'We've gotta show 'em!'

Graham and Derek stood up and cheered in unison. 'Yeah!'

Bill stopped himself. 'But how?'

Eric stroked his chin and let the silence draw them in. 'How many bandits are there at this Bandit Fortress? A lot?'

'Yes a lot,' said Bill. 'A lot a lot. More than enough to make a small army, I'd wager.'

'And what if we took that army and struck at the very people who seem to be funding this whole mess?'

Bill's face beamed with realisation. 'You know who that is?'

'I do indeed.' Eric tapped the side of his nose. 'So maybe I can talk some sense into this Bandit King. Get him to fight *against* the adventurers, rather than feeding them.'

'You can certainly try, it's your funeral.' Bill laughed and patted Eric on the shoulder, Eric's finger tensed on the crossbow's trigger. 'I'll admit Eric, we were planning on handing you over to The Bandit King ourselves for a cheeky little ransom. But now... maybe you can be more useful to us after all.'

Eric felt a pang of fear and relief. 'I'm glad you changed your mind.'

26

Chief Evoker Xenixala of Xendor, Forsaker of The Kin, Defeater of The Beast of Yensur and bachelor of crochet design at Histoon Night School for Women appeared in a puff of smoke in the streets of Porkhaven, her heels clicking onto the cobbles. The Scroll of Town Portal vanished from her fingers and she returned Wordsworth to her hands. He complained awfully if he spent too much time tucked under her arm, no matter what deodorant she conjured. The Royal District they had apparated into was the most bearable part of the city, and yet it still had the unmistakable whiff of piss. Some thought Porkhaven's aroma was part of its charm, Xenixala thought those people had a urine fetish. Still, at least the streets weren't coated in too much mud, which would save her boots, and most of the passers-by were sober, which would save her sanity.

A wall loomed before her, thick and layered with a lattice of granite blocks. Dozens of towers soured above it, shining in the midday sun. The Royal Palace. It reminded her of Porkwarts School For Witches Not Wizards.

'Xenixala will demonstrate to the class how to levitate down from the tallest tower. She will then cure herself of the unknown poison she just drank.'

Wordsworth wriggled free and plopped to the floor. 'What are we doing here?' he flapped. 'I thought we were looking for The Chosen One?'

Xenixala sighed. 'We are. It's in the prophecy isn't it?'

Wordsworth's pages remained motionless.

'Think about it, what does the prophecy say?'

Wordsworth cleared his throat or at least made the sound as if he actually had a throat to clear, then opened his pages wide.

'Have you heard the tale,
of The Chosen One? The Chosen One?
With highest Experience, and never undone.

'I didn't want you to actually sing the wretched thing. You sound like a cat being strangled by a wad of scrolls.'

He continued, unperturbed,

'The greatest adventurer,
Gentle and kind,
A stronger man you will not find.'

'Grenden the dragon,

Would rage no more,
When he shot its mighty maw.

'Our great King,
Learned of his might,
So sent him many beasts to fight.

'There,' Xenixala interrupted, tapping her foot with impatience. 'That verse.'

'The King?' Wordsworth's spine bent upwards into an uncertain arc. 'The King knows The Chosen One?'

'Exactly. I don't know why we didn't just come here in the first place.' Xenixala reached down and rested her hand on the cold cobbles. 'It's like The Nuub said, either he's done everything in the prophecy, or will do it. One way or another, we'll get some info.'

Her hand glowed orange, creating a burning ring around it. It grew outward from her palm, wider and wider. She clicked her fingers and the newly formed disc floated upwards from her feet, taking them with it.

The wall flickered by, up and up. Soon the whole of Porkhaven spread out into the horizon. Its wonky towers stood like a sea of soldiers, popping above the clouds of magic that coated the more dangerous and pungent districts.

'I could have helped you with that levitating disc enchantment you know,' said Wordsworth with a little shrug. 'It would have been much more stable.'

Xenixala rolled her eyes. 'My way's faster, we don't have all day.'

They were nearly in the clouds. Most men would have probably fainted, but for Xenixala it was exhilarating. The disk came to a halt with a flick of the wrist, right at the top of the tallest tower. Birds fluttered by, the wind whipped at her robes. She shivered and stepped from the floating platform through the open stained glass window.

'How many times do I need to tell you to improve your security?' said Xenixala as her eyes adjusted to the dim room. Paintings depicting heroic feats covered the walls, mostly concealed by an array of ostentatious furniture, the largest of which was a four-poster bed.

The King jumped and dropped his goblet. He was only a little man, which he compensated for with bushy whiskers over his thick lips. His reign had clearly taken its toll, turning his hair grey and deepening his eyes. To think Xenixala once considered him handsome. She was glad she'd kept her hands to herself.

The King pulled up his pantaloons and straightened his crown, the only two items he was wearing. 'For Mole's sake Xeni, couldn't you give me a bit of warning? Damn near killed me!' He flopped into a plush red chair and breathed out, hand on his chest. 'It's been a while. What do you want now? Another set of titles need updating?'

'No no, nothing like that.'

'You're not here to...to...' he paused and swallowed '...to kill me are you?'

'Lucky for you, you're more useful to me alive. I'm here on a quest.'

The King breathed a sigh. 'Ah, yes, a quest, of course. An awful lot of questing going on right now. Very profitable you know, or at least that's what Darkius tells me.'

'Darkius?' Xenixala immediately regretted asking.

'Darkius Doom. My vizier-slash-accountant. My income has nearly doubled since I hired him. Bleeding marvellous! Lord knows how he does it. Strange fellow though, very fond of pink skulls.'

Xenixala tried to change the subject. Politics was more boring than cart-spotting. 'I'm here because of a prophecy.'

'Which one?'

Wordsworth opened his pages and inhaled. Xenixala snapped him shut before he could start singing.

'The one about The Chosen One. Slew a dragon called Grenden, then ran some errands for you?'

'I do send a surprising number of adventurers on errands.' The King thoughtfully stroked his whiskers. 'Mainly to make them leave. They're always storming into my courtroom like they own the place. Snaffling my bread rolls from the kitchen and expecting me not to notice. The dirty rats.' The King stopped himself. 'Present company excepted.'

'Get on with it.'

'Ah yes, well I think I know the chap you mean. Can't remember his name though. I summoned him after he killed that Elder Dragon Grenden about twenty-odd years ago, got him destroying other troublesome beasts for me too. That was big news at the time, smiting the most vicious creature on the continent. I'm not sure you've even managed to slay one, have you?'

'Well there aren't any left now are there?' Xenixala made a mental note to look for an Elder Dragon on her next adventure.

'My advisors informed me that this was what sparked the little adventuring trend in the first place. Everyone wanted a good taste of that level of Experience. All excellent news for me of course, goblin hordes and dragons are finally a thing of the past! I lost three daughters to those ruddy dragons, shouldn't have kept them virgin you see. Also, now I get the extra taxes on the newly inherited riches these adventurers find. I can suffer some bread rolls for that!'

'I'm very happy for you.'

'I've been able to build three extra towers, three! I've got another on its way. It'll be the tower for my pet crabs...'

'And a *magnificent* tower it shall be,' came a voice from the shadows. A figure stepped into the room, a smile on his lips, a cloak draped across his tunic and a pink skull shining out from a pin on his breast. 'Even if it is an accounting mess.'

'Ah!' announced the King, 'This is the man I was telling you about Xeni, Darkius Doom my vizier-slash…'

'Slash-accountant, yeah.' Xenixala finished.

'A *pleasure* to meet you,' said Darkius with a nod. The air grew cold when he spoke. 'Your highness, if I could have a word?'

'Yes yes, of course. Xeni, what is it you want to know about this Chosen One fellow?'

'His name?'

'I told you I can't remember.'

This had all been a total waste of time. Xenixala rubbed her temples. What did she know? 'Wait,' she said triumphantly. 'Are there any parts of the prophecy he hasn't done yet?'

Wordsworth burst into song.

'He'd conquer the thieves,
Of the Bandit King,
And off his head with a piercing sting.

'The Fen Legion of dead
Falls at his knees,
With all his skill, done with ease.

'Great spiders of Wortwood,
Would he destroy,
Only a stick need he employ.

'Have you heard the tale,
of The Ch-'

Xenixala snapped Wordsworth shut and held him tight.

The King continued to hum the tune to himself. He stopped and looked up as if he had forgotten they were there. 'Ah yes, The Bandit King is still causing me a fair sum of grief on the roads. I presume he's still alive.' He tapped his chin in thought. 'The Fen Legion was wiped out years ago and Wortwood has been clear of spiders for a while too, Lord Egglewort won't stop boasting about it.'

'That's all I needed to hear.' Xenixala smiled and leapt out of the window.

Perhaps a little dramatic, but it pays to keep powerful people in awe of you. She cast a quick fall-damage cantrip as she plummeted and landed gracefully on the streets far below.

27

It was dawn by the time Eric, Bill and his two sidekicks Derek and Graham reached The Bandit King's Fortress. Birds had begun their chorus, but it didn't lift Eric's spirits. He felt like he was going to collapse from all the walking. Every part of him was stiff, every motion was pain. He winced and looked to where Bill pointed.

Even through the dense trees he could see the shoddy craftsmanship of the fort. Three-story high wooden poles made up the walls, sharpened to points at the end. Random holes punctuated the fortifications, the largest of which was a gateway at the centre. Dozens of bandits wandered around the base, ostensibly guarding, but mainly napping, chatting or playing cards.

'Here we are, Eric,' said Bill, 'Put this bandana on, it'll make you look more like a bandit.'

Eric took the grey cloth from Bill and wrapped it over his mouth and retched. The smell was somewhere between stale onions and armpits. 'You're coming with me?' he asked, hopeful.

'If we go together, you'll blend right in. Also, let's just say I'm deeply curious about your plan,' Bill smiled mischievously. 'I can't help myself. I gotta see how this pans out.'

Eric wondered the exact same thing.

The four of them approached the main gate, striding as if they were supposed to be there. Eric held his breath. Two bandits stood either side of the entrance. As they passed, one locked eyes with Eric.

Eric's stomach was in his throat. He shoved his hands into his pockets to hide the shaking and kept his eyes down. The door itself lay splintered across the dirt, covered in moss and cobwebs. They stepped between its remains.

Yet not a single guard moved a muscle.

'That was easy,' muttered Bill as they passed through the passageway and into the courtyard. The builder certainly had a fetish for overhead walkways. Random paths to nowhere zig-zagged above them, some of them with huge gaps splitting them apart. They seemed like a total death trap. Almost no guards were to be seen, and the ones that were visible vacantly stared off into the distance.

Bill led them over to a fence with a walkway built head-height over it. 'The Bandit King likes to be in the hardest-to-reach part of the fort, so you have to go through *everything* before you find him.' He winked at Eric. 'Luckily I know a shortcut.' He leapt onto the wooden wall, his lithe limbs bending effortlessly as he clambered up. Once he reached the platform he whispered. 'Come on up.'

Eric grunted as he heaved himself onto the platform, panting into the bandana until it was moist.

'It's funny, adventurers never find this way in,' said Bill, grabbing Eric's arm and pulling him the rest of the way. 'It's like they can't be bothered to climb or jump even the slightest bit.'

Once they'd all made it up, Bill opened a door at the end of the walkway and they crept into the darkness within. Lit torches lined the walls, flickering ghostly amber across the wood. They emerged into a gigantic hall, propped up by mighty columns topped by crossbeams, from which hung skeleton-filled cages.

Dozens of bandits milled around them. Some fought, some laughed, others sharpened swords. They seemed identical to his bandit guides, ragged, thin and fond of bandanas. Many of them moved items out of wagons and onto the piles of loot that lined the walls. Each pile was distinct, one for swords, another helms, another gold, another silver. Eric couldn't help but lick his lips. Different wagons were being re-loaded from the piles. These were green and labelled with the Adventurer's Supply logo.

Then the breath stopped in his throat.

Sat at the centre was the most disturbing mound of them all. A pile of skulls. As Eric's eyes adjusted to the light, he realised it was a *throne* of skulls, sat on by a thick-set man.

The man saw them.

The man's bone necklace clattered as he stood up. He tossed his black ragged cloak over his shoulder and stepped towards them, eyes burning. Or rather, eye. As one was missing from a gaping scar across his face. Bill pushed Eric gently towards the menacing figure, then took a step back.

Eric held his ground, grasped at his crossbow with one hand and wiped the sweat from his palm with the other.

The Bandit King stopped a few feet away, breathing heavily. 'What do you want, *maggots*? Stare at me like that any longer and I'll have your balls.' There was a look in The Bandit King's eye that seemed unhinged. His eye didn't keep still, but darted all over as if it was already engaged in a bar brawl.

Eric felt paralysed. He opened his mouth but nothing came out.

'Work your tongue, recruit, before I rip it out and have it for breakfast!' The Bandit King shouted, bringing the hall to silence. All eyes were on them.

Eric was very used to dealing with men or creatures who held positions of power. They had an ego the size of their castles and expected people to kneel to them unquestioningly. The trick was to bow and yet appear to be their equal, unfazed by their bravado. Only then would they listen. Or that was the theory anyway, it mainly worked on the goblins.

Eric cleared his throat. 'I've come to you to pay a ransom, you've captured someone very dear to me. There was a mix-up with a Main Quest, but I'm not an adventurer. I've got no gold to trade for her, but I do have a better offer if you'll hear it.'

The Bandit King sneered. 'My patience wears thin, filth. Get on with it or I'll have you ransomed up the wall.'

Eric nodded. 'Very well.' He spoke louder, knowing he had an audience, he needed them on his side too. 'Adventurers have plagued us for too long. My business is in ruins, the land is desolate and no-one is safe.' He gestured to the room full of wide-eyed bandits. 'Especially not for bandits. Even a tiny creature hiding in the deepest cave isn't safe. They kill every little thing in their path. And for what? Fun, sport, *Experience*. They have no care for life, just ending it and profiting. Most have more money than they even know how to spend.'

There was a titter amongst the crowd. The Bandit King growled and they went silent. 'What of it?' he said. 'We make do.'

'From what I hear, you've been helping the adventurers along. Making ransoms, filling forts for them to raid, sending your men to the slaughter.' Eric gestured across at some of the bandits who were covered in bandages or had missing limbs. They looked to each other and began nodding with agreement. 'Maybe if you stopped helping them you could end adventuring once and for all. Finally plunder in peace.'

The crowd became animated, chattering agreement and shouting curses.

'SILENCE!!' screamed The Bandit King. 'We're doing *no* such thing, maggot.' He turned to his minions and raised his voice. 'All of you, listen up. We've got a good thing going here. We keep the adventurers entertained and get a cut of the profits. Then we get the best rates selling what we loot back to the Adventurer's Supply shops. We're richer than ever.'

'It doesn't look to me like you're all that rich,' said Eric, pointing at the rotting walls. 'Do your men share in these riches?'

There was more muttering from the crowd.

The Bandit King scowled at their response. 'Get out of here before I lop off your head.' He drew his sword and pointed it at Eric.

'Well then... I guess that settles it.' Eric stepped back and raised his crossbow. 'All I ask is that you return my hostage, Daisy.'

'*Daisy*?' The Bandit King rolled his head back and let out a diabolical laugh. 'That mule we had to kidnap? Hahaha!' The Bandit King grinned wide, a disturbing satisfaction on his face. 'She's dead, fella. Long dead. We don't have time for silly animals.'

Eric felt his blood boil. His fingers shook, his jaw clenched. That was it, Daisy was gone.

'You think your pitiful crossbow can hurt me?' The Bandit King cackled, 'I've got more Experience than a *thousand* adventurers.' He twirled his sword. 'Did you know, I used to be an adventurer myself, many years ago? When I crush your skull, I shall enjoy taking your essence for my own. My power is...'

That was when Eric noticed the fire pit. The carcass rotating over the flames, golden and dripping blood. Were they cooking a whole horse? No, it was a mule...

Something came alive inside of him. The room melted away. All that was left was rage and hurt and pain. All that was left was the man gloating between his crosshairs.

Eric pulled the trigger.

The Bandit King's neck exploded as the quarrel flew straight through it. Blood sprayed everywhere. His head tumbled off his shoulders, stopping at Eric's feet. Eric stood, stunned. Heads don't come off like that. Had his father enchanted this crossbow?

The crowd went silent.

Time stopped.

Bill grabbed Eric's hand and held it high. 'All hail Eric, the new Bandit King!'

'All hail The Bandit King!' cried the crowd, who bowed low and cheered. *'All hail the Bandit King! All hail The Bandit King!'*

These kinds of folk worked on primal instinct. Kill the leader, you're the leader. It was a model which inspired the majority of orcish culture, which was one reason humans avoided orcs. That and the oral hygiene.

Eric raised his hand and the crowd went silent. One wrong word and they'd turn on him, they could get another Bandit King in a matter of minutes.

He cleared his throat. 'Are you sick of helping the adventurers?'

The crowd cheered.

Eric continued. 'They've destroyed everything good in this world. You should be fighting them, fair and square, not giving them quests and luring them into your home.' He gestured to the piles. 'Don't sell these weapons and armour to Adventurer's Supply, keep them for yourselves! Use them to defend against these questing lunatics. No more adventurers, no more quests and no more Adventurer's Supply!'

'Yeah!' the crowd shouted, fists in the air.

'Down with Adventurer's Supply!' came a voice.

'Raid Adventurer's Supply!' came another.

Eric waved his hands in disagreement. 'Well, maybe let's not *raid* anywhere...'

Bill jumped up onto the throne of skulls and addressed the crowd. 'We shouldn't be *selling* to these shops… we should be ruddy robbing 'em! Think of all the great gear we can get!'

'Yeah!' the crowd roared.

Bill continued, 'Let's go, right now, all of us, send the ravens to every bandit hideout in the land. We'll burn every last Adventurer's Supply to the ground, arm ourselves good and proper, then take on these adventurers, once and for all!'

'Yeah!'

'Wait, what?' said Eric in disbelief. 'I was thinking maybe more of a defensive protest...' But the cries and whoops drowned out his voice.

The bandits poured out of the room, weapons raised, whipped into a frenzy of his own doing. It was both a glorious and terrifying sight to behold.

28

Queen Warlock Xenixala of Xendor, denier of The Untruths of Old, Wielder of Time and a ten-year subscriber to Turnip Weekly, frowned into the images that appeared in her silver bowl. Could this be true? Was this Eric The Chosen One? She sat back. Sighing, she broke open another Elixir and drank it down, letting the pulse of happiness wash over her.

She was home, or at least the closest thing she could call home. It was the best witch's tower she'd ever had the pleasure of ransacking, and so had decided to tidy it up and move in. The hilltop had an unparalleled view over Porkhaven. Sure, she'd had to fend off the odd adventurer here and there, but that wasn't anything a few animated golems and spike traps couldn't sort out. She knew how adventurers operated, so she also knew exactly how to make defences to bamboozle them. Having no stairway was a big plus, as adventurers were notorious for needing a specific path to guide them through a dungeon or they would become pathetically lost. Sat atop the warren of boobytrapped and vacant rooms below, the inaccessible tower was where she spent most of her time, the only place she felt truly at ease.

Her thousands of trinkets and trophies filled the chamber around her. Creatures' head's, demons' horns, golden cups, silver rings, magic scrolls, enchanted books, haunted orbs, glowing balls, keys to kingdoms, jarls' pardons, college certificates, arrest warrants... she'd done it all. A lifetime of achievements. They were probably worth a small fortune, but she would rather die than pawn a single one, no matter how bad things were. Yet for some reason, they no longer gave her an ounce of joy.

'You will never amount to anything, Xenixala. You are worthless. You can barely survive these punishments. Drink another poison. If you aren't the best, you are the worst.'

She looked back into the silver bowl, whispering the spell once more. The images appeared again, flickering as the liquid silver moved. She was back in the bandit fortress, looking down on the figures below. Her vision was limited because it depended entirely on the well-trained crow she'd sent to spy on The Bandit King. Annoyingly, the crow spent far too much time glancing around at insects rather than focussing on the task at hand.

Eric pulled the trigger.

The crow looked at the head of The Bandit King as it rolled to the ground, obviously curious at the fly that had landed on the corpse's nose.

Xenixala drummed her fingers. She couldn't believe the mettle of this unassuming man. He'd actually gone and killed The Bandit

King, exactly as the prophecy foretold. It *had* to be him, but she could hardly believe it. She was expecting some kind of hulking goliath or mighty wizard. He was supposed to have slain an Elder Dragon for Mole's sake. But for all intents and purposes, the person who had shot off the head of one of the most feared men in the land was just… plain. Everything down to his wispy middle-aged hair to his grubby overalls made him plain. Nothing about him screamed "Chosen One" in the slightest. Maybe that was what made him so special?

There was no way he was the world's most Experienced adventurer. It must be some kind of mistake.

Bill got up onto the ostentatious skull throne and shouted about destroying all the Adventurer's Supply shops. The bandits cheered in agreement and stormed out of the room.

Wait. No more Adventurer's Supply meant no more Elixirs. That was bad news. Very bad news indeed.

She'd spent many years trying to recreate the Elixir formula, to little success and a scalded oesophagus. She even tried to find out who their supplier was, but that led to a dead-end too. It was infuriating.

This had to be stopped.

She'd have to confront Eric immediately and put an end to this nonsense. Hopefully he'd be the nemesis she so sorely desired, but it didn't seem very likely. He looked pathetic.

She needed to be the best. He had to be the great foe she must conquer.

What was even more worrying was that she had just finished off her last Elixir. She'd need some more, and fast.

Xenixala set the bowl aside, stood up and snatched the napping Wordsworth from the table.

Wordsworth stretched with a flap of his pages. 'Where are we off to then?'

'To kill this Chosen One and become the most Experienced adventurer of all time.'

'Oh, excellent.' Wordsworth's bookmark licked his front pages. 'But we'll get a few Elixirs first, right?'

29

For the hundredth time that day, Skwee the goblin twisted his neck to try and stretch out the ache, but it didn't help. He was tempted to drink an Elixir for it, but he daren't. The punishment for stealing from the shop was a fate worse than death. Or so he'd been told on his training.

He leaned back in his chair and sighed. Today had been a slow day at Adventurer's Supply. Even when adventurers did come in, interacting with them was dull as dishwater. He had to stick to a very particular script, such as, *'Good day weary traveller, can I interest you in some wares?'* or *'I've the finest swords in the land,'* a boast he never understood as every Adventurer's Supply shop touted it. Deviating from the said script was also punished with a fate worse than death. In fact, every penalty seemed to be a fate worse than death. Some crafty minions must have realised if they put a low value on their own life, you could get away with anything.

Skwee put quite a high value on his own life. Or at least compared to the other goblins he met working for The Dark Master. He hadn't done his jobs properly and it had got him killed three times. In a lot of ways, he was lucky to be alive. It had been his own fault: first, he hadn't remembered his master's biscuits, second, some adventurers had nearly lopped his head off, and then he'd broken protocol and hidden under a pile of his fallen comrades, only to be suffocated. The taste of their blood still haunted him to this day. And finally there had been the unfortunate altercation with the ogres. Each resurrection had somehow been more painful than the last. Goblin Resources ("GR" for short, but not to be confused with "Gnome Research") had offered him counselling sessions, but he had turned them down. He was fine and there was no need to make a fuss.

That was the main reason they'd re-trained him for the retail division of The Dark Army, a role that was usually reserved for gnomes. GR seemed particularly concerned with his mental health for some reason, and decided he needed a break from "hostile work environments".

He found his new position much more relaxing, and over the past few weeks his little shop had begun to feel like home. A place all of his own. It was small and dingy, but he took pride in keeping things tidy and dust-free. Or at least the bits he could reach. The overloaded shelves took half the day to wipe down, and he often cut himself on a sharp axe or sword. Helmets and shields were his favourite thing to polish, something about their round shape made it highly therapeutic. He kept the potions and balms under the counter, which he lined up into a perfect grid in a wooden box. They never needed cleaning as he'd usually get through a fresh box a day. Adventurers couldn't get enough.

The magical force field at the back of the shop blocked off the more exotic items for sale, but he never had to deal with that. The fancy weapons and armour somehow always stayed shiny. He suspected they were just for show, as an adventurer was yet to buy any of them. In fact, he wasn't even sure how to get past the barrier. He presumed it would magically know when it needed to open.

The smell of the place took a while to get used to. Magical items and enchantments had a metallic tang to them, which was jarring at first and made his nostril hairs stand on end. But he got used to it. On the rare days that he did leave the shop, he felt himself missing it.

The doorbell tinkled and a middle-aged man in a grubby apron walked through the door. If it weren't for the large crossbow on his back, Skwee would say a cobbler had got lost and gone into the wrong shop.

Skwee straightened up to see better over the counter and smiled. 'Good day weary traveller, can I interest you in some wares?' he spoke in his friendliest voice, but knew it would come across as patronising. They'd made him practice his tone for hours. 'Some armour perhaps? I've the finest swords in the land.'

The man fumbled and hesitated. 'Ah, no, I'm alright thanks. Listen, you're in danger. You should probably leave here or you might get your head caved in.'

There was nothing in the script for this. Was he being robbed? He'd dealt with light-fingered adventurers before. He had an enchanted panic lever under the counter that summoned the Porkhaven city guard for exactly this sort of thing. They arrived so fast the thieves didn't even have time to leave the shop.

Skwee rested his hand on it and maintained his smile. 'I've got my eye on you adventurer.'

The man continued. 'I know you'll try and summon the city guards, but they won't come, every Adventurer's Supply in Porkhaven is under attack. In fact, every shop in the land is under attack. The bandits have gone crazy. It's not safe for you here.'

Skwee pulled the lever. 'Certainly traveller.' He smiled and waited.

Nothing.

'Bandits will be here any second,' the man continued. 'Please, you've gotta come. I didn't want this. I have to save someone, *anyone* from this mess. You're the first shop I could find that hasn't already been ransacked.'

'Stay safe on your travels adventurer.'

'Please.'

'Stay safe on your travels adventurer.'

The door burst open and three men charged in. Finally, the city guard. They'd get rid of this maniac and leave him in peace.

Why were the city guards wearing bandanas over their faces? Did they hire bandits these days?

Oh no.

The men screamed and swung their clubs into the shelves, splintering his beautiful displays. Their eyes turned on him, glinting with bloodlust.

'Have it your way,' said the man as he flung a powder from his bag.

Skwee's face burst with pain, Lights sparkled in his view.

Then darkness.

30

Eric placed the unconscious goblin onto his desk in the Beast Be Gone shop and hastily closed the blinds. He wiped his brow and breathed in the familiar scent of home. Safety, security and dust, now blended with a hint of mimic urine. Eric grunted at Larry, who was disguised as a tall lamp. Larry leapt into life, flashing his bulb and came hopping across the room.

'Oh. You're back,' said Larry, as his light flickered off.

'Yeah,' said Eric. He looked down at the goblin. 'And this little guy.' But no Daisy, he thought to himself. He pushed the pain away and tried to focus. She was gone and there was nothing he could do about it. At least he could help this creature, one less death on his conscience.

Larry bent over the goblin, his lampshade almost touching the creature's long nose. 'Urgh, a goblin? Why'd you bring such a horrid little thing?'

'Goblins aren't horrid,' said Eric with a sniff. 'They're just misunderstood.'

'Shouldn't we tie him up? What if he does something, you know… evil?'

'Goblins aren't evil, either. That's a stereotype.'

'But they do *so much* evil.'

'Admittedly, they do a lot of evil, yes.' Eric produced a rag and wiped the pixie dust from the goblin's face. 'But that's mainly because of their socio-economic standing.'

'Socio-eco...what now?'

'This one was making an honest living as a shopkeep, so he can't be all bad.'

The little goblin stirred, his pointy ears flickering. His beady eyes opened and regarded them with horror, then screamed.

'Shhh,' Eric lulled. 'We're not going to hurt you.'

'I might,' said Larry.

The goblin writhed on the desk, slapping Larry's lampshade away with his scrawny arms. 'A talking lamp!?' it cried.

'Don't worry,' said Eric, 'he's just a mimic.'

'A *mimic*!?' The goblin flailed even more.

Eric cleared his throat. 'A *friendly* mimic. Ain't that right Larry?'

Larry straightened himself up and hopped back. 'Sure, mostly anyway.'

The goblin stopped moving but kept his eyes fixed on Larry. 'So… if you're not going to kill me, then what do you want?'

Eric pulled a chair over, and sat down, bringing him to eye-level with the goblin on the desk. 'I only wanted to save you. I accidentally let the bandits loose on the Adventurer's Supply shops. All of them. So I'm afraid you're out of a job.'

The goblin laid his head back onto the wood and closed his eyes. 'I'll have to retrain *again*.'

'What's your name little fella?'

'Skwee.'

'I'm Eric, this here is Larry the mimic.' He pointed his thumb.

'Just Larry,' said Larry. 'I don't call you Eric The Human.'

'Yeah, sorry,' said Eric. 'Well, Skwee, maybe we can find you a job somewhere else.' Eric's heart went out to the little minion before him. He probably didn't have a soul in the world who cared for him. 'I've got some pamphlets on relocating, I bet there's a goblin warren somewhere you can...'

Skwee shook his head. 'Nowhere's safe for me. I can't desert The Master. Do you know what they'd do to me?'

'A fate worse than death?'

'How did you know?'

'Textbook minion control strategy,' said Eric. 'I've even had to use a few of them myself at times. Last resort of course. Who's your master?'

The goblin rolled away and put his head in his hands. 'I can't tell you.'

'Or it's a fate worse than death?'

'A fate worse than death.'

Eric massaged his temples. 'Alright, have it your way. But if you want me to help you, you have to help me.'

'Why do you want to help me anyway?'

'I'm in pest control, it's what I do.'

'You're not an adventurer?'

Eric spat. 'Definitely not.'

'Oh. Most of you humans seem to be.'

'I know what you mean.'

Skwee hung his head. 'That's on reason I went into the Dark Army in the first place. It's the only safe place away from them.'

Eric stopped. 'What's this about a Dark Army?'

'Ah... I... I've said too much. I should be going now.' Skwee sat up and looked around the room in confusion. He tried to pull himself off the desk but fell with a *clump* onto the floor.

Eric leaned down and pulled him back up. 'You ain't going anywhere. That pixie dust I threw at you is a powerful muscle relaxant.'

'I swore an oath,' Skwee clasped his hands together. 'Please don't make me talk. *Please*.'

Eric stood up. He wasn't going to force poor Skwee to talk. Adventurers who described themselves as "chaotic" liked to force people to talk. Anything to give themselves a bit of edginess, but Eric suspected they were really just sadists. And besides, he wasn't too bothered about what he had to say. There were more villainous masters out there than there were rats in Porkhaven.

'Alright Skwee, settle down. You can stay here while all this looting goes on, then we'll find you a nice new goblin clan somewhere, or return you to your master.'

Skwee breathed out. 'Oh, um. Thank you,' he stammered.

There was a crash outside.

Eric sensed something in the air. Something wasn't right.

The tang of magic.

He delved into his Sack of Clutching and pulled out some essentials. This included witchbane, an anti-arcane stone and some resistance potions. He stuffed them into his pockets, then took out a rope and slung it over his shoulder.

'Larry, keep an eye on Skwee here would you?'

'Sure thing,' said Larry, who had already turned into a footstool and was hiding in the corner.

Eric ran over to the front door and pulled it open an inch. He peeked out and shivered at the fresh air.

A woman stood on the street with a tome in her arms, staring fiercely at the shop. Her lightning-blue robes glimmered in the sunlight, complemented by her piercing black hair. He would have described her as beautiful if there weren't something so ugly about the way her face contorted with anger. She stepped forward, staggering.

'Eric!' she called out, slurring. 'Come out and faace me, *Eric*. Oh Chos'n won. I know you'rrre in there. Come ouuuut.' She smiled, stopped and pulled out an Elixir from her bag, then poured it into her mouth. Most of it went down her robes. 'Look wha you mad me do Eric.'

Eric opened the shop door and stepped into the street. Passers-by quickened their steps, obviously avoiding the drama. He smiled at the strange woman as best he could. She needed careful treatment, she was unhinged. 'I'm Eric, what do you want?'

'I noh you're Eric. I'm Xe-ik-zalla. No. Zen-in-clalla. Xenizlaala. Whateva. Breaker of things, killer of... whatyoucallit. You know. Defender of aaaall this.' She twirled her arms around. 'I'm here to fight you, oh great warrior man. I'ma taking your Essperience.'

This woman was out of her mind. 'You've clearly had a lot of Elixir, miss. But you have the wrong Eric, I'm afraid, I ain't a warrior and I don't want no trouble.'

'Oh I've-' She hiccuped and wiped her mouth, 'I've got the right Eric all right, tha's you. Cho's won. We fight and it will be amaz'n. Best dual evver. I guna be best. The best.' She flicked open her book.

Eric's hands moved so fast he didn't even have to think about it. First, he scrunched witchbane leaves in his ears. Second, his fingers rubbed an anti-arcane stone in his pocket, it vibrated in response. And third, he leapt aside, rope in hand.

He moved just in time to dodge the fireball that exploded into the stables behind him.

The potion of fire resistance flew from his fingers, shattering over the stable roof. The fire went white, flaring bright, then disappeared altogether.

Eric turned and lunged towards the witch. She mouthed spells, but he didn't hear her, the witchbane working magic of its own.

The witch scrunched her face in confusion, backing away.

Eric grinned. Magic users relied so much on their spells. They never bothered learning anything else. Why would you when you could summon minions to do your bidding?

He threw his rope, whipping it at her feet. She stumbled backwards. Eric ran to her, spinning the rope around, dancing to avoid her jabbing and scratching hands. But she was close now, he heard her spell.

The world turned sideways as he flew back. He crashed against the shop wall.

Moaning, he stood up.

The witch cackled as a glowing wolf emerged from her fingertips, green smoke emanating from its body. It pounced, eyes beaming, jaws snarling.

Eric rolled to the side. His hips screamed as he hit the ground. The summoned wolf flew past with a yelp, then turned.

The witch grinned and helped herself to another Elixir. The street was empty now, everyone knew to stay away. Drunken magic duels were a common sight in Porkhaven and a stray lightning bolt was no laughing matter.

The wolf levelled his gaze on Eric. Not breaking eye contact, Eric rummaged through his Sack of Clutching. Carefully, he tossed a pork jerky at the animal's feet.

The wolf sniffed the meat, enchanted by its scent, and snaffled it up. It let out a whimper, crumpling to the floor as it dissolved into ash.

Dispelling salts were worth every penny.

Now it was Eric's turn to grin. He turned back on the witch, rope ready.

He stopped.

Her skin was already bright green as she lay twitching on the floor, foaming at the mouth and sparks flying from her nostrils. Her robes twisted over themselves, soaked in vomit and gutter water.

The Flux.

He knew exactly what he had to do.

31

Night Prophetess Xenixala of Xendor, crusher of Fatigue, taker of The Forty Winks and author of 'How to Keep Account of All Your Sheep', squinted. The world was a blur. Figures stood over her. They put things in her mouth and made her sick. The taste was bitter, like bile. Like Elixir. She needed an Elixir. She tried to say it, but all that came out was a croak. Who were these shapes? Was that a talking lamp? Why wouldn't they listen? Eyes closed.

She was out adventuring, Wordsworth in her arms. Goblins appeared, she needed to kill them. Get the Experience, take the loot, move on. She opened her mouth... but nothing. The spells wouldn't leave her. She thrust out her hands, yet no magic came to her fingertips.

She screamed, there was only silence.

She was back at school. The classroom was dark and musky. Professor Mogg held out a potion. An Elixir.

The class chanted.

Drink.

Xenixala batted the potion away. But it reappeared in the teacher's hand.

Drink.

If you're not the best, you are the worst.

Drink.

She drank.

Breathless, she turned over. A figure wiped her dripping brow. How long had she been like this? The bed smelled stale and rancid. She needed to magic it clean. Maybe tomorrow. Close your eyes. Do it tomorrow. Eyes closed.

Adventuring again. A kobold ran at her, pleading. Its furry nose wet with tears. A spell. Kill it with a spell. Her arms were empty. Where was Wordsworth? Had he abandoned her? She went to look, rolling frantically. Where was he? Figures held her down. They told her to relax. They wiped her brow again. They made her drink. It was delicious and horrid. Eyes closed.

No more dreams.

* * *

'Where am I?' Xenixala spoke, but it was more of a rasp. She lay in a bed of tattered sheets in a barren room. What in hell's name had happened? A man sat beside her, looking at her with concern.

'Awake at last.' The figure held a cup to her mouth. 'Here, drink this.'

She accepted his request, gulping and spluttering. 'Urgh, what is this, piss?'

'Drink a lot of that do you?' The figure smiled. 'It's greywillow bark, ash and a little Elixir residue. Good for a retreating Flux.'

Xenixala ignored him and tried to sit up, but found she could hardly move her arms. 'Who are you?' she whispered, resting her head back into the pillow. 'And where am I?'

The man frowned. 'You really don't remember anything?'

Xenixala shrugged. She glanced around to try and answer her own question. The man was being intentionally unhelpful, but her surroundings were even less so, being only a tiny box room with a bed and a cupboard in it. Peeling beige paint covered the walls, the beams holding it all together thick with dust and cobwebs. The window was open and it sounded like chaos outside. Screaming, explosions and steel on steel. Normally those familiar noises would excite her, bring a flutter to her heart and a grin to her face. Now they sounded like trouble. She was far too weak for trouble. She sighed.

'I'm Eric,' said the figure, unnecessarily pointing a thumb at himself. 'You're in my house above my pest control shop. You came here to fight me for some reason.'

Eric The Chosen One. Pest control. Of course. She nodded. 'Oh yeah, I defeated you. Why are you still alive?'

Eric laughed. His face was so bland, the smile seemed to disappear. His wispy hair had probably once been quite nice. He was so forgettable, Xenixala felt like she'd seen him a thousand times, and at the same time, never before. It was oddly reassuring.

'Not even close,' he replied with a smug look on his boring face.

Xenixala's head felt like it had been hit with a mace. 'I need Elixir.' She winced and held out an expectant hand. 'Gimme.'

Eric batted it away. 'No more Elixir for you. Not in the state you're in. You get a little dose with your medicine to ease things through. That's it.'

Xenixala scoffed. 'You sound like my mother. I said *gimme*. Or I'll turn you into a toad.'

'Do your worst.'

Xenixala raised her hand mumbling incantations. She stopped. 'Why are you smiling?'

'No reason.' Eric stifled his moronic grin and pointed at the empty cup. 'Although I did put witchbane in your drink there. Didn't want you casting spells in your fever. With the amount I've been feeding you, you'll be spell-less for a few days.'

Xenixala cursed under her breath. 'That's cheating. No fair.'

'Since when was magic fair?'

'Always. Where's Wordsworth?'

'Your pet book?'

'Familiar.'

'Your pet *familiar* is upstairs, clamped shut. You can see him when you're better. I don't want you magic-ing all over us.'

No Elixir, no magic, and no Wordsworth. Great.

'You should probably get used to the idea of no more Elixirs,' said Eric. 'I don't think they'll be around much longer anyways.'

Xenixala's eyes widened. 'What do you mean?'

Eric made a serious frown. 'There was an... *incident* with the bandits. Which may or may not have been started by me - accidentally of course - so Adventurer's Supply is urm… gone.'

'*All* gone?' Her breathing stopped. No more Elixir forever.

'As far as I'm aware, they're the only guys making the stuff.'

'*I know,*' she snapped. 'Oh Mole.' She put her hands over her face, which took the last of her strength. Her arms collapsed to the sides. How was she going to live? Surely she could hunt some down? There must be stockpiles somewhere. Okay, so it wouldn't be fresh, but it would be better than nothing. She'd have to find who was making the stuff and fast.

'I need to go,' she said, trying to shuffle out of the bed. Her body felt like it weighed a thousand tonnes. Eric held her still with one hand.

'You need to rest. Besides, it's not safe out there.'

'Out where?'

'Anywhere. But especially Porkhaven.' Eric gestured to the window. The shouting and clashing outside seemed to grow louder. 'It's been full-scale rioting after all The Adventurer's Supply shops got looted. The newly armed bandits are running rampant and the adventurers are going crazy without their precious potions. The whole city's on lockdown. It's warfare out there.'

'How long have I been asleep for?'

'About two days. I've never seen The Flux so bad.'

Thoughts swirled in her head. Hazy, but forming slowly. 'Right, I remember now.'

'Remember what?'

'The bandits, you killed The Bandit King.'

'How'd you know that?'

'I spied on you with a crow.'

'You *spied* on me?'

'People spy all the time.'

'Not on me they don't.'

'You'd be surprised.'

Eric paused, his face had turned beetroot. 'Why'd you wanna spy on me anyhow?'

Xenixala was rarely one for subtle. She very much enjoyed watching lords squirm at her candidness during their pretentious banquets. Telling them they looked like oversized peacocks in their frocks or pointing out that their wive's gaze was clearly drawn to the servant boy. That sort of thing. To hold back the only piece of information she had over this man would take energy, which was something she no longer possessed. 'Well, you're not going to believe this, but… you're *The Chosen One*.'

'Chosen what?'

'One. You know, prophesied to save the world, the most powerful and Experienced adventurer. There's a few Chosen Ones as it turns out. Anyway, you're one of them and you're the best.'

'I don't believe you.'

Xenixala cleared her throat. She didn't sing, but spoke rhythmically as if there were music. *'Grenden the dragon, Would rage no more, When he shot its mighty maw.'*

Eric sat up a little straighter. 'Sure, I killed Grenden, but he killed my father first. What of it?'

She continued. *"Our great King, learned of his might, so sent him many beasts to fight.*

'He had a rat infestation and I…'

'The Fen Legion of dead, Falls at his knees, With all his skill, done with ease.'

'Anti undead scrolls really worked a charm on them.'

'Great spiders of Wortwood, Would he destroy, Only a stick need he employ.'

'Lord Egglewort still owes me for that one…'

'He'd conquer the thieves, Of the Bandit King, And off his head with a piercing sting.'

'It was an *accident*.'

Xenixala levelled her gaze on him. 'See?'

'Could be a coincidence.' Eric humphed and crossed his arms. 'Or maybe you wrote this song yourself. You have been spying on me.'

Xenixala let out a snort. 'Don't flatter yourself.' She looked Eric up and down. 'I wouldn't have believed it either. I was expecting some kind of mighty warrior.'

'Well, I did defeat you.'

'No you didn't, I passed out. It was a draw. Nobody defeats The Great Xenixala. *Nobody*.'

'If you say so.'

'I'll take you on any day, you wouldn't stand a chance.'

'Oh yeah?'

'Yeah.' Xenixala lunged but barely managed to sit up. Eric pinned her down with three fingers while she tried to wriggle free. Eventually, she stopped and laid back, panting. 'You cheated.'

'If this is cheating, then spells are cheating too.'

'I shouldn't have had so much Elixir, it made me sloppy.'

'You can say that again. You were a total mess.'

'Next time I'll have the perfect amount. Then I'll kill you in an instant.' Her hands shook under the bedsheets. She clenched her fists but it wouldn't stop. How did this man defeat her? He should be dead. No one had ever fought her and lived to talk about it. No one (except maybe The Nuub, but that didn't count.) The fight with Eric was a blur in her mind. How had he done it? 'I want an Elixir,' she said, determined.

Eric shook his head, a serene sadness on his dull face. 'You don't need that stuff. You need help.'

'Nobody tells me what I need Eric. I'll do what I want, when I want.'

'If you say so. But look what it does to you. I've seen it many times. The world's better off without Elixir and without adventurers. Running around, destroying and looting, murdering innocent creatures for a sniff of glory. It's disgusting.'

Xenixala could hardly believe the cheek. Who did he think he was? He has the gall to claim he beat her, then keep her locked in his bedroom like a pervert. AND he wouldn't even give her some desperately needed Elixirs. Then he insulted adventuring, too. The cheek.

'Well let me tell you something, *Eric*,' Xenixala spat. 'Want to know why there are so many adventurers? Hmm?'

Eric looked at her, confused. 'I suppose.'

'It's mainly because of *you*, Eric, or should I say, *Chosen One.*'

'You're having a fever dream again.'

Xenixala grinned. 'That's what the prophecy says, *"Have you heard the tale of The Chosen One? With highest Experience, and never undone."* Your level of Experience is *legendary* to adventurers, Eric. We all aspire to get to the highest possible power level. We want what *you* have.'

Eric stood up, looming over her bed. 'That's not possible.'

Xenixala continued, savouring every word that dug at her captor, like twisting a knife in his belly. 'Did you think you could just kill an Elder Dragon without absorbing an insane amount of Experience?'

'Grenden was an *Elder* Dragon?'

'I bet you'd drunk an Elixir too, giving you a hundred times more.'

Eric hung his head. 'I had to, I'd have been dead otherwise.'

Xenixala snorted, it all made sense now. 'No wonder you beat me, you had all that Elder Dragon power lolling around inside you. I bet you've had a whole bunch more Experience from exterminating all those creatures over the years too. Pest control isn't so different from adventuring, if you think about it.'

'It's totally different,' Eric snapped. 'I do everything I can to make it painless, and killing is a last resort. You adventurers are the exact opposite.'

'If you say so. Either way, you've inspired countless murders of kobolds, wolves, goblins, ogres, dragons, bandits… and the rest.'

Eric went silent.

Xenixala smiled and closed her eyes. Maybe she'd get a bit of peace now.

32

Eric couldn't believe his ears. Could it be true? How could it be true? The witch was lying. She had to be. And yet the prophecy rhymed. *Real* prophecies rhymed.

Xenixala was pretending to be asleep. He cleared his throat.

'What?' she snapped, scowling but keeping her eyes closed.

It was a shame that she was so aggressive all the time. She had probably been quite the beauty once, but every line on her face made her look like she was permanently disgruntled.

Eric folded his arms. 'How?'

'How what?'

'How have I got so much Experience?'

Xenixala smiled, clearly savouring his displeasure. 'I told you, you killed an Elder Dragon.'

'But that was... years ago. I was only a kid.'

'Don't look at me. You're the one who did it.'

The dragon that killed his father was an Elder Dragon? It was no wonder his father had been so serious about it. They were practically living gods, and only came into existence once in a millennia, or so the stories went. Eric wished he'd never been so foolish. To think that he and Freddy thought they could kill one on their own. They wanted glory. His Father knew it was wrong to kill in cold blood, but even then he'd screamed to shoot it as the flames roasted him alive. Eric had hesitated. Holding the crossbow high, fingers wet with sweat, hands shaking. Then it was too late. Father was a charred husk and it was his turn to scream. He'd fired the crossbow, caught the dragon's eye, just like father had told him to. The only weak spot. And only weak because of the sedatives his father had put into sheep that the dragon had been foolish enough to eat.

Eric paid a heavy price for his father's lessons. Never underestimate a dragon, never kill in cold blood and never go adventuring. He'd sworn to heed those lessons, and to never drink another Elixir ever again, even if it meant dying.

'How did you kill an Elder dragon anyway?' Xenixala's words snapped Eric back to reality.

'He was heavily sedated. It killed my father and I shot it with my crossbow.'

'Simple as that eh?'

'I barely made it out alive, it took my father months of planning and…'

Xenixala cut him off with a wave of a hand. 'I'm sure I could have done it with a few spells.'

'They're spell resistant.'

'Whatever. I'd think of something.'

This woman was so cock-sure it was painful. 'Are you not in the least bit worried that your strength relies solely on magic tricks? Anyone with half a brain can stop magic. Then you're nothing.'

Xenixala yawned. 'I dunno, no-one seems to bother. Most people consider anti-magic *unsporting*.' She gave Eric a scathing look.

'Magic's unsporting in the first place.'

'It's called being smart.'

Eric rubbed his eyes. This was going nowhere, as she was completely deluded. Maybe that meant he could disregard what she said about him. But deep down he suspected it to be true. There hadn't been many adventurers before then, but every year since there seemed to be more and more. His act of violence inspired them to do the same, to kill merely for the Experience. He felt sick to think about it.

A sharp knocking came from downstairs. More looters? He'd already barred the door and told Larry to stand guard.

'Wait here,' he told Xenixala and hurried downstairs into the shop below. He took the crossbow from the wall and loaded it while the rapping continued. He pointed it at the door, nudging Larry who was in the shape of an incongruous ottoman. Larry sprung awake, legs rattling to attention. Eric hissed at him and nodded towards the noise.

'I know you're in there, my *dear* Eric,' came the voice through the door. 'I saw you through the window.'

Eric froze. He knew that pompousness anywhere. Lord Egglewort. He really didn't have time for this right now.

He opened the door and two burly humans fell inside, two more followed behind carrying an open-top litter. Sat atop it was the rotund Lord Egglewort, bending so as to not hit his head on the ceiling. His robes were dusty and torn and his once large chin looked narrow and sharp. He bit into an apple and chewed loud enough to be heard over the racket from the street outside. The door swung closed behind them.

'Good to see you again Eric,' said Lord Egglewort, flecks of apple ventured into the air as he spoke. 'How have you been?'

Eric lowered his crossbow but kept his finger on the trigger. 'I've been better. How'd you get through the city?'

'With a little difficulty. These riots are most startling. But I've got these able-bodied sorts to keep me safe.' Lord Egglewort flapped his arms, signalling the men to lower him to the floor. They did so, then stood against the walls. Lord Egglewort remained seated and beamed up at Eric. 'These mercenaries have been on retainer for months and I thought I might as well get my money's worth. I came as soon as I heard about the fall of Adventurer's

Supply. I had to see it for myself! Top work old boy. But the job isn't over.'

'Isn't it?'

'Not by a long shot. If anything, it's worse than before. But we need a storm to bring the harvest. Isn't that so?'

'I suppose.'

'Then we're agreed.'

'I agreed to something?'

Lord Egglewort's rosy cheeks wobbled with glee. 'I seem to recall you murdering one of my loyal subjects and dropping him at my feet...'

'That was an accident...'

'I don't care. We had an agreement to stop the adventurers. You finish the job, or I get The King to lock you in a dungeon so deep and dull, not even an adventurer would bother finding you. Do I make myself clear?'

Eric had an awful sense of foreboding. 'Crystal clear.'

'Excellent,' Lord Egglewort took another bite of his apple and chewed triumphantly. 'So no more dilly-dallying, now's the time to strike. You told me you had a hunch about a Dark Master?'

'Something like that.' With all the excitement and distractions, Eric had completely forgotten about this supposed evil villain. 'I was... uh... sidetracked.'

'Understandable given the circumstances.' Lord Egglewort glanced around the room. 'Didn't you have a little, uh, comrade?'

'She went to work for Freddy Glorp.' Eric's head dropped. The thought of Rose made him feel sick.

'Good plan! Team up with your pest control rival to take on a common enemy. Textbook adventure tale wouldn't you say?'

'I don't read all that much.'

Lord Egglewort tossed his apple core to the ground. 'Well, it's settled then, off you go to Freddy Glorp's, and together you put a stop to this nonsense once and for all.'

'But…'

'No buts.' Lord Egglewort clicked his fingers and the heavyset guards surrounded him, casting glares at Eric. 'I *don't* want to have to ask you a second time.'

Eric sighed. 'Alright then.'

'Don't fret, dear Eric, once I get my lands back I'll be sure to reward you handsomely.'

Eric licked his lips. 'Very kind of you.'

'Oh, what a lovely ottoman.'

'I wouldn't touch that if I were you.'

Fortunately, the guards raised Lord Egglewort up before he could molest Larry. 'I shall take my leave. I need to get out of this hell hole of a town. Tally ho.' The guards clustered closer as he pulled a Scroll of Town Portal from his sleeve. He muttered the incantation, and they all disappeared into a puff of smoke.

Eric spluttered as the cloud dissipated. He went to shut the door, but looked outside first. A family ran by, children screaming. A cart sat ablaze with no horses in sight, broken windows, and glass strewn everywhere. In the distance, he heard the unmistakable sound of a fireball exploding. Down the road, two paladins and a barbarian were in the process of attacking six bandits, thrusting swords and launching arrows. Their fighting styles were haphazard and involved more rolling on the floor than actual fighting. You'd think they'd have been more practised.

Eric closed the door. He'd caused all this. Him. And it was his job to fix it. Chosen One or not. If that meant going to Freddy Glorp, then so be it. It would probably mean seeing Rose again too. He hesitated. No, if she got him in this mess in the first place, she could damned well help. And as much as he hated admitting it to himself, he missed her. Somehow she made him feel a little younger, happier, calmer. Even if she was a little annoying. And a traitor.

Eric stormed upstairs, two steps at a time.

He burst into the witch's resting chamber that used to be his spare room. 'Xenixala,' he announced, 'I'm going to leave you here for a while. I'm on a mission to stop these adventurers once and for all. You stay here and Larry the mimic will keep you guarded.'

Xenixala blinked. 'Larry the... mimic?'

'So don't touch any of the furniture. Oh, and there's a goblin living in the stable, I rescued him from working at Adventurer's Supply, so be nice to him. Don't leave. I'm taking your magic book…'

'Familiar.'

'…magic *book,* with me in case you decide to run off. Collateral. I'll be back soon.'

The strange book had been kept hidden inside his Sack of Clutching the entire time. He wasn't sure what happened when you put sentient magical objects into the bag. He suspected it would be fine.

Xenixala frowned. 'What have you got against adventurers anyway?'

'They're all a bunch of ogres boils.'

'I'm an adventurer, you know.'

'Oh, I know.' Eric winked, turned and ran down the stairs, not waiting to see if Xenixala sneered. He told Larry to stand guard, then left the shop, being sure to snatch his trusty crossbow on the way out.

33

Skwee rolled over and wriggled deeper into the hay. Bliss. Eric's stable was the perfect size for him and was already beginning to smell like home. Probably because he'd defecated in the corner a few times.

He truly couldn't believe his luck. He'd almost died again but had been saved by possibly the nicest human he'd ever met. This Eric fellow was what humans *should* be like. This kind of good nature was what goblins took advantage of all those centuries ago. Raiding loot from unwary travellers. Of course, now the hunters had become the hunted, which was why all humans were so mean. The golden age of goblinry was long gone, not that he had been alive to witness it. He only heard about it from the older goblins, who wouldn't shut up about how things were better in their day.

Eric hadn't even tortured him to find out more about his Dark Master's plans. That's how nice he was. Skwee wouldn't have minded much either way. Torture was a normal part of life back at The Master's Lair. Everyone had to endure a bit, so you kind of got used to it. He was sure a few of the minions did things wrong on purpose so they could get some time with the Master's Torturer. Torture punishments had to be observed by the offender's whole team, which they called *Team Building Exercises*. Skwee watched some of his comrades stifle their grins as they were bound and whipped. One had even called the Torturer "Father". They'd been beheaded for that.

The door to the stable creaked open, shining light into the room. Skwee pushed the hay back and squinted. 'Who's there?'

'Hello there little goblin,' said the figure. It was a human woman in robes. She looked like some kind of sorceress. 'I hear you work at Adventurer's Supply?'

Skwee gulped. 'Worked. I think I'm out of a job.'

'That's good to hear.' The woman moved closer, kneeled down beside him, and caressed his tufty head. Her hands shook, her face was pale. He flinched away and tried to sit up. She pinned him down. 'Now now,' she cooed, 'Relax. We need to have a little chat.'

'Do we?'

'Yes, we do. You know something I want to know.'

'Do I?'

'What's your name, goblin?'

'Skwee.'

'Well, Skwee, why don't you tell me who your master is? I need to know how he makes Elixir. And soon.'

Now it was Skwee's turn to shake. 'I can't tell you that. I'm under a sworn oath, under penalty of...'

'A fate worse than death?'

'Yeah.'

'Would you like to know what's worse?'

Skwee tried to wrap his head around it, but it made his head hurt. 'Is that even possible?'

A sickly sadistic grin grew on Xenixala's face. 'Would you like the good news or the bad news?

'Good news?'

'I can't cast any spells right now.'

'Oh. And… the bad news?'

'I'm still *very* good at making people talk the old-fashioned way.' From her robe, she produced a small serrated dagger. She levelled it at his face.

Skwee swallowed and closed his eyes. He got the feeling he was about to find out what "a fate worse than a fate worse than death" actually meant.

34

Eric hurried down the alley and stopped against a wall, panting. Some unknown substance dripped on him from above. He wiped it off his forehead with his sleeve and looked up at the wonky guttering.

If only Daisy were with him. The thought that he would never see her again made his stomach hurt. Pull yourself together, he thought. You deserve to walk after what you let happen.

He stepped aside, then leaned around the corner into the light of the main high street. A group of bandits screamed and ran by, followed by a barbarian wielding two inhumanly large axes. Eric wouldn't even have been able to lift one of them.

Porkhaven was no stranger to random acts of theft and violence, yet this level of chaos was beyond anything Eric had ever seen. The streets were a mess of bodies and broken shop fronts. The air was thick with the taste of smoke and magic. The houses of Porkhaven had always been a misshapen sprawl, but now most seemed on the brink of collapse. A few were ablaze and others wobbled dangerously with the wind. Some locals were trying to prop them up with ladders and beams, while others emptied their worldly possessions onto carts, keeping a keen eye out for bandits and wild adventurers.

Eric hopped over a puddle of blood and ran across the open ground, keeping his head low. An explosion resounded nearby. Eric threw himself to the ground, bringing him nose to nose with the lifeless body of a bandit. The man's bandana covered most of his face, his eyes dull. When they hid their faces like that, they didn't seem like people anymore, just generic bad guys. Eric supposed that's why people didn't have such a problem killing bandits.

He stood up and dusted himself off, looking around to see what set off the explosion. He changed routes and dashed the opposite way. He wasn't taking any chances. Fortunately, he knew the streets like the back of his hand. But only his left one.

Eric backtracked and took the second alley out of the Alchemy district, towards the merchant quarter of Porkhaven where Freddy Glorp had his shop.

After two more detours and a few threats from an angry bard, Eric found himself at the Glorp & Co. Pest Control shop. Shattered panelling and beams lay strewn on the floor outside, revealing the shop within like a doll's house.

Eric heard the chuffer before he saw it. Rose's metal contraption huffed and whizzed as its hundreds of little legs scuttled across the rubble, bashing into three hapless bandits. They seemed to be enjoying the game of catch, taunting the young woman atop it.

'Come on little one, we won't 'urt ya!' spat a bandit, as he tossed his sword from hand to hand in an unnecessary display that presumably signalled his swordsmanship.

'*Yeah*,' sneered another. 'Give us your big metal bug and we won't lay a finger on you, bandit's promise.' Eric noticed the man had his fingers crossed behind his back as he winked at one of his cohorts.

'Get lost, the lot of you!' shouted Rose. She turned the chuffer around, and with a huge burst of steam, ran at one of them. The man stepped aside, laughing and raising his sword.

Eric strode towards the fray, puffing out his chest. 'Leave her be, boys. Move along.'

One bandit turned to him, eyebrow raised. 'Oh yeah? Says who?'

'Says me. Eric. Your new Bandit King.'

The bandits audibly swallowed and lowered their weapons.

'*You're* Eric?'

Eric raised his crossbow and levelled it at them. 'I shot off The Bandit Kings head with this crossbow only a few days ago. Want me to show you how I did it?'

The bandits exchanged glances, then one lowered his head and spoke. 'Sorry Eric, we was only having a bit a fun.'

'That's what I thought. Now run along, grab your loot and go back to your hideout to fence what you've already stolen. I'm sure you've got more than you can carry anyway.'

The bandits nodded and hurried away. They didn't look back.

Rose beamed at Eric. 'You're back!'

Eric went over to the chuffer and patted it on the side. The metal was surprisingly warm. 'Let's just say I'm in need of an apprentice.' It wasn't as if he had much of a choice. He needed all the help he could get, even if that help was from someone who utterly betrayed him.

Rose jumped down and smiled at him. 'You're the big lump, Eric.'

Eric cleared his throat. 'Things have been a bit… hectic since you left.'

'You're telling me. Freddy's livid.' She sighed. 'I should never have agreed to work for him. Now I'm stuck in this contract and I have to put up with all his tirades.'

'Doesn't surprise me. He always did have a temper.' Eric explained everything. How the bandits had killed Daisy. How he'd killed the Bandit King and accidentally started the riots. How he'd somehow ended up saving a goblin and a witch who were both convalescing in his house. How he was some kind of Chosen One and how he'd inadvertently inspired adventurers to hunt endlessly for Experience.

'Yikes,' said Rose once he was done. 'So what are you going to do about it?'

'About the adventurers?' Eric tightened his fist. 'I'm gonna put an end to them once and for all. And you're gonna help me.'

Rose smiled back. 'Damn right I am.' She paused. 'Sorry about… you know. Spying on you and everything. I was only doing what I was hired for. I didn't really want to.'

'Let's put it in the past.' Eric tussled her head, but did it a little too aggressively, breaking the pristine hair bun. Rose pushed him away, shook her head and realigned her hair into its familiar shape. Eric looked back at the shop. A figure emerged from the dilapidated front, cowering. He walked towards them, head flitting in search of danger.

Rose sighed. 'Freddy.'

'Ah, Eric,' said Freddy, ignoring Eric's outstretched hand. 'Why am I not surprised to see you here, begging for a job?' Freddy whipped his violet cloak to the side in a flourish of belittlement, his golden locks remained motionless and smarmy face demanded a punching. Eric resisted.

'I'm here to stop the adventurers,' said Eric. 'Thought you might like to help.'

Freddy scoffed. 'I already tried that old boy. Didn't do much good, did it?'

'You mean you paid Rose to get me to do it for you.'

Freddy absentmindedly neatened his already perfect sleeves. Eric could see why he was in trouble, he must have spent the last of his coin on clothing. 'Precisely,' said Freddy, 'and look how that turned out. You were the only man for the job, a dragon slayer and adventurer yourself. And you even managed to keep the business alive after all these years. I knew I could never ask you to stop the adventurers, you'd need to be *coerced*.' He waved a gentle hand to the ruined street around them. 'But whatever you did doesn't seem like it worked. The adventurers are running amok. What can we possibly do now? We're both ruined.'

Eric scowled. Still the same old Freddy. 'How about you stop complaining and help us put an end to it once and for all?'

'And how on earth do you expect to do that?'

'We know who's behind this whole thing. A Dark Master is working with the Doom Bank somehow. We need to go after 'em.'

'Rose was babbling this nonsense as well.' Freddy stifled a grin. 'You *really* think a bank is behind all this? Don't be so absurd. Sounds like you've spent too much time huffing kobold dung. It's gone to your head.'

Eric clenched his jaw. Freddy had wanted him to waste all his time and resources solving the problem with Rose while he lay around. Then once adventurers were out the way, Freddy would swoop in and put him out of business. Typical Freddy.

Eric knew it was a lost cause. 'Have it your way, Freddy. But I'm taking Rose with me. And her chuffing thing, too.'

'Chuffer.' Rose chimed.

'Yeah, chuffer.'

Freddy rolled his eyes and waved a dismissive hand. 'Take her for all I care. In fact, she's still contractually obliged to me to sort out these adventurers, so I suppose you could call this *win win*.' Freddy laughed and patted Eric on the back. Eric flinched at his touch. 'She's been the bane of my life ever since she's been back. She won't stop going on about all your adventures. It's been exhausting. Good riddance I say.'

'We're agreed then,' Eric looked down at Rose. 'Assuming you *want* to come and help me?'

Rose grinned. 'It's the least I could do after what I did.' She scrambled up onto her machine and pulled down her goggles. 'Ready when you are.'

Eric looked up. 'Can I get a ride?'

'I *thought* you hated Western enchantments?'

'Desperate times call for desperate measures.' Eric winced, hauling himself up onto the great mechanical carapace. The bronze was smooth and he began to slide across over the other side. He slapped his hands harder onto the metal, making them squeak with friction as his stomach lurched. His face flushed, and he avoided looking at the inevitably smirking Freddy. Instead, he sat up while the chuffer lurched and moved down the street. It was a smoother ride than he was expecting. Especially as the thing had to clamber over so much debris.

Rose turned back and spoke loudly over the spluttering machine. 'What happened between you two? After the dragon?'

Eric squinted and waved a hand in a futile attempt to get the steam out of his face. Rose hadn't even offered him her goggles. 'Freddy ran off. Stole a good few things from the shop before he left too.'

'What a tool.'

'Yeah, quite a lot of tools.'

'I said, *what a tool*.'

'Oh. That too.'

Rose pulled a lever and the chuffer veered around a corner into anarchy. The street thrummed with bandits clashing with adventurers, rogues shot bows from up high, fighters spun their swords and wizards flung bolts of lightning. Such exaggerated displays of battle were being thwarted by the bandit's overwhelming numbers and basic ruthlessness. One group of bandits wielded a long wooden plank, ramming it into the twirling adventurers, knocking them to the ground. Eric was pretty sure they were aiming between the legs too. Rose pulled another lever and the chuffer sped up, dashing around the fights and making the brawlers fall aside in shock.

A moment later and they were back at the thankfully intact Beast Be Gone shop. Eric jumped down and let out a sigh. Motionless ground had never felt so good.

He went through the door and stopped dead in his tracks.

Skwee hung upside down from the rafters. The witch Xenixala stood over him like a cat toying with a half-dead mouse.

'Ah, Eric,' said Xenixala, without looking up from the squirming goblin. 'You're back. How did it go?'

35

Major Elementalist Xenixala of Xendor, Binder of Souls, White Princess of The High Castle and heiress to a small farm two miles west of Mudwell-On-Sea, stared at the plain-faced Eric. He stood in the doorway like a taxidermied trollop, mouth wide and motionless. Eventually, he spoke. 'What in hell's name do you think you're doing?'

Xenixala smiled and held up her feather. 'Just a little light coercion. Your little goblin friend here's been *most* helpful.' She looked Eric up and down. 'What are *you* doing? I suggest you close your gob before a blot-fly lays eggs in it.' He'd returned much sooner than she'd thought, he'd made it sound like he'd be gone for weeks. Xenixala was relieved. She could get Wordsworth back and be out of this dump.

Eric stormed over to the bound and gagged Skwee hanging upside down from the ceiling. 'Get him down right now, *witch*.'

Had Eric had some kind of a stroke? It sounded a lot like he actually valued a goblin's life. A goblin. Literal scum. A creature so evil it would rather piss on you than shake your hand. Eric was an odd man indeed and most unusual for a Chosen One. You would expect a boring peasant hero like him to be at least some kind of secret heir to the throne. In fact, that was how the current King ended up in power. The nobility had been furious when he showed up in rags demanding the whole kingdom bow to him.

Xenixala folded her arms. 'I've been feeling much better, by the way, thanks for asking.'

'But still magic-less from the witchbane I suspect.' Eric grabbed the ropes around Skwee's ankles and struggled with the knots.

'Which I'm still mad at you for *by the way*,' she said. She felt wretched. It was as if a part of her soul was missing. She was as helpless as her days before witching school.

'You are weak, Xenixala.'

Eric managed to get one foot free and began work on the other. 'Does this look like the face of concern?'

'If you mean concern for that wretched creature, then yes.'

Skwee fell unceremoniously to the ground with a thud and a yelp. Eric took off his gag and lifted him upright. 'You okay little fella?'

Skwee shook his head. 'Not really. But I've had worse.'

Xenixala clicked her tongue. 'It was only a little tickling.'

'Tickling?' Eric looked at her, incredulous.

'Okay and I stabbed him a bit too. But he's so scarred already it won't make any difference. He's just lucky I didn't use poisons.'

Skwee nodded agreeably. 'Probably true. The tickling was the worst part really. Stabbings are what I'm used to.'

'See?' she said, triumphant.

'How is that better?' Eric raised his voice. 'It's torture! Are you some kind of sadist?'

'A little,' said Xenixala with a shrug. 'But mainly I wanted information. You'll never *believe* what the little thing has to say for himself.'

'I don't care what he has to say! I'm trying to save the world from adventurers, not listen to goblins moan about their mean masters.'

A girl appeared in the doorway with the stance of a precocious teen, a lump of Westerner technology strapped to her back. Arrogant Westerners, thought Xenixala, just what this conversation needed. A tiny cloud of steam floated around the girl's tidy hair, she pulled a lever and the backpack stopped chugging. 'What's going on, Eric?' said the girl. Xenixala clenched her jaw at the infuriating accent.

'Ah,' Eric stuttered. 'This is uh, Xenik...uh.'

'Xenixala,' said Xenixala.

'Yeah, that.'

'Nice to meet you, I'm Rose,' said Rose, cheerily with a nod. 'Eric's Apprentice.'

Xenixala grimaced and ignored her.

Eric smiled weakly at Rose. 'I saved Xenixala here from The Flux. And I saved Skwee here from an Adventurer's Supply. It's all I could manage before the bandits started ransacking.'

Skwee sat up straight as if remembering he existed. 'And I greatly appreciated it, Master.'

Eric frowned. 'I'm not your Master.'

'But goblins always have a Master... or a very big goblin at least. So you are Master Eric.'

'No, I'm not.'

'As you say, Master.' Skwee bowed his head, his pointy ears flopping along.

Eric sighed. 'Well aren't we a merry bunch.'

Rose grinned and jumped with excitement. 'Will these two be helping us stop the adventurers then?'

The thought of getting rid of all the adventurers actually did appeal to Xenixala. She'll have all the Experience, and wouldn't have to deal with bards singing their nonsense, poncy thieves sneaking around and getting in the way, or clerics blabbing on about The Holy Mole. She could have every quest to herself and become the most Experienced adventurer of all time. Especially if she got rid of this Eric fellow in the process. The problem, however, was the Elixir. No adventurers meant no demand. Which meant she wouldn't be able to get it as easily. If at all. Her Experience gain would fall dramatically without Elixir.

She also needed to get out of this stinking shop. Her hands shook, she could feel the sweat dripping down her back, her mouth was dry. If she couldn't get an Elixir soon she'd scream. A plan began to formulate in her head. Perhaps these morons may be useful after all.

'Xenixala will be on her way soon,' said Eric with a sneer.

Xenixala tutted. 'I'll be on my way as soon as you give me Wordsworth back, you stubborn little man.'

'Here, take your damn book.' Eric thrust his arm into his Sack of Clutching, rummaged around and pulled out Wordsworth, who had been cruelly bound shut with twine. He tossed him at Xenixala, who set him free from his bonds.

'Ah, that's a relief.' Wordsworth's pages flapped with a sigh. 'You wouldn't believe the amount of junk in there. And the *stench...*'

'Now you know why I had to bind him,' said Eric.

Xenixala ignored his comment and put on her best persuasive tone. 'Actually... you're in luck Eric, I may be able to help you. Skwee here's been quite forthcoming on the adventurer craze. He worked as The Dark Master's personal assistant for a few days, didn't you Skwee?'

Skwee looked nervously between them. 'I shouldn't say... I've been sworn to secrecy...'

Xenixala rolled her eyes, 'Oh, come *on*. You literally just told me, it's too late to play coy. You only have one hope now, and that's to help us defeat your ex-master. Then he won't come after you with that fate-worse-than-death.' It had taken an hour of tickling to break Skwee. Xenixala was impressed at his resistance. Although his knobbly skin probably helped resist the tickles.

Skwee pondered on this for a moment. 'I suppose I hadn't thought about it like that.'

Xenixala felt a strong urge to stab the green thing again, somewhere squishy and painful. 'Go on then, tell them.'

'I... shouldn't,' Skwee whimpered.

Xenixala held up her feather. 'Do we really have to go through this again? *This* is your new master now, and he wants you to tell him what you told me.'

Eric leaned in and made no objections. In spite of his moral high ground against her interrogation methods, he clearly wanted to hear what Skwee had to say.

'Alright then,' said Skwee, resolute. He cleared his throat. 'My old master, The *Dark* Master... has a financial interest in adventurers.'

'This is about money?' said Eric.

'Of course,' Skwee continued. 'He says everything's about money for humans. He runs The Doom Bank, which in turn controls its sister companies Adventurer's Supply and Geiston & Geiston.'

Eric clapped his hands together. 'Geiston & Geiston are part of this! I always knew they were up to no good.'

'I don't understand?' said Rose.

'I'm a little unclear too if I'm honest,' admitted Eric.

Xenixala cut in. 'Basically, it's one big scam. This Dark Master gets adventurers to plunder treasure across the whole world, who sell it at rock bottom prices to Adventurer's Supply, who *then* sell the exact same junk back to the less experienced adventurers. When they die, they spend all their money on resurrections and buying even *more* loot.'

'Seems rather elaborate,' said Eric. 'How do Geiston & Geiston fit in?'

Skwee chimed up. 'There are properties everywhere that are unliveable because of creatures inside. Castles, caves, dungeons, temples, everything. The lords usually don't even bother declaring property taxes on them. Then once the adventurers have cleared them out, they have value again. And so Geiston & Geiston come to collect what should be paid to the crown, inflating the price with fake offers and valuations, taking a cut of the profits for themselves. They even seize the properties when the owners can't pay up. So now The Dark Master has nearly half the whole land. Then all of it can be rented out to monsters to live in.'

Eric sniffed and sat up a little straighter. 'The Doom Bank is about to take my shop too. With all that land he can proclaim himself a new ruler.'

Skwee continued, 'They do the same thing when an adventurer finds a family heirloom like an amulet, sword or ring, in a cave and gives it back to the owner, usually some farmer. The Doom Bank tracks the owner down and demands the inheritance tax. They can never afford the taxes, so the banks fines them, *and* takes the heirloom. Then they sell it back to the adventurers the very next day at an Adventurer's Supply.'

Eric scratched his chin in thought. 'Incredible.'

'Does The King know about this?' said Rose in disbelief.

Xenixala shook her head. 'I know him all too well. He's a buffoon. He'll be oblivious to the whole thing. Wouldn't know his breeches from his taxes.'

'That's true,' said Skwee. 'The Dark Master is also The King's accountant-slash-vizier. So he's the one really pulling the strings.'

'Wait, I met him!' exclaimed Xenixala. 'He was with The King when I went to the palace the other day.' She racked her brain. 'Is his name Darkius Doom?'

'I think so,' said Skwee, uncertain.

Rose started to pace up and down the shop, her backpack jangling with each stride. 'The Doom Bank sponsors the Guild, they're even training up the adventurers.'

Skwee nodded vigorously. 'Each part of the adventurer's "customer experience" is there to turn a profit. We train them up, get them hooked on expensive Elixirs and they won't ever stop. You can only buy Elixirs at Adventurer's Supply. They're made exclusively inside The Doom Bank HQ here in Porkhaven, and only The Dark Master knows the secret recipe.'

This was the part Xenixala had been most interested in. This monopoly The Dark Master had created was a stroke of genius. But Elixirs were a particularly cunning touch. She needed that recipe, and The Dark Master was the only one who knew it. If she could start her own business selling it, she would be richer than ever and would have an endless supply of Elixir to herself. She smiled at the thought.

The Dark Master would surly be a worthy advisory. If she defeated him, perhaps she could be the best adventurer there ever was.

Skwee continued, 'Problem is, the craze went too far, there weren't enough places left to be adventured. So The Master had to make new dungeons, ones that magically refresh, breeding monsters for slaughter, forcing bandits out on pointless raids, even making fake quests that had no end. It got out of control.'

'So what you're saying is, he's weak.' Eric furrowed his brow. 'The bandits destroying every Adventurer's Supply shop would have been quite a blow. Now's the time to strike.'

'Great!' said Rose, jumping up and down. 'So what's the plan?'

'That's a good question.' Eric looked at Skwee. 'Where is this Dark Master?'

Skwee seemed to flinch at the thought. 'He lives inside the Doom Bank's flagship store in Central Porkhaven. My old home.'

'He even *lives* in a bank.' Eric smiled. 'Doesn't get much more evil than that.' He stopped, then pointed to the mirror in the corner. 'I have an idea. Larry?'

Xenixala had been very aware that the mimic had been there the entire time, and was not surprised. She also knew that unless provoked directly, mimics were far too scared to do anything but remain hidden and out of trouble.

Larry burst into life, hopping from corner to corner, somehow defying gravity as a rectangle. Xenixala wondered if he did fall, whether he would shatter.

'What's up?' asked Larry, through a small mouth shape in the gold detailing at the top of his frame.

'I've got a plan,' said Eric. 'Although you're probably not going to like it…'

36

Skwee looked up at the foreboding building he once called home. Now it somehow seemed like a strange and oppressive place. The walls were simple thick-cut blocks centred by a vast door blocked by two guards. Above it, in a large, no-nonsense font, the words Doom Bank were embossed and punctuated with their signature pink skull logo.

Skwee pulled the lever on the chuffer, just how he'd been told. The confusing machine stopped moving and went quiet, giving him a moment to think. He didn't like this plan one bit.

Behind him, the chest whispered, 'I hope you know what you're doing.'

The two goblin guards blocking the door came towards the chuffer with confused looks on their faces.

'*Please* be quiet, Larry,' said Skwee, voice low.

'Is that you Skwee?' said one of the guards in the unmistakable high-pitched goblin tone. For the life of him, Skwee couldn't remember the goblin's name, and he suspected his life was indeed on the line.

'It is,' said Skwee with a smile trying to conceal his trembling lips. 'I've got some treasure here for The Master. Including this lump.' Skwee kicked the chuffer with his heel. It probably would have hurt quite a lot if he hadn't lost most of the feeling in his legs from all the torture. 'I got this off a Western adventurer a few weeks back.'

'Weren't you placed on Shopkeep duty?' The guard's eyes narrowed.

'Um.. well yes… but there aren't exactly shops left to keep now, so I grabbed the most valuable stock, to go back to the treasury.'

'Those damned bandits.' The guard shook his head. 'Alright. You know where to go.'

Skwee wiped the sweat from his brow and pulled a lever. The chuffer lurched forward and into the darkness of The Doom Bank.

37

'Don't kick me!' came Xenixala's voice in the darkness. 'That's my leg.'

'It's *not* me,' Eric insisted.

Eric felt like lashing out, anything to get out of this hellish box. There was barely an inch to move. His breath was short, and the air tasted stale.

'Sorry, I think that's my claw,' said Rose.

Something wet stroked Eric's back. 'Larry are you *licking* me?'

A wave of light and freshness gushed over him. Silhouetted was Skwee's unmistakable pointy ears. 'Quick,' Skwee said quietly, 'Come on out.'

Eric, Xenixala and Rose stumbled out of Larry's open lid, panting and dripping with sweat.

Xenixala gave Eric a dirty look. 'That was you making those smells, wasn't it?'

Eric wafted his overalls, taking deep breaths. 'Of course it wasn't,' he lied. 'Larry, were you salivating?'

Larry shuffled back. 'You humans are quite delicious, and you were sitting right in my mouth!'

'Shhh,' hushed Skwee, finger to his lips.

'Sorry,' Eric lowered his voice. They were in a long vaulted room packed full of wooden crates and boxes. He could only imagine what lay within them. The Doom Bank must have access to all kinds of riches.

'If you don't mind...' said Larry in chest form, his lid flapped as he spoke. 'I'll hide here and guard the chuffer?'

Eric rolled his eyes. 'Larry, I wouldn't expect anything less.'

Larry's lid turned into a sort of grin, then he bounced over to a stack of boxes beside Rose's chuffer and went still. He blended in surprisingly well.

'What are we actually going to do to this Master?' asked Rose.

'Kill him,' Xenixala scoffed. 'Obviously.'

The sorceress looked dangerously pale, and she clung to her spellbook as if it gave her magical protection. The last of his Flux remedy would be wearing off by now, and she'd be going into withdrawal. There wasn't any more Elixir, so she didn't have much choice. The best thing he could do for her now was to keep her mind off Elixir with the mission. She would probably be quite useful if she could resist vomiting and actually cast some spells. Although they probably wouldn't be that effective with all the witchbane he'd been feeding her. It wouldn't entirely leave her system for another few weeks.

'Surely we're not *actually* going to kill him?' said Rose. 'Just send him to jail or something?'

Eric hadn't thought that far ahead. He assumed he'd be able to talk The Dark Master out of what he was doing. Either way, he decided to load his crossbow. 'We'll cross that bridge when we come to it.' Eric turned to Skwee. 'Which way to The Master's office?'

Skwee nervously twiddled the hem of his Adventurer's Supply uniform with one hand. 'It's right around the corner. There'll be a few guards, but we can knock them out with a quick bash on the head.'

'What do you mean, knock them out?' said Eric.

'You know, bash them on the head.' Skwee mimed it. 'So they're unconscious for a bit.'

Eric tutted. 'That could kill them. Do you know how damaging a concussion can be? It could leave them a vegetable, or worse! *No* murders if we can avoid it. I've got a few sleeping spores, we can use those if we have to.' He turned to the group. 'Right guys, I'll lead, and Skwee, you come behind me and point the way. Xenixala, you guard the rear.'

Xenixala sighed. 'Whatever.'

'And try to stay quiet,' said Eric. 'We don't want to alert the guards. Skwee says they'll mostly be downstairs in their nests about this time, but there may be some wandering about.'

The gang, which verged on being an adventuring party, nodded in unison.

Skwee pointed to the end of the room. Eric took the lead and crept over to the doorway, opened it slowly and looked around the corner. There was no one there. He waved, and the others snuck along behind him.

The walls of the corridors were thick with soot and odd scratches. Eric identified them as a demon's marks. From the looks of which, the claws seemed to have been trimmed, so it would have been a domesticated creature. He shuddered at the thought. Perhaps this wasn't such a great idea after all. His finger tightened over the crossbow trigger.

They reached a junction and Skwee pointed to the right. Eric nodded and looked around the corner to be safe.

He nearly dropped his crossbow in shock.

Walking towards them was Sylvia, the interior designer. Her neat pink frock barely moved as she glided along in her heels.

Eric turned back to Rose and whispered, 'It's Sylvia, I know her! You know her! You met after we did the kobolds for Lord Egglewort. Remember? She could help us.'

Finally, someone with a bit of sense. She'd understand, she'd know what to do. Perhaps she could tell them more about this Dark

Master. She must have been remodelling the horrible interiors for him.

'No, Eric!' Rose whispered back. 'Throw a sleeping spore. You don't know...'

But Eric didn't hear the rest. He strode up to Sylvia with his crossbow lowered. She stopped dead in her tracks, mouth agape.

'Hello, Sylvia,' said Eric. 'We need your help.'

Sylvia looked over the top of her pink, crescent-moon shaped spectacles. 'What on *earth* are you doing here, Eric?'

'We're here to stop The Dark Master. He's been causing the adventuring craze all along! So you're here redesigning his bank? Not a bad gig. I'd start with trying to make it look a little less evil...'

Sylvia tutted. 'Oh, poor innocent Eric. I'm redesigning everything.'

'Everything?'

'I wouldn't expect you to understand, darling. I've got a good thing going here. You're not going to screw it up. Guards!' she hollered with surprising volume. 'Guards!'

Eric froze, stomach in his throat. 'Quiet!' he pointed his crossbow at her, and she obeyed. Rose jumped around the corner, her backpack whizzing, metal arm outstretched for a fight.

'What are you doing?!' Eric hissed at Sylvia.

'What I have to,' she replied with a wave of a hand. 'Do you know how much work I'm getting from renovating what the adventurers destroy? It's a dream come true. The Dark Master is the best thing that's happened to me, and I'm richer than you could imagine.'

'This... is about money?'

'Everything's about money, darling.'

A clamour came from both ends of the corridor. A sea of goblins appeared, all wearing matching uniforms smattered with pink skulls. They scurried towards them, brandishing pikes, daggers and pointed teeth.

'Uh, Xenixala,' said Eric, his voice failing him. 'Now would be a great time to use your magic... maybe a freeze spell or something?'

There was no response.

'Xenixala?'

'I think she's run off,' said Rose, defeated. Sure enough, only Rose and Skwee were beside him, cowering from the circle of steel.

'Ah.'

Skwee fell to the floor, sobbing.

Sylvia grinned, towering over the wall of goblins with her hands on her hips. 'Oh, poor Eric, it has been nice knowing you.'

She clicked her fingers, and the goblins descended on them.

38

Keen Magiker Xenixala of Xendor, Light Bringer of The Dark, Dark Bringer of The Light and known by many as a woman who arrives exactly when she means to, strode along the passageway, head held high, Wordsworth under her arm. She was confident of where she was going, as she'd been through evil overlords' palaces like this a hundred times before, and they all had the same basic layout. They'd probably hired the same architect. Bland, torch-lined walls, endless corridors to nowhere, rooms with no discernible purpose, a distinct lack of windows, and most importantly, severely linear circulation routes. She followed this particular route to the right and into a gloomy antechamber with three doorways.

Having finally shaken Eric and the other losers, she could get on with her real quest. Finding Elixir. During her interrogation, Skwee had said they manufactured it somewhere on this floor but had been uncertain on specifics. She sniffed the air. When in doubt, always follow your nose. A wizard had told her that a long time ago, right before he'd had the misfortune to stumble into the mouth of a honey dragon. The door to the right had the unmistakable aroma she was looking for. Acrid tang and spicy bitterness. Elixir. She'd know it anywhere.

The smell brought up a burning desire inside her. Her stomach turned in knots, sweat dripped down her back, but the thought of getting her hands on Elixir filled her with vitality.

'I will not accept failure in this classroom, Xenixala. Drink another poison. The class will wait until you finish every drop.'

She flipped her wrist at the door. But it didn't move an inch. She tried again. Nothing. She cursed under her breath.

'Terrible wrist technique. I knew you were worthless.'

'You know,' said Wordsworth. 'You could push the door open with your hand.'

'Like a barbarian?' Xenixala tutted. 'Don't be absurd. I can do it, I'm just... not feeling my best right now.'

'If you're not the best, you are the worst.'

Wordsworth muttered something about being lucky to have arms at all, then went quiet.

Eric had filled her with his cheating antimagic, and it was ruining her. What he'd done was a crime against humanity. He acted like he had the moral high ground, yet he'd stripped her very essence, her power. They deserved to face this Dark Master alone. She didn't care if they stopped him or ended up killing themselves. It was all the same to her. So long as she had her Elixir, she'd be fine. And with the recipe, she'd be unstoppable. She needed to be the best, no matter what.

She concentrated, drawing up the energy from within. Focus. The tingling began in her chest and crept into her fingers. Usually the sensation of magic came so fast she didn't even notice. But now it felt thick, like tree sap oozing out of her. The door wiggled and clicked open.

Xenixala grinned. 'See?'

Wordsworth ruffled his pages. 'Xeni, do you ever wonder if we've had... too much Elixir?'

Xenixala stepped through the now-open doorway, it led to another generic corridor. 'Don't be daft.'

'I've had a lot of time to think while trapped in that bag of Eric's. And, well,' he paused. 'Maybe we failed to defeat The Chosen One because…'

'Eric?'

'Yeah, Eric. You think that we failed to defeat Eric because Elixir jaded us?'

Xenixala's heels echoed as she paced down the corridor. 'Not possible. Elixir makes us stronger, gives us more Experience.'

'So does bedding a man, but you've seemed to have given up on that front.'

'Priorities, Wordsworth. Priorities.' She had considered bedding Eric, but his bland face made her reconsider, even if he did have a certain unkempt charm.

'If what the goblin says is true,' said Wordsworth carefully, 'Then Elixir was invented by this Dark Master to make adventurers addicts, and not to help them, so maybe it's been weakening us this whole time.'

'Once I get the recipe, we can modify it to be less addictive and more potent.' Xenixala licked her lips. 'Problem solved.'

'Perhaps we're better off without it?'

Xenixala stopped dead and looked down at Wordsworth. 'What?'

Wordsworth's spine quivered. 'I mean, you know. We did so much better before we had our first Elixir. Don't you remember the good old days? Back when it was just us, no big parties lumbering along. All these new adventurers have slowed us down. Made us lazy, complacent.'

Xenixala didn't know what to think. But he was right about one thing. It had been better before. 'And you think this is because of Elixir?'

'Not only Elixir. Everything. Our quests and adventures have become so bland. The Dark Master has drained the fun from adventuring. He's commercialised it, taken its soul for profit. Remember the days where we would be happy to stroll alone up a mountain just for the fun of it?'

'I do.' She quickened her step.

'Now we're only content with flashy deaths and explosions. Fast raids, the same thing over and over. A quick fix, unchallenging and repetitive. Subdued with Elixir and thirsty for blood and action. Numbing our mind and soul.'

Wordsworth was starting to be a real downer. She forced him back under her arm and carried on walking. 'Oh, shut up. What does it matter? I'm happy. We're happy.'

'Are we?' he said, muffled by her armpit. 'I can feel what you feel and I don't feel much anymore.'

'I knew you were worthless.'

Xenixala ignored him. Before her was a metal doorway, its bolts coated with green rust. It smelled of heaven. The source of all Elixir must be right behind it. She was so excited she actually opened the door with her hand.

Her senses went into overload. Every part of her tingled with the fever of Elixir in the air. It was electric. It was wild. It was beautiful.

Before her sat a gigantic iron vat at the centre of a cavernous chamber. The container hummed and glowed green. Pools of stale Elixir wallowed on the floor. Goblins ran to and fro in funny tunics, carrying all sorts of ingredients, bottles and boxes. Thousands of empty Elixir vials ran down a metal contraption towards the vat in the centre. Nobody seemed to notice her.

Wordsworth shuddered in her arms. 'The source of all Elixir,' he murmured. 'What a sight.'

'Indeed,' said Xenixala. Her heart raced. 'You, minion!' she called out to one of the goblins, who pointed to himself. 'Yes, you, come here.' The goblin's ears drooped submissively and he obliged.

'Wha-wa-what can I help you with, mistress?' whimpered the goblin, head bowed.

Goblins were so pathetic. It was no wonder they were so easy to enslave. They'd believe anything a human told them. It was like they wanted to be taken advantage of.

'The Master sent me. He wishes to see the recipe for uhh, Elixir.'

The little goblin scratched the back of his tufty head. 'I don't understand mistress… doesn't he already know it?'

'He forgot.'

'Oh.'

'Yeah, so give it to me. Or he'll be very mad, and it's a fate worse than death for you.'

The goblin's eyes went wide. 'Oh, crikey. Righto. Come this way.' He led her over to a noticeboard on the side of the vat. On it were a series of crude drawings.

'That's it?'

'Why, of course.'

'What language is that?'

'It's not a language mistress. It's drawings to explain what we need to do to make Elixir. We can't uh… read.'

Xenixala rolled her eyes. 'So why don't you tell me what it says.'

'Right you are.' The goblin looked intently at the board. 'The first picture of four elderberries, that means four parts elderberry. Then two parts witchbane, seven parts boiled flumbut root, a dash of honeyworm, and a sprinkle of powdered drake bone.'

Xenixala already knew that based on her research, aside from the elderberries that were clearly there for taste. 'Yes yes, I know all that, what's that last part, the bit with the red drop?'

'Oh, but The Master would surely remember that part.'

'Tell me.'

The goblin gulped. 'That part is a secret known only to The Master.'

'Really?'

'Really.'

Xenixala sighed. 'Looks like we'll have to pay this Master a visit then Wordsworth. Let's hope those fools haven't killed him already.'

Wordsworth jiggled in her arms. 'Let's not be hasty Xeni… how about we treat ourselves to an Elixir first?'

'Excellent idea Wordsworth.' Xenixala dashed over to one of the stacked boxes with a potion painted on the side, then pried it open. Dozens of bottles stared back at her, glinting.

Down they went. One after another, the glorious tang sliding down her throat, burning its numbness from the top of her head to the tips of her toes, lightening sparkling on her tongue. It made her feel alive. It made her feel power. Another, and another. The box was almost empty, dizzying joy and flavour. There were thousands of bottles. Maybe she could stay forever, drinking straight from the source. Maybe she would finally be happy.

She reached for the very last vial in the box, but a firm hand planted itself on her shoulder.

'Do you know who I am…?' she said, turning around.

The vial in her hand shattered onto the floor.

It couldn't be.

'Hello, *witch*,' said Edwardius, a knowing smile on his face. Behind him stood Felina, who looked equally smug. 'Long time no see.'

39

Skwee let out a sigh. It was strangely good being back home in The Master's lair. It felt safe, comfortable somehow, even if it did mean being locked up with his funny human friends. The cell was rather spacious by his standards. A human could nearly lie down, and the hay was at least a month fresh and had hardly gone mouldy at all. Plus the gruel the jailor had thrown on the floor had been rather tasty. Although Rose and Eric had been too snobby to lick it up, they didn't understand how much worse it could get. They should have considered themselves lucky.

It hadn't even been a whole day, and the humans were already going insane. Rose whimpered, trying to get as far as she could from "defecation corner", while Eric paced back and forth endlessly, muttering and grumbling. Every now and again he would rattle the iron bars on the door, but they wouldn't give way, and he'd get himself flustered.

Skwee knew there wasn't anything he could say to cheer them up. He wasn't used to humans at all and hadn't the foggiest idea of what they were thinking. Talking had usually ended in beatings from his old masters, so silence seemed to him to be the best option.

After an exceptionally long streak of silence, Eric tutted. 'I can't believe Xenixala abandoned us like that.'

Rose sat up. 'I can. She hates us, you can tell. Of course she'd save her own skin. By now she's probably a hundred miles away with my chuffer.'

'No,' said Eric gravely. 'I know where she went.'

'Where?'

'To find some Elixir.' Eric rubbed his temples, seemingly in some deep head pain. Humans had such weak skin. 'She's an adventurer, so she's addicted. This is where they make Elixir, and with Adventurer's Supply gone, it's the only place she can get it. She'll be no good to us now, even if she wanted to be, which she doesn't.'

'I can't believe you trusted her.'

'I trusted *you,* didn't I?'

'Exactly.' Rose laughed and shook her head. 'You're far too trusting, Eric. Look what happened with Sylvia.'

Eric rolled his eyes. 'Sylvia was a friend, how was I supposed to know she'd gone bad?'

'It's obvious! She had bad written all over, just like Xenixala.'

'What does that even mean?'

Rose groaned and stood up. 'Eric, you know everything about creatures and nothing about people.'

Eric raised his voice and pointed a finger. 'And you ain't nothing without your gadgets neither.'

'That may be, but you need to calm down.'

'How am I supposed to stay calm when I'm stuck in prison with someone who betrayed me like you did?'

'I said I was sorry!'

'No you didn't!'

'Alright, *I'm sorry.* Happy?' Rose slumped back down to the ground. 'I didn't have a choice. I know it was wrong, but I didn't know you back then and I needed the money. I really do want to stop adventurers.'

Eric thought about this a moment. 'Apology accepted.'

Rose got back up and opened her arms. 'How about a hug?'

'What? No.'

'Go on.'

Eric winced and let Rose hug him. Skwee thought he saw him smile, but it was gone so fast he wasn't sure.

'I'm not used to seeing you without that lump on your back,' said Eric as they parted. 'It wouldn't make hugging easy.'

Rose backed away and leant against the wall. 'It's a shame they took everything, my backpack could get us out of here, no problem.'

Skwee had been rather impressed by all of Rose's trinkets. He'd never seen anything like them. Something about steam was rather thrilling. Maybe it was the constant danger of being scalded that excited him.

Eric went over to the door and rattled the bars yet again. 'Still nothing.' He sighed and poked his head through the gaps. 'So close and yet so far.'

'What do you mean?' said Rose, looking up.

'They've left our stuff on a shelf right in front of us and no guards to keep watch. Probably to be annoying.'

Skwee nodded to himself. That was indeed the policy.

'Of course! What am I thinking!' Rose leapt up, bouncing with newfound energy. 'My pack is thought-activated!'

'Thought what now?'

'Thought activated. How else do you think I control it? It performs hundreds of advanced commands. Did you think a couple of levers could control all that?'

Eric scratched his chin. 'I guess I hadn't thought about it.'

Rose went over to the door and squeezed her tiny head through the bars, standing on the tips of her toes. 'I can see it! Here goes nothing.' She made a barely audible clicking sound with her teeth, then quivered with concentration. She let out a moan and took her head away from the door. 'It's not working. It's too far.'

'Try again,' said Eric. 'What have we got to lose?'

'They could punish us with a fate worse than death?' said Skwee, and judging by how they both looked at him, immediately realised he'd said the wrong thing. 'Or, you know, cut off our skin.'

Rose shuddered. 'See? Quite a lot.'

'Well, at least give it another go,' said Eric. 'It didn't look like you were even trying.'

'I was trying!'

'Oh yeah?'

'Yeah.'

'Well I reckon you're too scared,' Eric spoke with a malicious tone. 'You'd rather stay here and feel sorry for yourself.'

Skwee felt like Eric hadn't said the right thing, but wasn't too sure why.

Rose drew an intake of breath. 'Oh, forgive me for being scared. We're gonna have our skin ripped off!'

'Listen to me, Rose.' Eric went over to her and took her by the shoulders. He stared into her eyes, speaking calmly. 'We're going to stop this Master no matter what. Got it?'

Rose looked sheepish. 'How can you be so sure?'

'Because…' Eric hesitated, then sighed as if his realisation was in some way painful. 'It's my destiny. Or something.'

'Because the sorceress said you're the Chosen One?'

Eric nodded. 'She knew things, and there was a rhyming song and everything. But more importantly… It felt right. If you know what I mean.'

Rose smiled. 'I do.'

Skwee thought this was rather a touching moment. Suddenly his eyes seemed to be leaking, he wiped away the liquid from his eyelids and made a mental note to find a shaman to check his eye holes as soon as possible.

Rose went back to the door and put her head through the bars again. This time she grunted as she tensed, her whole body poised.

'Come on,' Eric said with the kind of encouraging tone a goblin warlord uses on his minions before a battle. 'You can do it.'

Rose trembled, pushing herself even higher onto her toes. She yelped. 'It's working!'

A faint hiss came through the door, then a pattering and scraping sound. There was a clunk.

'Step back,' said Rose. A pointless statement, given the size of the room.

The clunking grew louder. The three of them pressed themselves against the wall.

There was a crash as the door flung off its hinges.

Skwee exhaled. The door had landed right beside him, inches away. Steam billowed in, which dissipated to reveal Rose's backpack, arm outstretched and cocked like a swan's neck.

'Well I'll be damned,' said Eric.

Rose high-fived the metallic claw, turned around and let it crawl onto her back. The straps flipped into place automatically, and soon she was her usual half-mechanical self. She beamed at Eric. 'Now let's get this son of a harpy.'

* * *

Yet again Skwee found himself leading the humans towards his Ex-Master's chambers. Down another passage, left turn, stay quiet, right turn. Screams echoed in the distance, followed by dull groans. Judging by their tone, Skwee figured it must have been about two o'clock, toenail plucking followed by lunch. He knew precisely which corridors had the least foot traffic and was sure to take these routes. He didn't want to repeat his last mistake. But if Eric wanted to go and talk to anyone again, this time he'd know to run the other way as fast as he could.

Eric fondly fondled his Sack of Clutching as he crept along. 'I can't believe they just left all our gear on a shelf right in front of our cell.'

Skwee put his fingers to his lips. They needed to be more careful, and silly mindless talk was not careful. They turned another corner.

There was The Master's door. It was tall and dark, with hundreds of expensive-looking human skulls sculpted into it. Each painted pink.

'Here we are,' said Skwee, hushed. His heart pulsed so hard his ears throbbed. 'It's two o'clock, so Master will be having his brooding time. He'll have dismissed the guards for an hour or two.'

Eric raised an eyebrow. 'How handy.'

The Master spent most of the day brooding, looking out over the city with his fingers to his lips. Considering his immense power, it was odd that he needed guards at all. Skwee suspected they were mainly to make him feel less lonely while he had his tea.

Skwee turned to face his friends. 'I'll watch the door and make sure no one comes in. I'll tell anyone who comes that The Master's having a nap.' There was no way Skwee was going back into his Ex-Master's chambers. Not only would the memories be too painful, but he still valued his skin. And besides, he wasn't sure what more he had to offer. 'Oh, there's something you should know...'

Eric looked at him, concerned. 'What?'

'The Master, um… he's quite… powerful.'

'What?' Eric and Rose said in unison.

Skwee put his finger to his lips again.

'What?' Eric and Rose whispered in unison.

'Now you tell us!' said Rose, hoarse.

Skwee shrugged. 'I thought you knew. But it's just occurred to me that you don't.'

'I was kinda counting on Xenixala's magic for this.' Eric had already returned to his signature indifference. 'We've come too far now.'

'You're right about that.' Rose pulled the lever on her backpack. The claw whizzed harder than ever. 'Kinda feels like we're on an adventure don't you think?'

'Unfortunately, I suppose it does.' Eric spat on the ground and lowered his crossbow. 'Now's the time for me to embrace my title.'

They smiled at each other.

Skwee figured that meant they were ready, so he reached up to the door. His little green hand shook as he rapped against the obsidian panelling, giving the code that signalled The Master's tea was ready.

'Enter,' came a booming voice.

Skwee turned the handle shaped like a severed demon's fist and strained to push open the door. 'Good luck,' he whispered to the humans and hopped aside.

The humans both gulped, then stepped into The Master's chambers.

Skwee closed the door behind them and wiped the sweat from his brow.

Why did he get the feeling that this was all a terrible mistake?

40

General Spellmaker Xenixala of Xendor, Translator of The Scrolls of Knowledge, Mistranslator of The Scrolls of Oversight and founder of The Noticeboard Society, backed away. Surely her mind was playing tricks on her? Was it from drinking all that Elixir at once? That must be it. She hadn't had any in days. It must have gone to her head.

But they were too real. There was no denying it. It was them.

'What are you doing here?' said Xenixala to the all-too-familiar paladin and bard. The fresh Elixir she'd drunk was like nothing she'd had before. She could already feel it racing through her.

Edwardius frowned, his armour glinted in the low light of the Elixir factory. The machines continued to thrum in the background. 'We could ask you the same thing.'

Felina drew her little pixie daggers and glared at Xenixala, saying nothing.

'I assume you're still trying to get this Dark Master?' said Xenixala.

Edwardius puffed out his chest. 'Always, for it is our quest, our purpose.'

Xenixala rolled her eyes. 'Me too.'

'Is that so…?' Edwardius stroked his chin with a gauntleted hand. It couldn't have been comfortable. 'I know we've had our differences… but perhaps we could join forces?'

The tiny Felina exploded, which looked so adorable it made Xenixala stifle a laugh. 'After what she did to you? To *us*?!'

'We need all the help we can get my sweet,' Edwardius cooed. 'We know how powerful he is! Does the Holy Mole not teach us to forgive?'

'Not for things like *that*,' spat Felina. 'She's pure evil. The Holy Mole tells us to destroy evil.'

Xenixala grinned at her. 'Good luck with that.'

'I'll have your head off, *witch*.'

Edwardius held Felina back with ease while she thrashed towards Xenixala.

Xenixala kept Wordsworth ready just in case. The electricity in her veins tingled with power. A small part of her considered his offer. Perhaps they *could* defeat this Master and restore some sanity to the land. Maybe she *was* better off without Elixir. But those thoughts dissolved into the wave of joy that licked her senses.

'How'd you get here then?' she asked. 'Followed me?'

Edwardius let Felina go, and she went straight into a fighting stance, breathing heavily.

Edwardius put his hand on his sword hilt. 'The Nuub showed us to another Chosen One,' he said. 'Who'd had a vision about The Dark Master and how we could find him. We've already wiped out the castle minions, and we're looking for his study. If you can't join us, perhaps you could tell us where it is?'

She still needed his secret ingredient. 'I do, but I won't. He's all mine.' Xenixala smirked. Right behind them was a door labelled *The Master's Study*. Her hands no longer shook, her head light and free. She felt like she could take on the whole world.

'It's like that is it?'

'It is.'

'In which case, you leave us no choice.' Edwardius drew his mighty sword. 'It seems as though you are evil after all.'

'That's what I've been saying this *whole time*.' Felina finally smiled, brandishing two daggers. 'I'll enjoy this.'

The pair charged, swinging their weapons.

A green haze fell across Xenixala's vision. The world seemed to slow, like it was the first time she ever tried Elixir. She remembered it like it was yesterday. The perfect sensation. Bliss. Wordsworth snapped open.

Fire rained down from her lips, she was at one with the magic, at one with the power. Electricity toppled from her fingers, wrapping pain around her victims.

She breathed deep, letting the air fuel her destruction.

Goblins ran in all directions, as the room became alive with brimstone of her own making. A haze of devastation. All her hate, all her resentment poured out of her. She pushed forward, forcing the magic harder, bending it to her will. Wind and flames flew, blood spattered her face, some green, some red. Metal and Elixir erupted from the machines, the great vats disintegrated, whipped into the wind, flying in the air.

Further, harder, more. Wordsworth laughed. She laughed. Tears of joy streaming from her eyes.

She would show them her power. She would be the best.

The room was bright. Sheer light.

Then darkness.

Then nothing.

41

Eric held his breath. This was it. Time to be the hero he never wanted to be. Do it for Daisy if nothing else.

He stepped into The Dark Master's chamber, and Rose followed, her backpack hissing as if it were afraid as well. He couldn't stay mad at her forever, what good would that do them now? There was a job to be done, and she was almost all he had left. He was startled by something surging through him that he'd never felt before. A fatherly feeling. He frowned and focussed back on the room.

At the far end, a man sat behind a desk while a fire crackled beside him. He wore a cloak that collected on the floor, with a banker's tunic and a pink skull shining out from a pin on his breast.

Eric found himself surprised by how tasteful the furnishings were, sleek and minimalistic, very impressive craftsmanship. For a split second, he thought about asking The Master who his carpenter was.

The man, who was presumably The Master, looked up, drumming his fingers against the wood. 'What *is* it?' he said, wearily, before pausing. He stared more intently at Eric and Rose. A grin crept onto his face.

Eric kept his gaze fixed on the man who had caused him so much pain, so much torment over the last twenty years. The man who destroyed the land and every living thing in it, big or small.

The Master stood up and clapped. Slowly at first, then faster, never breaking eye contact with Eric. Eric shuffled his feet but refused to look away.

The Master stepped away from his desk and walked towards the pair, his claps echoing around the chamber. He stopped not ten feet away.

'Eric and Rose.' The Master spoke in a patronising tone. He smiled, baring dagger teeth that jutted through his pointed features. 'How I've looked forward to meeting you.'

'Likewise,' said Eric, his fingers tensed over the crossbow trigger.

'Eric, ever since you defeated my lich, I've been watching you. I should thank you, really. Now my minions can no longer be dispelled, repelled or expelled. Trickery can't stop my underlings any more.'

'You're welcome.' After Xenixala's spying shenanigans, Eric had resigned himself to the idea that, as a Chosen One, there were probably quite a lot of people who knew what he had done or would do. Although the thought of wizards watching him on the loo still made him shudder.

'You've been quite the thorn in my side Eric. These bandits have been most *inconvenient*. You've nearly cost me my entire operation.'

'I figured it would have.'

'You see, my plan was *perfect*, Eric. Would you care to hear it?'

'Not really.'

'I used to be an alchemist, all those years ago. But so few people wanted my masterful healing creation, *Elixir*. I tried to sell it to the military of course, a potion to increase your power with every kill, while keeping you alive! It was perfect for war. But of course, there was far too much peace in the world.' The Master sighed. 'The King laughed at me when I tried to explain it to him all those years ago. Then an alternative practically fell into my lap. The war on creatures. Adventuring. It was perfect, and people were already desperate to do it. All it took was an inspiring tale of a man becoming the most *Experienced* adventurer.'

Eric swallowed hard.

The Master continued, 'Naturally, I had to tweak the story to make it seem more *grand*. Said it was a great knight who slew Grenden the Elder Dragon, that sort of thing. I created demand, a burning hunger for power. All they had to do was keep killing and keep drinking. Elixir sales grew and grew.'

Eric looked down at the weapon he pointed at The Master. Maybe if he blamed the actual crossbow for slaying the dragon he wouldn't feel so guilty.

'To begin with I borrowed money from the bank, but soon I had enough money to *buy* a bank. We invested in or bought up companies dealing with everything to do with adventuring, from tax collectors to castle renovators, from goblin breeders to sword smiths. Then we pushed adventuring across the globe.'

'We already know that bit.'

The Dark Master twiddled his moustache. 'Everyone got a cut. Everyone got rich. It wasn't long before Adventurer's Supply took off too, and we were selling addictive potions, expensive resurrection stones and enchanted helms.'

'Yeah, we kinda figured it out.'

'Adventurers went out and *found* loot for us! Then they sold it back at a rock bottom price, and we sold it to the next adventurer for double what we bought it for!'

'One of your minions told us everything.'

'But things got out of hand. We were too successful. There were too many of them. We needed more dungeons, more quests, more mentors. We've invested untold sums filling caves with invincible goblins, resummonable undead and rejuvenating demons. As soon as they die, they return to life, ready to be slaughtered again.'

Here was a man who liked the sound of his own voice. 'Why are you telling us this?'

'That was until *you* came along Eric Featherwick.' The Master snapped. 'You and your bandits destroyed all my shops and sent my operation into colossal debt.'

'Serves you right.'

'For what?'

'For *murdering* countless innocent creatures.'

The Master scoffed. 'I gave people hope, and a welcome release from their miserable lives. I give people escape. I give people freedom! Who would want to be a farm boy or shopkeep when they could be out slaying monsters? I am *saving* people, Eric. The King enslaves them into servitude. I am breaking their shackles of oppression.'

'*I* wanted to be a shopkeep.' Eric jabbed a thumb at himself. 'You've just given them a new kind of suffering. And you destroyed the natural world while you were at it.'

'Perhaps, but now they *choose* it. And that makes all the difference.' The Dark Master stepped a little closer. His voice went softer. 'Why don't you join me? I need able men like you to manage my countless creatures. You'd be richer than you could possibly imagine.'

'Never.'

'A pity.' The Master clicked his tongue. 'It's a new world. You're too late. To undo my work would only bring chaos. What good would come of stopping me now?'

'The satisfaction would be more than enough.'

'The satisfaction will be all mine.' The Master's lips twisted into a smile. 'I've prepared a special treat for you, Eric. Although I was hoping it would wait until it was fully formed, I wasn't expecting you to escape from our dungeon like that. I'm impressed. It's a shame, this will make an awful mess of my study.'

The Master snapped his fingers. A low rumble sounded at their feet. Rose yelped and leapt to the side. Eric steadied himself on a column.

A crack split the floor, thundering and splintering the floorboards. It exploded, wood flying. Eric dove to the ground as a gigantic scaled beast rose through it. The Master clambered onto its neck, then beamed down at Eric and Rose.

A dragon. A ruddy big dragon.

Its pale, gaunt face was riddled with sores and horns. Pus oozed from its scales, a faint glowing hue circling its ragged wings. Somehow it looked oddly familiar. It couldn't be.

'Remember Eric?' The Dark Master shouted with delight. 'Remember... Grenden?'

'No,' Eric spoke under his breath. 'That's not possible.'

'Everything's possible with a bit of dark magic, Eric. I have a great many necromancers making all sorts of creatures for me. This

Elder Lich Dragon is the first of its kind. I thought it would be a poetic way to enact my revenge.'

The dragon opened its maw, teeth bared. A blaze of white fumes blasted towards them. Eric and Rose leapt to the side, the breath so cold it blistered their skin.

Eric rolled on the floor. His arm felt like it was on fire. He clenched his teeth and got to his feet. This was no time for crying.

The dragon turned its long neck towards them, dripping ectoplasm across the floor.

'Rose, get back!' Eric cried.

Rose's backpack raced into action, forcing a jet of steam out from its base. Rose shot across the room, just in time to evade another wave of frost.

An undead frost dragon was not what he signed up for. It even smelled the same as all those years ago, sulphur and blood, now combined with a rotten icy overtone. Eric decided they were very much in over their head and escape was reasonable. But when he saw the door behind them, his heart sank. It was now a sheet of thick ice, blasted by the dragon's breath. They were trapped.

The Master cackled, rubbing his hands together. 'You can do better than that, Eric. Come on, at least *try* and defeat me! I *dare* you. For you see, you're only the most Experienced *adventurer*. Not the most Experienced *person*. For every time someone gains Experience with Elixir, *I too* gain some of that power.' He laughed again. 'You don't stand a chance against me!'

Eric thrust his hand into his Sack of Clutching and rummaged. It came to his hand in an instant. He smiled and pulled out the Greater Dispel Undead Scroll. He read it out loud. It had to be with confidence, that was key.

'*Lichus disspellus magicum exlodus!*'

Nothing happened.

Maybe he read it with too much confidence. He tried again as the dragon inhaled for another wave of ice.

Nothing.

Rose propelled herself at the beast. She flew through the air, mechanical arm whizzing and slicing. She landed on its back, her arm thrusting into the creature's decomposed flesh. The robot arm crumpled, crushed by the thick skin. The dragon swept a mighty claw, batting her away like a fly. Rose's robot arm barely worked enough to cushion her fall.

The Master stroked at his goatee atop the beast. 'Not bad Eric! Not bad at all, but not good enough. You can't use your silly dispels this time, no tricks. I had him thoroughly protected from your nonsense.'

In a rage, Eric fired his crossbow. The bolt hit the dragon's skin and rebounded. It clattered pathetically to the ground. Deep down, he knew it wouldn't work, but he had to try. He had one last option.

Back into The Sack of Clutching. This time a stone came to his fingers, Spirit Stone, Level Ten. He'd never had to use a level this high before. They didn't even make them higher than ten. Or at least not that he'd seen.

He held the stone high, brow furrowed as he channelled its power.

There was a flash of light and a high pitched wail. Energy exploded from the stone towards the dragon.

The smoke rolled away, revealing the dragon's teeth. Eric could have sworn it was grinning. Dragons didn't even have lips, so he knew it wasn't possible, but by The Mole that dragon looked smug.

The Master sounded like he could barely breathe through his laughter. 'I told you, Eric!' He wiped away a tear. 'Your tricks are no good now. Why don't you try to be an actual adventurer?'

As much as he hated to admit it, The Master was right.

He needed to do both. Pest control *and* adventuring.

Time to set up a trap, the dragon needed to be subdued. That's what father had taught him, although that advice had got him killed.

Eric scanned the room. Rose hid behind an upturned table while the dragon breathed a barrage of ice at it. Frost mounted up behind the wood, creaking and cracking.

He needed Rose. 'Quick, come here!' he called to her. She saw him and nodded, running over, her backpack bobbing limply. They both ducked behind a pillar, panting.

'Do you have your bombs?' said Eric, hopeful.

Rose nodded, her face pale. 'A fat lot of good they'll do. We're dead.'

Ice blasted the pillar behind them. It rumbled in complaint.

'I've got a plan,' said Eric quickly. 'Trust me?'

'Always.' Rose smiled and handed him three bombs. They were perfect spheres, glistening gold. 'That's all I have. What are you thinking?'

'We need it sedated, that's what I did the last time. Then his eyes will droop. That's our target.'

The pillar continued to hold but was now a creaking block of frost.

Eric produced a secret ingredient he hadn't used in many many years, dragon sedative. He wiped it over the bombs and handed one to Rose. 'On the count of three,' said Eric. 'One, Two… Three!'

They ran from cover, just as the pillar shattered, bringing down a good bit of the ceiling too. They hurled the bombs, which exploded into a bright white smoke. The dragon roared, rearing its head back.

Rose and Eric ran forward. This was it - last chance.

The dragon's eye was red, lid droopy. The smoke had left a fine blue crust over its face. The dragon writhed in pain, but Eric knew it wouldn't last.

He raised his crossbow, putting a foot forward. He focussed on adventurers, on the ravaged land, on the massacred kobolds, the betrayals, Old Ted, Wise Wally, The Bandit King and Xenixala.

But most of all, he thought of his father.

He pulled the trigger.

The bolt flew.

It hit the dragon dead in the eye. Eric tried not to smile, but he couldn't help himself.

With an ear piercing shriek, the dragon disintegrated into a mass of bones and pure energy. Skin fluttered into oblivion, and the creature was no more. The Master, however, had landed on the ground unscathed.

Eric spat. 'That was for Daisy.' The Master looked at him, speechless. Eric raised his crossbow and pointed it at him. 'Now you're going to come with us. Real slow like. No funny business.'

The Master just smiled and raised a hand. 'That was only for *fun* little Eric.' He tutted. 'Did you think you stood a chance? I told you, I'm the most *Experienced* man alive.'

A jolt of pain hit Eric in the chest. The air rushed from his lungs. Choking, he fell to the floor, trying to draw breath.

Faintly he heard his Master's speak as he loomed over him. It was distant like he was in another room.

And it felt an awful lot like a fate worse than death.

42

Top Wizardess Xenixala of Xendor, thinker of ideas, visitor of places, and owner of countless pointless accolades, awoke to the sound of a muted crash, her mouth rank with the taste of bile and Elixir. She sat up, face throbbing. The factory was now a flattened mess of metal and dried chemicals. Goblin corpses littered the floor, along with a decapitated Edwardius and eviscerated Felina.

Those poor holy fools. Why couldn't they have just left her alone?

One problem solved at least.

Although it created another. Elixir was well and truly destroyed. No one would be making it any time soon. Perhaps this was what she needed, a chance to rid herself of its clutches once and for all. Maybe.

She stood up and rubbed her temples. She'd had burnouts like this before. But her head had never felt like this. It was like a disgruntled ogre had decided to live inside her ear and refuse to leave.

A soggy Wordsworth leapt into her arms. 'I feel like death Xeni.'

'Tell me about it.'

'Where to now?'

'The Master's Study, I suppose.'

'You know the way?'

'Probably through that door labelled, Master's Study.' She pointed at an ornate doorway painted pink.

'Oh yeah.'

A thundering came from the direction of the door, followed by screams.

'Sounds like quite the commotion,' said Wordsworth. 'Let's not miss the fun.'

Xenixala went over and opened the door with a flick of the wrist. She strolled through and stopped at the sight.

In the huge study, an undead dragon evaporated into the air, unsummoned. A poncy-looking man, who must have been The Master, said something, then raised a hand. A spell flew towards a boring-looking fellow and a woman with a metal backpack. They both crumpled to the ground.

Poor Rose and Eric, they never stood a chance.

Xenixala cleared her throat, the man in the cloak whirled around. 'Who are you?' he said

'I'm known by many names.' Xenixala smiled thinly at him. 'But you can call me Xenixala. You must be this Master everyone's making such a fuss about.'

'The very same,' said The Master. His voice oozed false charm. 'I recognise your name. You were the one to topple the tyrant of Threndalfal?'

Xenixala nodded. 'The very same.'

'To what do I owe the pleasure?'

'I need the recipe. Give it to me, and I'll let you live.'

'What recipe, may I ask?'

'Don't play dumb,' said Xenixala, tutting 'Elixir's secret ingredient. I need it. Now.'

The Master's laugh echoed throughout the chamber. 'I'm afraid you cannot have what you seek. For you see, the secret ingredient is *my own blood.* I gain Experience from every kill when Elixir is in your belly. You think you stand a chance against me? I'm more *powerful* than you can imagine!'

Xenixala didn't know if she should laugh or cry. It was so perfect. No-one could steal the recipe. No one could replicate it. And the world needed him alive. Although if she did kill him, she could gain a lifetime's worth of Experience. She would be the best adventurer there ever was. The best witch there ever was. The best everything.

'If you ever want Elixir again,' The Master continued, 'you'll have to let me live. And as an adventurer, I'm sure that you do. Leave, I'll get back to making it, and you'll have your precious Elixir again. It's very simple.'

Everything could go back to the way it was. The way before Eric meddled with her fun. Before she ever knew about this wretched Chosen One. She thought back to how adventuring was before Elixir, how it had been about the joy of the fight, the thrill of discovery and pride in the kill. Now it was a meaningless grind, an endless search for more and more Experience with no end in sight, subdued and numbed with a potion that controlled her. No one controlled her. No one. Never again.

'I have a better idea.' Xenixala flipped open Wordsworth.

'So be it.' The Master stood tall, face blazing red. A wind circled him, lifting up his cloak. He pointed a finger at her, and spoke in a deep, hypnotic tone.

Finally, the battle she'd been waiting for.

She was too fast for his simple incantation. His magic bounced off her counterspell with a flash of sparks.

But he'd already cast another, she only just had time to duck as the fireball raced by.

Xenixala chanted, '*Libris Floaticous Maximus*,' and the words lifted from Wordsworth's pages, turning in the air, swirling larger and larger. In a moment they spread across the entire room, twisting in a whirl of confusion. The Master spun his head, frantically searching the floating words. Xenixala let out a hearty chuckle. She ran in as words parted before her, a tunnel of spells ready for her taking. She plucked one from the air, tossing it at the man.

He caught the word in his hand. He grinned, then flung it back.

It hit her flat in the chest, sucking the wind from her. She fell, mumbling the counterspell, knowing exactly which word it was that had cursed her. He was powerful indeed. Maybe a little too powerful.

Her head pounded. Concentrate.

The Master began charging a larger spell. It glowed in his fingertips as the ball of energy grew.

Her pain grew too. She needed Elixir. She needed its power, she felt like death. Her hand moved to the pocket in her robe, feeling an unmistakable lump. One Elixir left.

She jumped aside, dodging a shard of ice and pulled the last vial from her pocket. She hesitated. This could be the last one she'd ever taste. She'd better enjoy it.

Hold on. That was it. His blood was in the potion.

'Wordsworth,' she said, countering another ball of energy flung from The Master. 'Find me a connecting curse, quick.'

'On it,' said Wordsworth, pages fluttering. 'Page three-five-two.'

It was unusual, but it could work. She wove her fingers over the Elixir, reading the curse, forcing her will onto it, lashing the energy of the nearby Master. She drove her loathing into the green liquid, her salvation, her disgust, her agony.

'I will not tolerate failure in this classroom.'

Professor Mogg appeared in her mind. The poisons she'd made Xenixala drink. The punishments. The pain. Her peers laugher and mocking.

'I knew you were worthless.'

She muttered the paladin's prayer she'd learned from Edwardius. That felt like a lifetime ago.

'If you're not the best, you are the worst.'

She hurled the vial at The Master.

He caught it.

The world stopped.

The Master laughed, looking down at the Elixir. 'Are you trying to *heal* me?' He crushed the vial in his hand.

Blood showered in all directions.

The Master was no more.

All that was left was a red puddle.

Xenixala wiped her face on her sleeve, shut Wordsworth and breathed out a deep sigh. She stared down at her long-since ruined robe. There was no use worrying about that now.

She stood for a moment, taking in the scene of debris and blood. Somehow, there was a serenity inside of her. A silence. As if the voices from the past had evaporated.

Snapping back to life, she bent down, scooped up a splash of red goop into a vial, tucked it in her belt and went over to Eric and Rose. She muttered an anti-freeze charm, and the pair burst into life, gasping for air.

They looked around, confused.

Xenixala!' Eric exclaimed, standing up. 'You came back for me... I mean, us.'

'Sure,' said Xenixala. No need to tell him the truth, it would only get the poor man riled up.

'Thank The Mole!' Rose exclaimed. She leapt over to Xenixala and hugged her.

Xenixala felt a strange warm tingling sensation, not unlike Elixir. She patted Rose on the back, which clunked her hissing backpack. 'Don't mention it.'

Eric narrowed his eyes. 'Where's The Master?'

Xenixala gestured to the bloody mess on the floor. 'You're looking at him.'

'Ah, guess that's it then.'

'Yeah.'

'Just like that.'

'I suppose so.'

Eric shrugged. 'So, what now?'

'Well,' said Xenixala with a sigh. 'I'm going to go and lie down. My head is killing me. Then I'll drink my weight in beer.'

'Sounds like a good plan,' said Eric. 'And after that?'

'None of your business. What about you two?'

'Likewise.'

'Alright then.'

'Alright.' There was an awkward pause. 'Well,' said Eric, expectantly. 'You know where to find me if you have any problems with the... you know.'

'The Flux?' Xenixala shivered. 'I'm sure I'll be fine.'

Eric looked a little disappointed. 'If you say so.'

Xenixala produced a Scroll of Town Portal from her bag. 'See you around.'

Eric looked around at the debris. 'Aren't you going to loot the room? You are an adventurer after all.'

'Nah,' said Xenixala. 'I have everything I need.' She read her scroll aloud and disappeared into a puff of smoke.

43

Eric glanced around the throne room, the ornate finery turning his stomach. One of those tapestries could feed a thousand mouths, but instead, they hung on a wall gathering dust, merely to titillate lords who'd forgotten they were there. It reminded him a little of The Dark Master's chambers, all those weeks ago. Although his memory was a bit hazy on the whole thing.

The King looked them up and down as they approached. Eric, Rose and Skwee moved painfully slow on account of Eric's limp. Each step was agony, but Eric bit his lip and carried on. He couldn't make a scene, not in front of The King and his court.

The crowd on either side roared as they passed by, which had been incessant all the way through the streets of Porkhaven. The whole thing seemed over the top. He wasn't even the one to actually *kill* The Dark Master. It was probably too late to bring that up now.

They reached The King at the end of the procession, stopped, then bowed just like they'd been shown that afternoon. The fanfare stopped, and the crowd went blissfully silent.

The King cleared his throat. He was only a little man, compensated for with bushy whiskers. Eric felt sorry for all the crimson jackfloofs that had to die to make his cape.

'Ah my heroes,' he began, whiskers twitching. 'Thank you for ridding the land of this Dark Master. I can't believe he was under my nose this whole time, Darkius Doom. My vizier-slash-accountant. Who would have thought?' He tutted and shook his head. 'Although I must admit his goatee was a little suspicious. What a terrible beast he was, profiting so much from all this mess.'

Eric didn't fail to see the irony of The King's statements, considering he hadn't worked an honest day's work in his life. The taxes on all the adventuring would have made him plenty of coin too.

'The land owes you a great debt Eric, Rose and Skwee,' The King continued, 'Now things can go back to the way they were. Farmers and craftsmen will be adventuring no more. In fact, adventuring will now be strictly regulated. Anyone found adventuring without a permit will be executed.'

The crowd cheered, and Eric, Rose and Skwee bowed again. Eric winced standing back up, his leg complaining. The fight with The Master had been far too much physical activity for his liking.

The King placed wreaths around their necks, and the crowd made a final cheer. The King then stood up and beckoned them into a side chamber. The crowd's excitement became muffled as the thick door closed behind them.

Rose, Eric, Skwee and The King were alone. The antechamber was a miniaturised version of the grand hall they had departed.

The King slumped into a plush armchair. 'Ah that's better, take a seat. We can speak candidly now.'

Eric followed The King's lead and plopped into a comfy looking settee. Rose remained standing, and Skwee sat on the floor with a vacant look on his face.

'What a mess, eh?' said The King. 'We've finally managed to round up the last of your bandits. Thank you for talking to them like that. For some reason, they really listened to you.'

Eric nodded. The bandits seemed surprisingly keen on leadership hierarchy. As the new Bandit King, they did whatever he told them. Some people yearn to be led.

He couldn't wait to go home. No more of this attention. No more fanfares. A warm fire and a tasty whisky. Was that too much to ask for? But no, he had to be paraded around like a hero. He'll never hear the end of it. His eyes darted to the door. Maybe he could sneak out while The King wasn't looking.

'They've all agreed to become part of The Royal Army,' The King continued. 'Which amounts to the same degree of murder and theft, only it's against our enemies, so they seemed quite pleased with the idea.'

Eric was sure that a large amount of the newly armed bandits were still at large. But he didn't want to dampen The King's excitement.

'Also,' said The King. 'Lord Egglewort spoke very highly of you, Eric. He seems to be claiming that this was all his idea and that he should be greatly rewarded. Is this true?'

That certainly sounded like Lord Egglewort. 'I suppose so.'

'Alright, then. And uh…' The King hesitated and looked around. 'And what about your other *companion*?'

'You're sitting on him.'

The King shrieked and leapt up as his chair came to life.

'Nice to meet you,' said the chair. 'My name's Larry.'

The King shook. 'What in the name of The Holy Mole?'

'Larry's a mimic,' said Eric. 'He helped us too.'

Larry did a kind of bow which involved bending his legs in an odd angle.

'Oh,' said The King, hand on his chest, wheezing. 'A pleasure Larry, although that wasn't the companion I meant. I was wondering about…' he gulped, 'Xenixala The Sorceress.'

'What about her?'

'Where did she go? I was informed she helped defeat The Dark Master too.'

'Sure, she helped a little,' said Eric. 'But I ain't seen her since. I think she wants to be left alone.'

'Ah,' The King sighed with relief. 'Probably for the best.'

Eric was also quite relieved to have Xenixala out of his life too. She was the very definition of chaos, even if she did have her own sort of charm. A small part of him hoped he might see her again, but he pushed those thoughts deep down.

'Well then,' The King clapped his hands together. 'Time to discuss your reward. Luckily enough, the crown's coffers are positively brimming with gold at the moment. So nothing is off-limits. What'll it be?'

'The honour alone is enough,' said Rose with a bow. 'Although I could do with some upgrades to my machines.'

'I'll have my engineers take a look at once,' said The King. He turned his attention to Skwee on the floor.

'I'm not sure I'm allowed things,' said Skwee, surprised at being given any attention. 'I'm a goblin.'

The King nodded. 'That's true. Alright then, your reward is that you are henceforth allowed to have things. Um, here, have this.' He fished something out of his pocket and handed it to Skwee.

Skwee beamed.

The King turned to Eric and looked at him expectantly.

Eric rarely knew what he wanted in life. Most of the time, he concerned himself with simply avoiding what he *didn't* want, and that was most things.

Now he wanted to be home. Back with all the things he'd had to pawn off. Back when he didn't have any debt. Back to clearing out dungeons the good-old-fashioned way. Back to riding Daisy lazily to the next job. Back to enjoying a good beer in a bad pub. Back to how things were all those years ago.

At that moment, he knew exactly what he wanted.

'I want everything to be back the way it was,' he said resolutely.

The King smiled. 'Consider it done.'

44

Skwee hopped down from the chuffer and looked up at the fort before them. He did a little wiggle of satisfaction with his landing, then turned back to his friends.

Rose slid down from the chuffer too, and Eric dismounted his new donkey, a gift from the royal stables that he'd named Maisy. Both steeds had freshly painted *Beast Be Gon*e banners draped across them.

'I've missed this,' said Eric. 'Feels like I haven't had anything to sink my teeth into in a lifetime.'

The fort loomed a shadow across the clearing. Vines crept up the sheer stone walls and down over the gate that lay shattered on the ground. From the darkness within, a series of tiny figures appeared, their ears unmistakably pointy, their weapons unmistakably blunt.

'Hello there friends,' Eric called out to the concealed goblin horde. 'Your Master's long gone, so there's no need to run and hide any more. I have many relocation programs and work schemes here for you.' He waved the pamphlets in his hands. 'The King has offered all goblins immunity with co-operation.' Eric held the crossbow in his arms ready, which seemed excessive to Skwee. But Eric insisted that goblins had a thing about power. He'd said it with such conviction that Skwee felt a surge of excitement.

There was a murmur from the darkness of the doorway.

Skwee stepped forward. His heart raced, his mouth dry. It was time to prove himself to his new Master. He held The King's toothpick aloft with pride. 'Comrades!' he called out theatrically. 'I too was a minion, so I understand what it's like. I know the fear and pain. But it's pointless to keep up his scheme when he's dead. There will be no "Fate Worse Than Deaths". Throw down your weapons, join us and finally be free!'

Eric nodded with approval. It had taken almost two hours for Skwee to memorise the speech the night before. His tone and confidence still needed a little improvement, but Eric had said it was an excellent start for a junior apprentice.

A spear hurled its way from the darkness. Rose leapt into action, her repaired robot arm whizzed. Skwee opened his eyes to the spear caught a few feet from his face.

'Thanks,' he murmured.

'Don't mention it,' said Rose with a wink. The golden claw snapped the spear and discarded it. Rose pulled some kind of metal ball from her belt and held it ready.

Eric levelled his crossbow at the dark doorway. 'Looks like we're doing it the adventuring way after all.' He smiled and pulled the trigger.

EPILOGUE

The Great Witch Xenixala of Xendor, Vanquisher of The Dark Master, Defeater of The Nuub and founder of the new Xenilixor Health Tonic, tossed the last of her ale over the man tied up in a witchwood chair before her. The man awoke, spluttering.

'Wha...?' mumbled the man who used to be called The Master. His tragic goatee dripped as he frantically looked around Xenixala's study. 'Where am I?' Or at least that's what he was trying to say. It came out more like. 'Uhh am ehh?'

Xenixala smiled. 'Is that really important? You're in the tallest tower of my impenetrable home. I wouldn't worry any more than that.'

That was when he noticed his fingers. Or lack of them. He wailed and writhed, pulling desperately against the bonds that held him to the chair. He screamed through his tongueless mouth.

Xenixala hushed. 'Quiet, you're only going to tire yourself out.'

The man didn't settle, so she sent a small spark his way. He yelped in pain and stopped, panting deeply. He glared at her with a fire in his eyes. She found it quite pleasing.

'I'm sure you remember me,' she said. 'So let's cut to the chase. You're here now, and there's nothing you can do about it.' She strolled over and took him by the chin, savouring how he flinched away. 'There'll be no spells coming from you... not after my little *modifications*.' She looked down at him. 'No tongue and no fingers. There isn't a magic-user in the world who can invoke after that.'

The man still wore his old tunic, now coated in dried blood. It was disgusting. She'd probably have to find him a sack to cover him up.

'I still need my Elixirs *Master*,' she continued. 'And nothing will stop me. Do you understand? *Nothing*.'

The man stayed silent. Sweat gleamed on his face.

'But now I have your blood, the final piece of the puzzle I've been looking for all these years. An endless supply of Elixir. All for me. I'm even going to sell some of it. Then I'll have more money than I'll know what to do with. Thanks to you.'

He mumbled something and she patted him on the shoulder.

'But I'm not a monster, I'll give you plenty of the supply to ease the pain. If you behave, of course.' Xenixala pulled back his head and poured an Elixir into his mouth. Half of it dribbled down his face as he gargled. Then she produced an ornate gutting knife and held it up to his eyes, which went wide. 'Don't forget, I can resurrect you. Again and again and again. Unlimited money and Experience. I'll be more powerful than an Elder Dragon by the time I'm done with you.'

Finally, she'd be the strongest adventurer in the world.

His screams echoed around the room. He writhed so hard he kicked over one of the collection buckets on the floor.

Wordsworth, who sat on the table beside them, stuck out his bookmark and ran it along his pages. 'Time for another Elixir. It's been a while.'

'No time to waste then, eh?' said Xenixala as she plunged the knife into the man's left kidney.

THE END

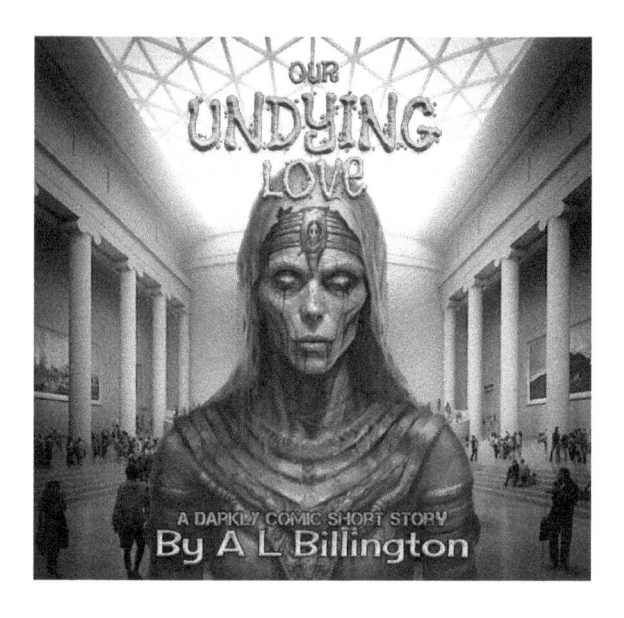

Want More Comedy?

Get A **Free** Short Story By A L Billington:

OUR UNDYING LOVE

"Jeremy was in love with Queen Ninatutu the Third. Ever since he saw her on his first day at work those twelve-and-a-half glorious years ago, he knew he was in love. Unfortunately, she didn't love him back. How could she? She was dead..."

As a thank you from Billington Publishing, we would like to offer you **free** access to **Our Undying Love,** A L Billington's short comedy horror story.

Simply go to **BillingtonPublishing.com** and sign up to the newsletter. Enjoy!

ACKNOWLEDGEMENTS

I would like to royally thank the following delightful people for all their proofreading efforts and support, as they had to endure this book at its worst.

In alphabetical order so they don't get jealous:

Dr Andrew Billington, Henry Billington, Sangeeta Bhatia, Renee Brandson, Nick Holloway, Cheryl Lanyon, Asher Macdonald, Elena Makarenko, Assaph Mehr, Alex Newman, Dr Richard Newman, Scott Rhine, Caroline Robertson, Victoria Rose, John Taenzler, Peter Thomson, Emma Van Straaten, Nicole Williams and Andrew Youngson.

Billington Publishing

If you would like to get in touch, please email us at:
info@billingtonpublishing.com

ABOUT THE AUTHOR

Who is A L Billington? Some say he is just a myth, a phantom, a whisper on the lips of a kindly gentleman. Or maybe he's just some bloke with access to a word processor and too much time on his hands. Who calls them word processors these days anyway? Turns out A L Billington is old enough to use the term 'word processor', yet only ironically, which should tell you exactly how old he is. He's also the one writing this bit, so it's very strange that it's in the third person.

In case you were wondering, the 'A' stands for Arthur, and the 'L' stands for a secret that he'll never tell you unless you get him drunk at an awkward party.

Anyway, you all have access to your own word processors, so you can look him up using the magic of the internet. He's the cheeky chap who set up 'Billington Publishing' (in case you hadn't made that connection based on the narcissistic naming), therefore you can find his updates at *billingtonpublishing.com*.

Well done! You actually read this last boring bit. Does anyone actually care about the acknowledgements and this sort of nonsense? It's just a list of names, so I suppose it's a bit like watching the credits. In a way, this silly bit is like the bonus at the end of a Marvel film. What I'm trying to say is that this book ought to be as famous as Iron Man 2.

Please tell your friends it's better than Iron Man 2.

AUTHOR REQUEST

Can I ask you for a very small favour? Would you consider leaving a review on Amazon and/or Goodreads? It's very simple, you just need to log onto Amazon, click on your name at the top and go to your orders page.

If you are reading this on Kindle, at the end of this book, Amazon will display a "Before you go" section, asking you to "Rate this book". Please spare a second to simply click on the stars to rate it.

Your feedback is important to me, and will really help the book get noticed!

Many thanks!

A L Billington

ERIC AND FRIENDS WILL RETURN!

Here is a sneak peak from the sequel:
BEAST BE GONE - UNDEAD DON'T DIE
Available now at an online retailer near you!

-

Skwee the goblin retched for what felt like the thousandth time. Even though death was a stench he was strangely familiar with - an occupational hazard of having worked for numerous Dark Lords. In his last career as a minion, there had rarely been a moment that he hadn't witnessed some kind of blood, which, on a good day, wasn't his. However, this smell was somehow a *lot* worse. It was death, but somehow fresher, almost as if it had been repackaged into a scented candle.

Eric, Skwee's newest boss and all-round-lovely-human, had given him a peg to put over his nostrils. However, as Skwee's goblin nose accounted for about half of his face, the peg uselessly sat atop the bridge of his snout, wobbling back and forth as they stalked through the cave, providing no relief from the smell. Because Skwee had to devote so much time to balancing, he could barely watch out for zombies. It had been very kind of Eric to offer him the peg, so Skwee hadn't had the heart to tell him it was pointless. Therefore, Skwee continued his acrobatic act while desperately trying not to throw up in the zombie-infested cavern. This was especially important after Eric's stern warnings about bodily fluids attracting the undead.

'... and even snot.' Eric continued as he led the way through the cave's darkness, followed by Rose, his young human apprentice. A metal contraption, which Skwee still didn't entirely trust, chugged on her back, emitting a steady flow of steam. As they walked, their torches flickered through the many stalagmites-and-or-tites, casting ever-changing shadows. The cave was silent apart from their footsteps and the ever-dripping dampness leaking through millennia of geology. The trio each wore matching overalls and white shirts, all were faded and patchy from attempts to purge the disgusting splashes that their work attracted. Emblazoned on their chests were the words:

"Beast Be Gone - Adventuring Pest Control"

They were the first ever company in the land of Fen-Tessai to combine Adventuring with Pest Control. After squashing the rampant outbreak of Adventurers (a story so long and winding you could have written a whole book on it, according to Eric), Beast Be Gone had gone from strength to strength (again, according to Eric). Skwee wasn't so sure that their new method of Pest Control was much different from what they'd done before, but Skwee hadn't been around for that part, so he had to take their word for it. The main difference seemed to be that this time, they had a backup crossbow if the traps and repellent didn't work.

'Why are we here again?' Skwee whispered, glancing at a particularly spooky rock feature. He shivered as a breeze passed, making his long ears stand to attention and feel even colder in the process.

'We've been through this, Skwee.' Eric sighed. 'It's your classic zombie infestation. The King wanted this cave cleaned out for a soon-to-be profitable mining operation.'

It was difficult for Skwee to notice any defining features in Eric. It was confusing enough that all humans looked alike. But Eric looked as if the features of every other human had been blended together to make him. His wispy brown-smattered-with-grey hair, however, would be highly desirable to the average goblin, as well as the patches sprouting from his ears, arms and neck. Unfortunately, he was stocky in a way that goblins weren't. His arm was probably about as wide as Skwee's whole body, and his hands were bigger than Skwee's entire head.

Rose chimed in. 'So keep an eye out for clues that might lead us to the necromancer who controls them.' The peg on her freckled nose made her Western accent even more nasally, to the point that Skwee thought she sounded almost goblin, which he found oddly reassuring. She was short for a young human but made up for it by having a lot of opinions. Skwee wondered how long her dark hair would be if she ever let it down from the bun she always wore. 'Stop the necromancer and we stop all of his or her zombies.'

Skwee was still confused but decided to stay quiet so as not to cause a fuss. He just enjoyed being included.

A cold hand gripped his shoulder. Skwee smiled. Finally, his mentor, saviour and boss had decided to give him the physical contact he so desperately craved.

Although come to think of it, Eric and Rose were quite far in front of him.

'Eek!' he screeched, stumbling away.

A figure loomed over him, arms outstretched. Strips of flesh dripped off its body, clothes tattered and grey, its skin as pale and green as his own. The thing was the opposite of alive.

Skwee turned and ran.

He collided with Eric and, being half his height, went headfirst into his stomach. Instead of fleeing, Eric simply chuckled to himself and shook his head.

'Don't worry, Skwee,' he said, lowering his crossbow. 'Just watch.'

There was a *whoosh*, a *thunk*, a *groan* and a *thud*.

The zombie lay motionless on the ground, a crossbow bolt protruding from its head.

'Nice shot,' said Rose.

Rose pulled a lever on her backpack, producing a mechanical arm that simmered in the torchlight. She described her backpack as "standard issue" in The West, where she was from. The arm whirred, reached toward the newly corpsed corpse, then plucked the bolt from the mush - and handed it back to Eric. Eric winced, wiped the bolt with a rag - and put it in his bag with the others.

'Waste not, want not,' he said.

Rose tutted. 'Such an Eastern expression. In the West, we say: *Waste not, why not*?'

Eric ignored her. 'This is today's first lesson: always aim for a zombie's head.'

Skwee didn't understand. Surely, everything dies when you hit it on the head. He'd learned that the hard way when he got his first pet rat. 'But why… *wouldn't* you go for the head?'

Eric smiled. 'Good question. Zombies are the only time you do. Heads are small, see? Plus, any creature with a bit of sense has a thick skull or wears a helmet.' He tapped his temple with his forefinger. 'Zombies wear rags, have skulls like melons, and kindly move nice and slow. Even a child could get 'em in the head, which is quite handy because destroying the brain is the only thing that stops 'em. That and fire, but then you've got a fire to deal with.'

'That makes sense.' Skwee found himself agreeing with whatever Eric said, even when it didn't make any sense.

'That's why zombies are a breeze,' Eric continued, 'Level One Minion, maybe Two, tops. You've got nothing to worry about.'

Eric had concocted an elaborate monster rating system that Skwee was still trying to memorise, although he suspected that Eric changed the rules every time he brought it up. He once described goblins as *Level One* and had gone red as a beetroot. He'd muttered, "Well, not *all* goblins," then had avoided explaining the system again ever since.

Rose sighed. 'Well, that is a relief.'

'We can't relax just yet,' said Eric, loading another bolt into his crossbow. 'They can still bite ya. Then, you'll end up dead with a strange urge to wander around. Let's press on, shall we?'

'Was… that not the only one?' Skwee stammered.

Eric laughed and patted him on the back. 'We've only just got here! One zombie isn't an infestation. This cavern could have hundreds more, maybe even thousands.'

Skwee gulped. How was Eric able to stay so calm? He must have been insane, which made sense, as Skwee had yet to meet a sane human.

Rose tightened her nose peg as she stepped over the rotting corpse. 'They smell worse than that hobgoblin nest we cleared out.'

'Someone needs to educate hobgoblins not to defecate where they eat,' said Eric, 'and about bathing. Which is strange, considering how much they use bidets.' Eric stepped over the body, too, prodding it with his crossbow and muttering, 'Oh, and always make sure they *are* dead-dead.'

They continued deeper into the damp depths of the cavern. Every few paces, Skwee was sure that the air got thicker, and the faint groans and hissing sounds grew louder

Rose squinted at her map. 'I think if the necromancer *is* here, they'll be surrounded by the strongest lurchers in the big end chamber. Right, Eric?'

'Lurchers?' Eric scoffed. 'What's a lurcher?'

'That's what we call them in the West, lurchers. On account of all the lurching.'

'That's ruddy stupid.'

Rose tutted. 'Calling them zombies is a bit stupid if you ask me. It's not like they *zombie* around, is it? Like, what does that even mean?'

'Doesn't have to mean 'nuffing. It's just a name, like goblin - oh uh, no offence, Skwee.'

Skwee didn't see anything to be offended about, although he did like his name being mentioned.

Rose continued, 'I've never actually seen a *lurcher* in the flesh, or whatever flesh is left, but I was always told they were quite fearsome.'

'The pong certainly is,' said Eric, wafting the flies away from his face. 'But so long as we know our exit strategy and don't take on too many at once, we'll be right as rain. Have you both put on *extra* comfy shoes, like I told you?'

'Yes,' said Rose and Skwee in unison.

'Good,' said Eric with satisfaction. 'We may need to do some light jogging, which is famously the best way to avoid 'em.'

They arrived at a large chamber. Eric lifted his torch high, revealing the lurching forms within. They murmured and turned towards them, eyes glazed and glinting in the light. Skwee felt his knees tremble.

'Right,' said Eric, 'Pass me the rope.'

By the time the zombies came close, Eric had attached a rope to both sides of the cave wall. It reminded Skwee of the ropes put out in front of posh inns that played loud music and needed your name on a list before they would let you in. However, this rope was far less your "fancy-red-velvet" and more your "tie-up-your-donkey-hemp".

Miraculously, the wall of zombies and/or lurchers reached a total standstill once they hit the line. It held them right by the waist, blocking their path, so all they could do was shuffle their feet and stretch out their hands, desperately trying to reach the trio. Skwee was startled by the sheer variety of their rotted outfits: bakers, farmers, blacksmiths and even Men of The Holy Mole dressed in their moleskin mole costumes. There was a zombie for almost every profession, including one dressed as a giant chicken with a butcher's logo on the chest. Had they been buried in these clothes? There was no way of knowing without listening to Eric try to explain it.

'Now,' said Eric, 'Take your pointy stick, and let's have fun.' He paused. 'Just watch out for the mess.'

Skwee's pointy stick felt heavy in his hands, but it was of a reassuring length, the key sign of a premium pointed stick. He watched Eric plunge his stick into the nearest zombie's face, disintegrating it into a splatter of dark ooze. Skwee gulped and followed suit. He thrust the weapon, accidentally cutting off his target's ear. The next thrust he did with his eyes open, which hit the mark, showering him with stinking, bitter blood. He immediately regretted keeping his mouth open. The corpse fell to the floor, and another lumbered forward to replace it.

'Well done!' said Eric with a red-splattered grin as he swung his stick simultaneously through two zombies. 'And don't worry, I brought plenty of towels.'

Rose darted back and forth, jabbing her stick while the claw on her back sliced and whirled with a mind of its own. 'This is actually quite fun!' she exclaimed.

'See, I told ya they ain't no bother,' said Eric, unfazed by the zombie that had made it past the rope and held at arm's length by Eric. Its arms spun like a windmill, but Eric just laughed and kept it still. 'All their muscles have rotted away. They're weaker than kittens.'

'Why do these necromancers even bother?' said Rose. 'They know that clockwork exists, right?'

'They do,' Eric replied with a smile. 'I think they just have a death fetish.'

Soon, piles of re-deadded-dead filled the cavern floor, and the groans went silent.

Eric wiped his brow. 'Now let's check they're all definitely back to dead, and we can move on.'

They continued like this for hours, shoring up a rope and splatting zombie after zombie. Sometimes, there would be one or two lumbering alone, but most seemed to stay in packs, which made

Skwee very grateful for Eric's rope trick. After a while, Skwee's fingers became coated with blisters, but not in a good way. His back screamed for a lie-down in some hay, and his joints demanded a good soak in a puddle. By this time, the trio had more red on them than not, making it look like they'd been to a vampire's ball. Eric kept grumbling about how he should have brought more towels.

After what felt like days (and without any sunlight, it may have been), the three mercifully arrived at the final section of the cave. It was a gigantic space big enough to fit at least ten goblin warrens, depending on how big the goblin family was, of course. Skwee slumped to the ground and massaged his hands.

'Right, here we are,' said Eric with a sigh. 'Nearly done. I don't reckon the necromancer will be here, though. It doesn't seem nice enough. They prefer to be at the top of plush towers.'

There was a stirring in the darkness.

Then, the sound of clinking metal and a guttural clamour.

Rapid footsteps.

A mass of bodies surged towards them, moving at what could only be described as top speed.

Rose squinted, 'Are those... lurchers? But they're running! What are they waving? Are those weapons? Can they... hold things?'

Eric scratched his head. 'I uh, oh. No? Maybe? No. Their arms are too weak.'

The creatures careered closer, now bathed in the light of their torches.

Rose spoke fast. 'And they've got helmets, and armour and...'

'By The Holy Mole,' exclaimed Eric. 'They're Ex-Adventurers!'

Skwee tugged on Eric's overalls. 'Wha... what do we do now?!'

Eric looked down at him, face white as a demi-lich. 'Time we use our comfy shoes... and run.'

Milton Keynes UK
Ingram Content Group UK Ltd.
UKHW032358031124
450530UK00001B/6